Grounded Eagles

Helena P. Schrader

Table of Contents

Grounded Eagles: Three Tales of the RAF in WWII

Copyright © Helena P. Schrader, 2021. All rights reserved.

Cross Seas Press
91 Pleasant Street
Blue Hill, Maine 04614
www.crossseaspress.com

ISBN: 978-0-989 1597-8-4 (eBook)
ISBN: 978-0-989 1597-9-1 (paperback)

Library of Congress Control Number: 20219198869

Grounded Eagles

Three Tales of the RAF in WWII

A Stranger in the Mirror

Shot down in combat in September 1940, David Goldman awakes to find that not only is his face burned beyond recognition, he will also never fly again. While the plastic surgeon recreates his face and hands one painful operation at a time, the 22-year-old pilot must decide who he really is.

A Rose in November

Rhys Jenkins, a widower with two teenage children, has finally obtained his dream: Ground Chief of a Spitfire squadron. But an unexpected attraction for an upper-class woman threatens to upend his life.

Lack of Moral Fibre

In late November 1943, Flight Engineer Kit Moran refuses to participate in a raid on Berlin, his 37th 'op.' He is posted off his squadron for "Lack of Moral Fibre" and sent to a mysterious DYDN centre. Here, psychiatrist Dr Grace must determine if he needs psychiatric treatment – or disciplinary action for cowardice.

Foreword and Acknowledgements

Grounded Eagles brings together three novellas that revolve around non-flying RAF personnel during World War II. The tales are unrelated, although there is some overlap of secondary characters. Two of the stories deal with grounded aircrew, while the third focuses on RAF ground crew. More about the background of the individual novellas can be found at the start of each.

I wish to thank my editor Rhonda Shore, my cover designer Hazel Horne, and all my test readers, each of whom provided unique input based on their respective backgrounds. I am particularly indebted to Leslie Wood (RAF aircrew), Steven Mathews (pilot), Stephen Tobin, John Orton and Diana Page, all of whom helped make this a better book.

Cover Image

The photo is a composite image created by Hazel Horne from multiple photos. The Spitfire under maintenance is based on a photo provided by Chris Goss. The damaged Hurricane is also from the collection of Chris Goss. The bandaged pilot is a composite image developed from open-source images. The Lancaster crew is a composite based on two original photos provided by the International Bomber Command Centre (IBCC) Digital Archive belonging to a collection of photographs concerning Sergeant William Frederick 'John' Burkitt (1922–1944). Burkitt flew as a flight engineer with No 9 Squadron from RAF Bardney.

Helena P. Schrader
Blue Hill, Maine 2021

A Stranger in the Mirror

Helena P. Schrader

HELENA P. SCHRADER

A Stranger in the Mirror
Foreword and Acknowledgements

A Stranger in the Mirror was inspired by first-hand accounts of pilots who were severely burned when their aircraft caught fire as a result of combat during the Battle of Britain. With plastic surgery still in its infancy, these young men underwent multiple, torturous plastic surgery operations to recover their faces and regain the use of their hands. Perhaps the most famous account is that of Richard Hillary in his wartime classic *The Last Enemy*. Yet there are many others such as Geoffrey Page's *Shot Down in Flames*.

While David "Banks" Goldman was a fictional character, the outline of his treatment is based on the accounts of Dr. McIndoe's patients, who called themselves the "Guinea Pigs." While Banks was only a minor character in *Where Eagles Never Flew*, he plays a more important role in my forthcoming novel on the Berlin Airlift. Telling the story of his recovery is both a means of explaining what happened to him in the gap between the books and is intended as a tribute to the pilots who were so horrendously disfigured while defending the UK from a Nazi invasion.

The psychological response of men to devastating wounds is always individual. Each man responds differently in accordance with their circumstances, character and psyche. Banks' story is his own, complicated by his confused national identity and his difficult relations with his father. Likewise, while Ginger Bowles is fictional, his role is one that many people who have lost loved ones will recognize.

I wish to thank my editor Rhonda Shore for her meticulous and gentle interventions. I am also deeply indebted to Hazel Horne for the evocative cover collage.

Cover Image

The photo of a Hurricane under attack is used with the permission of the copyright holder Chris Goss. The image of a bandaged pilot was created by Hazel Horne. Combination and photo editing also by Hazel Horne.

HELENA P. SCHRADER

Chapter 1

Queen Victoria Cottage Hospital
East Grinstead, September 1940

The incendiary bullets set fire to the engine and the flames reached back towards the cockpit. The pilot struggled to escape, but the fire embraced and consumed him. Then he fell out of the burning wreck and the canopy of a white parachute unfolded. It gently brought him, swaying and lifeless back to earth. What landed was a charred remnant of a human being. It was taken to hospital and tended. Only a spark of life remained in it.

His delirium was a kaleidoscope of disconnected voices and images drowning in a tempest of emotion. The physical pain had been smothered by morphine, but the emotional pain of failure and loss raged. It collided with terror of the future. The shockwaves knocked him down a black abyss of despair and hopelessness. His screams of defiance died in whimpers too weak to hear. Only the others spoke.

"We're losing him!" the doctor warned urgently.

"Break! Break!" Ginger shouted, followed by Kiwi booming out: "Hit the silk, mate! Hit the silk!"

"We've got to stop them!" Ulli pleaded. "The Nazis are destroying everything!"

Ginger echoed him desperately. "We have to stop them! That's London burning!" Burning.

"I should have known you'd fail again," his father scoffed.

"I've got my wings, Father! I've passed the wings test!" he was so proud of that.

"Flying is a sport not a profession!"

"Don't listen to father, you look wonderful!" his kid sister Sarah assured him.

"My God! His face is gone!"

9

"What's his name?"

"David Sebastian Goldman, but he goes by the name of 'Banks' in the RAF – apparently his father owns a bank in Canada."

"He's Canadian then?"

No, German, Banks tried to tell them, but they couldn't hear him.

Youthful voices chanted, "*Jude verrecke!*"

British voices answered: "No first-class club admits Jews."

"The ground crews know you don't fire more than twenty to thirty rounds a flight. You can't do any damage with that."

"Failed again."

"I'd like to recommend you for a transfer to Training Command."

"Morphine!"

"Don't give up, Banks!" Ginger pleaded. "M'Dad's coming."

"You don't need to come back, David. Not, if you fail again."

"He'll never fly again, poor chap."

"If I can't fly, I'll die!" Banks protested.

"Maybe it's better to die?" Who said that?

"Don't give up, Banks, m'lad. Don't give up now. You've almost made it. You're in good hands." The voice was rough and uncultivated, but emotion made it deep and forceful. It broke through the fog of the delirium and drew Banks towards it.

He opened his eyes, but they swam with murky tears blurring his vision. It was dark. The blackout blinds were firmly shut. The only light came from a shaded lamp. The blinds diffused and dulled the flashes that accompanied the steady thud and crump of bombs going off in the distance. They were hitting London again.

His gaze found the hulking figure in the chair beside his bed. The visitor's big hands were stubby, his dirty fingers played unconsciously with his brimmed hat, and his brow was creased.

"Mr Bowles?" Banks asked, distrusting his own eyes. Why on earth would Ginger's father be sitting with him here in the hospital?

"Banks?" The man's face lit up with relief, and he jumped to his feet. "Banks? Are you awake?"

"Yes. What are you doing here?"

"Ginger sent me. He woke me up out of a deep sleep. Shook me that hard that I couldn't stay asleep. 'You've got to get to Queen Victoria Cottage Hospital in East Grinstead, Dad,' he said. 'Banks needs you.'"

"But ..." Banks didn't have the strength to put his thoughts into words. Ginger couldn't possibly have done or said any of that. He'd been nailed by an Me-110. His Hurricane had flamed and crashed into the burning dockyards during the first big daylight raid on London. That must have been two weeks ago, or more.

"Been here for nearly 24 hours," Mr Bowles continued. "The doctor was worried you wouldn't pull through. I'll go and find the night nurse and let her know you've come round." He was out of the door before Banks could stop him.

Banks tried to see his surroundings, but it was dark, and the flames must have damaged his eyes. They had put him in a single room, an indication that he was in critical condition. Otherwise, he perceived only the sterility of a hospital and the smell of antiseptic. He looked down at his hands, half hoping his memories of them as black claws had been only a nightmare. Rigid crow's feet on the white sheets wordlessly shattered his hopes. The tannic acid applied immediately after his admittance to hospital was still there. If his hands were so severely burned, then his face was gone too. Just like his future. He would never fly again.

Since his eyelids had been incinerated, he could only roll his eyes back into his head and try to find sleep again. He didn't feel strong enough to carry on a conversation. When Mr Bowles returned with the night sister, he didn't move, feigning sleep.

A cool hand reached out and professionally pinched his wrist, evidently taking a pulse. Then a soft but competent female voice concluded, "He's gone back to sleep, Mr Bowles, but it's a good sign that he recognised you. I think we can assume the crisis has passed. Why don't you go and get some rest yourself?"

"You think he'll be all right for a little bit?"

"I do, Mr Bowles. Get some sleep. I'll inform Dr McIndoe of this development when he does his rounds tomorrow."

Their footsteps faded as they retreated down the hall together.

Banks breathed deeply and waited for sleep to overtake him. While waiting, he tried to trace his journey to this sterile room in a foreign country.

He'd been born in Wilhelmshaven, but his family had moved to Hamburg just before he went to school. When someone said the word "home," he still pictured the sumptuous, two-story, stucco house with the long, green lawn stretching down towards the Aussenalster. That was the place he went "home" to on holidays from boarding school in Switzerland.

Yet there had always been something awkward about going home. A sense of being more on his best behaviour there than at school. A sense of alienation from his strict, cool and elderly father. A desire to please that was never fulfilled.

"Oh, David," his mother pleaded in her soft, cultivated voice, "couldn't you just once exert yourself a little more at school?" She sat in her study with the sun pouring in through the tall French windows opening onto the back terrace. This was the room with her books and her desk and, very discreetly, a narrow bed that Banks knew she used more than the one in the master bedroom. Her lovely blond hair swept up onto the back of her head, held in place by pearl-studded clips, and her dress was sheer, patterned silk over a rust-coloured, satin shift – the height of understated, aristocratic fashion. She was always perfectly coifed and dressed, and when he kissed her, a faint whiff of an expensive perfume used sparingly breathed back at him.

"You'll never succeed in life with sports alone," she advised him.

He'd pointed out that professional athletes earned huge salaries, but she had dismissed the thought with a wave of her graceful hand. "Impossible! Your father would never allow it."

Just as he wouldn't allow David's sisters to go out without chaperones or cut or perm their hair. Just as he wouldn't allow David's older brother Karl to study drama or go to tea dances. David's father was a serious man, and David's memories of him were all of him frowning. He was always busy, too. Having a family, Banks imagined from his hospital bed in East Grinstead, had been an afterthought – or an obligation – for the successful banker. His father had certainly had little time for either his children or his beautiful wife. The four children, two boys and two girls, spent the school year at boarding schools and the holidays entertaining themselves or visiting with cousins. Twice they had gone on a "family trip," once to Rome and once to the South of France. They'd travelled by private railway car accompanied by a throng of servants but without their father.

Outside the hospital, the German bombers withdrew, leaving London in flames again. Banks took a deep breath of relief and sought happier memories: The glider club. Joachim with his open, cheerful face and freckled nose; Ulli, lank and long-faced, with silky dark hair; and Andreas the epitome of "German youth," with bright blond hair and a strong, squarish face. Joachim's father had plans for him to join his ball-bearing business, Ulli's parents wanted him to go to the seminary and become a Jesuit priest, while Andreas was supposed to become a sea captain. Instead, they had been as keen as David himself about flying. They had been willing to take risks and spend every penny they could scrape together to build their own glider. During every spare minute of their school holidays, when it wasn't raining or snowing – and sometimes even when it was – they were down at the club. If they weren't actually flying or working on the glider, they were reading about flying, aerodynamics and aircraft design.

Unfortunately, none of those topics were taught at school. David's grades were terrible, and his father was furious. His father had forbidden him from setting foot in the glider club ever again. David had responded by declaring he would not open a book, much less take his exams unless he could go to the club. His mother had negotiated a compromise: David would do enough schoolwork to pass his exams (if barely), and his father would allow him to continue at the club. It was a bitter truce rather than peace between them.

Then the world economic crisis came. Unemployment skyrocketed. The barricades went up on the streets of Berlin, Hamburg and Leipzig as workers called for a socialist revolution. The perpetually fragmented Reichstag became deadlocked by infighting. Governments came and went before policies could be implemented. At eleven, David didn't understand what was going on or why, but the tensions and the uncertainty were palpable. His parents dismissed some of the staff. His father had always been distant and disapproving; now he was acerbic and caustic as well. The very fact that David didn't care about anything except gliders only made things worse.

"You may think politics has no impact on your life," his father warned him ominously. "But the day will come when you will be confronted by political reality."

The banker had been right, of course. Hard as David tried to run away from it – and his Swiss boarding school was a comparatively safe refuge – politics caught up with him. It came in the form of the Hitler Youth. By the time he turned fourteen, half the members of the gliding club were wearing Hitler Youth uniforms. At first, they just snubbed him. Then they became verbally abusive. Andreas stood up to them. His father was a shipowner; his mother was Danish. The family was cosmopolitan, liberal and democratic. They were appalled by Hitler and his followers. They could not grasp what made him popular. Hitler was a madman, a poorly educated, crude, bombastic little man who understood nothing except creating fear and hatred. Andreas left the club in indignation.

Ulli left next. He left sadly, saying the immorality and corruption around them were so appalling that the only escape he saw was in the Church; he entered a Jesuit school in preparation for the seminary.

But David just wanted to fly. He didn't want confrontation or escape. If he could have joined the Hitler Youth, he would have, just to avoid problems. Joachim stood by him, at the price of himself becoming a target of insults and hostility. The others called him "Jew-lover" and worse. Then they sabotaged Joachim and David's glider and nearly succeeded in killing them both. Fortunately, they crashed before the glider went very high. They suffered nothing more serious than bruises and scratches – and acquired a new understanding of politics. Three months later, Hilter was chancellor, and David was officially thrown out of the glider club.

Within a year, David's father obtained visas for Canada. Ulli showed up on the doorstep four days before the family was due to sail. Wearing his black school uniform, Ulli looked more serious than ever. "I couldn't let you go without telling you how sorry I am that it has come to this," Ulli told him solemnly.

"I know," David mumbled. "I'm sorry too." He hated leaving.

"I truly believe that God will triumph over this pagan regime," Ulli declared forcefully, strong words that only a fifteen-year-old would dare utter so baldly, so sincerely, in Nazi Germany.

David looked around hastily to be sure no one was listening before answering, "I wish I could believe that." He didn't because he didn't believe in God at all. His father's Judaism was nominal at best, more a fact of heredity than conviction, while his mother never spoke of her Catholic heritage. The daughter of debt-ridden, aristocratic parents, she had married for money, status and security. With the clarity of those near death, Banks recognised that, in the process, she had sacrificed more than her own identity. She had sacrificed her convictions.

Joachim and Andreas stopped by the day before David was due to depart. David's family had been preparing to move into a hotel for the last night, and they had little time to say anything. Andreas, more radicalized than ever, declared his intention to fight for "the real Germany." Joachim, on the other hand, talked about all the good things Hitler was doing. "His policies against the Jews are wrong. That's his Austrian background coming through," Joachim argued. "But most of what he's doing is good. He's going to make Germany great again," Joachim insisted. Without the glider, Banks reflected, their paths had already started to diverge.

While he had grown apart from Joachim, Andreas and Ulli, at least they shared a past and a passion for flying. In Canada, David discovered he hardly understood what his fellow students were talking about. They played different sports. They read different books. They listened to different music. They made fun of his "Oxbridge" accent, acquired from his British teachers at the Swiss boarding school, and they mocked him as a "Kraut" too. His grades went from bad to worse. Yet, this no longer enraged his father. Too late, David discovered there was something worse than his father's anger: his indifference.

In Canada, David's father gave up on him entirely. David's elder brother Karl had dutifully given up his dreams of acting and buckled down to do his duty as the eldest son. He had top grades in everything from literature and languages to mathematics and physics. He was accepted at Harvard with the expectation of continuing through Harvard Business School. During school breaks, he worked at the bank. He would be a partner one day. David, on the other hand, was superfluous.

Anticipating that his second son would not find admittance to any university, David's father allowed him to take proper flying lessons. At last, David excelled at something. He earned his wings at seventeen, and bursting with pride, showed his father his flying licence. His father shrugged. "So what? Flying is no different from driving or ploughing. It is menial labour for the unintelligent."

David doggedly continued, secretly encouraged by his mother and sister Sarah. He qualified on twin-engine aircraft at eighteen. He obtained his commercial licence at nineteen. After a year looking unsuccessfully for work as a pilot, his father's partners hired him to fly for the board of directors. Yet, even then, when he came home delighted to wear a uniform displaying his wings, his father only snapped at him to change into "proper" clothes for dinner.

At least flying for the bank meant he was often away from home. The bank had branches in Ottawa, Windsor, Montreal and Vancouver. When he flew one of the partners out to Vancouver, they had to cross the Rockies. That kind of flying was challenging – at first. After two years of being a "glorified chauffer" (as his father put it), David started to get bored.

Then one day he read an article in a newspaper about the RAF giving Short Service Commissions to qualified pilots from anywhere in the world. David had folded the newspaper open to the article and set it beside his father's place at dinner.

"What's this?" Goldman senior asked sharply, scowling.

"I thought you might be interested in the article, sir."

"What? About the RAF?"

"Yes, sir."

"I can't see ..." But he put on his reading glasses and scanned the text. Still frowning, he turned the page to read to the end. He closed the newspaper with a rustle and laid it neatly folded beside his place again. "You think you could do that? Go to England and fly for the RAF?"

"Yes, sir."

Their eyes met. There was surprise in his father's eyes, surprise and a flicker of – well, not respect, exactly, but David thought it was approval. At length, his father admitted it: "This is the first time I've ever been proud of you."

His father arranged for the bank to give him indefinite leave from his job while paying half of his salary into a Barclays account that he could draw on while in the UK. His mother added a gift of a thousand pounds so he could cope with any "unexpected expenses." The bank also paid his passage on a liner bound for England, but only his mother and sister Sarah came to see him off. His sister stood waving from the quay with a bright yellow scarf for at least a quarter-hour. He knew she would miss him; now, she would be alone with her rebelliousness.

Barely eight weeks after he'd shown his father that article, he was commissioned in the Royal Air Force and put on an RAF uniform with the thin stripe of an (Acting) Pilot Officer on his sleeve. He'd had no trouble with any of the exams, not even the written ones. He understood aeronautical engineering, radio technology and navigation. His father might not consider those valuable subjects, but the RAF did. He also passed the flying exams with ease. The only awkward moment had come when the examiners asked to which flying branch he wished to be assigned. When he had said "fighters," they had been taken aback. "But you're qualified on twin-engine aircraft," the examiners replied.

"It's against my principles to engage in bombing," Goldman answered, inwardly so nervous that his stomach was tying itself in knots. He'd come to England because the paper had said England was about to be invaded. He'd come to fight a defensive war against the forces that had swallowed, crushed and deformed his real homeland. He wanted to fight the Nazis, but the thought of bombing Hamburg or Wilhelmshaven – both legitimate targets – was unsettling. David didn't think he could do it.

The RAF officers had looked skeptical but said nothing. He had been left in the dark about what they had decided. First, he was sent to learn drill and military protocol at a two-week course with other new recruits like himself. Only on his arrival at an Operational Training Unit did he learn they had given him his wish: He'd been assigned to Fighter Command.

Chapter 2

Queen Victoria Cottage Hospital
East Grinstead, September 1940

The pain was coming in waves. It seemed pervasive and overpowering, like the throbbing of unsynchronised engines. Or was it a new raid coming in?

In his mind, the sky spread out from horizon to horizon dotted with German aircraft, large and small. There were hundreds and hundreds of them droning forward at a steady pace. They grimly held formation as only the Germans could do, Banks thought ... dogged, determined, oblivious to the flak. They were contemptuous of the RAF fighters that swirled and danced and dived around them, too.

The fighters seemed too few, too small, too helpless. The light rattle of their machine guns could barely be heard above the rumbling of the bomber engines.

The Skipper claimed that dozens of squadrons converged on the bombers from different fields in staggered attacks that ensured the RAF fighters couldn't all be caught on the ground at the same time. The RAF deployed in squadron strength, he said, for maximum flexibility and to keep up the pressure. Banks accepted that the Skipper knew what he was talking about. He was a squadron leader. He'd been in France. He had ten kills and a Distinguished Flying Cross. But Banks could not escape the *feeling* that the RAF offered only a frail line of defence, and he remained awed and intimidated by the German air armadas.

Nor could he escape the conviction that Joachim, Ulli and Andreas were up there. Surely, Andreas would have learned to hide his political opinions by now, while Ulli would not have had time to complete seminary before being absorbed into the bloated Wehrmacht. Germany had universal male conscription from the age of 18. With their experience on gliders, Banks reasoned, they would automatically have landed in the Luftwaffe. Andreas and Ulli were both serious and steady by nature. They would have been assigned to bombers. Joachim, more daring and flamboyant, might have become a fighter pilot. Banks could picture him in an Me-109. For all he knew, Joachim had been flying the one that shot him down.

The shudder of the cannon shook the whole bed. Jolted, Banks heard the explosions in the armour-plating behind his head. Then the engine blew up in his face.

The heat blew back at him like something physical. It took his breath away and ignited searing pain. He struggled to evade it, but it had attached itself to his face. His face was burning. The heat penetrated to the bone. His bones felt as if they were slowly turning to charcoal. His brain started melting.

"Hit the silk, mate! Hit the silk!" Kiwi shouted in his ears.

The voice yanked him out of his fatalistic paralysis. The need to escape overcame everything else. He reached up to push back the canopy hood, but something pushed his arms down and held them in place. He struggled to free himself, thrashing and groaning inarticulately. He had to get out. He had to get over the side.

"Doctor! Help! Doctor!" A female voice cried out.

"Release him, you fool!" another woman ordered sharply. "You're making him panic!"

"But I need to change the bandages," the first woman protested. "He tried to fight me off."

Banks sank back on the bed. He sensed the matron beside him. She put a hand on his shoulder and spoke calmly. "We have to change the bandages, Banks. It's for your own good."

Banks nodded, but the thought of what was to come made him rigid with terror. The raw nerve ends would scream as if the flames were eating at him again. He went rigid in anticipation and sweat streamed from his neck.

"Try to relax," the matron suggested and then turned and called over her shoulder, "Bring more morphine, nurse."

Banks sighed with relief as he felt the needle slip into his arm.

Banks had no sense of time. It might have been hours or days later when Dr McIndoe arrived to find him lucid. The famous doctor sat down to have a chat with him. He was encouraging but blunt. "You're out of mortal danger now. It's just a matter of patching you up again. We can do it. But it will take time."

"How much time?" Banks asked.

McIndoe didn't want to be specific. "We need to rebuild your face and replace the skin and muscle on your hands. That means a series of operations."

"How many?"

"I really can't say right now. Depending on how your body reacts to the grafts and your tolerance for pain, we can sometimes double up on operations. On the other hand, we sometimes have to slow down, or even suspend work, to let your body recover and adjust. At a guess, I'd say we'll need to operate at least ten to twelve times, but probably more. I suspect we'll be seeing a lot of one another over the next year."

"But at the end I'll be fit for flying?"

"I didn't say that," McIndoe warned, looking grave and disturbed. "I can give you back a face that is human and hands that function, but I don't think you should plan to return to flying, much less to operations."

That left Banks feeling despondent, as though he didn't have a future to look forward to.

Then one day, when the matron had removed his bandages to let his face "breathe" while she prepared to remove some sutures, Banks looked up and saw a beautiful young nurse entering his room. She was still laughing about something that someone had said to her in the hall. She seemed like the most beautiful creature he had ever seen in his life. A flicker of happiness quivered deep inside, and he was remined of his pretty little sister, his beautiful mother, and Hazel, the Women's Auxiliary Air Force (WAAF) plotter he'd had so much fun dancing with at the squadron's last party.

Banks smiled at the nurse as she turned towards him, and abruptly her beautiful face froze. An expression of intense revulsion crept across it. The exquisite features twisted and became distorted. "Oh my God!" she gasped, clapping her hand to her mouth. She hunched her shoulders and doubled over.

"Get out, nurse!" the matron ordered sharply, dropping what she was doing to intervene. "Get out this minute!"

The matron blocked Banks' view of the fleeing nurse, but she couldn't obliterate the sound of someone retching and heavy liquid splattering on the floor. Nor could she cover up the smell of vomit.

"Pay no attention to her," the matron ordered firmly.

"All I wanted was for her to smile at me," Banks defended himself. "Just one smile."

"Isn't my smile pretty enough for you?" the matron answered, her face lighting up for him.

Banks appreciated her effort, but he felt shattered, nevertheless. "I want to see a mirror."

"No, you don't," the matron countered. "It's too soon."

"It's my face. I have a right to see it."

"This isn't about your civic rights, young man, it's about what is best for your recovery."

"You think seeing my own face will have a negative impact on my recovery?"

"Yes, I do."

Banks thought about that. His face was so hideous that it made women sick just to look at him, and his hands would never be strong enough to enable him to fly again. He had no future. Why on earth was he enduring all this pointless pain? "Can't you put me out of my misery?"

"You don't need more morphine at the moment," the matron responded firmly. "I will be removing the sutures myself, and you know how gentle I am."

It was true; when she removed the sutures the pain was bearable. But she couldn't always be here when this was necessary. The others made him feel like a victim of the Spanish Inquisition. There just wasn't any point in subjecting himself to this indefinitely. "I don't mean more morphine, sister. I mean an overdose of morphine."

"I'm going to pretend I didn't hear that. This is a British hospital, and I am a registered nurse, not a murderer."

Banks turned his head away and closed his eyes. He wanted to die.

Chapter 3

Queen Victoria Cottage Hospital
East Grinstead, September 1940

"Banks?" The voice was definitely upper class, gentle but not patronizing. It was familiar but did not belong to any of the hospital staff. It pulled him upwards. "It's me, Colin." Colin was the chaplain at RAF Tangmere and a good friend. Colin continued, "Kiwi and Squadron Leader Priestman have come, too."

Banks couldn't believe his ears and turned his head slightly. They were there. The Skipper looked shattered, and Kiwi had lost weight. With a wave of guilt, Banks realised that while he'd been wallowing in self-pity, they'd been facing the Luftwaffe day after day. How long was it since he'd been shot down? Three weeks, at least. Suddenly, he felt guilty for abandoning them. The tension of readiness surrounded him again. It felt as if any second, the squawking of the tannoy or the jangle of the telephone would shatter the stillness of the hospital. They would be gone instantly, running to their Hurricanes, leaving him here.

Then he remembered that he had to thank Kiwi for saving his life before they disappeared again. "Thank you," he gasped.

"Surely you knew we'd come," Colin replied with a smile, and Banks felt affection embrace him like a warm wind. Colin's smile was what the nurse had failed to give him. It was a smile that saw past his visage to the person underneath. Kiwi was smiling too and cracking jokes about the English weather. The Skipper, on the other hand, looked shocked and distressed, but it was nothing like the nurse's revulsion. The Skipper' shock expressed sympathy and concern. That too was restorative, in a different way.

A sense of gratitude overwhelmed Banks. He felt privileged to have known these men, however briefly. He felt honoured they would take the time to drive all the way here to visit him. Their voices calling him "Banks" were a balm for the wounds left by those who'd called him "Jude." He'd feared the RAF might nickname him "Jew" or "Hun" or "Jerry."

Because he was emotionally incapable of saying much, however, his friends did most of the talking. Kiwi told him about the crazy things they'd done. The Skipper explained the military situation, the shifting of the attacks away from the airfields to essential war industries, particularly aircraft factories and London. Colin brought greetings from Hazel and another WAAF. Banks felt too weak to respond, yet he basked in the warmth of their presence like a lizard in the sun. It didn't matter what they said; all that mattered was they were here.

Inevitably, however, someone looked at the clock and announced it was time to go. They promised to return. The Skipper said his fiancée would come to visit one day soon. They started for the door, and Banks realised he hadn't asked about the others – Reynalds, Tolkein, Green and the rest. Suddenly he was afraid they might be dead. He called after his friends, "You aren't hiding anything from me, are you? Is the rest of the squadron OK?"

"The squadron is a bloody wreck!" Kiwi retorted. "When I tell the others that you're lying about being looked after by very pretty nurses all day, they'll probably go on strike for equal treatment."

"All of them?"

"Oh, I suppose you're right, Sutton would oppose a strike on principle, but—"

"I mean are they *all* still with the squadron?"

The Skipper interrupted Kiwi's nonsense and assured him seriously, "Yes, they are." Their eyes met. The Skipper understood.

Banks reached out to this figure of authority like a drowning man. "I don't want to be invalided out, Skipper. I want to stay in the RAF, and I want to fly again."

"I'll see what I can do, but first you've got to get well."

They were gone. Banks sank back on his pillows, but he felt better. He felt the bonds of belonging, and he trusted the Skipper. Maybe he was right about getting well first and then worrying about being passed fit to fly.

"Mr Goldman?"

Why did the nurses insist on calling him Mr Goldman rather than Pilot Officer Goldman? Did they want to remind him that he would never fly again? Or had he been expelled from the RAF already because he'd never fly again? No, the Skipper had promised to try to help, and, at the worst, there were plenty of ground jobs. He wasn't going to answer to Mr Goldman, Banks resolved. He kept his eyes closed and did not move.

"Mr Goldman?" The voice was closer and a little urgent.

Banks resigned himself to his fate and forced himself to turn his head in the direction of the nurse. It was one of the civilian volunteers, very young and shy. "Yes?"

"Mr Goldman, do you think you could help us with a new patient? He's just been brought in, and he speaks only German. The doctor needs to get some answers from him – blood type, religion and that kind of thing."

Banks pushed himself up more. "German?"

"Yes, he crash-landed and then couldn't get the hood open without help. He's in quite bad shape, not only burned but with several bullets in his left arm, as well. The doctor wants to operate sooner rather than later, but he's lost a lot of blood. Blood tests take time. Fortunately, he's still conscious."

Banks struggled to sit up and the nurse came to help him. "How did you know I spoke German?"

"Squadron Leader Priestman told us. He was the one who saved the German pilot and told the ambulance drivers to bring him here. He got his hands burned getting the German out of the cockpit." The nurse broke into Banks' thoughts. "We're looking after him now, then the doctor wants him to get some rest. He says he'll lock the door and throw away the key rather than let him rush back to the fray." She laughed a little nervously, as she described the doctor's unorthodox threat.

Banks' feet had found the floor and the hospital slippers. With the nurse helping to hold him upright, he shuffled out of his room dressed only in pyjamas. Out in the hall, there seemed to be a lot of commotion, nurses bustling about looking important. Banks was led in the opposite direction from his usual "stroll" to the lavatories. He passed a ward where a half-dozen men lay flat and motionless with bags of fluids hanging over them to drip food, blood or painkillers through needles in their arms. In a lounge area, living mummies, sat and flipped listlessly through magazines or played desultory games of cards with one another.

The nurse brought Banks to a room crowded with nurses. Flying boots stood just inside the door. A burnt-smelling leather jacket had been dumped in a heap beside them. Several nurses were trying to remove the remainders of the man's clothes. The German was not resisting but he seemed confused and on the brink of panic. His eyes were swollen shut in a face that was a mass of raw, blistered skin.

"Relax," Banks called out to him in German. "Everything's in order. They're trying to help."

"Where am I?" the German asked. "What's going on? What is going to happen to me?"

"You're at a hospital for burn cases, but they need to get the bullets out of your arm first. The doctor will need to operate. Don't worry. You're in good hands here."

"Are you German too?" The newcomer asked with a trace of hope in his voice.

Banks hesitated. How should he answer that? He decided on, "No, I just went to a Swiss boarding school."

The senior nurse interrupted. "Can you ask his name, age and blood type, please?"

Banks obliged, learning additionally that the German pilot was only 20 years old and a mere lieutenant. This was not one of their so-called "experts," just a lowly pawn like himself. After relaying the required information back and forth, the nurses bustled off. Before they left, however, one suggested that Banks stay and talk to the patient for a few minutes. "It will calm him down while we prepare the surgery."

Banks lowered himself into a chair by the bed. Since the German patient was a pilot like himself, he opened with the most obvious question. "What did you fly?"

"Messerschmitts, the 109."

Banks nodded, then realised the other man couldn't see him and said, "I see. I flew Hurricanes. Have you been flying long?"

"Are you an intelligence officer?"

"No, just another pilot. Burned like you."

"Oh." A pause. "I'm sorry."

"No need to be." Goldman responded automatically, but then he thought about it a moment and added, "You don't need to apologize for my burns or thinking I'm an intelligence officer, but you ought to be sorry for trying to conquer England. You have no business doing that."

"I'm only following orders." The German pilot sounded more miserable than defiant, adding, "Hitler didn't want this war. He begged England to accept the new world order and even offered to let you keep your colonies."

"Let us keep what we already have? What is ours anyway? And why should we accept a 'new order' based on racism, hatred, brute force and bullying?" Banks demanded indignantly. Then he remembered the nurse wanted him to calm the patient. Swallowing down his anger, he announced. "This is no time to argue. Maybe after your operation we can talk again. For now, let's talk of something else. Where are you from?"

"Cottbus."

A pity, Banks thought. If it had been somewhere he knew, somewhere pretty, he could have said something nice about it. He looked for a new topic. "Tell me about your family."

"My father's a plumber." Nothing in common there, either, but it reinforced his impression that this young man was just a pawn, the pawn of an unscrupulous dictator.

The German volunteered. "I have three sisters, two older and one younger than me."

At last, something in common, Banks thought, and at once volunteered, "I have two sisters. One older and one younger. My older sister is married and has moved far away. My baby sister is nineteen now." He pictured Sarah as she'd looked waving from the quay with her yellow scarf. She would be devastated to see him now.

"My younger sister is just twelve," the German said into his thoughts, adding, "It's my fiancée I worry about. We've only been engaged a week, eight days exactly." It came out almost as a whisper and Banks felt sorry for him. What girl would want a man whose face had melted away? Aloud he said, "I'm sorry. That's very bad luck, but you'll be able to write her via the Red Cross. She'll find out you are alive and will wait for you."

The other man didn't answer. He probably shared Banks' assessment of how a woman would react to the sight of his face. That nurse had said it all by vomiting. After a moment the German said, "Please, would you be sure someone thanks the people who rescued me. They risked their lives."

"Of course."

The nurses were back with a trolley and orderlies. "Tell the patient we are taking him to the operating room and will be giving him an anaesthetic."

Banks did as he was told and watched them roll the German away.

The nurse who had brought him had disappeared, so he made his way down the hall back to his room on his own. It registered abruptly that he was on his feet and unattended for the first time since his arrival — and there was a washbasin with a mirror over it in the corner of the room. Banks could not see into that mirror from his bed, and the nurses never let him approach it. They always escorted him to the lavatories where the mirrors had been scrupulously removed.

Banks hesitated only for a moment, and then approached the mirror with firm, determined steps. An image took shape in the glass. A mummy with glistening, shifting eyes. There was something inherently terrifying about a moving mummy because it suggested the return of the dead, something unnatural. Yet, he had seen so many other moving mummies in the hospital since his arrival here that he was not particularly shocked. It wasn't his bandaged face that had made the nurse vomit, but what lay underneath.

Colin came to visit every few days. He kept Banks informed about what was happening at the squadron. By mid-October, the German offensive had shifted to night raids. While there were still some day raids, they tended to be minor affairs or just fighter sweeps. Tangmere squadrons were scrambled less and less frequently, and often only to patrol or to provide cover for a convoy. Casualties had fallen to almost nil.

Then one day Colin brought a surprise. "Banks, I've brought a special visitor," he warned.

Banks had had the first of his promised operations the day before and wasn't in the best of spirits. He wanted to decline, but Colin looked so pleased with himself that he couldn't bring himself to say no. Had he had a face, his expression would have warned Colin that this was not the best time, but no one could be expected to read the mass of bandages and the ever-watering eyes.

Then Banks saw her and part of him recoiled at the thought of her seeing the living mummy he was now, while another part of him soared with pleasure at the sight of something so lovely, young, fresh and glowing with happiness. He struggled to sit a little more upright and Colin helped him. She swept into the room smiling straight at him, as if he weren't just a mass of bandages but still the good-looking young man he'd been before. Of course, she'd been warned. The others would have told her what to expect.

"Banks! I wanted to come sooner, but it wasn't easy to arrange. Fortunately, Colin offered to bring me with him today." She tossed Colin a smile.

Colin took the opportunity to announce, "If you'll excuse me, there are a couple of other patients I promised to look in on." The RAF chaplain was out the door.

"It was very kind of you to come at all," Banks answered, remembering her name just in time to add, "Miss Pryce."

"Mrs Priestman, now," she corrected. "Robin and I got married a little over a month ago."

"I'm happy for you both." Banks meant it. He had never known her as anything except the Skipper's fiancée. Many of the other pilots thought she wasn't Priestman's 'type' because she wasn't rich or glamorous. She had light brown hair and eyes and a face that was gently lovely rather than strikingly beautiful. Yet Banks understood the attraction. The other pilots were like moths around the bright-haired girls with easy laughs who offered distraction and excitement, the challenge of the chase and the triumph of conquest. Mrs Priestman, on the other hand, was calm and thoughtful. That might seem dull to most of the pilots, but the Skipper had more depth than they. Emily was a quiet harbor in the midst of the storm around him. She was exactly what the squadron leader needed.

Banks was too busy thinking to speak, so Mrs Priestman held up the conversation. Smiling she announced, "Robin asked me to tell you that your transfer to Training Command has been approved."

"The orders must have been cut before they knew I'd been shot down," Banks snapped back, unable to keep the bitterness out of his voice. "Look at my hands!" He held the black claws attached to his arms up in her face, only to let them fall back on the bed and turn his head away, ashamed. He shouldn't have done that. He started to cry. He hadn't cried in a long time. Not since he'd received his father's letter filled with withering contempt. But once he started crying, he just couldn't' stop.

After a while he became aware that she had her hand on his shoulder, although she said nothing.

He gasped, "I'm sorry."

"You have every reason to be bitter. Robin was so angry when your orders arrived too late, he wanted to shoot up the Ministry. Fortunately, he thought better of it and strafed a German airfield instead."

Banks turned back to her. "He did what? When was that?"

"Oh, weeks ago. He got a ticking off, of course. Didn't bother him. Still, he thinks it's important that you have the transfer. He says you'll only need to prove to the Medical Board that you're fit to fly training aircraft – light aircraft – not operational fighters, much less bombers. He thinks you'll have an easier time being passed fit to fly if you're going to Training Command. Something about a restricted flying category, if that makes any sense."

Banks stared at her. What a wonderfully encouraging thought! It was like dawn breaking after a terrible, cold night. Leave it to the Skipper to know exactly what he was feeling, what was most important to him.

"Robin says," she was speaking again, "You may need to start slowly, but even if you only start on old biplanes, you should see them as a stepping stone to better things."

Banks was still too choked up to say anything, but he nodded. Finally, he managed. "I don't mind starting with training aircraft. The thought gives me hope again." He paused. "I have a message for him as well. The German pilot he rescued sends his thanks."

"Oh! Of course. You're able to talk to him! What's he like?"

"He's just a frightened 20-year-old who loves to fly and believes everything his government and teachers and parents told him."

"Have you told him about yourself?"

"No – well, not that I'm a Jew. Mostly I talk about Canada and my Swiss boarding school and gliders. Things like that."

"Don't you want him to know?"

"Eventually, I suppose. It would be hard on him just now. I'm the only one who can talk to him. If he knew I were a German Jew, he would become confused and unsure how to behave."

"Maybe it would be good for him to be confused and ashamed. Maybe he'd start to question all the things the Nazis told him."

"I've thought about that, but, you know, I'm the enemy to him already, seeing as I'm RAF. Why would he believe anything I say?"

"Because you're being nice to him, when there's no need to be. He's the one who attacked us, not the other way around."

Banks remembered something. "Didn't the Skipper say you speak German?"

"Oh, good heavens, no. I studied it in Cambridge, but that was years ago. I haven't used it since."

"Too bad. Ernst was engaged to be married just before he was shot down, and he's desperate to get a message to his fiancée. The Red Cross telegram went to his parents, of course, and they don't even know about his girl. I can't help him because I can't write any more than he can. All you'd have to do is write down what he says. He'd probably prefer to dictate to a woman than a man."

She looked skeptical but conceded, "I could try, I suppose. I'd certainly want someone to do the same, if ever Robin landed in a German hospital, but what about you? Would you like me to write a letter for you?"

She was clever, Banks registered. "Yes, if you wouldn't mind? I don't want the nurses doing it, and I want to write in German."

"Of course! Do you have writing paper..." she was already looking about and concluded rapidly. "No, of course not. I'll go and see if the receptionist has anything. I'll be right back."

Banks was glad for the break. He needed a few minutes to collect his thoughts. Ever since he'd received his father's letter, he had been writing answers in his head. He had mentally composed many bitter, angry, accusatory, shrieking, pain-filled letters. He was glad he had not been able to write them down. This letter would be simple, it would be straightforward, and it would be short.

Mrs Priestman was back. She had brought a large magazine, so she had a firm base to write on. She took a pen from her purse. "So, let's see. Today's date. Do you want me to put the hospital name or just East Grinstead?"

"The hospital."

"Done. Dear?"

"No 'dear.' I'll dictate in German, please."

"I'll try, but you may have to correct my spelling."

Banks nodded and started slowly and precisely in German. "Very honoured Herr Dr Goldman. This is to inform you that your son David Sebastian Goldman is dead."

"Banks! What are you saying – doing?"

"I've given this a great deal of thought. I'm tired of letting him hurt me. I don't want anything more to do with him. If my mother or brother or sisters want to communicate, they will find a way. That's why the hospital name is good. But I want him to understand that I am beyond his reach from now on. Please continue."

With a deep breath and an expression of doubt, she poised her pen over the page and waited.

Banks dictated: "'The fact that the sacrifice of his face and hands was insufficient proof of his value caused complete heart failure—'"

"Slow down. That's too fast," Mrs Priestman protested. She repeated aloud what he had said as she wrote it. When she finished, she looked up at him expectantly.

"'Before dying, he renounced all rights to support or inheritance.' New paragraph please. Then: 'In the future, any person going by the name of David Sebastian Goldman is no relation to you whatsoever. He is the son of Mr George Bowles of Devon, who has been visiting him weekly at great expense to himself and is repairing and redecorating his house so that said David Sebastian Goldman has a home to go to in the future.' New paragraph please."

"Wait, wait ... 'a home to go to in the future.' Good. Continue."

"'In the unlikely event that you should come to England, you need not fear' – no, not 'fear' – um – 'you need not be concerned about encountering anyone resembling your deceased son. It will take an estimated fifteen operations to reconstruct any kind of face.' Am I sounding too bitter? Maybe I shouldn't add the last sentence?" Banks asked Mrs Priestman.

"I don't know, Banks. I honestly don't know." She sounded very distressed

"Ah, Colin! Perfect timing! I'm dictating a letter to my father. Please read it back to him in English, Mrs Priestman. Let's see what he thinks."

Colin looked alarmed even before Mrs Priestman started reading. As she finished, she stopped and looked at him expectantly.

"Is it too bitter?" Banks asked.

"No," Colin answered firmly. "Not in the least. But I think it is enough."

"Yes. I'm getting riled again," Banks admitted.

Mrs Priestman brought it to him to read. He made corrections and she wrote it out again in a clean hand. Banks nodded and then turned to Colin. "Would you sign if for me? Write my name, 'David Sebastian Goldman' and then in parenthesis underneath write i.V. and your own name, adding 'because the signee's hands are' – how should we word it? Immobilised by tannic acid?"

"No, I'll say 'inoperable for the indefinite future,'" Colin decided, taking the letter and pen from Mrs Priestman.

Mrs Priestman gaped at the padre, but Banks smiled inwardly. That was friendship. Colin was as furious and outraged at his father as he was himself.

Chapter 4

Devon, April 1941

After the first eight operations, the doctors decided Banks needed a break from the hospital. He was given a months' convalescent leave. That was too little time to get to Canada and back, even if Banks had wanted to go. Instead, Banks decided it was time to go to his 'adopted' home, Mr Bowles' cottage in Devon.

It was a journey of almost 250 miles and Colin, whose family had a house near Exeter, obtained a 72-hour pass so he could drive with Banks 'via the scenic route,' showing him a little of England along the way. He planned to return by train leaving Banks' Jaguar with him for future use. He arrived with the Jaguar early Saturday morning and loaded Banks' few things in the boot while Banks took his leave of the staff and the patients he had come to know. One patient was missing. Lieutenant Ernst Geuke was no longer at the hospital; he had been deemed fit enough for transfer to a POW camp. Banks had never found the right moment to reveal his identity.

By now, the bandages were gone, and in their place were strips of grafted skin that simulated eyelids, lips, and covered his forehead, nose and cheeks. For every strip of skin on his face, he had a new scar on the inside of his thighs or arms where skin had been removed for the graft. In addition, the tannic acid had been removed from his hands, and skin grafts created a patchwork across the back and front. While his hands had regained some mobility, they remained weak and extremely sensitive.

Since all the burn patients were allowed to go out in the evenings or on short passes as they made progress, the residents of East Grinstead had become used to them. In contrast, people in the small, provincial towns that Banks and Colin passed through on their drive west were still surprised when confronted with a visage like Banks'. Children cried or ran away. Women caught their breath or crumpled up their faces into expressions of horror or pity. Men tended to gape in blunt curiosity. Very few people could simply treat Banks as if he were normal.

By midday, when they stopped for lunch and the waitress exclaimed, "Oh! You poor dear! How you must have suffered!" Banks found it difficult to reply in a civil tone.

"A little, yes," he choked out resentfully, and Colin smoothly took over, chatting with the waitress about what she recommended and how many food stamps they needed.

As she disappeared to place their order, Colin put a hand on Banks' sleeve and urged gently, "Try not to blame them. Humans have been conditioned to respond to one another based on facial expressions. We know how to read young faces, old faces, happy faces, angry faces, but – for the moment – your face is unreadable. That disorients and discomforts them. It makes them do – and say – insensitive things."

"You think that's all it is? Surely, it is more than that? Humans like beauty. I'm the opposite."

"Of course, people appreciate beauty, but most of us aren't particularly good-looking and we all age poorly. Look at me!" Colin joked. He had thick glasses and a long, narrow face. When Banks gazed back unconvinced, he tried again. "When was the last time an attractive woman went up to an ugly man and exclaimed: 'Oh, you poor dear! How you must have suffered!'"

Banks laughed and conceded, "I suppose you're right."

"Nor do they say things like, 'We'll get the bastards that did that to you!' either." Colin reminded him of the petrol station attendant they'd encountered earlier.

Banks sighed again. After a moment, he admitted, "You're right. I shouldn't blame them. When I look in a mirror, I feel like turning away, weeping with pity or threatening revenge too. I certainly don't recognise myself. A stranger looks back at me." He paused, thought about that and then added, "My state would seem to give credence to you men of religion, who argue there is an immortal soul unconnected to our bodies. If I can remain me, when I look nothing like myself, then the soul's relationship to the body – or at least the face – is ephemeral."

"Certainly," Colin agreed with a smile. "Yet, while you say your face is alien, it is hardly unrelated to your soul. Rather, it is reshaping your soul."

"Are you trying to tell me I've become a hideous patchwork monster inside as well as out?"

Colin laughed but then turned serious and firmly told Banks, "Nonsense! Our souls are no more a *reflection* of our exterior than vice versa. But you will not be the same *internally* after this experience, any more than you will be the same externally."

"Neither will you, Colin – although your face is unchanged."

"True," Colin admitted ruefully, "very true." They let it go at that.

Despite intermittent showers, the day had turned into a lovely, late April day with bright, warm sunny spells between the rain. The countryside was green and the daffodils in bloom. They stopped in Winchester, and Colin conducted a tour of the castle and cathedral. "One day you should ask Mrs Priestman to show you around," he suggested. "She read medieval history at Cambridge and knows so much more than I do."

Banks thought he would have liked a personal tour from Mrs Priestman. Although she had seen the hideous, stitched-together mask that now was attached to his skull, she never made him feel ugly or pitiable.

Colin broke in on his thoughts. "She said she would like to visit you in Devon. She said, even if the Skipper can't get leave, she'd come down for a couple of days."

Banks drew a sharp breath.

"What's the matter?"

"You know what Mr Bowles cottage is like!" Banks answered irritably. When they'd taken the news of Ginger's death to his father, they'd been shocked to find that Mr Bowles lived in a rundown, cluttered, dirty cottage with outdoor plumbing. It was little better than a rural slum. Banks knew he would have a hard time adjusting to these conditions, and he did not want to think about Emily Priestman visiting him there. He realised with a start that he felt just as Ginger had done: Ashamed of his 'father.'

"You've never lived in such a humble house, have you?"

"Of course not, but I refuse to let something as immaterial as an outhouse or threadbare furniture weigh more heavily than a good heart. Mr Bowles saved my life as much as anyone else. He has offered all he has, and I will take it as it is."

"Very commendable," Colin agreed, "but sometimes we humans find that material comforts, or the lack thereof, make a difference. I worry that despite your best intentions, you may find it difficult to live with Mr Bowles. After all, you hardly know one another."

Banks stared ahead at the road for a long time. He should have known

Colin would intuitively grasp the situation; he so often did. Banks was acutely aware that the only thing he really knew about Mr Bowles was that he'd loved Ginger so much that he could conjure up his ghost and was willing to come halfway across the country to sit by the bed of his son's friend when the latter was thinking about dying.

"Sometimes," Colin remarked in a soft voice, "even great love is worn down by petty things." He paused, but Banks still would not answer or look at him. So, he continued, "I want you to know that I've already told my aunt to expect you. If you feel that you need to get away, even if just for a short spell, you will be welcome at her house. I've put the address and telephone number on a card inside the glove compartment already."

Banks looked first at Colin, and then leaned forward to open the glove compartment and remove the simple white card with the arms of Exmouth embossed (but ungilded) at the head. The address (it was a castle) was written in Colin's neat handwriting along with the name and titles of his aunt. "Aunt Louisa is a widow and she'd be delighted to meet you," Colin explained as Banks studied the card. "In fact, I'd appreciate it, if you would visit her once or twice, if only for tea. She's quite lonely. I've already spoken to Mrs Priestman about her, and that's where she and the Skipper will stay, if they manage to get away for a weekend."

"That is very kind of you, Colin," Banks answered cautiously, unsure how he felt. He returned the card to the glove compartment. After a moment he asked, "Did you warn her I was a Jew?"

"No. I didn't think it was relevant. It's not how I think of you." Colin paused and looked over at Banks intently. "I never got the impression that your religion was particularly important to you."

"Religion? Being a Jew has little to do with religion in today's world. People who have been baptised and gone to church all their lives are still labelled, discriminated against and ostracised as Jews." The bitterness bubbled out of the depths of his soul.

"In Nazi Germany, yes, but you aren't in Germany any more," Colin reminded him.

"It was English pilots who told me I didn't belong in a 'first-rate flying club,'" Banks retorted.

"And an Englishman who put them in their place. You can't blame all of us for what some stupid teenage boys said once. Did Ginger ever make you feel like 'a Jew'? Or Mr Bowles? Or Mrs Priestman or myself?" Banks looked down ashamed. Colin continued softly. "You know, if you are serious about cutting all ties with your family, you can decide exactly who it is you want to be from now on. You could, if it is truly what you want, choose not to be a Jew."

"With a name like Goldman?" Banks shot back, his face trying to twist into a cynical parody of a smile.

"In the RAF you'll always be 'Banks,' but that isn't what's at issue here, is it?"

Banks' ravaged face gave no indication of what he was feeling, and he registered that there were some advantages to this artificial patchwork plastered onto his skull after all. At length he had collected sufficient calm to reply. "I'm finding it more difficult to forget my family than I expected. I knew my father would never reply to my letter, but I had thought – hoped – that my mother or my little sister Sarah would write."

Colin looked over sharply, and then swiftly pulled the car to the side of the road and pulled the hand brake as he switched off the engine. He focused his attention on his friend, but Banks didn't dare look back. He was too close to tears. He supposed it was all the morphine and pain and emotional stress of losing his face, his career, his future... .

"Do you want to talk about Sarah?" Colin prompted softly.

"She's three years younger than me. Very pretty, lively. She was the only one who could get my father to smile. She seemed to find his soft spots instinctively, particularly when she was little. As she grew up, it became harder. She couldn't talk him into letting her cut her hair or go places on her own or even go to university. She had much better grades than I ever did, but he said it would be a 'waste of money' because she was just going to get married and have a family."

"Many men of his generation think like that," Colin pointed out sensibly.

"Sarah wanted to become a doctor," Banks answered.

"Well, that would astonish most fathers. Didn't he let her go to nursing school instead?"

"Never! She would see naked men, he told her angrily. When she replied that she'd see the same thing if she married, he corrected her, saying: 'No, then you'll only see one naked man, not thousands.'" Banks paused, lost in memories.

Colin waited patiently, and at length Banks continued, "After eight months in hospital, I realise that Sarah isn't suited to be a nurse, much less a doctor. She would have been like the nurse who vomited when she came to change my bandages. But she has other talents. She loves chatting with people and can make people talk to her. She'd make a good newspaper reporter. Instead, the only job my father would allow her to take was as a sales clerk in a jewelry store owned by a family friend. The shop is very small, very exclusive and quiet. There are hardly any customers, just cold stones. She was miserable there." He paused. "When she saw me off at the ship, she said she wanted to come to England to join the WAAFs or Women's Royal Naval Service or whatever. She said: 'I want to fight the Nazis too!' Then she'd hugged me hard, her eyes swimming in tears."

"And you've heard nothing from her since you left Canada?"

"Before I was shot down, I had three letters, but two had been censored by my father."

"Censored?"

"Yes, he always insisted we submit our letters to him before sending them anywhere. He did not want us 'disgracing' him in any way. Of course, he couldn't enforce that on me after I was flying around the country, but Sarah had no choice. Still, she managed to write one letter from the shop. It was different from the others. She was angry about being treated like a child and claimed she would 'escape.' She also said she was very proud of me."

"Of course, she was," Colin commented softly.

"That was before I was shot down without doing anything," Banks reminded him with a shrug.

"Statistically, 90 percent of our pilots are shot down before they bring down an enemy aircraft. At least that's what my uncle at the ministry says."

That got Banks' attention. He looked over sharply. "Are you serious? Ninety percent of our pilots don't succeed in shooting down the enemy! How can we ever win the war?"

"Well, there's also a small percentage of our pilots who are very good at it, like the Skipper, Sutton and Woody. Besides, how many times have you heard the Skipper tell sprogs 'your job is just to survive'? He knows what he's talking about, Banks. If the sprogs can survive two or three weeks, eventually they learn to shoot too, but usually not before they've been on the receiving end of machine gun and cannon fire that forces them to jump." He paused and before Banks had a chance to say anything, added, "I know your case is different, but that's the reason the Skipper got you posted to Training Command, where you can still make a significant contribution to the war effort without tormenting yourself. The point is, you shouldn't feel ashamed about being shot down before you could bring down any of the enemy. You are in very good company."

Chapter 5

Devon, April 1941

By the time they reached the Bowles' cottage the light had nearly gone from the April day. Inevitably, Banks and Colin were reminded of their last trip – arriving in the grey of pre-dawn, utterly exhausted, still in shock, and dreading the confrontation with Ginger's father. Despite all that, they had been appalled by the state of the cottage because neither of them had ever encountered such poverty before.

Banks sensed a change immediately. The wood pile, which had been just a heap of wood before, was now neatly stacked under a hand-made shelter. The path leading up to the front door was no longer missing bricks. There was no moss on the thatch any more either. Colin and Banks glanced at one another. "He said he was cleaning it up for you," Colin reminded Banks.

Banks nodded, still not believing the transformation would extend very far. He reached forward and knocked on the door. Like last time, he dreaded this confrontation, if for a different reason: Mr Bowles had not seen him since the bandages had been removed.

At once, the barking of a dog answered, then Mr Bowles' voice shouted at the dog to 'behave.' Finally, the door opened, and Mr Bowles stood beaming in the doorframe. "Banks! You came! You really came! I thought you might change your mind."

Not for an instant did the old farmer quail at the sight of his son's friend. His eyes seemed to see right through the grafting to something underneath. It was as if he'd been expecting what confronted him, although that wasn't at all logical. A sense of relief flooded through him as Banks assured his host, "no, of course not." Lying only a little, he added, "I've been looking forward to this."

"Come in! And you too Colin! Are you staying the night?" Mr Bowles asked Colin at once. "I can make up a bed for you here in the sitting room." As he spoke, he backed up into the sitting room that on their last visit had been a disorderly collection of broken-down furniture covered with dirty and tattered blankets. Old magazines, dirty plates, broken tools and discarded clothing had cluttered the corners covered in dust and cobwebs.

The wooden floors had been obscured by threadbare rugs thick with dog hair.

The room that confronted them now was spotless, almost barren. Where the dirty rugs had been there were now polished floorboards; in place of the clutter was empty space. The dirty blankets had been removed to reveal sagging and worn upholstery on mismatched furniture. Yes, Mr Bowles was poor, but he had cleared out the junk, the dirt and the cobwebs. Something of the cottage's potential charm shone through the small windowpanes that let in the last light of the fading day.

"What a lovely cottage, Mr Bowles!" Banks exclaimed in surprise and relief.

"Do you like it?" the older man asked back hesitantly. "You think it's better like this?"

"Oh, very much so," Colin jumped in. "Those beams! They must be at least sixteenth century. I hadn't noticed that before."

"The vicar come down and helped me out a bit. He said most of the things I had here weren't worth saving, you see, and he said that less clutter would show the house off better. He said the same thing you just said, Colin, that the cottage must be very old. He was going to try to find out something about it from his records, but I suppose he hasn't had much time. But come with me, Banks, I want to show you something." He gestured eagerly towards the back behind the stairs.

Banks followed warily.

With great pride, Mr Bowles threw open a door and revealed a water closet complete with free-standing bathtub, upright washbasin, and a lavatory – none of which matched in any way. Clearly, this had been a shed of some sort and the walls were still rather uneven and cracked, but Mr Bowles declared excitedly, "and it works!" With childish delight, he pulled the chain over the lavatory, producing a satisfying rush of water.

His mood was so infectious that Banks tried to smile back and exclaimed. "It's marvelous! How did you manage to get the fittings with all the wartime restrictions?"

"I went round bomb sites!" Mr Bowles explained, bursting with pride. "The tub come from a hotel they hit down in Torquay, and the toilet from a posh house over Plymouth way. Whenever there was a raid these past six months, I scavenged till I found something useful. Then all I had to do was get permission from the police. Most times, a firm was responsible for clearing away the rubble and they were happy to have someone take things off their hands. And it's all yours, Banks. The staff at the hospital told me how important it is that you don't get any infections. I'll use the old outhouse, and this will be your private domain – and yours, too, Colin, if you want to stay?"

"I've promised my aunt to spend the evening with her, I'm afraid," Colin answered.

"Well, that's all right then, but you'll stay for tea, I hope? I've cleaned up the kitchen too!" Mr Bowles led them into the kitchen, which, while less transformed, was in a more sanitary and serviceable state than when last seen. The cupboards still hung a little crookedly, not all the doors closed properly, and the countertops were scratched and gouged, but everything was neatly put away, and the surfaces wiped clean. Banks was beginning to believe it might not be so bad to live here for four weeks. "You've worked very hard, Mr Bowles." he acknowledged.

The older man nodded, but his face grew sad. "It was overdue. I shouldn't have let things get so rundown after m'wife Daisy died. The way I lived made Ginger ashamed of me." He turned away and started getting out the tea things.

Colin and Banks exchanged a look, and Colin spoke up. "He was never ashamed of you, Mr Bowles."

The older man kept his back turned toward his son's friends. He opened the tap to fill the kettle through its spout. He spoke toward the window rather than his guests. "I've had lots of time to think since … it happened. Ginger was ashamed of me and rightly so. I let him down."

"No, Mr Bowles! I can assure you that's not the way he saw it!" Colin protested.

"He loved you deeply," Banks chimed in.

Mr Bowles lit the gas and shook out the match. He placed the kettle on the stove. When he turned to face them, his eyes were watering. "Yes, he loved me. I don't doubt that. But he was ashamed to bring his friends here, especially fine young men like you. I should have done more to make him proud. Now, it's too late — except for trying to help you, Banks."

That night Banks lay in Ginger's bed and stared at the ceiling, feeling desperately lonely and confused. The room was filled with Ginger – his childhood toys, model airplanes, aircraft recognition charts from the last war, a shelf with books, even his clothes. The collection of things hinted at an individual with many facets Banks had not had a chance to learn about. Ginger and he had not had that much time together, and the war had dominated everything. They had shared their thoughts and feelings about flying, fighting, the Germans, the war, other members of the squadron, even their views about God and death. But what did he know about the Ginger who collected stuffed animals? The Ginger who read Treasure Island and Rudyard Kipling?

He could never replace Ginger to Mr Bowles, Banks reflected, any more than Mr Bowles could be a father to him. Their worlds were too different. Pretending he was 'home' here was even more ludicrous than pretending he was 'home' in Hamburg. He was an orphan, drifting alone through life, trying to make friends but unable to hold onto them. His memories of Ulli, Joachim and Andreas were fading. He remembered them as youths, and they were now men. Ginger would always remain twenty, of course, but how long would he remember their few weeks together? And how much of Ginger had he known at all?

Very gradually, but unavoidably, Banks started to feel something strange. He sat up and looked around the room. He had the strong feeling that someone was in the room with him. The boards creaked as though someone was moving around slowly. The model airplanes turned gently on the air as if someone had walked by. Banks remembered what Mr Bowles had said: Ginger had shaken him out of a deep sleep to tell him to go to East Grinstead.

Banks had never believed in ghosts. He didn't want to believe in them. He resolutely dismissed his feelings. They were nothing but the after-effects of so much morphine, he told himself. They were the product of emotional and physical exhaustion. He was imagining everything.

Banks turned over and pulled the bedcovers over his shoulders. The cottage might have been cleaned and tidied, but it was still draughty. This was England at the end of April, and the air was chilly and damp.

Banks drifted off only to wake again with a start. Something had awoken him. He looked around the room as fear held him in a rigid grip. There was a noise outside the door, and Banks went stiff with terror. No, it was just the dog, Bessie. She slept with Mr Bowles in the bedroom across the landing. She had apparently slipped out and had just returned.

He closed his eyes, but his ears strained for other noises. He heard footsteps, and sat bolt upright, searching the darkness. There was no one in the room.

Ginger spoke from right beside the bed. "Thank you for coming, Banks. I know you could have gone to Colin's Aunt."

The voice was completely human. It was not breathy, quavering, echoing or distant. It was clear and resonant.

This cannot be happening, Banks told himself, not daring to move. Surely, if it were a ghost, he'd see something? But the room was utterly empty; there were no eerie lights, shadows, or transparent figures. Banks closed his eyes and lay down again, his heart thundering in his ears.

"Dad doesn't expect you to replace me," Ginger continued reasonably. "He knows better than to think anyone can do that. He knows you have your own life and will go your own way. Just stay for a day or two, or as long as you like. I think you'll like the moors."

Banks sat up again and searched the room, but Ginger was gone. He lay down on his back and stared at the ceiling for a long time. Before he could make sense of what had happened, exhaustion overwhelmed him, and he fell asleep.

Chapter 6

Devon, April 1941

In the bright light of day, Banks convinced himself he had simply had a vivid dream because he was sleeping in Ginger's room. The dream, he told himself, was his subconscious telling him to relax and enjoy a holiday in the English countryside, in a quaint old (sixteenth century, to be precise) cottage. He told himself to enjoy being away from telephones and air raid sirens, away from nurses and syringes, away from the smell of antiseptic and the sounds of other patients sobbing, whimpering and groaning.

When he went downstairs, Mr Bowles hastily slipped something into a wooden box and stood to greet him. "How would you like your eggs, Banks?"

"Is there any way to do powdered eggs other than scrambled?"

Mr Bowles grinned. "Got real eggs! Six chickens out the back."

"In that case, fried would be divine," Banks answered, and they went into the kitchen together.

Mr Bowles cheerfully set to work cracking four eggs open over the skillet, while Banks found the chipped and mismatched crockery in the cupboards and laid the table.

"Now, I don't want to get in your way," Mr Bowles declared as he turned the eggs carefully. "You've got wheels and all, so don't feel like you have to stay here in the cottage all day. I've got a carpentry job for a neighbour that'll keep me busy for a week or more. Won't be home until after dusk while it lasts. Just help yourself to whatever you like in the house and come and go as you please. No need to lock up. Ain't nothing to steal here. In weather like this, though, you might want to go for a walk. Ginger always went for long walks when he was home."

Ginger had talked a lot about his walks on the moors. He had gone for long walks whenever he was confused, frightened or angry. When the other children made fun of him at school, he took refuge in nature. When his dog died, he found comfort in nature. When he feared he wasn't going to be accepted in the Volunteer Reserve, he'd gone for 'the longest walk of his life.' Ginger had talked about how alive the country was, with rabbits, mice and birds. Banks had not understood half of what Ginger was talking about, but when he looked out of the kitchen window, Banks understood Ginger in a new way.

Besides, he was reluctant to drive on his own and dreaded contact with people. It was so much easier to stay here at the cottage surrounded by the simple beauty of his surroundings. After Mr Bowles left, Banks cleaned up and then went for a walk. He followed a narrow footpath that led down the slope on the far side of the barn behind the cottage – and got lost in the English countryside.

At first, it was only figurative. Banks stopped thinking consciously and just let the sights, sounds and smells lead him. As he wandered, the war was forgotten, replaced with fragments of poems and melodies and pleasant memories. When he discovered a creek gurgling contentedly as it carried off last autumn's rotting leaves, he sat down on a rock and let the sun soak his face. He wondered if the different strips of skin would absorb the sunlight at different rates, exaggerating the effect of the patchwork or if a tan would help smooth over the differences. He dozed off for a bit.

Banks was awoken by a breeze that stirred up the debris of autumn and swirled it around him. Clouds were rolling in from the West and the temperature had dropped. He got up, stiff from the damp and the hard rock. He started walking back the way he'd come but soon came to a hedgerow he didn't remember and couldn't cross. He turned around and tried a different path. This brought him to a stone wall he had not seen before. He had utterly lost his way.

By then, the sky was almost completely overcast, and a cold, brisk wind was blowing. Banks decided to follow the wall, thinking it might lead to a house. It didn't. In the distance, he spotted a road, and he crossed a muddy, ploughed field to reach it. By the time he stepped out onto the dirt road, his feet were soaked, his trousers muddy, and fog had settled over the entire landscape.

Banks was hungry and frustrated. All the pleasure he had experienced earlier while discovering the beauty of Ginger's countryside had evaporated. He wanted to get out of his wet and dirty things. He wanted to get off his sore feet. He wanted to curl up alone on a sofa and read a book, not wander about in the damp and cold.

A house loomed out of the fog. It was a moderately large, red-brick Victorian house in much better condition than Mr Bowles' cottage. It had a doorbell rather than a knocker. Banks went up the path, took a deep breath and rang the bell.

No one answered.

Banks turned around to look back the way he'd come, trying to find a clue to lead him back to Mr Bowles' cottage. It was hopeless. Fog smothered everything.

"Who's there?" A rough male voice barked through the closed door.

"You wouldn't know me, sir. I'm a stranger to these parts, staying with Mr Bowles. I went for a walk and lost my way. I haven't a clue where I am or how to get back to the Bowles' cottage. I was hoping someone could point me in the right direction."

"Staying with George Bowles, you say?"

"Yes." Banks found himself remembering all the things Ginger had said about people looking down on his dad.

The door was pulled open, and Banks was confronted by a frail, middle-aged man sitting in a wheelchair; he had no legs. The man recoiled sharply at the sight of the younger man, and then he stared with morbid fascination. When he had at last satiated his curiosity about the wreckage of Bank's face, he announced, "You must be the visitor Bowles has been going on about for months, a friend of his boy Ginger. Kept telling everyone – whether they wanted to hear it or not – that some fine gent was coming to stay with him. Rich man's son, he said." He squinted up at Banks, clearly not convinced that this Frankenstein-like face could belong to a rich man's son.

"Yes, that's right." Banks kept his tone neutral and polite. "Ginger and I served together on the same squadron."

"Hmphf! Didn't believe Bowles. Thought he was making it all up," the man admitted, his tone scornful, while his eyes remained riveted on Banks' face. "Huns did that to you, eh?"

"Flames from my engine did it to me," Banks corrected.

The man's eyes narrowed a little before he declared, pounding his fist on the arm of his wheelchair, "The Huns did this to me! Somme, November '16."

Banks heard the bitterness in his voice, but he knew the price Germany had paid too. His mother had lost two of her brothers, their housekeeper in Hamburg had lost three of her four sons and his nanny had lost her fiancé. Before the churches of every town, the legless beggars clustered, and the graveyards of even the tiniest village marked the slaughter of a generation. He said simply, "I'm sorry."

"Everybody's sorry!" The legless man snapped back. "A lot of good that does me. Doesn't give me back my legs or my life, does it? Did you bag the bastard that hit you, at least?"

"I didn't even see him," Banks admitted.

"Got plenty of others first though, I hope? I certainly did."

"Good for you," Banks uttered without feeling. He was still picturing the faded photographs on the endless tombstones in his mind.

The legless man's eyes narrowed again. "You're an odd bugger, just like Bowles and his kid." With a contemptuous gesture, he concluded, "If you want to get back to the dump Bowles lives in, just go down there," he pointed to the right. "After about a quarter of a mile, you'll come to a crossroads. Turn left there and keep walking."

"Thank you," Banks said politely and walked away.

He had been cold before he rang the bell, but the encounter with the man in a wheelchair chilled him to the bone.

When he returned to the Bowles cottage, he went up to his room to change out of his wet things. Quite unintentionally, he caught a glimpse of himself in the mirror, and he caught his breath. Instead of an ill-made leather mask, the glimmer of a human expression looked back. The pieces of his face appeared to be molding themselves more to his skull, and the slabs of skin seemed to be transforming themselves into a coherent whole. The visage was awkward, stiff and hideous still, but it was no longer completely dead. With a shudder, Banks recognized the face of the legless man reflected back at him — a face stamped by bitterness and self-pity.

He turned sharply away from the mirror. He didn't want to end up like that: embittered, hopeless, living on hate.

He looked down at his hands. He could move his fingers, and he could hold a knife and fork. If he forced himself, he could use a pen. Maybe, if he pushed himself even harder, his fingers would become strong enough for him to drive and, eventually, to fly. He mustn't give in to his injuries, to his depression, he told himself, and he mustn't succumb to bitterness.

Chapter 7

Devon, April 1941

When Banks told Mr. Bowles about getting a little lost in the fog, the farmer wasn't the least bit surprised. "Easy to do that, 'specially in the fog," he told his guest. "Even Ginger used to get lost – or pretended to so he'd have an excuse for being late to dinner," he added with a wink and a smile. "What you need is a dog."

"Oh, no," Banks shook his head. "We never had dogs." His mother had grown up in the countryside with dogs and horses, but his father was a professed urban dweller. He forbade all pets in the house and was particularly adamant about dogs. "They chew things, scratch the furnishings, stink and leave their hair everywhere. Disgusting creatures. I cannot understand why any civilised being would want such a dirty animal living inside their home."

Mr Bowles was still speaking, "Bessie, here," he looked down at his dog, "always was a two-man dog, just me and Ginger. She hasn't taken well to losing Ginger. She clings to me more than ever. You need your own dog."

"They don't allow dogs at the hospital."

"You can leave it here when you go back and collect it when you go on a squadron again. Lots of blokes have dogs with them, Ginger said."

That was true, but Banks didn't particularly want one, so he let the subject drop.

He'd underestimated M. Bowles' persistence. Three days later, when Mr Bowles needed to go to town to get some supplies for the job he was doing, Banks naturally offered to drive him. Since he didn't know his way around, he simply drove where Mr Bowles told him and soon found himself at the dog pound. More bewildered than anything, he stood awkwardly looking at the rows of kennels while Mr Bowles discussed various options with the dog catcher. Banks decided that Mr Bowles wanted a second dog, and he was just the convenient excuse for getting it, so he did not attempt to interfere. Eventually, Mr Bowles called Banks over and showed him a medium-sized dog with long golden hair on its back and white fur on its belly.

"Some kind of collie mix," the dog catcher thought. "We found him wandering around after the bombing one night. Had a collar too. Name's Sammy. We always post notices about animals found after a raid, but no one came for Sammy here."

"How long ago was that?"

"Oh, over two months now. If we don't find a home for him in the next thirty days, we'll have to put him down. It would be an awful shame. Nice dog like this. He's very well mannered. Never hear him bark."

"How old do you think he is?"

"Oh, no more than four, I'd say. But sad. He's not been eating much. Beneath that hair, he's all skin and bones. He wasn't like that when we found him. He's wasting away from grief."

Mr Bowles asked some other questions, but Banks and the dog were staring at one another. Tentatively Banks held out his scarred hand towards the dog to see how he would react. The dog sniffed and then started licking vigorously and systematically. Banks had the impression Sammy recognised the hand was wounded. He'd heard that licking was a dog's way of dealing with injuries.

"So, what do you say, Banks?" Mr Bowles asked.

Banks just nodded. Mr Bowles completed the formalities. The kennel was opened, and Mr Bowles clipped a spare lead on Sammy's collar. Then he turned the leash over to Banks, and they went back out to the car.

Sammy knew about cars. He jumped in as soon as Banks opened the back door. He sat primly beside the window and waited. All the way home, he sat beside the window looking out. At the cottage, Mr Bowles told Banks to release Sammy, so Sammy and Bessie could get to know one another and come to their own terms. It went remarkably well, Mr Bowles assured him. So, they went inside to feed both dogs. Mr Bowles carefully explained all about feeding dogs to Banks.

That evening, the topic of dogs gave them something to talk about, but Banks remained skeptical about the experiment. They bedded Sammy down in a basket by the fire with a bowl of water ready at hand, and Mr Bowles explained that it could take a few days or even weeks before Sammy felt 'at home.' "You've got to help him make the transition," he urged, "make him feel welcome."

Banks went down on his heels beside the dog and stroked his soft head. Sammy did seem sad and mournful. He's an orphan too, Banks realised. And homeless. He started warming to the dog. "Can he sit beside me on the sofa, while I read a bit?" Banks asked.

"Of course, just pat the seat beside you."

Sure enough, Sammy sprang up beside Banks and curled up at once. Banks stroked him some more. He put his head on Banks' lap. Banks felt affection stir in him.

But it wasn't until the middle of the night when Sammy found his way onto Banks' bed that the bond was forged. Banks was awoken by a soft whimpering outside his door. He lifted his head in alarm, then realised what it was but decided to ignore it. The dog had a perfectly nice bed. He didn't need to come in here.

But the sound was too pitiful. Eventually, Banks got up and opened the door. Sammy padded in and jumped straight up onto the bed, curling up on the warm indentation Banks had left behind. "Now, where am I supposed to sleep?" Banks asked, annoyed. "That's my bed," he told the dog.

Sammy blinked at him once but then dutifully jumped back down. Banks lay down, covered himself, and told the dog he could sleep beside the bed. Sammy lay down with his head on his paws looking mournful again. Banks turned his back on the dog, the covers pulled close around his shoulders, and he fell asleep.

He woke up sometime later to find Sammy stretched out beside him, licking his hand. "What the devil?" He pulled away angrily. Sammy looked up at him with big pleading eyes. Then he lifted his head and licked Banks' face. Banks yanked his head away in disgust, but Sammy's tongue found his face again, caressingly. Understanding dawned: Sammy wanted to heal his face as well as his hand. It was that simple. He lay back down and put his arm over the dog. "It's all right, Sammy," he told him. "There's nothing you can do."

Sammy licked his hand and then laid his head down, drew a deep breath and sighed with profound relief.

"Yes, you're home now, Sammy," Banks assured him, stroking his shoulder. "We may both be strays or abandoned or orphaned or however you want to put it, but we have each other, and we have a home here."

Chapter 8

Devon, May 1941

Sammy's joy of life was utterly infectious. He loved waking up in the morning. He loved walks. He loved chasing birds, rabbits, mice and even insects. He loved car rides. He loved food. And he loved Banks and Mr Bowles. His wagging tail, alert ears, excited leaps and caressing licks were better than morphine. By the time Banks drove down to see Colin's aunt with Sammy sitting happily in the "second pilot" seat beside him, Banks was feeling better. He was learning to put people at ease when they stared at him. He was learning to joke about his face. He was forcing himself to write and drive because both increased the strength in his hands, the prerequisite to flying again.

Colin's aunt was a different kind of balm. She was actually Colin's great aunt, a woman in her seventies, who had married a certain Graf Walmsdorf in 1889. "It wasn't at all unusual back then," she pointed out. "The English and Prussian royal families were so close that there were always Germans at court. My husband and I met while fox hunting with the Prince of Wales."

She had lived nearly fifty years in Germany before returning to England after her husband's death. She had lost a son and son-in-law in the First World War, spoke flawless German and detested the Nazis. "Every decent German detests the Nazis," she told Banks emphatically.

"Proving conclusively," Banks quipped back, "that the majority of Germans aren't decent."

They were having tea on the terrace behind the house with Sammy stretched contentedly at Banks' feet. Honeysuckle climbed up the latticework attached to the brick Elizabethan manor that had long since lost its fortress character, despite still being called a "castle."

"I beg to differ with you, young man," Aunt Louisa insisted firmly. She was ramrod straight and elegantly dressed in a grey raw-silk skirt and lace-trimmed blouse. Pearls studded her ears and encircled her throat. She reminded Banks of his maternal aunts. Like them, she had managed large estates through the last war, confronted deserters and revolutionaries, and overcome inflation and economic depression. She was the kind of woman who could have commanded battalions or managed a bank with equal competence. The table in the parlor they had passed through was stacked with the latest editions of not only the Times but the *Zuericher Allgemeine* as well. "Hitler never did win a majority of the popular vote," she reminded Banks.

"His popularity, however, increased with each of his victories after all elections were suppressed," Banks countered. He found it surprisingly liberating to be able to talk about Germany with someone who understood it.

"True enough. Success is a powerful, seductive elixir," Aunt Louisa admitted, "but he has suffered his first defeat, thanks to you and your colleagues." She nodded towards the wings on his tunic.

"I wonder if he – or anyone in Germany – has even noticed," Banks questioned.

"What do you mean?"

"Well, he always claimed he didn't want war with England. Rather than admitting he was defeated, I'm sure he tells himself – and Goebbels then tells everyone else – that he simply chose not to invade last fall. Besides, we can't be certain he won't invade this summer. If he sends the Luftwaffe over in the same strength this year as last, there is no guarantee that the RAF will win," Banks warned.

"You are wise to be cautious," Aunt Louisa noted, "but we also need to be optimistic. It's hard to get through a war without some kind of hope."

"May I ask ..."

"Yes?"

"How did you, well, get through the last war, as an Englishwoman in Germany?"

"Remember, by the time the war came, I'd been married and living there for a quarter of a century. On our estates in Mecklenburg-Vorpommern, I was quite simply the 'Frau Graefin.' My husband was in the army and my sons were in the army – fortunately fighting in the East more than the West."

"I meant emotionally," Banks clarified his question. "Didn't you have divided loyalties?"

"Not really. I was on the side of my family – regardless of which side they were on. It helped, I suppose, being in the East. We were sincerely afraid of the Bolsheviks, and I was appalled by the terms of Versailles. The betrayal and double-dealing of the allies at Versailles shattered my faith in British 'fair play.' I might have been ambivalent about the war, but not the peace. Things only changed after Hitler started to gain support. When he seized power and disbanded the Reichstag, my alienation from Germany increased almost daily. I could not feel at home in a nation that admired, indeed adulated, such a crude, corrupt, hate-filled bully. With each new outrage, I rediscovered my Britishness. It got to the point where I simply had to leave. I tried to persuade my husband to come with me, but he didn't have the luxury of being British. He was utterly incapable of abandoning 'the Fatherland' even though he suffered to see it misused and misled. Among my many grievances against Hitler, the most bitter is the fact that he ruined the last years of what had been an excellent marriage up to then." She paused to think about her words, with her eyes turned inward.

Then directing her gaze at Banks, she asserted. "People make far too much of nationality. Having two countries that you love is a blessing, not a curse. It widens your horizons, your perspective. It gives you greater scope for action. If at some time in the future Germany is freed of Hitler, you will have the option to return. Meanwhile, you are here and can fight against him. Colin tells me you want to be passed fit for flying again."

"Yes, very much."

"I can understand that. I have a grandson roughly your age who was absolutely mad about flying. He could think of nothing else as a teenager."

"What happened to him?"

"He's in the Luftwaffe, of course."

That shook Banks. "But then ..." She understood. She understood precisely what it was like – and Colin knew it. No wonder he had wanted them to meet.

"Yes, exactly," she answered with a wry smile.

"Your grandson, do you know what he flies? Where he is now?"

"No, I have no idea where he is now. I've had no contact with my daughter since the first day of the war. Before the war he flew hunters – fighters – of some kind. He's my daughter Sophie's second son. I have a picture of him if you're interested."

"Very!"

She went inside and returned with a silver-framed photo of two teenage boys on tall, elegant horses. Both youths smiled out of the picture, one dark and one fair. The dark-haired youth seemed more serious, his smile almost shy, and he bent to stroke his horse's neck. The fair-haired boy looked full of himself and decidedly saucy. "The dark one is Philip, the elder boy, he went into the cavalry and was in General Staff College when I left. The blond is Christian, now in the Luftwaffe." Her eyes lingered on the photo, then she put it down and focused on Banks. "Some more tea? Or should we open a bottle of champagne to drown our sorrow?"

"I think I better stick with tea."

"I was afraid you'd say that."

Chapter 9

Devon, May 1941

At the start of Banks' third week of leave, Ginger came again. Banks had been sleeping soundly, comforted by Sammy's warmth and unwavering acceptance. Then suddenly, he was yanked from his sleep to find Sammy whining and trembling beside him. The dog was looking at the door, but it was closed. Banks felt fear creep over him. His heart raced, but he could not move. The model airplanes swirled slowly on the ends of their strings. The floor creaked.

"I need your help, Banks."

"Ginger?"

"Please. My Dad's in trouble, and I don't know who else to turn to."

Banks was too terrified to answer. He could not deny what he was hearing. It was Ginger's voice. It was right here in the room with him, and Sammy sensed him too. Furthermore, this time he was saying things that Banks could not have imagined.

Ginger continued. "He's run up debts everywhere – the butcher, the chemist, the grocer, the builders' supply shop … He's so far in arrears, they're threatening to cut off his electricity and water."

Were those the papers he kept hiding in the wooden box?

Ginger spoke rapidly as he'd always done when agitated – like when he'd talked about Spitfires shooting down an unarmed German rescue plane or when the auxiliary pilots had made snide remarks about the Skipper behind his back. "M'Dad was never good with numbers. Bills confuse him, so he ignores them."

"He was fixing the cottage up for me," Banks thought guiltily.

"No, that's not it." Ginger answered his thoughts. "It's that he forgets to bill people for the work he does. He's uncomfortable about writing and he doesn't like asking for money. If people don't voluntarily pay him cash, he doesn't get paid. This last job, he had to buy a lot of supplies, but the Dalbys haven't paid him back, much less paid for his time. Do you think you could help? I don't want you to pay his bills for him, Banks, just see that he collects what others owe him."

"Yes," Banks answered in his head. "I can do that." He was still too frightened to speak aloud.

"Thank you, Banks. I knew I could count on you." Ginger's voice changed a little. He was audibly smiling. "And don't be frightened, Sammy. I won't hurt you." Then he was gone.

Banks could not sleep for a long time afterwards. He could not pretend to himself it had been a dream or figment of his imagination. It had been Ginger. And as the terror of an encounter with the dead receded, Banks found himself a little elated. It was comforting to think that Ginger wasn't completely gone – and that there was something he could do to help repay Mr Bowles for his kindness.

In the morning, he waited until Mr Bowles had left to do some errands, then he went into the sitting room and opened the mysterious box Mr Bowles had on his lap every morning when Banks came down for breakfast. Instead of bills, he found only Ginger's letters, all neatly removed from their envelopes and arranged by date. The first one was from Upavon on being mustered with the RAF after the start of the war.

Banks put the box back on the table and started a systematic search of the cottage. At last, in one of the kitchen cupboards, he found a stack of utility bills. There were six of them altogether. Although the sum demanded was not large, it was long overdue, and in the last notice, they threatened to cut off the electricity by the fifteenth of the following month if no payment were made. Banks slipped the final warning into his wallet and went out to his Jaguar, Sammy eagerly at his heels.

Banks knew in England many bills could be paid in the post office, so he went there and inquired about paying utility bills. Although Ginger had said he was not to pay the bills himself, Banks did. He had money. A lot of money. He had almost no expenses, and in addition to his RAF salary, his father's bank was still paying him for some reason. Furthermore, he still had almost all the money his mother had given him. He went to the grocer's, the butcher's and the other shops that Mr Bowles frequented and settled all the accounts. Altogether it came to well over forty pounds. That was a lot, but Banks didn't have any other use for the money, and it was easier than trying to confront people he didn't know about not paying Mr Bowles. Finally, he stopped at the pub for lunch and sat outside with Sammy in the May sunshine. Only now did he stop to think about what he should tell Mr Bowles. He decided not to say anything at all.

Three days later, his deeds caught up with him. The grocer cheerfully told Mr Bowles what a wonderful young man "that friend of Ginger" was, adding that he had paid all of Mr Bowles' arrears. Mr Bowles was too shocked to say anything beyond mumbling agreement with the grocer, but he was hopping mad by the time he got home to the cottage.

He confronted Banks angrily. His bills weren't any of Banks' business, he said. He was an honest man. He paid his own way. He'd never taken charity from anybody, and he wasn't going to start now. He wanted to know exactly what Banks had spent. He was going to pay him back down to the last farthing.

"I never doubted that for a moment, sir. As soon as you've collected what's owed to you, you can pay me back, but we didn't want the electricity cut off in the meantime," Banks countered.

"Who told you I haven't been paid?" Mr Bowles demanded angrily.

"Ginger."

Dead silence. After a long pause in which his anger dissipated, Mr Bowles asked, "He came to tell you that?"

Banks nodded.

Mr Bowles sank down on the sofa so heavily that it creaked. He wasn't looking at Banks anymore, just staring. After another long pause, he noted, "He must be worried about me."

"Yes, he is. I'd like to help in any way I can. I have the money—"

"I don't take charity!"

"It's not charity, Mr Bowles. I'm helping a friend, who has helped me more than anyone could ever repay."

"I'll pay you back," Mr Bowles insisted doggedly.

"I know you will," Banks paused, "maybe you could start by asking the neighbours you've been working for these past few weeks at least to pay for the supplies you've bought on their behalf."

Mr Bowles looked at him with a heavy frown and declared stubbornly, "I don't like asking people for money!"

"But it's money they owe you."

Mr Bowles frowned more intensely. "It's none of your business."

"Ginger made it my business. He asked me to help." Banks found himself wondering how many of Mr Bowles' neighbours had taken advantage of him over the years? How often had their contempt for his intelligence and disdain for his simplicity been based on the fact that he hadn't noticed they were cheating him?

"I'll handle this in my own way!" Mr Bowles growled, hauling himself to his feet and stomping out of the room.

Banks drew a deep breath, suspecting he would do nothing. Part of him wanted to champion Mr Bowles, to confront the people who had looked down on him and made Ginger so miserable growing up. But if he did face these people, wouldn't they just say, "typical money-grubbing Jew?" With a sigh he accepted there was nothing more he could do.

Chapter 10

Devon, May 1941

The weekend before Banks was due to return to hospital, the Skipper and Mrs Priestman came to visit. They were staying with Colin's aunt, but they drove over in the Skipper's red MG, arriving after lunch. Because Mr Bowles didn't have a telephone, they could give no warning. Their unannounced arrival set off wild barking from Bessie and Sammy and brought Banks and Mr Bowles tumbling out of the house in excited surprise. Mr Bowles was beside himself with delight, and Banks had the impression that a visit from the king and queen wouldn't have pleased him more.

Mrs Priestman smiled and kissed Banks on both cheeks as if his face were completely normal. "I've missed my visits to you!" she declared with every appearance of sincerity. "No one else in the squadron will talk about anything except Spitfires!"

The Skipper held out his hand. "How are you doing? You look rested." His discerning eyes registered both the positive changes to the scar tissue and also pierced through the tortured flesh to the calmer man underneath.

"It is wonderful here," Banks answered without reservation, making Mr Bowles glow with pleasure.

"The house is marvelous!" Mrs Priestman agreed, taking it in with knowing eyes. "Fifteenth century, is it?"

"Colin thought sixteenth, but we haven't seen any evidence yet," Banks answered.

"You show them around, while I make tea," Mr Bowles urged, adding, "In weather like this, we'll have it out in the yard."

So, Banks took the Skipper and his wife inside, showed them the front sitting room and the lavatory, and then took them up the creaking stairs. Mrs Priestman expressed delight at nearly all she saw. She loved old buildings almost as much as she loved history.

"That's Mr Bowles' room," Banks noted, waving his hand in the direction of the master bedroom, but not venturing into Mr Bowles private space. "And this is where I stay. In Ginger's room." He opened the door but stood back to let the guests file in.

Mrs Priestman was drawn to the window and the view across the moors. "How lovely!"

But the Skipper stopped in the centre of chamber, his head almost touching the low beams. Smiling faintly, he tapped one of the model aircraft hanging from the ceiling and sent it slowly circling. "Just like me," he remarked softly.

They returned to the ground floor and went out the back door to find Mr Bowles busy laying tea things on an old picnic table in the cobbled yard. Mrs Priestman offered to help, but Mr Bowles wouldn't hear of it, so they sat on the benches. Mrs Priestman's eyes fell on the barn that sat at right angles to the house, partially enclosing the yard. "What a wonderful old barn! Do you use it for anything?"

"I don't think so," Banks admitted. He'd never gone into it nor seen Mr Bowles enter it either. They got up and wandered over.

"A barrel roof!" Mrs Priestman exclaimed with enthusiasm. "They're so rare these days – most have been torn out or covered up! And the windows are original too, I think. Oh, look! The floor is flagstone. This is a gem!"

The pilots looked blankly at one another.

Mrs Priestman called Mr Bowles over. "This is a wonderful example of fifteenth-century rural Devon architecture. Is it listed?"

"Listed?"

"With the National Trust."

"But it's just an old barn," Mr Bowles replied, baffled. "When I was little, m'dad had three cows and our plough horse, Matty, in here. She was a sweet mare. Haven't had any animals in here in thirty years, though." He looked sadly across the room that still had four wooden stalls with troughs and a hayloft. Some old equipment stood in one corner.

"Have you ever thought of renovating it and turning it into a guest house, Mr Bowles?" Mrs Priestman asked. "It's the kind of place where people would love to stay. You could turn the loft into the bedroom, put a small kitchen where the troughs are and make this whole area a cosy sitting room." She expressed her enthusiasm with her expansive gestures. "May I climb up to the loft?" she asked.

"Of course, but the tea will get cold."

"Oh, we don't want that! We can have tea first, and I'll have a look later. But I'm serious, Mr Bowles. I can think of a dozen people who would pay ten bob a night to stay in a place like this."

Her husband laughed. "And if you don't ask too many questions about the 'wives' they bring with them, they'll pay you twice that."

"Robin!" Mrs Priestman admonished in feigned shock.

They returned to the picnic table and settled down for tea and biscuits. Mr Bowles started chattering as he often did when he was nervous. "If I'd known you were coming, Mrs Priestman, I would have bought fresh scones from the tearoom in town. They make wonderful scones, and we could have asked Mrs Hollis, who lives just up the road a bit, for some of her home-made jam." He talked on about the fresh produce they had and the healthy air and hunting, telling Robin he could come any time he wanted. "Nice partridges hereabouts and plenty of hare."

The squadron leader demurred. "I'm afraid I never did develop a taste for shooting."

"Unless it has swastikas on it," Banks corrected, and they laughed.

"But others might like the hunting," Mrs Priestman noted. "Think of Woody and Sutton. They always try to get in some shooting when they have time off. So, in addition to history buffs —"

"and illicit lovers" (From Robin.)

"—your guest house would attract bird hunters," Mrs Priestman concluded.

"Bessie and Sammy would be in heaven," Banks noted with a smile at his dog, who had flopped down beside him, panting.

"But who'd want to stay in a barn?" Mr Bowles protested.

"It would have to be renovated first, but you have all the skills to do it yourself," Banks pointed out, the plans already forming in his head. "I can finance the materials and you can pay me back from the income."

"But I'd need someone to clean for the guests."

"Didn't Mrs Wells say she was looking for more work?"

"But it's so far away from everything and it hasn't got a telephone," Mr Bowles pointed out.

"Now that is the greatest advantage yet!" the Skipper proclaimed. "I'd pay almost anything to stay somewhere where there isn't a telephone."

"We could make it a joint venture, Mr Bowles," Banks persisted seriously. "I'll finance the cost of renovation and set up a joint bank account. That way we can keep the accounts straight." Banks was confident he would be the only one keeping an eye on the accounts and that, in this way, he could make the odd deposit without Mr Banks noticing. It would help Mr Bowles get back on a sound financial footing.

Mr Bowles looked towards the old barn. "It would be nice to have people here now and again, if you don't think they'd find it too primitive?"

"We will have to put in plumbing," Banks conceded.

"What about electricity?"

"No, oil lamps and candles are much more romantic," the Skipper insisted.

"Mr Bowles," Banks leaned forward and looked at him intently. "If this is a success, do you know what we'll do?"

The older man shook his head.

"We'll establish a memorial scholarship to Cranwell in Ginger's name. A scholarship for young men, like him, who didn't go to public school and whose parents can't afford the tuition fees."

"What does that mean?" Mr Bowles asked.

"It means that young men like Ginger, who would have liked to be commissioned in the RAF but cannot afford the tuition at Cranwell will get a scholarship that covers their tuition as long as they meet the requirements and pass the requisite exams. We will finance that with the money we earn from the guest house." Banks explained. "We'd call it the Ginger Bowles Scholarship, and everyone who applies will hear about Ginger."

"They'll put up a brass plaque with the names of each year's winner," the Skipper assured him.

"A plaque with an engraved picture of him, perhaps," Mrs Priestman joined in, with a glance at her husband to be sure she wasn't saying anything she shouldn't.

"You think we could make that much money?" Mr Bowles clearly couldn't believe it.

Banks didn't believe they could either, but that wasn't the point. He had other ideas for raising the money for the scholarship. Out loud he merely said, "I don't know, but it's a goal to work towards, don't you think?"

"Ginger would like the idea," Mr Bowles admitted hesitantly.

"Yes, he would," the Skipper agreed.

Mr Bowles looked from one to the other and then to Mrs Priestman. "You really think people would pay money to stay in my old barn?"

"Absolutely, if you get it done up! We'll be your first guests." She took her husband's burn-scarred hand as she spoke.

Mr Bowles, still looking a little bemused and skeptical, finally nodded and agreed. "Well, then, if you think we might raise the money for something that would be a memorial to Ginger, then I'd like to try."

Chapter 11

June - December 1941

Turning Mr Bowles' barn into a bed and breakfast became a joint project shared by Banks and Emily Priestman. She concentrated on getting the property listed with the National Trust and on developing architectural features in accordance with heritage preservation guidelines, while Banks developed a business plan and marketing strategy. The irony of working on business and finance did not escape Banks. He was voluntarily doing precisely the kind of things he had stubbornly refused to take an interest in up until now. He would rather have been flying, but since he was grounded and confined to a hospital for months to come, doing something useful with his mind was more appealing than other available pastimes. It was an added benefit that the joint project gave him an excuse to visit often with the Priestmans.

Whenever he had recovered enough to leave the hospital after an operation but was not well enough, or didn't have sufficient time before the next operation, for the long drive down to Devon, he would nip down to Bosham and stay with the Priestmans. They were looking after Sammy for him anyway, and Colin lived nearby, which meant that Banks and Colin could meet for a quiet drink in the evenings. Almost as importantly, No. 606 squadron still viewed The Old Ship just down the street from the Priestmans as their pub, so almost any evening Banks could find some of the pilots congregated there. They always greeted and treated Banks as one of their number, so dropping by made him feel he was still on the squadron.

Another attraction was that the Skipper and Kiwi shared a 16-foot sailing boat that they let anyone from the squadron use throughout the summer. Mrs Priestman was a novice sailor and only beginning to learn about this first passion of her husband, but she took to sailing like a duck to water. Banks liked it best when she and the Skipper sailed together because they were a good team. When Kiwi and the Skipper sailed together, on the other hand, it was a competition that could get quite dangerous.

As for his own role, Banks' hands weren't strong enough for sail work, and no one would trust him with the tiller, but he was happy just being a passenger. He would simply sit back, close his eyes, and let the wind and sun caress his mutilated face. He was convinced the sea air was healing it.

In his nightly inspection of the stranger in his mirror, he thought the old stitches had all but disappeared and the patchwork of skin was blending together into a single supple surface. Best of all, his hair had started to grow back. Strangely, it wasn't the same fine, blond hair he'd had before being burned. The hair that grew back was courser, darker and reddish in hue. Kiwi joked that they would have to start calling Banks "Ginger" on account of his red hair, and although it seemed odd, Banks wasn't unhappy to have hair more like Ginger's. It certainly made him look more "human."

But the guest house and sailboat weren't the only attractions. Banks freely admitted to himself that he was in love with Mrs Priestman. He viewed his love as a private, one-sided emotion that was fated to go unrequited. Banks knew, too, that if Mrs Priestman found out or suspected his feelings for him, she would feel compelled to put distance between them. Banks accepted that Emily would never return his love for her, yet he found it satisfying to discover he could love like this, without expectations of greater benefits than he already had. He treasured it all: The heartfelt smiles whenever he arrived, the hours spent together poring over the plans for the guest house, the jokes, the homemade meals, the sailing and the sympathetic ear for his frustrations. They were all healing him in their way.

Returning to hospital after a few days in Bosham, on the other hand, was almost unbearable. It meant leaving a dejected Sammy, whose tail sagged and head hung down as soon as Banks pulled his suitcase out from under the bed. It meant leaving the comfort and privacy of the Priestman's cottage and the company of friends and cutting himself off from the squadron too. It meant returning to the utilitarian, impersonal and excessively sterilised hospital. It meant yet more pain, more morphine and the nagging fear that something might go wrong. Too many patients had had setbacks – allergic reactions to drugs, grafts that didn't take, anaesthetics that didn't work ... or worked too well.

Bad luck caught up with Banks on the fifth surgery of his second series of operations. An infection took hold in his right hand. They couldn't seem to get it under control. The pain was excruciating, and the morphine seemed to have lost its potency. In the no man's land of pain-filled delirium, Banks thought he overheard the word 'amputation,' but maybe it was just his nightmares getting the better of him. In the end, it was agreed the grafts had to be removed, and they had to start anew on that hand. It would cost him another six months in hospital. His chances

66

of being passed fit for flying were almost nil.

Depression set in. Banks collected Sammy from the Priestmans and went back to Mr Bowles' cottage in Devon for a fortnight. But the magic was missing. All work had stopped on the barn for the winter, and the barn seemed derelict. It was a wet and dreary November. Banks could not shake off his mood. He wallowed in self-pity, crying spontaneously at odd times from sheer despair. The face that looked back at him from Ginger's mirror was more human but no less a stranger. The bitterness of the legless man was back, mixed now with a new cynicism that set a shiver down Bank's spine. At odd moments, it seemed as if his father were sneering at him from the mirror.

Mr Bowles and Sammy suffered mutely with him. Sometimes Sammy whimpered in sympathy, and Mr Bowles was apt to repeat helplessly, "everything will be all right in the end." Only, neither Banks nor Mr Bowles believed it. Ginger came nightly but said nothing. Banks felt his presence and his sympathy, but what could he say?

At the end of the fortnight, Banks returned to hospital for a new round of operations. When Christmas came, he was too ill to leave. No one could cheer him up, although the Priestmans, Colin and Kiwi tried.

Chapter 12

Queen Victoria Cottage Hospital
East Grinstead, February 1942

Several days after one of his operations, Banks was told he had a visitor. He looked up, expecting Colin or Emily, and was taken aback to see his little sister Sarah walk hesitantly into the ward in a smart suit and a chic hat over permed, blond hair cropped chin length. Despite her natty attire, she looked rather lost. Still there was no mistaking his sister, and Banks couldn't believe his eyes. "Sarah?"

She stopped abruptly and stared at him blankly, clearly not recognizing him. Then she gasped. "Oh, my God! David? Is that you?" she stammered, "But what—? Oh, David!" She rushed across the room to fling herself onto his chest and cling to him, sobbing.

Banks held her, unsure of what he felt. He was happy to see her. After more than a year of feeling utterly rejected by his family, it was wonderful to discover that Sarah, at least, had not cut him off. Yet, he was resentful too. Had it truly been impossible for her to write? Was it so hard to send a word of encouragement or sympathy? If not from home, then from her job, a friend's house or a public library?

She pulled back. "Oh, David! Your face! It's horrible! We had no idea!"

"Actually, it's much, much better than it was. Take a look around the hospital before you leave."

"You're bitter," she concluded, her eyes watering.

"Am I?" Banks shot back, feeling in that moment that he had every right to be bitter. Then again, he reminded himself, he didn't want to be, so he drew a deep breath and urged, "never mind. Where did you come from? How did you get here? Where and how long are you staying?"

She held out her left hand, displaying a large diamond ring and a slender gold wedding band beside it.

"You're married?"

"Yes. To an Englishman. Clive was the British Consul General in Toronto when we met, but he's now moved to a new assignment at the

Foreign Office. We left Toronto January 20 and we only arrived in London a couple of weeks ago. Clive's secretary contacted the RAF and tracked you down, so I came as soon as I could arrange a car and petrol." She looked around the ward, clearly horrified by everything she saw: The patients dressed like mummies, their hands still in tannic acid, others with faces lacking eyelids, eyebrows, lips or noses, others with these features all to obviously sewn on. "David, we have so much to talk about – but in private. Is there a private room, or could you get released, even if only for a few hours?"

"Actually, I'm due to be released for a few days tomorrow." Banks had been planning to go to Bosham, of course.

"Oh, that's wonderful! Surely, they'll let you come home with me? I've got a car and driver. I can take you straight to our flat in South Kensington. I'll just give Clive a ring to warn him. We have two guest bedrooms. Yes, that's the best thing. I'll ring Clive and tell him I'm bringing you with me." She was gone.

Banks found the bell that called the nurse and explained that his sister had arrived from Canada and he wanted to leave the hospital right away. The very-young nurse said she'd have to talk to the matron, but Banks got out of bed and started getting dressed anyway. His right hand was completely bandaged and unusable, but he had become adept at getting dressed with his left hand – and a little help from one of his roommates.

When he was almost ready to leave, Dr McIndoe stopped by. He did not beat about the bush. Nodding with his head at Banks' bandaged hand, he said: "You know the risks."

"I know the risks."

"I'd hate to have another setback with that hand."

Banks stared at him for a moment. Dr McIndoe cared deeply about his patients, yet he wasn't the one to bear the pain or the consequences of failure. The problem was that Banks had reached the point where he had so little hope that he wasn't willing to be careful anymore. He was tired of the whole thing, especially the pain that robbed him of sleep when he wasn't drugged; he was equally tired of the drugs that left him emotionally drained and fragile.

Increasingly, he found himself thinking that maybe they should just amputate the useless thing. Maybe an artificial hand would serve him better? Didn't the legendary Wing Command Douglas Bader fly with two artificial legs? Perhaps he could fly with an artificial hand? All he said was, "it's been twenty months since I saw my sister. I didn't know she was married much less in the country. I've never met my brother-in-law. I'm going to London with her. When do I need to report back for my next operation?"

"You are due to be operated on next Thursday morning."

"I'll be back Wednesday night." Banks picked up his little suitcase with his left hand and walked out to reception, his right hand cradled at his waist.

In reception, he found his sister still trying to get a connection. "The phones are terrible here!" she complained, then sensing the collective disapproval of those around her, she concluded. "It doesn't matter. I'm sure Clive will be overjoyed to have you with us."

"I'll only stay until next Wednesday. Then I'll have to return here."

"That's lovely!" she assured him as she took his elbow and leaned her head against his upper arm. "I'm so glad to have you back, David. There's so much to talk about. You'll love Clive."

The car and driver had been borrowed from a friend of Sarah's husband, and Banks got the impression that the less he knew, the better it would be. He and Sarah settled into the back seat behind a partition intended to prevent the driver from hearing the conversation of his passengers. Sarah turned to face her brother, her eyes searching his face with a kind of appalled fascination. "David, you have to tell me what happened. All we were told was that you had been shot down and injured. They didn't say how or in what way you were injured. I never dreamed you'd still be in hospital after all this time! I was so astonished that I assumed it must be because of a second injury, but the nurse at reception said you'd been here for more than a year."

"What do you mean, you didn't know what happened? The telegram said I'd been badly burned on the face and hands, and my letter was explicit, too. I said quite clearly that you would not recognise me, and that I had fifteen operations ahead of me. As it turns out, it will be more."

"What letter?"

"The one where I told Father I was no longer his son."

"What? How could you? And why?" She was appalled.

"After what he wrote to me when I was shot down, why should I want to have anything more to do with him?" All Banks' anger and hurt exploded with those words. "My face had melted to the bone and my hands were naked of skin! But all Herr Dr Goldman had to say was that after less than two months in the RAF, I'd 'managed to remove myself from the fray' – as if I had intentionally been shot down and was trying to avoid combat!"

"David! We – Mother and I – never saw that letter! We had no idea what he wrote to you. You have to believe me."

Suddenly it became clear to Banks that she was right. Of course, his father hadn't shared what he wrote to his son with his wife or daughter. Which meant, Banks registered, that his father would also have hidden his son's reply. But he must have said something. "Surely he told you I had written?"

"He said you were in hospital and were not able to write, that some stranger had written a short message without details. He said you'd be in touch when you were ready to correspond with us. I thought you had broken your wrist or some such thing." She waved her hand in a gesture of helplessness. Then frowning, she stopped and thought back on it. After a moment, she admitted, "maybe Mother knew or suspected more. She became very quiet and subdued. I caught her looking at photos of you once. I asked her if she were worried about you, and she said, 'of course,' and hastily put the photos away. She loves you very much, David, and so do I. If we'd known ..."

"Why didn't you just write? If you didn't know what had happened to me, you could have asked? You could have shown some interest, some sympathy. Or, if not that, you could have told me about your plans."

"I didn't have an address," Sarah defended herself. "Father said you were no longer on your squadron, and although I asked him for your new address, he answered vaguely, saying you hadn't yet been reassigned. He told me to wait. But then I met Clive and we started planning our wedding. Once I knew I would be coming to England, writing didn't seem so important. I knew I'd be seeing you once I got here, and besides it would have been impossible to say all I wanted to say in a letter. But Mother sent a letter. As soon as I told her Clive and I would be coming to England, she made me promise to bring you a letter. I have it with me!"

Sarah turned to her handbag, opened it, and removed a thick, sealed packet. It was cream-coloured with an elegant, printed return address; his mother's personal stationery. David took it with his left hand and put the letter in the breast pocket of his tunic to read later. He turned to his sister and suggested she share the news from home with him, thinking she would start with her husband and wedding.

Instead, Sarah eagerly talked about their siblings, cousins and friends. She did so nervously and with a brittle cheerfulness that suggested she was desperate to talk about anyone but herself. When she had nearly exhausted the news of even their more distant relatives, David couldn't stop himself from asking, "What happened to all your plans for joining the war effort?"

"I was terribly naïve, wasn't I?" She answered with an embarrassed laugh. "I've grown up a lot since then. For one thing, I realised I'm not the type to put on a uniform and take orders from ignorant people. I also hate being in groups. In the women's services, everyone sleeps in barracks with six or ten beds to a room and they share big institutional showers, too—"

"You sound like you're quoting Dr Goldman," David pointed out more sharply than he intended.

"You mean Father?"

"I no longer consider Dr Goldman my father."

They stared at one another. Then Sarah softened and reached out a hand to touch his sleeve gently. "Let's not fight, David. We've only just found one another again. This should be a happy reunion."

"I don't want to fight with you either – just accept that I have cut myself off from our father."

"But he hasn't cut himself off from you," she answered, meeting his eyes almost for the first time since she'd discovered his artificial and strange face.

"How do you know?"

"He told me to bring you his greetings."

"Just that? His greetings? Not his love? Not his regrets? Not his apology? Just 'Gruß aus Kanada' – like on the back of a postcard." Banks spat it out.

"Oh, David!" Tears welled up in her eyes again. "He's not really as terrible as you make him out to be. I'm sure he loves you in his way."

"Well, not in a way I find sufficient. I don't want to talk about him. Tell me more about yourself. You were just explaining how your personal life choices were more important than stopping the Nazis."

"David! That's cruel!" The tears in her eyes quivered on the brink of overflowing.

"Sorry." He didn't sound it. "I just happen to have lost my face and future fighting the Nazis, and I know a lot of very fine women who have endured more than communal showers to do their part." He thought of the WAAFs on the station, some of whom had given their lives.

"I will do my part! I'm more determined than ever to contribute to the war effort. But I'm going to do it in an intelligent way! I'm not just going to drive cars and answer telephones or any of the other silly things women do in the services. I'm going to use my brains and my skills."

That sounded much more like the sister he remembered. Yet Banks had far too much respect for the WAAF, the nurses, the Salvation Army and all the other services in which women were working tirelessly and selflessly to admire Sarah's attitude. His tone was edged as he retorted, "Oh, I see. Do tell me."

"Clive says there are lots of meaningful jobs for someone like me with a native command of German."

"Really? In the Foreign Ministry?"

"Among other places, yes."

"I see. Tell me about Clive. You seem to have gone out of your way to talk about everybody except your husband. Aren't you comfortable talking about him?"

"Of course, I am! I just don't know where to start.

"Then start in the beginning. How did you meet?"

Sarah launched into a description of her husband of fewer than six months. She called him 'handsome' and 'divinely charming.' She said he was 'ever so attentive' and 'sophisticated beyond measure.' It seemed they had met at a charity ball to raise funds for the Red Cross. "He swept me off my feet!" Sarah exclaimed.

"How did you ever get Dr Goldman's permission to marry at just 19?" David wanted to know.

"I haven't a clue what Clive said to convince Father. He contacted Father at the bank, and they went to lunch together. When Father came home that night, he first met with Mother alone in his office and then called me in to face them. Mother was crying and Father announced that 'Mr Clive Fleming' had requested my hand in marriage. He said that 'after due consideration,' he had told him he had no objections to the match and that the decision was now mine. I think Mother was hoping I'd say 'no,' but, of course, I flung my arms around Father's neck and thanked him. Then I rushed out and put a call through to Clive. Mother invited him to dinner shortly afterwards, and he brought the engagement ring." She showed it to David again. "Then we started planning the wedding. Because of the war, we kept it small, only 200 guests, and, of course, none of Clive's family could be there. I didn't meet them until I got here."

Sarah started talking about her new in-laws, but by then, they were already nearly to South Kennsington and before long, they arrived in front of the lovely, terraced house facing one of London's many garden squares. The driver pulled up to the curb and saw to David's suitcase, while Sarah rushed in to warn the cook and put a call through to Clive. This time she got through to his office, and she was visibly relieved when she announced he would be home in an hour or so.

Clive was tall, slender, debonaire and almost twice Sarah's age. Something about the way he greeted Banks with an "Oh, I say, how exciting! One of our gallant few!" grated on Bank's nerves.

Not that he wasn't a gracious host. Clive was hardly through the door before he offered to "rustle up" some drinks. A moment later, he was holding out a crystal glass complete with an ice cube floating in the golden liquid. "Kentucky Bourbon!" he announced. "I managed to bring back a crate of the stuff."

Sarah excused herself to help the cook with dinner. The smells from the kitchen were mouth-watering, reminding Banks how hungry he was and how long it had been since he'd had a decent meal. (Emily Priestman cooked wholesome workman's dinners rather than gourmet food.)

"You'll have to tell me all about the Battle of Britain," Clive opened the conversation. "I was in Toronto from before the start of the war until just last month, so I missed the entire show."

Banks had to resist the urge to say there hadn't been a "show" at all, but a bitter, bloody battle. Biting his tongue, he replied, "I was nothing but a lowly pilot. I have no sense of the overall situation. You'd be better off asking someone at the Ministry or Fighter Command for an assessment."

"Well, yes, obviously, but you were out there on the front lines doing all those things the prime minister raved about. It must have been quite exciting. You flew Spitfires?" Banks presumed Clive didn't mean to sound condescending, yet he certainly managed to do so.

"No, Hurricanes. Tell me more about yourself." Banks changed the subject. "You're with the Foreign Ministry, Sarah told me. Where else have you served besides Canada?"

"Oh, spent most of my career in the Far East — Bangkok, Peking, Tokyo."

"And Sarah is your first wife?"

Clive answered with an almost nervous titter. "Good grief, yes!" He laughed again and gave Banks a meaningful look that jolted him. Surely, he didn't mean that?

Just then, Sarah called them both to dinner, and they got up and went to the dining room, which was beautifully and tastefully appointed with select pieces of Asian art providing exotic highlights in the otherwise standard upper-class décor. With only the slightest encouragement, Clive talked about the Ming vase, the Thai Buddha, the lacquer trays inlaid with mother-of-pearl and the vertical, Japanese ink paintings. Sarah, Banks noticed, seemed remarkably comfortable in her role as lady-of-the-house. It was as if Clive's maturity had rubbed off on her. He found it a little sad, however, because Sarah had always said she didn't want to be "just" someone's wife.

Banks asked to go to bed early, explaining that his body was run down from frequent surgery, anesthetics and painkillers. Clive and Sarah were quick to excuse him, but Banks then had to explain he needed help getting undressed and changing into his pyjamas. Although Sarah jumped up and came with him, she was a clumsy helper compared to the nurses. She was nervous and uncomfortable with the situation and embarrassed by the intimacy. Banks was glad when she said good night and closed the door behind her.

At last, he sank down into a winged chair beside the lukewarm radiator and took out his mother's letter. When he opened it, a check for five-thousand pounds sterling fluttered out. It was signed by his father. Banks raised his eyebrows and set it on the table beside him. It might come in useful someday, but for now, the letter interested him more. It was twelve pages long, written in his mother's beautiful, elegant script. There were almost no errors in it. This was no spontaneous letter. She must have worked on it for a long time, he concluded, writing, rewriting, correcting and then copying it out carefully. He imagined she had drafted it many times in her head before she knew that Sarah would be able to deliver it in person. It amounted to a long apology for her whole life, a confession of failure, a plea for understanding and a surrender to her own weakness.

It left Banks feeling exhausted and sorry for her but uncomforted. He refolded the letter and pushed it back into the envelope. He picked up the check and looked at it. His mother had stressed this was not an advance on his inheritance but a gift to help him through 'such difficult times.' He supposed the honourable thing to do would be to send it back, but it would fund the Ginger Bowles Fellowship on its own. He put it in his wallet, lay down, turned off the light and tried to sleep.

The sheets were clean and crisp, the room almost too warm; it was much quieter than the hospital. But Banks couldn't sleep. He found himself wishing Ginger would visit him or that he had Sammy in his arms. He didn't feel comfortable here.

The alarm went off in the adjacent room before dawn, and Banks heard someone get up and go to the bathroom. He heard the heater ticking, the water running, the lavatory flush. He heard someone make his way downstairs and out the door. A motorcar moved off down the street.

Only then did he get up and go to the bathroom. Here he examined himself in the mirror for a long time, wondering why Sarah had been so shocked yesterday. Living most of his days surrounded by men with third degree burns on their faces or in all the early stages of plastic surgery, he had come to see his face as, well, rather nice. Indeed, McIndoe often pointed to him to encourage the young men arriving in a state of shock and horror only days after being incinerated in their cockpits. The stitching that had made his face look worse than Frankenstein in the early months was no longer visible at all. The strips of different skin had blended together almost seamlessly across his cheeks and chin, although, he had to admit, his eye-sockets still stood out as particularly pale, giving him a somewhat owlish look and his eyelids were maybe a trifle oversized and his eyebrows bushier than they had been. He had consciously let his course, reddish hair grow longer to fall over the seam at the top if his forehead — and because it reminded him of the way Ginger had worn his hair. He didn't think his face was the least bit terrifying any more, but he supposed the shock for Sarah was that it wasn't the face he sailed away with. Particularly, his nose was different, broader and more solid than the family nose. Well, she would just have to get used to it the way it was.

When he came out, he was startled to see his sleepy sister emerge from the room across the hall in her dressing gown. That wasn't the room adjacent to his own in which the alarm had gone off.

"Do you need any help?" she asked in a sleepy voice.

"Yes," he told her honestly. She came and helped him dress.

Gradually, over the next two days, the awkwardness between them began to melt. Sarah stopped seeing the artificial components of his face, and her memories of how he'd looked before were soon overlaid by the daily visage in front of her. Perhaps she also started to see beyond the surface just as the Priestmans, Colin and Mr Bowles did. She asked him to tell her everything that had happened since he'd arrived in England, and he did.

Eventually, David felt comfortable enough to ask Sarah about the separate bedrooms. "It's not a usual arrangement for newlyweds," he noted.

Sarah's laugh was strained. "Oh, did you notice?"

David didn't laugh.

Sarah grew serious, but she didn't meet David's eye either. She focused instead on looking into the teapot and then pouring a sample, putting it back and announcing they should wait another couple of minutes. David kept staring at her until she finally admitted, "It's because our relationship is entirely platonic, and that's the way we want it."

"What?"

"Yes. I told you I was determined to come over here. I mentioned that to Clive the day we met. We were dancing and, I don't know, something about him made me trust him. Besides, he was with the British consulate, so I started telling him about how you'd come here and explained that I wanted to come over too. He was sympathetic, but suggested a ball was a poor venue for a serious discussion, so we agreed to meet for lunch."

"Dr Goldman let you meet a man for lunch after meeting him only once?"

"Father knew nothing about it. I said I was going shopping with Judy, and she was prepared to lie for me. I met with Clive for lunch and poured out my whole life story. He said he would consult with his superiors and see what he could do for me, so we agreed to meet again a week later. We did that four or five times, before he formally called on Father and asked permission to take me to the theater. Father agreed, and so we started seeing each other socially, but by then, we'd already come to an agreement."

"An agreement? So, the formal proposal was a sham?"

"No, I wouldn't call it that. He had to do it to get Father to agree. We are legally married, and frankly it's no one's business but our own whether we share a bed or not. Clive and I are very fond of one another and we understand one another. He needs a wife if he is ever to be appointed ambassador, and I wanted to come here and do something meaningful."

"If Clive needs a wife to advance his career, why didn't he marry earlier?"

"Don't be dense, David! I'm sure you know perfectly well why."

David did, and it didn't make him feel any better about his new brother-in-law.

The night before David was due to return to the hospital, Clive raised the issue of his future. "So, old boy, you're going back to face the knife again. How many more times did you say it would be?"

"Just two, if all goes well."

"Hm. Meaning you'll be released in about two months' time?"

"About that, yes."

"And what are your plans then?"

"Then I face the Medical Board, which I hope will pass me fit to fly."

"Fly? You can't mean you want to go back to being just a pilot? I would have thought after all you've been through that you'd be beyond that 'fly boy' stage."

His father wouldn't have been able to say it better, Banks thought resentfully, and answered stubbornly. "No. Sorry to disappoint. I'm still in that 'stage,' as you put it. I very much hope to be passed fit for flying."

"But David!" Sarah burst out. "Why? It could all happen again! Why risk it?"

"Because, in case you haven't noticed, we're still at war with Nazi Germany. Indeed, we're barely holding our own, and the RAF is the most important component of the fight."

"No question about that at all, old boy," Clive chimed in. "But I don't think anyone alive would question that you've already done your part. As Sarah said, why take any more risks? There are lots of other ways to contribute to the war effort besides flying fighters."

"My ambition is to become an instructor at Training Command," Banks admitted.

"Well, that's a little better," Clive admitted, before adding, "and yet, there are a tremendous number of flying accidents. It would be a terrible tragedy if, having survived what the Luftwaffe did to you, you died because some student pilot made a stupid mistake. Why not consider something totally different?"

"Such as?"

"Intelligence. With your language skills, you would be invaluable."

Banks made a non-committal reply, and they left it at that.

Chapter 13

Bosham, March 1942

Sammy's antics at the sight of Banks verged on the hysterical. He launched himself from the front door and down the front steps with a single, soaring leap. When he reached Banks, he sprang up to stand on his hind legs only to push against Banks' chest with his front paws, spin about and sprint back to the house barking. He than sprang back on the porch wagging his tail furiously the whole time. He repeated this performance three times before he'd calmed down enough for Banks to go down on his heels and embrace him. Sammy at once started frenetically licking his face, thrashing with his tail so furiously that his entire body swung back and forth.

Enthralled by this unbridled expression of canine joy, it was several minutes before Banks looked up towards the open door of the cottage. One glance was enough to warn him something was terribly wrong. Emily stood in the doorway watching Sammy's antics with an expression so sad that it cut Banks to the quick. She also looked as though she'd been crying.

Banks stood and started for the door. "Emily! Not the Skipper?"

She shook her head once. "No. Kiwi." She broke off and turned away, entering the cottage.

Banks followed her inside with an already subdued Sammy in his wake. He set his suitcase down by the door and followed Emily into the kitchen. She was putting the kettle on for tea with tears streaming down her face.

"I'm sorry," she croaked. "I know it's bad form. I've got to pull myself together before Robin gets home. He had to belly land at Hawkinge and bashed his ankle again, though apparently not as badly as in France. He was taken to hospital, but I've spoken to him. He'll be fine. He should be back any time now. I must pull myself together before he gets here, but – I keep thinking – remembering – all the good times with Kiwi. I just can't stop remembering. You know – no, you don't. You were already in hospital," she reminded herself. "It was Kiwi who came to the church to explain why Robin didn't show at our wedding. He walked out of the dispersal saying they could 'hang him from the yardarm' for all he cared, but he wasn't going to leave me standing at the altar with no clue about what had happened." The memory triggered a flood of tears, and then the kettle started to screech. Emily took it off the stove only to set it down on the wooden counter in confusion. Her turned back was shaking.

Banks didn't dare go to her. He loved her too much. If he started comforting her, he was afraid of what might happen. And the Skipper might walk in any minute. So instead, he got up and took the kettle off the counter before it burned a mark on it. He set it on a cold burner and found the tea pot. As he worked methodically, Emily took a deep breath and wiped her face with a dishcloth.

Banks sat down again and said as calmly and gently as he could. "Tell me what happened."

"They were slaughtered. The whole squadron. They were close escort for some Bostons on a raid to Lille and they got jumped by a Gruppe of Focke-Wulf 190s and" she gave a shuddering shrug "— they were slaughtered. They lost three pilots over France and a total of seven aircraft. Robin, as I said, just made it back to Hawkinge with his oil temperature off the clock and the engine about to explode. Reynalds and Wizard also crash-landed, and their Spits were total write-offs. Pearce managed to put his Spitfire down in one piece and it will probably be salvaged, Mickey told me, but he had to be taken to hospital with bullets in his thigh."

"Did anyone see what happened to Kiwi?" Banks asked.

"I doubt it," the Skipper answered, coming through the door. Emily ran to him, and he wrapped his arms around her tightly. Banks looked away until he heard them separate. Robin sank onto one of the wooden kitchen chairs and thrust out his ankle, which was in a cast. Taking up the conversation as if there had been no interruption, he said, "We were heavily outnumbered. I was so busy warding off attacks from three of the bastards that I couldn't spare a glance for anyone else. I expect it was the same for the others. The Fw 190s are far superior to our Spits. They're faster when climbing, diving, and on the level nor can we out-turn them – not to mention they carry four canons. I don't know how any of us got out alive."

Banks gazed at him. The squadron leader looked drained and shattered, worse than since the height of the Battle of Britain. Banks calculated he'd been at it since mid-August 1940 without a break, except for the odd week of leave now and again. He was well overdue to be pulled off ops. Aloud, Banks remarked, "If no one saw what happened, then surely there's a chance that Kiwi safely took a walk."

"Yes," Robin conceded, looking around before dragging himself to his feet.

"What do you want?" Emily asked sharply, adding firmly. "Whatever it is, sit down! I'll get it for you."

"No, I need to ring Mickey, and see if we've heard from the Red Cross about the missing pilots."

"Why don't I ring Colin instead?" Banks suggested. It was clear that the Priestmans needed time alone together without him underfoot, and as a padre, Colin would have access to information from the Red Cross. "I'll see if we can't meet for dinner. I promise to wring whatever information there is out of him."

"Yes, that would be helpful," Robin agreed, sinking back into his chair. Banks slipped out of the kitchen, closing the door behind him. From the hall, he rang Colin and arranged to meet at the Old Ship. Taking Sammy with him, he let himself out of the cottage and walked across to the familiar pub.

At the Old Ship there were conspicuously fewer RAF uniforms than usual and none from 606. But Banks was no stranger to the locals either and Sammy was also a 'regular' here and was well-liked by clients and staff both. Banks settled into his usual corner table, and Sammy lay down in 'his' space between the table and the empty fireplace. He sat attentively, waiting for the waitress to bring him a bowl of water and a dog biscuit. These received, he lay down to wait, dozing now and again, until Banks was ready to depart. Banks ordered a pint and settled in to wait for Colin. It might be an hour or more, Colin had warned.

His thoughts circled around Kiwi, swinging from disbelief to a sense of fatalism. Practically from the day they met, Kiwi had seemed like a big, strong shoulder to lean on. Banks had come to count on it being there. Yet, objectively, it was a miracle that the big New Zealander had lived as long as he had. Just like the Skipper, he'd been in the thick of it for more than eighteen months and was now the senior flight commander.

"Have you ordered one for me?" Colin asked, putting a hand on Banks' shoulder.

"No, sorry."

"Don't worry." Colin went to place his order at the bar, and when he returned, he sank into the chair opposite. "I got through to the Red Cross," he opened, without preliminaries. "Needham was found dead in the wreckage of his Spitfire, and Eton managed to bail out and was picked up by the Germans. He's a POW. But there's no news of Kiwi. Nothing."

Banks considered that. "Is that good or bad?"

"I think it's good. The aircraft was found – and it was empty."

"So, he either got out before it crashed or afterwards."

"Exactly. The French have an amazing network of people willing to help downed airmen and spirit them back by a variety of different routes. It can take months, up to half a year I've heard, and in the meantime, there is silence. So, no news is good news. I think we need to stay optimistic about Kiwi until we hear something to the contrary."

Banks smiled at that. Colin was always the optimist. It was part of his job.

"Let me ring the Skipper. He'll be very relieved to hear this," Banks suggested and left to call from the payphone.

When he returned, Colin remarked in a low voice, "I expect Robin is taking this very poorly."

"He seemed completely dazed. I've never seen him look so bad."

"He's overdue for a rest. Long overdue. He's not going to like it, but he's being sent to Staff College."

"How do you know that?"

"I have an uncle at the Air Ministry, remember?"

"You didn't — "

"Good heavens! I don't have that kind of influence – or I would have had him pulled off ops months ago. The sad thing is that – just as in your case – his orders had actually been prepared before this disastrous sortie. He should have been relieved a week ago, but there was some mix-up with his replacement and his orders were delayed a week. Please don't say anything to him. The Station Commander will deliver the news tomorrow morning when he reports in."

"It will rather feel as if they're blaming him for this disaster though, won't it?"

"Hard as it may be for you pilots to believe, an assignment to the Royal Air Force Staff College is neither a form of punishment nor torture. It is actually considered an honour and an indication that the Air Ministry believes Robin is ready and able to take on greater responsibilities."

"He won't like staff work."

"Emily will."

Banks laughed but then grew serious. "Speaking of staff work ... I told you about my sister."

"Yes! Tell me more! We haven't had a real chat since you spent nearly a week with her."

Banks was glad for the opportunity to talk about Sarah. He did not hide his misgivings about the whole relationship and his brother-in-law, albeit without going into details. He ended by admitting, "he suggested that I should give up flying and take a job in intelligence instead." Banks watched tensely for Colin's reaction.

"Well, that's certainly a possibility, if you want it," Colin responded without missing a beat.

"Why do you say that?"

"You might pretend you've only succeeded at flying, but just listening to you talk about Mr Bowles' guest house has demonstrated that you've got a shrewd head on your shoulders. Your command of maths leaves me dizzy, if nothing else." Colin laughed.

"That's different. You know why I want the guest house to succeed."

"We all do, and Emily has contributed as much as you have with her intuitive sense of style and understanding of the historical context. But that's not the point. The point is you could probably succeed at anything you put your mind to."

"For someone called 'the dullard of the family' all my life, the notion of being in 'intelligence' would be comical, if it weren't so frightening."

"What's so frightening about intelligence? It covers a multitude of sins, after all, many of which are quite straightforward."

"Such as?"

"Well, with your native command of German, you could be used to interrogate downed German pilots."

Banks remembered Ernst Geuke and how the German had suspected him of being an intelligence officer. He thought back to their conversations. It had been good for him at the time, but he didn't want to face one German pilot after another. Of course, he might run into Andreas, Ulli or Joachim, but he was far more likely to encounter all those former Hitler Youths who'd chanted *Jude verrecke*. Maybe it would give him satisfaction to confront them as POWs? But he doubted it. The fact was he didn't want to face individual Nazis. He didn't want to have to confront them as *people*.

"There are lots of other jobs, too," Colin spoke into his thoughts. "We are constantly monitoring German radio and newspapers and other communications. Even those media that are heavily censored often provide gems of intelligence for the trained reader. I understand simple things such as advertisements from manufacturing firms sometimes inadvertently give away technical details. Someone like yourself who thoroughly understands aircraft would be in a superb position to sift through the German technical journals and suchlike."

Banks smiled, inwardly relieved that he could smile at all. His skin had gradually become supple enough. "Somehow that doesn't sound like much fun."

Colin laughed but added seriously, "If you want something more exciting, someone with your command of German and French could be employed on clandestine operations."

"With this face? I doubt it. Too distinctive."

"You may be right about that, but there are many more people who help plan and organise missions than actually take part in them."

Banks stirred uneasily in his seat, and Colin observed, "your resistance to work in intelligence has nothing to do with the work itself, does it?"

Banks shook his head.

"What is it then? The flying?"

"The flying, yes, but its more than that. Even if I can't fly, I want to remain in the RAF so I can be among fliers. They can't take my wings away, you know. Even if I'm not in a flying job, people will know I once did fly, that I'm qualified to fly."

"And that's so important to you?"

"It's who I am, Colin. It's a part of my identity. I've lost so much else — my homeland, my family, my face. Being a pilot is all I have left."

"I think you're putting the case a little strongly," Colin demurred. "Far from having no homeland, you have three: Germany, Canada and England. You may have cut off your ties with your father, but you have a sister and a mother. And you do have a face. It may not be the same face you had two years ago, but it is not an unattractive face. In fact, I think I like it better than your old face."

"You would say that — even if I still looked like Frankenstein."

Colin just laughed and announced, "What I trying to say Banks, is that you are who you want to be. You have the right and the means to shape your future. It is up to you to make the most of it. Now, I'm going to order another round and see about a meal. Can I get you something?"

"Bring something we can share with Sammy," Banks answered.

Chapter 14

London, End of May 1942

The Central Medical Establishment crouched beside the Middlesex Hospital, surrounded by reminders of the Blitz. In the waiting room, scores of young men waited nervously to face the RAF Medical Board. The fresh, young faces of schoolboys hoping to be passed fit to enter the RAF wandered restlessly about the room, while the pain-lined faces of wounded veterans anxious – or dreading – a return to the fray hovered about the tables. The two groups segregated instinctively, keeping a wary distance from one another.

Banks nodded to others like himself, men whose faces weren't quite natural. They were involuntary members of the same club. Even if they did not know each other's names, they felt a natural kinship. He sat down next to one of them; the other man smiled stiffly and pushed a dog-eared magazine in Banks' direction. "Looking for a bowler hat or a flying category?" he asked.

"Flying category," Banks answered firmly.

"Me too."

Before they could deepen the conversation, a name was called, and his new-found companion jumped nervously to his feet. Banks had time only to wish him luck before he was led away, never to be seen again.

After another indefinite period that felt quite long, Banks' turn came. He was taken to a door labelled "Adjutant." The orderly opened the door for him, waved him through and closed it behind him. Inside the dingy, cramped room he was told to take a seat. The flight lieutenant behind the desk had a thick file in front of him, which evidently contained Banks' medical records. Looking at the documents rather than at Banks, he remarked. "Let's see. Third degree burns over face and hands. Right hand festered and needed repeat treatment ... hm." At last, he looked up. "You'll have no difficulty getting a discharge."

"I don't want a discharge," Banks protested.

"Oh, one of the gung-ho types, are we? Had a couple of you today already. It must be a contagious condition. Look, the RAF needs fully fit pilots, not invalids. We have hundreds of young chaps who can't wait to get at the Hun. It's better for everyone, if you take your discharge and look for other work."

"But that's not what I want," Banks insisted.

"Well, last I heard, the RAF isn't here to do what you want it to do, but rather to win the war. Go and take a seat again. You'll still need a complete physical before you get your discharge papers."

Stunned, Banks walked back into the waiting room and sank into a chair, unable to formulate any clear thoughts. He had not considered the possibility of being kicked out of the RAF altogether. He had assumed they would let him do a ground job — controlling, adjutant or the like.

At what seemed like a haphazard intervals, he was called to various offices to provide blood and urine samples, to have his lungs, blood pressure and reflexes tested, to take an eye examination and a hearing test, and so on. The afternoon dragged by as the waiting room gradually emptied. Shortly before 6:00p.m., Banks was called and escorted to a door with a sign stating the occupant was Air Commodore so-and-so and Chairman of the Board of Medical Examiners.

Unlike the adjutant, he wore medical insignia and projected a polite and gentlemanly manner. "Pilot Officer Goldman, have a seat." Smiling, he added, "There's no need to be nervous. If it were allowed, I'd offer you a brandy. As it's not, we'll just have a nice chat, shall we?"

"Yes, sir."

"Now, you have a rather thick file here, and by the looks of it you've had a very rough time these past eighteen months. However, I understand from the adjutant that you would like to remain in the RAF."

"Very much so, sir."

"Well, we're always pleased to have officers who are as keen on the service as you are."

Banks felt some of the tension ease. Even if they didn't let him fly, apparently they wouldn't throw him out altogether after all.

"Moreover," the air commodore was continuing. "except for your injuries, you appear to be in excellent physical condition – eyesight, hearing, and all the other bits and pieces seem to be in excellent working order."

"Yes, sir," Banks agreed emphatically.

"I'm also happy to tell you that a number of other pilots who suffered similar injuries and returned to flying status have performed far beyond expectations. We're seeing more and more of them nowadays." Just when Banks was about to relax, he added, "However, in your case, there are two impediments preventing a return to flying status."

After the initial encouraging remarks, the statement took him aback. "But, sir..." His voice faded away as the air commodore lifted a hand to halt his flood of protest.

"First, Dr MacIndoe does not think your right hand will ever regain sufficient strength to handle the instruments of a modern fighter, much less a bomber, under combat conditions."

Banks could have pointed out that the Spitfire did not take any strength to handle, but he preferred to focus on his personal objectives. "I'd be perfectly happy with a restricted flying category, sir. Just before I was shot down, I had been posted to Training Command. That's all I'm asking for now," he declared, adding without even stopping to take a breath, "I can certainly handle elementary training aircraft under training conditions."

This elicited a smile from the air commodore. "That's very refreshing to hear. We need good instructors – though, of course, you'll have to convince Training Command that you are up to the task."

"Sir?"

"If you decide to pursue that path, you will have to pass a flying test with the Chief Flying Instructor at Central Flying School Upavon."

Banks nodded seriously. "Yes, sir. Of course."

"However," the Air Commodore again quashed his growing hopes. "I mentioned two impediments. The second is more unusual. I have a note here suggesting you might be better suited to other kinds of work entirely. Specifically, that you might be better suited to intelligence than flying."

"Who put that note in my file, sir?" Banks asked, stunned.

"I'm not at liberty to disclose that, Pilot Officer, but I can assure you it is a gentleman in a very senior position within the Secret Intelligence

Service, or MI6 as some call it."

Clive, Banks registered, and his skin went cold. Then he roused himself. "Sir, I fell in love with flying as a child. I built gliders before I was fourteen. I obtained my pilot's licence at seventeen. I had qualified on twins by the age of eighteen. I had a commercial licence at nineteen. I have over 1,200 hours flying in my log. I came to England for the sole purpose of flying with the RAF and joining the fight against Nazi Germany – as a pilot."

The air commodore considered him calmly and not unkindly, but Banks had the feeling he was not entirely sympathetic either – or did Clive wield greater power and influence than Banks could imagine?

At length, the examiner declared. "There's no need for you to rush into this decision. You are due for leave. I suggest you take advantage of the improving weather and get away from it all for a while. Visit friends or family. We'll send you a time and date to report to Upavon for that flight test with the CFI. If you don't pass, that will decide your fate for you. If you do, we'll revisit this issue. Sound fair enough?"

"Yes, of course, sir." What else could he say?

Chapter 15

Devon, Early June 1942

With the Skipper at the Royal Air Force Staff College, Emily had given up the cottage in Bosham to save money. She had moved with Sammy into the nearly complete barn at Mr Bowles'. Here she worked on furnishing and outfitting the future guest house to make it comfortable and attractive. Banks' unannounced arrival sparked off a frenzy of delighted barking and canine antics that drowned out the no less heartfelt human welcomes from Emily and Mr Bowles. Banks felt as though he had indeed come home, at least for a holiday.

That evening they sat at the picnic table behind the house in the warm, early summer air, watching the light drain from the sky and the stars gradually burn brighter. The serenity of the place, combined with the warmth of the company, made Banks feel that life was almost good. If only he could be sure he'd be passed fit for flying and not be forced into a career he didn't want by a brother-in-law he didn't like. Then with a pang of guilt, he remembered Kiwi and asked, "Any news of Kiwi?"

"Nothing."

"How's the Skipper doing at Staff College?"

"As you'd expect. He's top of his class. His mind was wasted on the RAF. He could have been a Cambridge don teaching theology, philosophy or God-knows-what. Rather like you, actually."

"Me? I couldn't even get into a university much less graduate from one!"

Emily snorted her opinion eloquently.

Banks retorted by explaining only half in jest, "You have to understand, Emily: flying is a disease. Once it takes hold of you, you're never entirely free of it."

To his astonishment, Emily answered wistfully, "I know. Don't you remember? When Robin was at Hawarden, he used to take me up in the Maggie with him. He let me take the controls once or twice. It was like nothing I'd ever experienced before – heady, elating – and addictive. If it had been peacetime or I'd been a man, I think I would have been no different than either of you."

"Why do you need to be a man? Women can fly."

"I know they can, but all the private flying schools where women used to take flying lessons have been absorbed into the RAF. There's nowhere in England nowadays where a woman can learn to fly."

"I heard from someone that the ATA is accepting women candidates for ab initio training," Banks remarked.

Emily looked over at him. "What?"

"The Air Transport Auxiliary. They—"

"Yes, yes. I know what they do, and I knew they had women pilots, but I thought they had all learned to fly before the start of the war."

"Initially, yes. But the demand for ferry pilots is greater than ever, and they've already exhausted the available supply of trained pilots not fit for military service – male and female. They used to have scores of Americans flying with them, you see, but after America got sucked into the war by the attack on Pearl Harbor, most of the Americans have gone home to join their own Army Air Force."

Emily hastened to ask, "Do you know how one applies to the ATA and where they do the training?"

"I haven't a clue, but it wouldn't be hard to find out."

There seemed no more to say, so they moved on to other topics.

Over the next couple of days, Banks sat down with Mr Bowles and went over his accounting. On his last visit, Banks had talked Mr Bowles into keeping a ledger where he jotted down what he spent on materials, the number of hours he worked on various projects and what he had been paid. It was too rough to show an outsider, but Banks had persuaded the older man that it didn't have to be "pretty" and that he didn't need to do 'the maths,' just keep a record. With Mr Bowles beside him, Banks patiently added the sums himself and showed him what he should have earned on each job compared to what he'd actually received. He was almost invariably short.

"People been cheating me for years, haven't they?" Mr Bowles concluded with wounded anger. "My own neighbours," he added bitterly.

Banks looked at the humble man beside him and felt his pain and humiliation. Too late, he realised that he might not be doing him a favour by showing him how his neighbours had made a laughing stock out of him while taking advantage of his simplicity. Banks looked desperately for some means to soften the blow. What would Colin have said? "I think, I think ..." Mr Bowles looked at him expectantly. "Maybe it wasn't intentional. I mean, when you go to a shop and go to the till to pay at the end, you take the clerk's word for it, don't you? You don't add it all up for yourself, do you?"

Mr Bowles shook his head slowly, defeat in his eyes. He couldn't add things up in his head, certainly not quickly.

"What I'm trying to say, George, is that people pay you whatever you tell them is fair. They don't question how you calculated it. I think, if you asked for more, they'd give it to you."

Mr Bowles stared at the ledger between them. With a dirty finger, he underlined one of the sums. "Ask for five quid more from the Dalbys.?" He sounded extremely scepitcal and shook his head, clearly uncomfortable. After a moment, he looked over at Banks with big, pleading eyes. "Couldn't you go round and explain the situation?"

Banks did not want to do that. He'd be the Jewish banker squeezing his debtors. "I don't think it would go down very well. We need someone from around here, someone people trust and respect."

"Why don't we ask Colin to help?" Emily suggested. She stood in the door to the kitchen with an apron on as she prepared to make them lunch.

"They don't know Colin either," Banks protested.

"But doesn't he know the local vicar? And even if he doesn't, he could talk to him, don't you think?"

"That's a good idea!" Mr Bowles declared, brightening. "The vicar's a good man. I'm sure he'd help, if you just explain things to him." His eyes pleaded with Banks.

At night, Banks waited for Ginger, but he didn't come. He tried conjuring him with his thoughts and then called his name softly, but there was no answer. Banks realized that Ginger's presence had been fading for some time now. It was as if his ties to the world of the living were weakening, or maybe he had stopped worrying about Banks and his father because they were helping each other now?

After a week at the cottage, Emily and Banks went together to visit Colin's Aunt Louisa. Emily had told her about the guest house, and the old lady insisted she had a house full of "superfluous" household items that she would be delighted to donate. All Emily had to do was come and sort through what she wanted. Banks left the women to look through the bath and bedroom linen, the cutlery and incomplete dinner services, the lamps, pillows and cushions. Instead, he took Sammy for a walk on the grounds of the old manor.

Getting the household furnishings was the last step to making the guest house operational, and Banks wanted it to open when Emily rejoined Robin at wherever his next assignment might be. It was important to Banks to see it up and running before he faced the next phase of his life. Some irrational part of him feared that his whole life was about to change again, and not necessarily for the better. He feared he might not be able to keep an eye on things as he would have liked. As he walked around the grounds, he felt restless and nervous as he had not done for a long time.

They returned to Bowles cottage with the Jaguar filled with an odd assortment of household furnishings to find a wing commander grinning at them as they pulled to a halt in front. Emily jumped out of the car and flung herself at Robin with a heartfelt "congratulations!"

"Nice, aren't they," he said, looking at the stripes on his sleeves before turning to Banks to remark, "You're looking better than I've ever seen you. Is the ordeal finally over?"

"The surgery is finished, but I haven't been passed fit for flying yet. I have to take a flight test with the CFI at Upavon first."

"That shouldn't be a problem, surely?"

"I don't know what he's looking for – or if he has instructions to fail me."

"Why should he?"

"It's a long story."

"In that case, let's have dinner first." Robin turned and called back towards the cottage, where Mr Bowles hung in the doorway, looking both happy and left out. "Mr Bowles, go and put on your best suit. I'm taking everyone out to dinner at a very nice restaurant in Exeter. I've already made reservations, and I've put champagne in the refrigerator for when we get back."

Grinning, Mr Bowles disappeared back inside.

"I'll need to change too," Emily concluded, "but first stop torturing me, Robin. You have your next posting. What is it?"

Robin drew a deep breath and responded with obvious disappointment. "Station Commander, RAF St Athans. That's in Wales and is the location of the School of Air Navigation."

Emily threw her arms around her husband, gave him a quick kiss on the cheek and said, "Training Command? You won't be going on ops?"

"Not for the foreseeable future, although I was promised a wing in six months or so."

"Now, I truly want to celebrate. I'll be down in a quarter of an hour."

By the time they returned, it was almost midnight. Mr Bowles, who rarely stayed up past nine at night, fell asleep in the back of the car. On arrival, however, Robin reminded them about the champagne and suggested they sip it together in the sitting room. Mr Bowles declined and started to go upstairs to bed. The young people decided to take the champagne over to the barn so as not to disturb Mr Bowles, but before they got out of the door, they heard something crash overhead and a heavy thud. Rushing to the foot of the stairs, Banks called up, "Are you alright, George?"

An inarticulate grunt answered him.

Banks and Robin bounded up the stairs together, but Mr Bowles was already pushing himself upright, mumbling an apology about "not being used to so much wine."

"You go down and open the champagne," Banks suggested to Robin, "and I'll see George to bed." As Robin withdrew, Banks helped Mr Bowles to his feet and guided him to his room. "Here, let me get your shoes and belt off," he urged over the older man's weak protests. Banks helped Mr Bowles undress down to his underwear. Then, flinging back the bed covers, he gestured for Mr Bowles to lie down and sleep it off.

Obediently, Mr Bowles swung his feet up on the bed and lay back, pulling the covers over him. Just as Banks switched off the light before going out of the door, he called out. "Banks?"

"Yes?"

"You're like a son to me. You know that, don't you? Just like a son. Looking after me and helping me like you do. Just like Ginger would—." His voice broke.

"No one can replace Ginger," Banks said gently. "I know that."

"No, no. Don't want you to. You just be you. I love you the way you are. I hope you don't mind, do you?"

"Mind?" Banks returned through the darkened room and went on his heels beside the bed. He took the older man's thick, rough hand between both of his own. "I am honoured to be Ginger's brother. I only hope that I can continue to be a son to you and won't end up making you doubly miserable."

"Just stay alive," Mr Bowles answered, tears welling up in his eyes.

"I'll do my best," Banks promised, squeezed his hand and then withdrew.

Banks found Robin and Emily had lit the oil lamps and candles and settled down on the sofa together. "Am I intruding?" he asked from the door, ready to withdraw.

"Not at all. We've been waiting for you to open the bubbly," Robin answered, getting to his feet again. Banks moved hesitantly into the room. The Skipper was pulling the cork out of the bottle while Emily held two tumblers ready. "No champagne glasses, I'm afraid," she said over her shoulder apologetically.

"Who cares about that?" Banks answered, taking the glass she handed to him as Robin filled the next. When they all had some, Banks offered a toast to "Wing Commander Priestman," and they clinked glasses and drank.

Then the Skipper turned to Banks and asked him directly, "So, what's this about the CFI at Upavon wanting to fail you? Why should he?"

Banks took a deep breath. "It turns out my brother-in-law is not a diplomat at all. He's someone very senior in MI6, and he thinks I'd be more useful to his service than to the RAF."

"From his point of view, he's probably right, but I gather it isn't what you want."

"No, it's not what I want. I didn't go through all the pain of these last twenty months to be stuffed into some ground job reading German technical journals or interrogating prisoners!" The champagne had loosened Banks' tongue, and his pent-up frustration found its voice.

"I suppose I could write a confidential memo to the ministry saying you have a severe drinking problem that results in you talking indiscreetly whenever you have so much as a sip of bubbly," Robin suggested.

"Good try," Banks answered with a faint smile, but he found he was too tense – despite the champagne – to joke about the topic. "It's late." He declared, putting his unfinished glass down on the table. "You two need time together. Thanks for dinner and the bubbly—"

"Would you sit down for a moment," Robin ordered.

Banks hesitated and then sat down, unsure what to expect.

"You need to do some flying before the flight test. Time to build your confidence and make sure you don't have a fit of nerves on the test. If they're truly trying to wash you out, they'll throw something like a Wellington or a Hampden at you."

"Bombers? But I've never flown one." Banks had never thought of that.

"Emily and I were just having a chat about the ATA. Emily's keen to try to get in, and I was reminding her they are often required to fly aircraft they've never see before."

Banks glanced at Emily; she didn't look upset. In fact, she looked rather excited, so presumably. the talk had gone well so far. He decided to do his part for her happiness. "I think Emily would make a splendid ATA pilot."

Robin laughed and clinked his glass with Banks'. "That makes two of us!" He drank and then added. "The point is Central Flying School might decide that any instructor should be equally versatile and expect you to demonstrate competence in an unfamiliar aircraft. They'll argue that training needs are increasingly for bomber pilots. They can't justify retaining instructors who aren't able to instruct at least twin-engine aircraft. How long before you have to report?"

"A little over two weeks now," Banks admitted.

"Good. As long as the weather holds, that should be enough time for you to get in ten to fifteen hours on different aircraft."

"Where?"

"St Athans, of course. As I understand it, there are a variety of aircraft there, and you're welcome to fly any of them you want."

"May I?" Banks could hardly believe his good luck.

"Of course. On one condition."

He should have known there was a catch, but it didn't matter. This was the most important thing in the world to him at this moment. "Anything."

"You have to give Emily some basic instruction on the Maggie in between times, so she'll have no problem passing her ATA flight test. Is that a deal?"

Banks laughed. "That would be a pleasure. He clicked his glass with Robin's. "It's a deal."

Banks slept soundly after the unaccustomed quantities of wine and champagne. When he woke, the birds were starting to sing, and dawn was breaking. Beside him, Sammy stretched, yawned, and made himself comfortable again to sleep a little longer. Banks turned over to go back to sleep and suddenly froze. The model airplanes were rotating gently, and the floor creaked.

"Don't let them ground you, Banks. It wouldn't be right." Ginger spoke clearly and forcefully. His tone urgent and solemn he added, "your gift is showing others the joy of flying and giving them the skills to stay alive." Then abruptly, he laughed, a sound Banks hadn't heard since his death. "Besides, if you're flying, I'll be flying with you."

Epilogue

Flying Training School,
Little Rissington, August 1942

The gaggle of acting pilot officers in brand new uniforms marched into the hall to be greeted by the Station Commander. The instructors stood at the side of the room, listening to the familiar welcoming remarks, and then watched as the new pupils crowded around the tables with assignment lists. They observed the way the young held themselves, the way they chatted and interacted. They recognized the poorly suppressed excitement, spotted the inadequately suppressed anxiety, noted the pretence of nonchalance and understood the looks of surprise, disappointment and elation. Eventually, all the students seemed to have found their names and noted their assignments.

The station commander told them to divide up according to their assigned "flight," pointing to three corners of the room for A, B and C flight, respectively. A dozen youths dutifully assembled in each of the corners and waited expectantly. At a nod from the station commander, the flight commanders and their three instructors went to their respective corners to introduce themselves.

In "B" Flight, the flight for training on twin-engine aircraft, Banks watched the expressions of the four young men assigned to him as they turned their attention to him. He read eagerness, wariness, respect and admiration, but not a trace of shock or repulsion. He glanced at the faces of the trainee pilots looking at his fellow instructors, but he could see no difference in their expressions. To these young men, he was just their instructor; the man who would decide whether they would be passed on for further training or grounded for insufficient flying ability. His face no longer elicited revulsion, fear or pity.

Glancing up, he saw his reflection on the glass surface of some framed official document. For a split second, he saw Ginger's face but then it was gone. The face that looked back at him was no longer that of a stranger; it was his own.

HELENA P. SCHRADER

A Rose in November

A WWII Love Story
for the Not-so-Young

Helena P. Schrader

A Rose in November
Foreword and Acknowledgements

Almost twenty years ago a reader complained to me that all love stories are about "young things." She had just married at age 55 and noted correctly that finding love at a mature age was just as beautiful as finding it when young. Furthermore, lovers with careers, children and emotional "baggage" from the past face different, more complex challenges than young lovers. Complex challenges translate into good novels. So, the off-hand comment piqued my interest as a novelist and inspired me to write a story featuring mature lovers.

The choice of characters and setting were dictated by the fact that I had only just finished writing *Where Eagles Never Flew*. The characters of that novel were still with me, talking to me, influencing me. Hattie Fitzsimmons, only a minor character in *Where Eagles Never Flew*, insisted firmly that her story was exactly the kind of thing I was looking for. I had to agree. She was so determined to have her story told, in fact, that once I sat down to write, I never lost my way or lost my inspiration for a moment. Hattie was beside me the whole time explaining the situation. Whether my skills as a writer are adequate to tell her tale is for you, the reader, to decide.

However, another important theme of this work is class-consciousness or class prejudice, and the RAF's role in breaking some class barriers down. While Britain remained a class society in the interwar years, at its inception the RAF exceptionally established an apprentice program to attract technically minded young men to serve as ground crews. The applicants came from the lower middle and upper working classes, and the programme was welcomed as a huge opportunity for these underprivileged elements to enter the glamorous world of aviation. Training lasted three years and in some ways the graduates of the apprentice program were as well educated as the officer graduates of the Royal Airforce Training College at Cranwell. This inevitably led to a blurring of the distinctions between the ranks, reducing the sense of divide between officers and other ranks. Furthermore, the RAF actively encouraged ambition by offering cadet scholarships to Cranwell for the three best apprentices each year. Another training scheme allowed flying training for outstanding ground crew, who thereby gained sergeant's stripes regardless of what trade they fulfilled on the ground. When the war started, roughly one quarter of the

RAF's pilots were regular sergeant pilots trained through this scheme. These factors contributed to the image of the RAF as a comparatively socially mobile meritocracy. In the novel, however, I explore the impact of professional social mobility on personal behaviour.

I wish to thank my editor Rhonda Shore for her meticulous and gentle interventions. I am also deeply indebted to Hazel Horne for the evocative cover collage based on contemporary photos.

Cover Image

The photo of a Spitfire being serviced by ground crew is used with the permission of the copyright holder Chris Goss. The images have been photo-edited and modified for this cover by Hazel Horne.

Chapter 1

November 1940

Rhys Jenkins was torn from a deep sleep and grunted audibly when the alarm woke him. It was still pitch dark beyond the black-out blinds. He swung his legs over the edge of the bed and switched on the light so he could wash and dress quickly and quietly without disturbing the kids. He had been dreaming vividly, and he tried to bring the dream back to his consciousness, as he let water into the basin from the two taps. Plunging his hands in to the lukewarm water, he flung water over his face and wiped it dry with the towel hanging beside the sink. The dream eluded him, but it had taken him back in time — so much so that as he went to shave, he found himself asking when his hair had gone so grey? Could he really be an ageing man when he felt like he hadn't yet started to live?

Wasn't he still the same young man who had scrambled up from a trench in late 1916 to give a downed pilot a hand restarting his engine? That too had been on a cold and dark November day. The mud of no man's land had been frosted in the first glimmer of dawn. They had heard the aircraft sputtering overhead and looked up in astonishment as it banked and set itself down on the rough stretch of mud. They were even more astonished still when the pilot clambered out and ran around to open the cowling of his engine. "Must have some kind of engine trouble", someone surmised as they all stood there staring.

Rhys had glanced towards the rising sun and reckoned the German artillery spotters would soon find the downed plane and start taking potshots at it. He handed his tin mug filled with lukewarm tea to one of his mates and scrambled out of the trench to jog over to the pilot. "Can I help, sir?"

The young man who looked over at him in evident astonishment was about his age. He had pushed his goggles onto his forehead, but they left huge, red rings around his eyes, making him look frightened and vulnerable. He was bundled up against the cold, but his hands were so numb and stiff they were practically useless. "Do you know anything about aircraft engines?" he asked in an accent Rhys had only heard from very senior officers — the ones who came and went and never said much anyway.

"No, sir, but I've tinkered with the odd car engine. If you tell me what to do...."

Somehow together they got the thing going again. He and the pilot turned the fragile crate around by the wing tips so it faced the longest stretch of more-or-less level ground they could find, and then the pilot started to climb back into the cockpit. He stopped and looked back over his shoulder, "I say, what is your name?"

"Lance Corporal Jenkins, sir. Royal Welsh Fusiliers."

"Ever think of joining the RFC?" That was the Royal Flying Corps.

"No, sir. Do you think they'd take someone like me?"

"They would if they had any brains, but you never can be sure with the blimps, can you? Thanks again and cheerio!"

The pilot and aircraft disappeared in the misty November morning, never to be seen or heard again. The idea of joining the RFC, on the other hand, wouldn't leave him alone after that. Eventually, he broached the subject with the company sergeant major.

The sergeant major took a dim view of the idea. "What do you want with the RFC, Jenkins? Those crates are bloody dangerous. Crash even when no one is shooting at them. You may think this life is lousy – which God knows it is – but the RFC is a damn sight worse. Take my word for it, at least we get rotated out regular, but those poor blighters have to keep at it, regardless."

But he didn't want to fly, Rhys explained. Quite the opposite. What attracted him was the idea of tinkering with engines, getting these complicated constructions of wood and canvas to leave the earth. He loved to watch them just as he had once loved flying kites. The mere thought of climbing aboard one and flying, by contrast, made him want to dive underground.

The desire to go below ground when things were difficult came naturally to Rhys. He came from a long line of miners and had left school at 14 to start work. He'd been working down the pit for almost four years when the war broke out. Although mining was a reserved occupation, Rhys had been swept up in the patriotism and ran off to join the army in 1915. He'd been wounded twice, and he'd had more than one opportunity to regret his decision, although he didn't. Despite the horror, misery and pain he had seen, the war had opened windows. His parents had never travelled more than 20 miles from the village of their birth, whereas he had seen London and Paris. His parents hardly spoke English and mistrusted anyone that wasn't Welsh – and half the Welsh as well. Rhys, in contrast, had met and learned to like and respect men from every part of the empire. After three years in the army, Rhys knew that he wasn't going back to the pit or to spend the rest of his life – if he had one – in the mountains of Wales.

Yet, for some reason, that brief encounter with the pilot was like an itch that wouldn't go away. Reflecting on it now, more than 20 years later, Rhys speculated that perhaps it had gripped him so because it was the first time in his life he had ever done anything out of the ordinary. As a boy, he'd been one of five brothers, the second to last. His parents hadn't seemed to remember his name most of the time, content with just calling him 'boy' as they did the others. In school, too, he was just one of the crowd, neither particularly good nor particularly bad at learning or sports. In enlisting, he'd broken away from his family a bit, but only with a horde of other youths. After that, everything had been merely more of the same: He was a cog in the wheel of a giant war machine.

But on that fateful November morning in 1916, when he'd clambered out of the trench to tinker with an aircraft engine until it sprang back to life while the others just looked on, he had stepped out of the ranks. For once, he had become someone unique. It was, Rhys knew, the defining moment in his life, and eventually, he'd convinced the company sergeant major. The sergeant had eventually been decent enough to find out what forms were needed and helped him get them properly filled in. Indeed, he must have recommended him because Rhys found himself transferred to the Royal Flying Corps (RFC) almost three months later.

He could still vividly remember the day he arrived at an RFC training unit. He had felt small and alone, shivering in a threadbare uniform on a dreary and bitter March day. Everything had been grey and dirty, just like in the trenches, but the air had smelled different: Aviation fuel and wood and glue rather than cordite and shite. A sergeant waved away his salute distractedly and informed him he was to be trained as a fitter. Rhys had nodded dutifully while wondering what in the name of God that was.

Now, as Rhys stared into the mirror, he couldn't grasp that he wasn't still that overly-thin young man with black hair and eyes, but rather a man whose face had become square with flesh and whose hair was silver-grey. He'd always been short (came from generations of crouching underground, his Mum said), but back then, he'd been as frail as a jockey as well. Now he'd grown stocky. Not fat, he told himself, sucking in his stomach and squaring his shoulders for the mirror. But he'd have to watch it, he reflected as he turned sideways and considered his figure more objectively. At least his hair was still thick, he thought resignedly, as he scraped away at the crop of stubble on his cheek, careful to leave his thick, drooping moustache untouched.

After washing, Rhys dressed quickly in uniform. He'd been wearing uniforms for a quarter of a century, the RAF one ever since the service had been founded in early 1918. He had worked his way slowly up the ranks until he proudly wore the stripes of a flight sergeant. He loved the service, and he loved his job. Unfortunately, Warrant Officer Whiley made his life less than satisfying.

From the day they met, Rhys had not been able to stand the man, and the feeling was mutual. Whiley was a nitpicking, petty man with the face and figure of a weasel. He had a whiny voice, eyes that squinted, and a nose that dripped interminably. He was the kind of man who learned regulations by heart and quoted them at you in the most inappropriate situations. He was a man who could not take a joke, make an allowance, or forgive and forget a mistake. He made going to work every morning increasingly difficult.

It was now getting on half-past six, and Rhys just had time for a quick breakfast before catching the bus to RAF Middle Wallop. Rhys lived off-station on account of the kids. Owain was thirteen and still in school, and Ellen was only seventeen. When her mother died, Ellen had stopped going to school. Rhys wasn't happy about that, and the thought made him frown as he came into the kitchen and found her making his breakfast.

"You don't need to get up for me, El", he told her for the hundredth time. "I'm quite capable of making myself breakfast." When he spoke, the Welsh lilt of his voice was very pronounced.

"But you don't make yourself a proper breakfast if you're left to yourself, Dad," his daughter countered seriously. Ellen took after her mother, Rhys reflected. She had her mother's round, pale face, dark, fine hair, and her pleasingly plump figure. Yet watching her as she efficiently took a plate down from the cupboard and deftly served him baked beans and canned cooked tomato, he rather wished she didn't take after her mother quite so much. Gladys had been a woman who rarely smiled. He certainly couldn't remember her laughing, and that was a sad fate for a girl on the brink of womanhood.

Rhys felt a weight of guilt settle on him and abruptly felt as old as the man he had seen upstairs in the mirror. He hadn't done right by Ellen. It had been too easy to let her pick up the burden of the household as her mother took to her bed and drifted towards death. At first, he had hardly noticed how much Ellen was doing. He was out of the house all day, and when he came home, everything was just as it should be. That Gladys had stayed in bed and let Ellen do the housework was something he only learned later when confronted by one of Ellen's teachers. The teacher had given him quite a lecture about taking Ellen out of school. Of course, he had the right to do so, the lady admitted, but Ellen was a good student, the lady said, serious and hard-working. With a school-leaving certificate, she could train as a secretary, bookkeeper or telephone operator. By taking her out of school prematurely, he had blocked her way to well-paid, respectable work. She would end up in a factory or, at best, a salesgirl or waitress, Ellen's teacher lamented. Rhys had felt guilty about it ever since. He'd even made sporadic attempts to get Ellen to go back to school, but she resisted doggedly.

"And who would look after you and Owain then? Besides, I'm learning what I'll need to know best: How to look after a man and household."

It was hard to argue with that. It was hard to argue with someone like Ellen or Gladys at all. They were self-contained and very, very sure of themselves. At least Gladys had been. He supposed that had to do with her strong religious upbringing. She was raised strictly non-conformist and considered his own rather easy-going form of faith little short of atheism. In the early days of their marriage, he had provoked her once or twice into calling him a 'Godless Communist'. At least all the moving around they'd had to do with the RAF had prevented Gladys from raising Ellen as strictly as she had been raised herself. Gladys had gone to the same chapel with the same minister for the first 20 years of her life. She'd been buried by him too, back home in Wales.

Rhys sighed and turned his thoughts from wife to daughter again. Although Rhys had given up trying to talk Ellen into going back to school, he still felt guilty about her looking after him. How was she ever going to find a husband if she spent all day in the house alone? He had to convince her train for a job. It wasn't right for her to be looking after her old father and teenage brother at seventeen.

He kept his thoughts to himself as he kissed her goodbye and went out into the bleak November day. The buildings were just starting to separate themselves from the sky, hulking, black shapes against a dark grey sky that was barely growing lighter behind the solid overcast of cloud. It looked and felt like sleet was in the air. Just what we need, Rhys thought to himself, turning up the collar of his coat against the damp wind.

It was full daylight by the time he passed the sentry at the gate to the RAF station, and freezing rain had started seeping from the low clouds. Across the field, ground crews in oilskins were tightening the tarpaulins. The field was evidently closed for flying, and Rhys presumed the same weather had closed in over the Luftwaffe's fields on the other side of the channel.

He dashed up the steps of the admin building and ducked gratefully inside. He removed his fore-and-aft cap and shook it out with his left hand, while running his right through his hair to remove some of the sleet. He'd hardly had a chance to take a deep breath before a WAAF (Women's Auxiliary Air Force) appeared and told him in a self-important fashion, "Squadron Leader Sewall wants you to report to him at once, sir."

Once or twice Rhys had thought about suggesting Ellen join the WAAFs. Her lack of school-leaving certificate would be no barrier here, and she could train to do one of many interesting jobs. But then again, he didn't like the idea of her living in a mess with a bunch of other girls. He knew that most of the girls were nice, but some weren't – the ones you saw giggling in the corners of the hangars at odd hours of the day or sneaking out of unlikely places fussing with their hair and stockings. He wasn't sure he wanted Ellen mixing in such company. Nor was he sure he wanted her among so many young men either. Again, he knew that most of the lads were all right, but the atmosphere could still be pretty raw. He'd wanted something better for Ellen – like working in a proper office or a nice tea room with classy customers.

His thoughts still with Ellen, he knocked on the squadron leader's office door and entered at the call to "come in." The squadron leader was sitting behind a solid desk stacked high with wooden in and outboxes. The telephone was almost lost amidst the overflowing piles of paper, and Rhys recognised the exasperated expression of a man who hated paperwork but was now forced to confront it. Sewall's expression cleared at the sight of Rhys, however.

"Flight Sergeant Jenkins! Glad to see you. I have some good news. Good news for you, that is, although the rest of us will be sorry to see you go."

"Go, sir?"

"I've got your orders here. You're being given a squadron of your own, 606 at Tangmere. Apparently, they've just been fitted out with Spitfires, and want a chief who has experience with the kites. So, there you are, posted immediately, report ASAP."

Rhys could hardly believe it. Although there was nothing unusual about such a transfer, Rhys hadn't been expecting it. He'd been on the squadron for the last two years. He'd been on it in France and throughout this past summer during the Battle of Britain. He'd watched three squadron leaders come and go – one killed, one wounded, one transferred. Nine months ago, when Warrant Officer Kelly had been badly injured in a car accident in France, Rhys had hoped for the promotion. He'd been disappointed to have the weasel put in charge and a mite resentful too. Once or twice, after downing a pint too many, he'd thought about putting in for a transfer, but then the whole bloody show started.

Once the Germans smashed through the Ardennes, Rhys felt it would simply be wrong to leave the squadron. He owed it to the crews and the pilots to do whatever he could to keep it at peak efficiency. In the event, he'd been awarded the Distinguished Service Medal for his efforts and success in getting the ground crews out of France after the pilots had flown the serviceable kites back to England. It had been a close-run thing, and they had lost two men during the final days at Dunkirk. Still, under the circumstances, they had been lucky, and he was proud of them.

But the orders said ASAP, and there was never any point in lingering. Rhys had long since learnt that dragging out goodbyes only made them worse. He'd keep in touch with the men he liked best, the others he wished well and that was that. What preoccupied him as he packed his kit and took his leave was finding a solution for the kids. They would have to move, of course, but Tangmere had been mauled by the Luftwaffe this past summer, and he'd heard that RAF housing was scarce. He resolved to go there, appraise the situation, find suitable accommodation and then return to help with the move. That meant leaving Ellen alone with her younger brother for several weeks, however, and he wasn't entirely comfortable with the thought.

"Do you think you can manage, El?"

"Of course, I can, why shouldn't I?" came her solemn answer. The expression in her eyes made him feel he was insulting her to doubt it.

"Well, Owain can be a handful at times."

"I can handle him, Dad."

"Well, if he gives you trouble, all you have to do is ring me. I'll come straight back and sort him out."

"I'm sure that won't be necessary, Dad. It won't take you more than a couple of weeks to find somewhere for us. We'll be all right for that long."

"I'd better go over to the school and let Owain know what is happening. It wouldn't be fair for him to come home and find me gone."

"I'll pack your things for you while you do that, Dad. Is one suitcase enough?"

Rhys walked over to the school and explained the situation to the headmaster. As his son shuffled into the headmaster's office, Rhys was shocked by the way he hunched his shoulders. How often did he have to tell the boy to stand up straight? Worse was the guilty look the boy wore – as if he'd committed any number of misdemeanours and was wondering which one had been discovered. The boy was astonished to see his Dad.

"What are you doing here?" he asked at once, and then with a nervous glance at the head, he asked, "I'm not being expelled, am I?"

"No, of course not," Rhys answered without thinking. "I've been posted to Tangmere as Chiefy—"

"Are we going to have to move again?" Owain interrupted him in a whining voice that put Rhys' nerves on edge. If he'd ever used that tone of voice with his father, he'd have been nursing a sore jaw for a week – or he would have been unable to sit down, depending on whether his father went for the quick ear-boxing or the belt on the backside. But Gladys had been against any form of 'brutality' against the children.

"That's right," Rhys told his son in a tight voice, hurt that the boy thought only of himself rather than sharing his father's pride in the promotion. "As soon as I can find us somewhere to live and get you enrolled in school."

The boy grimaced, and Rhys' sense of helpless frustration grew. Owain had been a sweet child, but he'd taken a wrong turn since his mother's death. It wasn't Ellen's fault. She did the best she could, but there seemed no getting through to the boy. His marks in school had dropped steadily, and he had no interest in anything outside of school either. In fact, he had turned into a sullen, introverted child who seemed to lack any motivation, ambition or direction.

"You have to obey your sister while I'm away. She's in charge, and if you give her any trouble, you'll have me to answer to. It shouldn't take more than a couple of weeks to find something suitable. I'm sure we'll be together for Christmas.

Owain just shrugged and shoved both hands deep into his pockets, a sullen expression on his lips. "Is that all then?"

"For now," Rhys answered.

"Better run then. That was the bell." Without even waiting for an answer, Owain ducked out of the door and was gone.

Rhys was humiliated by his son's behaviour before the headmaster. He just shook hands with the head without meeting his eyes and mumbled, "you'll be hearing from me when I've arranged for him to change schools. It should be before Christmas."

"Very good," the headmaster agreed.

The sleet was worse as he made his way back home to collect his suitcase. Ellen was waiting for him at the door, already dressed in a coat, hat and gloves. "We have to hurry if you want to catch the 12:35 to Southampton, Dad."

"You've checked the schedules?"

"Of course, Dad. The 12:35 has the best connections to Chichester. Otherwise, you'll have to go via Winchester and change twice."

Out into the sleet again. "Your brother doesn't seem very happy these days, does he?" he ventured cautiously.

"I haven't noticed any change."

Maybe she was right about that. It was a long time since Owain had been that cheerful little kid that had brought so much sunshine into his life. A long time ago. Where had the time gone?

Rhys felt again the jarring contrast between the man he was now and the young man who had left the ranks one cold morning in 1916 to make himself into someone different. Sometime between that morning and this afternoon, he had become an ageing widower with two teenagers who needed something from him he couldn't even identify, much less give. He loved them both, but somehow that wasn't enough. He was failing them. He could sense it – almost taste it – but he didn't know what to do.

The railway station was damp, dirty, crowded and confused. Today was particularly bad because too many people crowded inside to avoid the cold and sleet. Wet wool, dripping Wellingtons, squalling infants and metallic, unintelligible announcements pressed in around them. Rhys felt an intense, fierce desire to take his daughter in his arms and hold her to him, to tell her out loud that he loved her and was worried about her. But Gladys had abhorred all public displays of affection and trained him to avoid them. The children were her product. Distant and self-possessed, Ellen saw him to the train.

"Now, I'll ring the phone box on the corner every evening at 9:30 sharp. If I don't get through, I'll call again at 10 pm and then 10:30 until we connect. I'll give you the number of the Sergeant's Mess when I ring through tonight. Understood."

"Of course, Dad." Then, with only the barest touch of her cheek on his, she urged him to go aboard. "You'll want to get a seat. It's almost two hours to Southampton".

Dutifully, Rhys climbed aboard. But the train had come in from farther west, and all the seats were already taken. People were sitting on their suitcases in the aisles, and it was near impossible to find a place even to stand.

Rhys fought his way to a window as the train lurched into motion. He shoved it down despite the outraged protest of an elderly woman passenger. He leaned out as the train started to gather speed and waved frantically to his daughter, still standing primly on the platform in her hat and gloves. Ellen waved back calmly and unsmiling, but Rhys felt a terrible, weighty premonition of impending change. He sensed that he had just left his whole life behind. There on that platform was the last 20 years of his life embodied in that seemingly mature young woman who was really only a seventeen-year-old girl – and he was being carried away from it all at increasing speed.

For a moment, he thought he'd made a mistake and wanted to get off the train again, but it was too late. All he could do was close the window and return to his abandoned suitcase in the aisle in a dazed state. Numbed, he sat on it, closed his eyes and surrendered himself to his fate.

Chapter 2

November 1940

By the time Rhys reached Tangmere, both the premonition and the sleet had been left behind. The stars shined through tattered clouds. Not having seen Tangmere since before the war, he was shocked to see the skeletons of two hangars gutted by German bombs and note that one wing of the Airman's Mess was in ruins. Evidently, the large number of Nissan huts was the alternative to a proper reconstruction of the damaged buildings, at least for the winter. All the more reason to find a place for the kids off-station, he thought, as he entered the Sergeant's Mess.

Built during the First World War, it was comfortable and well heated. Rhys put his suitcase down at the reception, his hat in his hand. "Flight Sergeant Jenkins. I was told to report—"

"Of course, sir. We've been expecting you. Flight Sergeant Rowe's quarters have been made ready for you, sir. Devitt!" the receptionist called to an airman who was sorting mail in the room behind him, "Come and give Chiefy a hand with his things and show him to his quarters. You'll want to get something to eat, of course; the dining room is just along there, sir. You can get a hot meal until 9:oop.m. And I'll let Squadron Leader Priestman know you're here, sir. Welcome to Tangmere, sir."

That was a pleasant welcome, and the quarters were an agreeable surprise as well. He had a bedroom and sitting room to himself, with views looking over the field. Of course, the room was sterile at the moment, bare of anything personal, but somehow it had a cosy feel about it on a night like this. The mess was centrally heated, too, a rare luxury. Rhys could hear music coming up very faintly from below or perhaps from the Officer's Mess just across the way. It made him feel not so alone, despite this being the first night he'd been away from his family since he'd returned from France.

He unpacked quickly – he didn't have much stuff anyway – and hurried down to the dining room to get something hot before the kitchen closed. Over the years, he had often found himself a stranger in a new mess, and there was nothing particularly intimidating about it any more. But this time, the mess steward's attentiveness and the polite nods of the others reminded him he was finally a senior non-commissioned officer (NCO) of an active RAF fighter squadron, which was special ... and distancing.

This was the job he had dreamed of ever since he'd found out what a fitter was. Things had happened so fast this morning, and his worries about the kids had so overshadowed his elation that he hadn't had a chance to savour the sense of accomplishment. He certainly hadn't had an opportunity to celebrate this promotion with anyone, and now he was among strangers.

What was more, these strangers were men whose trust and respect he needed to win – at least the men in 606. There were three squadrons stationed here at Tangmere, and as yet he could not tell which of the men around him were attached to his squadron and which to others. Only one thing was certain: They all knew who he was and were surreptitiously watching him.

His suspicions were confirmed when two sergeants approached him as soon as he finished his meal and was preparing to leave the dining room, "Flight Sergeant Jenkins?"

"Yes?"

"Newbury, sir." The first man introduced himself and held out his hand. The man beside him held out his hand as well and gave his name as "Fogerty." They invited him to join them at the bar for a beer.

Rhys accepted guardedly. He was acutely aware there was only a fine line between being friendly and being fawning, and he was suddenly very protective of his dignity. This was his chance at last, and he did not want to make a mistake right at the start.

But he soon relaxed. Newbury was the senior fitter and Fogerty the senior rigger in the squadron. They introduced him to the head armourer, then to the other senior NCOs of the squadron. After the third round or so, the others, who were very much on their best behaviour at first, started to loosen up a bit. Rhys gained the impression that this was a well-functioning team, at ease with one another, but not with him yet. This boded well, despite the cautious complaining about inadequate training on Spitfires for the riggers.

The other thing that struck Rhys was the evident enthusiasm for the CO. In his experience, the commanding officer of a squadron had minimal impact on the ground crews, and it was rare for them to identify with him. After all, most crews had almost nothing to do with him. The Chiefy represented the crews to the CO and, in return, shielded them from him. The Chiefy, not the squadron commander, was the usual focal point for the ground crews. The evident devotion of the men to this CO suggested either the squadron leader was a particularly strong character or Rhys' predecessor had been exceptionally weak. If the latter, he might find that the squadron was not up to par, but if it were the former, he might have a hard time following his own course. He would just have to wait and see what sort of man the CO was.

Just before 9:30pm, Rhys excused himself. He was feeling tired but cautiously optimistic. He went to the phone boxes and put a call through to Ellen. She sounded sleepy. "Tired, El?"

"A little. Is everything all right? Is it a nice station?"

"So far. How are things with you and Owain?"

"Fine, Dad."

"You're sure you've got enough money for the next fortnight?"

"Yes, Dad. Don't worry about us."

"All right then. I'll ring again tomorrow at the same time." He rang off and went up to his new room. It was chilly now, the central heating evidently turned down for the night, but still, he felt amazingly comfortable here.

After he was in bed, it struck him that Ellen had forgotten to pack the picture of Gladys that he had kept in a silver frame by his bed ever since her death. With a twinge of guilt, he realised he was glad she hadn't. Gladys had been dead three years. It was time to get on with a new phase of life. He drifted off to sleep thinking it would also be good for the kids to get away from the house where their mother had been ill and died.

Rhys was due to report to his new CO first thing in the morning. He dressed for the occasion in his best uniform and slicked down his hair with Brylcreem. He thought he didn't look quite as old today as he had yesterday, although he didn't feel quite so young now that he was in a position of such responsibility.

Having heard that the CO was a Cranwell graduate, Rhys delivered his best parade ground salute as he reported, and the first thing that struck him about the CO was his eyes. They were deep, dark, penetrating – and touched with amusement. He returned the salute smartly enough and then held out his hand. "Pleasure to have you aboard, flight sergeant."

Priestman was extremely good looking, with wavy dark hair that he wore unconventionally long so that a curl was hanging onto his forehead. He wore a silk cravat tucked in the front of his tunic, and the top button was left carelessly undone. He had sunk his left hand in his trouser pocket already. In short, he matched almost perfectly the stereotype of a fighter pilot that the newspapers had created in the last months – and he was young enough to be Rhys' son. (The RAF had a policy, not consistently enforced, that fighter squadrons should not be commanded by men older than 26.)

For all that, Rhys sensed an intensity and alertness that was very much at odds with the light-hearted and happy-go-lucky press image. For a man of 24, Priestman was marked as only men who had stared death in the face – probably more than once – were. Rhys had seen it before, in the trenches in '15 -'16, with the RFC/RAF in '17 -'18, and in the last seven months.

"It's a pleasure to be here, sir," Rhys answered automatically while taking all this in.

Priestman indicated a leather chair and came around from behind his desk. Rhys settled himself somewhat tensely in the chair, and the squadron leader, leaning against the front of his desk, offered him a cigarette from a felt-lined cedar box. Rhys was tempted, but he noted that the CO's fingers were not stained with nicotine as the hands of most RAF personnel were; instead, they were covered with the thin, discoloured and stretched skin of recent burns. Somewhat intimidated by those marks of recent pain, Rhys shook his head to the cigarette, and Priestman replaced the box without taking one for himself. Despite the scars, his hands were wonderfully steady for a fighter pilot with a Distinguished Flying Cross (DFC) and Bar, Rhys noted.

"You come from 55 Squadron, Middle Wallop."

"That's right, sir. We were in France, but managed to get back in the nick of time—"

"I saw that. Well done."

Rhys found himself blushing like a schoolboy at the compliment. It took him a second to collect himself – realizing that Priestman had actually read his records. He continued cautiously, "as you know, we were in 11 group, Hornchurch, until September 1. Since then, Middle Wallop."

"When were you outfitted with Spitfires?"

"When we were pulled out of 11 Group, sir."

"That's just over two months. At 55 you were senior fitter, but you trained as a rigger as well. How comfortable do you feel with the Spit?"

"Very, sir." Rhys looked him square in the eye; he wanted this job, and he wasn't going to risk having it taken away from him.

"Good. Then you must have some questions for me." Now the squadron leader smiled almost wickedly, "after all, you weren't given a chance to read my files."

Rhys relaxed just a bit. "Can you tell me the operability of the squadron's aircraft, sir?"

"I'd be a bloody poor CO if I couldn't," Priestman countered almost sharply, but then he softened it with a smile and added, "at the moment we're at 100 per cent. In fact, even at the height of the party this summer, we rarely fell below 80 per cent. Flight Sergeant Rowe had an admirable record in that regard."

"I see, sir. You must regret losing him."

"Not particularly. Flight Sergeant Rowe put machines ahead of men. Under Rowe, this squadron lost one airman in a fatal accident and another was paralysed from the waist down. I suspect both accidents could have been avoided, but I wasn't on the squadron yet. Certainly, Rowe would have dragged a man before a court martial just because he tried to go home without leave — ignoring the fact that it was Rowe who had denied his repeated requests for leave. That's not my style, flight sergeant, and I hope it isn't yours. I know perfectly well what pressure we were under this past summer, and I think we all gave our best – which is not the same thing as being 100 per cent all of the time. No one can be that. I can't be anyway, and I don't expect it of anyone else either. What I do expect, is that we are honest about it. If I ask something of you — or your men — that they honestly can't give, I want you to tell me that."

"Yes sir," Rhys said with conviction. He was beginning to understand why the others liked and respected Priestman so much. He'd met squadron leaders who tried to be chummy with their NCOs, others who were patronising, and some who were indifferent or even negligent of their ground crews. But he'd never been treated so like an equal before.

"If any of the men have a problem, I expect to hear it from you – not from them or their pilot."

"Yes, sir." Rhys almost smiled, noting that this was precisely the way he felt about things too.

"And that goes for you too."

"Yes, sir."

The squadron leader seemed to relax a fraction. He ran his hand through his hair with a suddenly abashed smile. "I seem to be doing all the talking again. Don't you have any questions for me?"

"Well, sir, are the crews up to strength?"

"Not quite. We're short one fitter, two riggers, an armourer and three batmen – although my pilots think the WAAFs should step into that department."

They exchanged a grin.

For a moment, Rhys seriously considered mentioning his concern about housing, but then he decided against it. He was supposed to be concentrating on his job, not worrying about his family, no matter what the CO said about no one being 100 per cent. "Well, sir, I'd like to meet the men and look around a bit. You know, see the lay of the land and then I'm sure I'll be back with a lot more questions. If you don't mind?"

"No. That seems a very sensible approach to me. Good luck." He held out his hand again.

Rhys got to his feet, shook hands, and went out feeling oddly invigorated. He'd been motivated before he went into that office, but he felt downright inspired now.

After meeting the CO, Rhys faced the squadron itself. The men were called together in the one hangar that was still standing. It was cold, and everyone stood about bundled in non-regulation bits and pieces, mittens, boots and even earmuffs. Their breath was visible, but their faces were shaded. Rhys had the impression that most of the men in front of him were wary. He was glad he knew what the CO had told him about his predecessor. Rhys was a man who thought actions spoke louder than words. He opted not to keep them standing here for long in the cold. He kept his introductory remarks to a minimum and then dismissed them. He withdrew to the chiefy's office on the side of the hangar and had the section leaders report to him, trying to get a feel both for the most pressing tasks and the men.

He had been ploughing through a pile of maintenance reports on his desk when the WAAF who served as his clerk put her head in the door and asked, "do you want anything from the Salvation Army, sir?"

Startled he answered "What?" Then, letting the words replay in his head, he realised how ridiculous they were, and modified his response to, "what should I want from the Salvation Army? I'm stone cold sober at the moment."

The girl laughed. "No, the mobile canteen, sir. The Nazis hit the airman's kitchen and Naafi back in August, and ever since the Salvation Army brings us a hot meal a day. The cook-house has since been fixed, but fortunately someone forgot to cancel the Salvation Army and they still come. The canteen's here now, sir."

Now that she mentioned it, he was starving. "I'll come out and see this for myself," he announced, taking his cap and following her out. A van had driven right into the hangar, the side opened, and food was being distributed to a line of airmen with plates and cutlery. Rhys took his place at the end of the queue, lured by the smell of cooked food.

As he inched his way forward, he was conscious of the volleys of laughter that erupted again and again from the front of the queue and noted that most of the airmen turned away grinning. As he got closer, he realised that the two women serving addressed the men by name and joked with them in a familiar manner. It would have been flirting in younger women, but both these women were the wrong side of 30 and matronly.

One of them had an infectious laugh, and when she threw her head back to chortle, you could see a nasty gap in her teeth. She was quite unattractive, really, and her accent spoke of the poorest backstreets of some industrial Midlands town. That was just what the young airmen liked about her, Rhys suspected, watching the way they teased her and exchanged insults. She was like the aunts and grandmothers of their childhood – tough, rough-tongued and warm-hearted.

The other woman was of a different class and calibre altogether. She was stocky and hefty now, but her face had a symmetrical grace that suggested she had been an attractive young woman. Indeed, in a way, Rhys found her attractive even now. She, too, had a friendly word for everyone by name but in an accent that clearly put her in the officer class. She probably was an officer, he decided, remembering that the Salvation Army had ranks just like a real army.

By chance, she was the one to serve him, and she guessed who he was instantly. "You must be the new Chiefy. How are you settling in?"

"I only just got here last night", Rhys replied with a smile.

"I do hope everyone is being kind. Fitzsimmons, by the way," she held out her hand to him.

Rhys found himself juggling his plate to offer his hand. "Jenkins."

"And where have you come from, Flight Sergeant Jenkins?"

"Middle Wallop was the last posting, Ma'am."

"Will your family be joining you soon?"

"As soon as I can find them a place to live, Ma'am. I'm a widower, you see, and I've got two kids. I don't want them living on-station. I've got to find something for them close to a school."

"Indeed," she agreed, and with a nod, indicated the man behind him who naturally wanted to get his meal.

Rhys joined the others at the tables. The meal was tasty – better than most messes. It was pork and prunes in a white sauce on mash with brussels sprouts — not burnt or overcooked or too salty either. When he finished, he glanced over his shoulder, wondering if seconds were allowed. Mrs Fitzsimmons caught his look and waved him over.

He got up and returned at once. "Any chance I could have seconds, Ma'am?"

"As it happens, there is just a little bit left." He gave her the plate, and she refilled it, adding as she did so. "So how old are your children, Flight Sergeant?"

"My girl's seventeen, ma'am, all grown up really. Since her mum died three years ago, she's been keeping house and looking after me and her little brother. Left school to do it, though I wish she hadn't. I tried to talk her into going back, but she wouldn't hear of it. But maybe here, in a new place and all, she'll reconsider. Or at least start learning a trade. I mean, it isn't right for a young girl to take care of her old Dad. She ought to be out starting her own life. Meeting a young man of her own, and all." Rhys suddenly noticed he was rabbiting on about his personal problems to a total stranger, and embarrassed, he snapped his mouth shut and swallowed awkwardly. "Sorry to burden you with my problems, Ma'am."

"Not at all. And your son?"

"He's thirteen and still in school. But he's lost interest in everything since his mum died. I rather hope a change will do him good, but I've got to find a place where he can walk to school, and Ellen, that's my girl, can get to the shops and all. Are you from this area, Ma'am? Do you know where I could start looking for a flat?"

"I was born and brought up in Portsmouth – which is not where you want your daughter these days. Chichester would be better. Or Bognor Regis. Or one of the smaller villages. If you like, I could look at the advertisements and see what's on offer."

"I wouldn't want to impose, Ma'am. I—"

She waved him silent in a mildly imperious manner. "I know you wouldn't, but I was just thinking how difficult it must be for anyone to make sense of advertisements without knowing the area. I think the best thing would be for me to screen them, select half a dozen suitable abodes, and then drive you around to see them. I have a car and petrol rations. Would that suit you?"

"I couldn't possibly impose, Ma'am," Rhys said more firmly, deeply embarrassed.

"You aren't. I'm volunteering. My sister would tell you it's a pathological weakness of mine. She thinks I 'interfere' in other people's lives and have a 'helper's complex'. No doubt she is right, but there it is. Eat up before it gets cold."

Chapter 3

November 1940

Over the next week, Rhys was so engrossed in learning about and starting to put his mark upon his squadron that he didn't even think about housing – except at odd moments when he guiltily reminded himself he really must do something about it. On his nightly calls, Ellen reassured him all was well and soothed his conscience so that another day slipped away without him making an effort.

When Mrs Fitzsimmons reached him Saturday morning and announced she had found six places he should look at and asked if he could get the afternoon off, he was so grateful he didn't think of saying no. If she'd gone to so much trouble already, what was the point of it anyway? It would have been rude. She asked that he catch the bus to Chichester station and told him she would pick him up there.

Rhys dropped everything, rushed across to the CO's office and managed to catch him just before he went out to lunch. He asked for the afternoon off to look for housing and was given it without further ado. Then he dashed back to his quarters, changed into a better uniform and shaved for good measure. Mrs Fitzsimmons was a lady – whether she was in the Salvation Army or not.

At Chichester station, it took him several minutes to find her. She was not in uniform as he had expected. In a neatly-tailored, double-breasted navy coat, she looked trimmer. She also wore a hat with netting that came part way down her face, which made her look very chic. She was definitely an attractive woman, Rhys noted, doubly glad he had taken the time to change and shave.

"Mrs Fitzsimmons." He held out his hand to her. "I really can't tell you how much I appreciate this. I've been meaning to do something, but somehow, I never find the time. I was starting to get quite a guilty conscience."

"Really, I'm quite happy to help," she told him and indicated an ageing Morris Minor, which had seen much better days. She got in behind the steering wheel, and Rhys dutifully climbed in the passenger side.

She did not start the engine right away, however, but instead handed him a stack of clippings and scribbled notes. "Now those are the places I've selected. I've rung just about all of them. They all have three bedrooms, and none costs more than 3 quid a month." He wondered how she knew what he could afford as they had never talked about it, but he didn't get a chance to ask. She was continuing. "The first three are here in Chichester and we'll start with those. Then there are two in Bognor and one right in Boxgrove. Oh, and the last one is probably unsuitable as it's an isolated cottage, but when she said there was a dinghy landing – well, I thought we could look at it. But, of course, we can leave it out. It's just I remember that when Robin was thirteen, he was mad about boats. It occurred to me that your son might be the same."

"Is Robin your son, Mrs Fitzsimmons?" Rhys asked softly, watching her intently.

She caught her breath and looked over, almost alarmed. Their eyes met. "It's Miss Fitzsimmons, flight sergeant. I never married. Robin is my nephew, my sister's son. His father was killed in the Battle of Jutland, and my sister and I more or less raised him between us. Not having any children of my own, he's been very important to me, but of course he's a grown man and married now. No doubt that's why I've taken to extravagant charity again, as Lydia would put it."

"Well, I'm very grateful to you for it, Ma'am." Rhys told her seriously, thinking that she was not at all the robust woman she appeared in her Salvation Army uniform.

She turned the key in the ignition, and they began their odyssey across town. Rhys found Miss Fitzsimmons' driving hair-raising and the flats depressing. Housing seemed to be at a premium here, and the wartime shortages of building materials impacted the state of repairs. The first flat had been left in appalling condition by the evicted previous tenants. The second was so poorly insulated that the windows were frosted on the inside, and the third was dingy and cramped.

"Well then, on to Bognor," Miss Fitzsimmons decided determinedly.

"Would you mind terribly, if I drive, Miss Fitzsimmons?" Rhys asked, in fear of his life, if she didn't turn the wheel over to him.

Miss Fitzsimmons seemed astonished by the question and then sighed and handed him the keys, remarking with resignation, "I don't know what it is you men have about my driving, but Robin won't get in a car with me behind the wheel either."

"I think I'd like your nephew, Miss Fitzsimmons," Rhys suggested with a smile.

"I'm sure you would," she countered seriously and then added more lightly, "no doubt you'd like his pretty young wife too."

"Oh, I don't know about that. I'm not a man for silly, young things. Even my Ellen's not silly. Too mature for her age, really. But I suppose that comes of her mother getting so ill when she was only thirteen."

"I'm sorry about your wife, flight sergeant." Miss Fitzsimmons said it so sincerely that it was almost embarrassing.

Rhys shrugged it off. "She's been gone three years. Life goes on. If only it hadn't been so hard on the kids. I mean, I have to bring home the bacon and this last year, well, you know what that was like for the RAF."

"I do, yes. We started with the mobile canteen in mid-August, a week after Tangmere was bombed. I was told that 606 squadron lost its CO, a flight lieutenant and two other pilots all on the same day."

"Crikey! 606?"

She nodded. Rhys let out a long whistle. No one had told him that. "And that was when Priestman arrived?"

"That's right. AVM Park considered pulling them out of 11 Group, but then he yanked Priestman out of an OTU and sent him to see what he could do with them instead. He chopped three pilots on his first day."

"What? Why?"

"Oh, you'd do better to ask the men of the squadron about that. I've only heard things second hand. Besides, you were telling me about your children. Who was looking after them while you were working around the clock?"

"When I was in France, I sent them to my mother in Wales, but I didn't want them to stay there. I don't believe in shunting responsibility onto others. They're my kids, and I want them with me. Even if they didn't see much of me this past summer, I tried to make them feel like I would be there, if they needed me."

He paused, thinking about this. Things took on a different reality when you said them aloud sometimes. Now that he had put it into words, he felt compelled to add, "Of course, that wasn't really true. I mean, if they had rung me when we were trying to refuel and refit between scrambles, I would have exploded. Fortunately, they never did. Maybe they didn't dare." Rhys was frowning unconsciously and concentrating on the road, but he could still feel the woman next to him considering him intently.

When she spoke, it was in a low, gentle tone, "I think it's very admirable that you can be so honest about it. No, they probably didn't dare, but I bet they were also very proud of what you were doing."

Rhys glanced over at her and admitted to himself that he was more attracted to her than he had been to any woman for as long as he could remember. What had gotten into him? She was so obviously upper class. She wouldn't have anything to do with him as a man. So why was she so dressed up to go and look at flats? He concentrated on the road again, and they didn't speak again until they reached Bognor.

The flats here were no better. Miss Fitzsimmons was embarrassed and started apologizing about doing such a terrible job. Rhys had the feeling her disappointment was greater than his own, and that reinforced his intuition: she had gone to considerable effort to please him.

"It's not your fault." Rhys assured her. "Why don't we stop for tea?"

"Oh." She glanced at him nervously.

She was really a very vulnerable woman, Rhys registered, and she wasn't the matron he'd taken her to be, either. In some way, she looked younger than his Ellen.

"Yes," Miss Fitzsimmons whispered, "tea would be lovely."

Rhys stepped on the brakes and swerved sharply into the drive of a cottage doing teas. The wheels screeched, and Miss Fitzsimmons grabbed the door handle. "And you claim I can't drive!" she protested.

Rhys laughed.

He went around the car to open the door for Miss Fitzsimmons, but she evidently hadn't expected this and was already getting out on her own. At the cottage door she hesitated, and he opened it for her. Inside there was a fire going, and the place smelt of hot spiced punch and home-baked apple tarts. "This is wonderful! I never knew about it!" Miss Fitzsimmons declared delighted.

"You can be sure I didn't," Rhys agreed and indicated a table near the fire. The only thing missing was someone to take their order. "I'll go and see if I can find the landlady," Rhys suggested. "Shall I order you some punch if I find her?"

"Yes, please." Miss Fitzsimmons looked up at him, her cheeks flushed from the sudden change in temperature and her eyes glistening to make his blood run faster. When was the last time a woman had ever looked at him like that? Not in a couple of decades. Had Gladys ever looked at him like that? No. Never. Not once. He turned away and went towards the back of the cottage, calling, "Hello! Is anyone there? Hello!"

A few minutes later, they had steaming hot punch and an apple tart (no custard, the landlady apologised, on account of the rationing) in front of them. Miss Fitzsimmons suggested she had looked at the wrong newspapers and said maybe she should go to an agent after all, but Rhys wasn't really listening. Instead, he was contemplating her seriously as he watched her from behind the steam of his punch.

She was an attractive woman. She was caring, warm-hearted, humorous and quick to smile. She was active too – not passive and spoiled as he'd always imagined upper class women. Most importantly, she was sitting here, clearly dressed up on his account. His wife had been dead three years, and she hadn't let him into her bed for five years before that. He might be going grey, but he wasn't ready for the grave yet. Why shouldn't he take an interest in another woman?

No reason other than this woman was so obviously from a different class. Still, she was the first woman to make him sit up and take notice. Maybe it was because he was away from the kids? He'd been feeling like a different man ever since he'd got here. Well, there was only one way to find out if he had a chance with her, and that was to take a chance. "Miss Fitzsimmons," he broke into her monologue. She stopped at once, holding her breath, looking at him slightly alarmed, as if she were afraid she'd said something wrong. "Miss Fitzsimmons, I greatly appreciate the effort you've gone to on my behalf, but—" The hurt in her eyes was so tangible that his instinct was to reach out and catch her hand. Only he couldn't do that. Gladys had him too well trained. Besides, she was a virtual stranger and a lady. No doubt she'd be offended. "Miss Fitzsimmons, what I wanted to say is that you don't need to go to so much trouble on my account."

"It's not that much trouble—"

"Miss Fitzsimmons, hear me out."

She fell silent, but she looked defeated already.

"What I'm trying to say is that I'd like to see you again – without all this business of looking for a flat. Though I'll have to do that too. But, well, I was wondering if you'd like to come to the dance at the station next Friday night?"

The answer came faster and harsher than he had expected. Like a burst of machine-gun fire, she said, "No, not that!" He was so taken aback he hadn't even had time to be insulted before she added, "Don't you see? Everyone knows me there. Everyone would snigger and tease. Let's go somewhere where we can be ourselves – not the chiefy and the auntie from the Salvation Army Canteen."

That left him stunned for a second too. It was a 'yes' more definitive than her apparent 'no' – and it was very wise too. He smiled.

"You're absolutely right, Miss Fitzsimmons! We'll do exactly that, and now I think it's time we used our Christian names, don't you? I'm Rhys. What's your Christian name?"

"Hattie."

Hattie? He was stunned – what a horrible name. Of course, it suited the 'auntie from the Salvation Army' – but that wasn't the way he saw her any more.

She seemed to guess his thoughts because she added, "Marie Henriette, really, but everyone calls me Hattie."

"Marie Henriette? That's a lovely French name!"

"My mother was French."

"You'll have to tell me about her. May I call you Marie?"

"If you like...." She sounded hesitant.

"Please."

"Of course."

"Marie, will you give me a number where I can get hold of you?"

"Of course. Portsmouth 25—"

"Wait a minute. I need something to write it down with."

She had her handbag out and handed him a pen and a little pad of paper. He wrote her number down and handed the pen and notepad back to her. He signalled for the bill and paid for both of them. As they went out, he took her elbow to help guide her through the door.

Outside it was already dusk. "Should I drive you home?" Rhys asked.

"Good heavens. That's all the way to Portsmouth! There's no service from there to Tangmere. Just drive back to Chichester station, and you can catch the bus from there."

"Right," he agreed, wondering if the real reason she didn't want him to take her home was that she was ashamed of him. No doubt she lived with her sister and didn't want to be seen with an NCO. Well, she wanted to meet him again, and he should be content with that for now. "I might be able to get an evening off during the week, would you like to go to the cinema and dinner?"

"Yes, very much."

"It might be on short notice, you understand."

"Yes, I understand. I do need a little notice, however. I help run a Seaman's Mission and often have evening duty. I'd need time to get a replacement."

"How much time?"

"A day's notice would be nice."

"Roger. I'll do my best."

"And shouldn't I look for flats for you?"

"Yes, of course, if you want." He looked over at her, and their eyes met. He smiled, and she answered it tentatively. She was very pretty when she smiled.

Hattie left Rhys at Chichester station and drove out of town on the A27, but when she saw the turn-off to Bosham, she flung the wheel over and plunged down the narrow country lane. She was far too agitated just to go home, not back to her little semi-detached cottage in Eastney with its echoing stillness and orderliness screaming "old maid." She needed to walk until her thoughts and emotions settled or to talk to someone who might understand what she was going through.

But what was she going through?

She was falling in love. It was as simple – and absurd – as that. At forty-five years of age, she was behaving and feeling like a silly, brainless schoolgirl. Oh, what wouldn't Lydia say to her if she found out?

Although Lydia was her younger sister by two years, she had the vast advantage of being a widow – which, according to popular opinion, automatically endowed her with a degree of dignity and presumed wisdom. The fact that Lydia had plunged headlong into a wartime marriage at the tender age of seventeen and lost her husband at the Battle of Jutland 10 months later was politely forgotten by everyone – especially by Lydia herself.

Hattie knew exactly how Lydia would react if she were to breathe a hint of what she was feeling just now. She knew because it had happened once before, back in '18. Even then, Lydia had reacted as if she were behaving 'ludicrously'. To the widowed 20-year-old, her older sister's 'affair' had been an embarrassment. She had been accused of 'making a fool of herself', of 'being a laughing stock' and of 'an utter lack of common sense and decency' – all because she'd had the nerve to walk out with an American officer a half-dozen times. He'd only kissed her once at the Harbour station before departing to rejoin his company in France.

So, what would Lydia say of her now, at forty-five and with a non-commissioned officer? It didn't bear thinking about.

Hattie had reached the village. Ahead of her, the road plunged into the waters of the bay. It was high tide, and there was a cold, November wind whipping up a rough chop in the little bay. Smoke was blowing horizontally from the cottage chimneys, and it was rapidly getting dark. Hattie drove the car onto the verge and pulled on the hand brake. She donned woolen gloves and replaced her pretty hat with a practical knitted one. Finally, she wrapped a scarf around her neck and set off on the path that circled the bay.

The wind buffeted her, and the waves crashed against the concrete base of the harbour basin, sprinkling her with saltwater. Seagulls cawed loudly as they wheeled overhead. Hattie clutched her coat to her and walked vigorously to keep warm.

After Michael was killed, she thought she'd never fall in love again. Lydia — for all that she liked to play the grieving widow — had spent most of the 1920s cocking her hat at one eligible bachelor or another, while Hattie had found a degree of solace in the Salvation Army instead. At least it had given a new focus to her life.

At some point, the grief for Michael had faded away. There was a scar still. If she took out the only picture she had of him or was foolish enough to reread the handful of letters she had, the pain returned. But it wasn't a feature of her life any more; it was history.

By the time the grief was gone, so was her youth. Besides, she had never been pretty like Lydia, and after a generation of young men had been slaughtered in the Great War, there were too many women to go around anyway. Even pretty Lydia hadn't been able to compete in that marriage market. It had been pointless for Hattie to hope and fantasise. She had just got on with things: The Salvation Army, the Seamen's Mission, being an alternative 'parent' to Lydia's little boy.

The wind was making something clatter terribly on the cottage to her left. Hattie looked over annoyed. It seemed one of the shutters was loose. She peered at the cottage in the near darkness, noting that it looked rather neglected. The garden had gone to weed, and there were no black-out blinds in the windows: It was just dark, empty. Was that a 'For Sale' sign? No, 'To Let'.

Hattie stopped dead in her shoes. It would be perfect for Rhys, she thought. Bosham was a proper village with all the shops his daughter needed, and there was regular bus service to Chichester where the schools were. Best of all, it was close enough to Tangmere to get there by bicycle. Of course, it might be too dear, being right here on the water. She went up the overgrown path and jotted down the telephone number of the estate agent. Tucking the notepad back into her handbag, she hurried back to her car.

She drove past the church to stop opposite the Anchor Bleu. She hurried up to the end cottage of a row of stone cottages nestled beside the millstream and knocked vigorously. A few minutes later, her nephew's bride of six weeks opened the door.

"Hattie! What a delightful surprise. Come in out of the wind!"

Hattie moved gratefully into the low-ceilinged room with its ancient beams and open fireplace. It was amazing how Emily had transformed this cottage into a cosy home in so little time. When they had first looked at it together, Hattie had found it depressingly dingy and cold, but Emily had read history at Cambridge and was enchanted by its character. Hattie liked plaster walls with flowered wallpaper, bay windows, pastel furnishings and parquet floors. She would never have moved here. But Emily had used carpets and hangings to lend the room warmth despite its stone walls and floors. The furnishings were sparse, and the main pieces were wicker – garden things really – but in the dark room they worked surprisingly well, preventing it from becoming gloomy.

"I hope you don't mind me dropping in unexpectedly," Hattie started as she pulled off her hat and gloves.

"You know I don't! We've seen far too little of one another since I married".

Emily had worked at the Seaman's Mission, and she had met Robin when he came looking for his aunt. Hattie liked to take credit for their meeting, but she would never have intentionally brought them together. Robin had been the kind of young man to go out with very glamorous women, and Emily was not glamorous. She was, Hattie noted now as the younger woman took her hat and coat, pretty in a subdued, subtle way, but her hair was a light brown, her eyes hazel, her mouth too wide and her teeth a little crooked. She had a natural grace and slender, shapely legs, but not the kind of hourglass figure to turn men's heads. Emily was elegant, not flashy, lovely, not stunning.

"Shall I put the kettle on?" she asked cheerfully.

"Yes, if I'm not keeping you from anything important."

"Important? Do you want to know a secret? I'm bored. You know I love Robin and I do want to be here for him, but I was used to having a job before and helping at the mission. At first, I had the cottage to do up, but there's not that much more I can do now. I don't think I'm cut out to just cook and clean. My mother worked full-time, you know."

"I'm not the least surprised. You're welcome back at the mission any time."

"No way to get there. Robin needs the car. I've thought of joining the WAAFs, but apparently they won't guarantee postings to the same stations as active service husbands." As they talked, they had moved into the kitchen. Hattie sat down at the solid table while Emily filled the kettle and put it on the stove. She also produced biscuits from one of the cupboards and set them in front of Hattie. "Was there any particular reason you called?"

Hattie's heart started to flutter, and she felt silly. She thought of denying it, but she also desperately wanted to talk to someone about it. She just didn't dare meet Emily's eyes, so she busied herself arranging the biscuits on the plate Emily had produced. "What would you think if I said I'd been asked out to the flicks?"

"That's wonderful!" Emily exclaimed at once.

Hattie looked up at her sharply. "Don't you think it's a bit ridiculous at my age?"

"Why? I mean, if you like him, if you want to go. Who is it?"

Hattie ignored the last question and concentrated on the rest. "Yes, I do like him. Very much. He must be about my age since he has a seventeen-year-old daughter. He's a widower of three years. He's candid and open-hearted. Yes, I want to go to the cinema with him. But it seems very strange." She looked up at Emily uncertainly.

Emily – bless her – turned the kettle off as it started to whimper and sat down opposite. She looked at Hattie very seriously and stated with conviction: "I think you are one of the warmest people in the world, and it's a terrible pity that you haven't had anyone to share that with – except Robin, of course. It's because you have so much warmth to give that you've been so active in the Salvation Army. But you spend most of your time there organising and administering and paying bills and – well, taking care of all the business aspects. That's no substitute for personal affection. Finally, there is nothing the least bit ridiculous about two people caring for one another and wanting to be together at any age. I hope to God that Robin and I will still feel affection for one another in our forties, fifties and sixties."

Hattie got up and gave her a big, heartfelt hug. "Thank you."

Chapter 4

November 1940

Rhys straightened his tie for the umpteenth time. He couldn't remember ever being this nervous before a date before. What had it been like with Gladys?

They'd grown up together in the same village. They'd gone to school together. At some point, they'd started 'walking out,' and then he'd enlisted and gone away. When he came home on leave, he called on her. That meant putting on his best uniform and combing down his hair and then sitting in the musty-smelling front parlour with her father while she and her mother made tea. Her father had asked him about the war but hadn't listened to his answers. He'd been more interested in telling Rhys about what had been going on at the pit and at chapel. Just before he returned to the front, he'd asked Gladys if she'd 'wait for him', and she'd solemnly replied, "yes, of course, Rhys Jenkins."

Not long after that, he'd been wounded and hospitalised in France. He hadn't seen her again for another year. When he came, it had been like before, only this time he'd asked her father for permission to marry her when the war was over. Her father had sucked on his pipe and asked. "You going to be coming back to the pit?"

Rhys had said he supposed so. He felt a little uncomfortable saying it. He knew he didn't want to come back but didn't know if he had any alternative. Things were so uncertain. It was hard to imagine surviving at all. Impossible to imagine what peace would be like. Maybe the war would go on forever. But his future father-in-law had appeared satisfied. He had nodded and sucked on his pipe some more.

"Do I have your consent then, sir?" He asked at last.

"Gladys don't fancy anyone else," came the answer. And that was that.

He had then spoken to Gladys directly, and she had solemnly accepted his proposal. They had kissed chastely.

No, Rhys concluded, there had never been a time when he was

nervous with Gladys. Not like now.

Rhys ran his finger around the inside of his collar and, for the first time in his life, wished he could wear a silk scarf the way the pilots did.

He knew the experienced pilots did it because the collar and tie cut into their necks when they tried to scan the skies while flying combat sorties, while the younger pilots did it to imitate the veterans. Mostly, he liked wearing a collar and tie because it was a symbol of his status. Miners didn't wear collars and ties except at weddings and funerals. Rhys was proud of what he had achieved.

But what were his modest achievements to a woman like Miss Fitzsimmons? Of course, he didn't know the first thing about her. He was judging her by her accent and manners alone.

Suddenly she was coming towards him on the platform, and he forgot all his nervousness as she smiled at him. Her smile was so uncompromisingly happy that it made him feel like Clark Gable and every hint of self-doubt vanished.

She was wearing a different hat today, one that sat more on the side of her head than atop, with a pheasant feather rearing up at a jaunty angle. She had leather gloves and leather pumps. As she gave him her hand, he caught a whiff of perfume. Very French, he thought with approval as vague memories of his only leave in Paris stirred in him. "You look smashing, Marie. That hat suits you."

"Do you think so?" Her hand went to it a little uncertainly.

"Absolutely wizard," he insisted and offered her his elbow. As she slipped her gloved hand through it, she glanced up at him with a look that was both uncertain and proud.

He had done some reconnoitering for the evening and selected a nice-looking restaurant. Not something fancy where he would feel out of place and sweat about the bill the whole time, but a place run by a friendly old lady with a limited menu printed on a card with hand-sketched flowers. He'd reserved the table in the bay window and ushered Hattie in. She looked about herself with evident approval. "What a lovely place," she declared.

"Let's hope the food is as good," Rhys countered. They consulted the landlady about the menu and what ration stamps she needed from them, and then settled down to enjoy the meal.

"Would you like a sherry?" he asked, feeling the man-of-the-world.

"Thank you, but I don't drink alcohol. Salvationist, remember."

"Sorry." He felt rather stupid for the mistake, but the woman opposite him just didn't look like that woman in uniform he'd met at the station on his first day.

"Don't let me stop you," Hattie urged him, on the brink of breaking her own rules for the sake of not offending him.

But Rhys replied with a smile, "I don't drink either, except beer, that is." Gladys had been a very strict non-drinker, considering even his beer a 'highly dangerous addiction', as she put it. But it was hard to be in the RAF and not drink anything.

They placed their orders, and Hattie announced happily, "I think I've found the right place for you and your children, Rhys. It's a cottage in Bosham, directly on the water with a very pretty but, at present, completely overgrown garden. It's been empty for some time, and the estate agent says he thinks he can talk the landlord into letting it for four pounds a month. He's asking for seven at the moment, but the agent admitted it was much too much for the condition it's in. You could manage five, couldn't you?"

"For the right place," Rhys conceded. It was twice what he was paying now, but he expected a promotion now that he was commanded the squadron's ground crew. "Is it near schools and shops?"

"Shops, yes, and there's good bus service to Chichester. Bosham is a lovely village." As Hattie talked on, her enthusiasm became contagious. Rhys knew he'd take the cottage unseen, just on her recommendation. Their first course arrived.

"And what do you hear from home?" Hattie asked, anxious not to talk too much and afraid she already had.

"Everything seems to be fine," Rhys answered, but he was frowning. "Ellen always sounds so calm and competent, but I can't help thinking I'm asking a lot of a seventeen-year-old. And Owain doesn't want to talk to me at all. All I get from him is a sullen yes or no to my questions." Rhys shook his head, all his worries and guilt crowding in on him again.

"I'm sure things will be better when they're here," Hattie assured him earnestly. "Just having you around will be good for them, and the schools in Chichester have a good reputation."

Rhys felt some of the burden lift at once. It was helpful just being able to talk about the kids to someone. Besides, Marie was a practical person with sensible advice. "Maybe you could talk to Ellen, get her to start some vocational training."

For a second, Hattie was so touched that he wanted her to meet his daughter that she hardly knew how to answer. Then, telling herself she was making too much of it, she replied, "my nephew's father-in-law is a teacher at a vocational school in Portsmouth. Your daughter could certainly get there from Bosham by bus quite easily. I'll ask him what courses are offered."

"That's a wizard idea, Marie! You're so full of good suggestions, I think I must consult you more often." He was grinning at her.

"Oh, some of my suggestions can be terrible."

"Such as?"

"No doubt you'll find out soon enough. How are things at the squadron?"

Again, Rhys frowned, and this time he looked down as well. Without realising what he was doing, he fussed with the napkin that had been folded on his plate. He'd known from the start that nothing could be as good as it seemed, but he'd never faced a problem like this before. Twenty-three years in the RAF and, in all that time, he'd worked his way up the ranks without ever failing to win the respect of the men under him. Now at the pinnacle of his career, he was astonished to find himself feeling superfluous.

"What's the matter? Aren't the ground crews up to your standards?"

"No, it's not that at all. They're good. They really are. It's just...." Rhys pressed his lips together and noticed that he was fussing with the napkin. He yanked his hands away, embarrassed and then noticed Marie had put her napkin on her lap already. He hastily followed her example, blushing slightly, reminded of the differences in their backgrounds.

"I'm sorry, it's none of my business," Hattie beat a hasty retreat, distressed that she had spoiled the good mood of just a moment ago. She could hear Lydia's high-pitched voice lecturing her: "That's why you never got on with men, Hattie. You're always trying to interfere in their lives, telling them what to do. Men don't like women treading on their territory."

"Tell me about yourself, Marie," Rhys said, changing the subject before the mood was poisoned. "I know almost nothing about you." Rhys' voice was suddenly deep and soft and slow.

Hattie looked back at him. He was meeting her eyes steadily, but in his request was a challenge. He was demanding that she position herself.

"There isn't really that much to tell. I was born and brought up in Portsmouth. I've never been farther than a day trip to France."

"I thought your mother was French," Rhys responded with surprise.

"Yes, but she abandoned my sister and me when we were very young. She went back to France. My father followed her, of course, but he claims he never found her. I," she hesitated, "I've always suspected he didn't like what he found. He never encouraged us – no – he actively discouraged us from ever trying to establish contact with her again. You see, my mother wasn't what one calls respectable."

"What does that mean?" Rhys knew what it would have meant at home or among the RAF ground crews, but he couldn't imagine it being the same for this upper-class woman.

Hattie took a deep breath. When was the last time she had told anyone about her mother? Emily – when she first got engaged to Robin. But that was different. Then she'd been explaining to a girl already head-over-heels in love with a wonderful young man about the 'skeletons in the family cupboard'. She could have told Emily that Robin's grandmother had been a convicted murderer, and it wouldn't have made her love him less. But what if Rhys was shocked? She looked at him, and he met her gaze steadily.

She took another deep breath. "My father was what one quaintly calls a 'captain of industry', which simply means that he owned a number of factories." Hattie saw Rhys recoil, and she hastened to correct any misconceptions, "once upon a time. He came from a good family in colonial service that made money in Malaysian rubber. After he became successful and well-to-do, he married a woman of independent means from a Liverpool shipbuilding family. His factories were up in the Midlands. But then, to everyone's horror, he fell in love with my mother."

"Your mother wasn't his wife?" Rhys asked, shocked despite himself.

"She was his second wife. But the affair had started two years earlier, and I was born out of wedlock." Hattie was very stiff, and she did not meet his eyes. She just waited for his reaction.

"It doesn't matter to me about your mother," Rhys said in a very low voice, "but it must have made life hard for you."

That insight took her by surprise. When had anyone ever sympathised with her about this? "When I was little, yes." She admitted, trying to answer matter-of-factly. "You see, my father turned his factories over to the adult son of his first marriage and moved away to 'start a new life', but, of course, everyone in Portsmouth knew who he was and who my mother was. She wasn't accepted anywhere, and neither were we. I can still hear my appearance being greeted with whispers of 'isn't that the little bastard'."

Rhys recoiled; his sympathies entirely with the little girl who was not to blame for her parents' sins. Spontaneously, he reached out and touched her hand in a gesture of sympathy because he couldn't put his feelings into words fast enough.

Hattie started, and their eyes met. Then she blushed and looked down.

Rhys withdrew his hand. "I'm sorry," he murmured ambiguously.

Hattie sat for a moment, trying to rein in her galloping heart. She was sure this was quite irrational and unhealthy. He'd barely touched her, and it had simply been a gesture of sympathy. It was perfectly absurd to be this disoriented. She swallowed and looked about helplessly for the waitress. Surely it was time for the main course? But there was no help coming, so Hattie continued. "My father had arranged for an annuity to be paid from the profits of his factories, but my mother's expenditures far exceeded it. He had to go into debt. She took to drink. When she abandoned us, it was a blessing. Things couldn't have gone on as they were. After she was gone, my father cut back expenses and gradually clawed his way out of debt, but we had to be very careful with our pennies. I don't mean we were really poor. I've worked in the Seaman's Mission for almost twenty years, and I know how privileged we were." She met Rhys' eyes now, and he glimpsed again the efficient, cheerful woman in the Salvation Army uniform that he had almost forgotten about.

"I'm not saying we were objectively poor. My nephew's wife, for example, is the daughter of two teachers and they had roughly the same income as my father did. But they were socialists, intent on helping the working classes and they lived among the dockyard workers and raised their daughter to expect to work all her life. Indeed, they raised her to view work as something virtuous and ennobling. My sister and I, on the other hand, were brought up to think of work as demeaning. We were brought up to think we were 'better' and that we should never have to work for a living. We were supposed to have servants and husbands who would 'provide for us'."

"And then the war came along," Rhys ventured.

Hattie smiled sadly. "Yes. But in my case, it probably wouldn't have made much of a difference anyway. Lydia was born after my parent's marriage. She was never 'the little bastard' – and besides, she was very pretty. I was never pretty. Not even as a young girl."

Rhys nodded solemnly, "I can believe that. You have too much character just to be pretty." He made 'pretty' sound like an insult. "But you must have been a very handsome young woman. I wish I could have known you then." He meant every word of it.

No one had ever said anything like that to Hattie before, and it left her almost dazed. She couldn't think how to react and only managed to whisper, "thank you."

Their dinner finally arrived. Rhys started talking about the various films showing and asked which one she wanted to see. Hattie knew it didn't matter where they went. This was going to be the nicest evening of her life since Mike.

It was only when he got back to his quarters that Rhys realised it was too late to phone Ellen. Or should he try anyway? Would she worry? Would she be waiting up? She was a sensible girl. She'd assume that something had come up, something to do with the squadron.

He changed into pyjamas, brushed his teeth and climbed into bed. But he didn't sleep. Instead, he lay on his back, reviewing the evening. They had held hands for the whole film, and it was the most wonderful thing that had happened to him in years.

He was glad he knew about her background. It was less intimidating than he'd feared. She'd never gone to a fancy school, had no fine degrees and she wasn't rich. Her father's annuity, she had explained while they had a last non-alcoholic nightcap after the flick, had ended with his death in 1922. After that, Marie and her sister had lived on the latter's widow's pension and whatever Marie could earn. Knowing about her mother made him feel he had nothing to be ashamed of, and most importantly, it made her accessible in a way she might not otherwise have been.

Accessible? Just what was that supposed to mean?

Rhys stirred uneasily in the bed, aware of something he hadn't felt for years and years – desire. Gladys had never – not even in the first years of their marriage – welcomed his marital attentions. The memories were oppressive in the chilly room around him. He had returned from France with a certain amount of 'experience'. They all had. There were so many girls willing to do it there, mostly for a fee. Not that they were whores. Rhys associated 'whore' with the girls who paraded up and down certain parts of big cities taking anyone who came along. He avoided them. They stank. They often had diseases. They were harsh, crude, cynical. But the girls in France, the two he'd slept with anyway, had been vulnerable, lonely, and desperate. They'd lost loved ones, homes, the world that had been before. They didn't know how else to get by in a world gone mad. Rhys had never looked down on them for what they did. He was sorry for them.

And they had made him eager for marriage — only to find that Gladys wasn't like the French girls. She didn't like intimacies, and only suffered them for the sake of children. After Owain was born, she'd made him sleep on the couch.

Other men would have sought comfort elsewhere, but Rhys wasn't like that. Besides Gladys would have found out somehow and it would have ruined his marriage. Gladys was a good woman in other ways. She was thrifty and worked hard. She was a stern but fair mother. She abhorred corporal punishment and had ruled by force of character alone. Yes, Gladys had had many virtues, he conceded, but she'd been dead for three years.

And here was Marie, a woman with warmth and wit and humour. What was more, she was positively crying out for a man's affection. She didn't know that herself. She wasn't the kind of woman who hung about at other people's weddings with big cow's eyes begging to be noticed, much less the type who tried to attract male attention with tight bodices and short skirts. But she did not avoid his touch.

He hadn't dared kiss her, but he had wanted to. When he saw her off on the last train from Chichester station, he had been tempted. He had held her hand tighter and held his breath for a second. For a moment, she had even seemed to expect it of him. She paused, glanced up and smiled timidly. Then some idiot of a conductor blew a whistle just a couple of feet away. Marie flinched at the sound and laughed nervously at herself.

She had turned away from him, hastily grasped the handle of the railway carriage and folded herself inside the compartment. The opportunity was gone.

He'd found himself alone on the platform, waving to a train disappearing in the darkness. He felt lonely and disappointed, disappointed not with what had been but with what had not been. They would just have to see each other again soon, he decided firmly, and with that thought, he fell asleep contentedly.

Chapter 5

November 1940

Rhys fell in love with the cottage for Marie's sake. She was so thrilled with it and so full of ideas on how to do it up that she reminded Rhys of a child with a new toy. He supposed that like any normal woman, she longed to do up a house but had never had the chance.

Hattie, noticing that he was watching her more than listening to what she said, became uncertain. "Is something wrong?"

He laughed. "I hope the estate agent is paying you a commission – because you are the best saleswoman I've ever met."

"But don't you like it?" Hattie asked uncertainly.

Rhys laughed again. "Of course, I like it," he admitted, looking about the parlour again. It was quite neglected – the wallpaper was peeling, the paint was cracked and flaking, the floors were scratched. He'd noted too that the drains needed clearing. In fact, there was a hell of a lot of work to be done, but it wasn't just Marie's fantasy that made this cottage special. Rhys had never in his life dreamt of living anywhere quite so 'fine' as this. This cottage had wainscoting, parquet floors, ceiling mouldings, and built-in cabinets. To Rhys, it was like the houses where 'gentry' and 'officers' lived. "What are they asking for it?"

Marie at once looked embarrassed. "I'm afraid the estate agent wasn't able to talk him down. He still wants seven quid."

Rhys frowned. Much as he wanted to rent the cottage, that was more than a third of his wages, and where would he find the money to do it up?

Marie, however, looked so crushed that he sighed and looked around again. Surely his promotion would come soon? And he needed something for the kids quickly. He'd been here for more than two weeks already. He'd promised the kids to have them moved by now. And Christmas was fast approaching. Nothing else he'd seen had been even half as suitable.

"Doesn't the RAF have the right to requisition housing?" Hattie suggested timidly.

"Only in an emergency," Rhys told her firmly. "Who is this landlord anyway? What right does he have to keep anything vacant in times like these?"

Marie sighed audibly. "I'm afraid it's the Duke of Norfolk. He has a lot of property in these parts and apparently this house belonged to his nanny. She died some time ago. The agent has the impression that he doesn't want to let it at all. He suspects the duke wants to keep it available for another deserving member of his household on retirement. That kind of thing".

The situation sounded hopeless to Rhys. A rich man that didn't need the money who could afford to leave the place vacant. Furthermore, he was a lord and wasn't going to negotiate with someone as insignificant as an RAF Flight Sergeant. He was going to have to pay the price or forget it. "Let's go and get some tea," he suggested to stop himself from getting depressed.

On the way back to the station, Rhys tried to work out how he could afford the cottage. It was a step up in the world. He'd be proud to take the kids there. They would hardly believe it, moving into somewhere so grand. His parents would almost faint if he could ever talk them into visiting him. Owain was sure to like being right on the water, and Ellen would love that big, sunny kitchen and having a real garden.

But seven quid! He only earned 18 quid a month. And if Ellen started vocational training, that would cost him something too. But where else could they live? His thoughts went round and round.

It was sleeting as he got off the bus at the station gate. He turned his collar up and saluted the sentry hastily, but the man called out, "Chiefy! You'd better get down to the hangar right away. There's been an accident!"

His heart missed a beat. Why did this have to happen while he was away from the station!? He tried to run, but at once, he slipped on the ice, and there was nothing for it but to go more slowly – agonisingly slowly.

Things only got worse as he entered the hangar. A crowd stood around a Spitfire crumpled to one side and resting on a wingtip. Below a huge hole in the Spitfire's wing lay an engine, while the crane's broken chain hung over the 'scene of the crime'. Worse still, medical orderlies were fussing about a man stretched out on the floor.

Rhys pushed his way forward with greater urgency than ever, only to find that the squadron leader was here before him. He was where Rhys felt he should have been – on one knee beside the injured fitter, a hand on his shoulder. The fitter, LAC Picket, was very pale and trembling. The medical orderlies were packing him in blankets while the MO himself examined his leg, which was clearly broken.

"What happened, sir?" Rhys found himself asking – and then feeling foolish, as it seemed pretty obvious.

The squadron leader looked up at Rhys reproachfully. "The chain broke at the wrong minute. You'd better find out why and get the crane and the Spit repaired as soon as possible."

It wasn't said angrily, but Rhys felt each word like a lash. "Yes, sir. Will Picket be all right, sir?"

The CO just glanced at the MO, who nodded confidently. "It's a bad break, but we'll have it set in no time." That said, he stood and nodded to the orderlies to lift the patient onto the waiting stretcher. The CO also got to his feet and fixed his dark eyes on Rhys. "I'll expect your report on the cause of the accident before I leave the station tonight."

"Yes, sir."

The CO turned and followed the stretcher out of the hangar. Rhys stood for a moment, his throat dry, and then – aware that all the ground crews were staring at him — turned to examine the Spitfire. One undercarriage leg had collapsed under the impact of the Merlin engine going right through the wing. High octane fuel was trickling out of the ruptured wing tanks onto the floor. The engine itself was oozing oil. He looked up at the dangling chain for a moment. Obviously, a link had given way. Why?

Rhys turned to the waiting crews and started giving orders. Detailing the men by name, he ordered several riggers to prop the Spit back up and start work on repairing the undercarriage and wing at once. Two fitters were ordered to take charge of the engine and look it over for damage, doing whatever was necessary to restore it. Lastly, all the pieces of the chain were to be collected and brought to him at a workbench on the side of the hangar. He then went over to the crane and lowered the arm.

It didn't take long to find the problem: The whole chain was badly rusted. Why hadn't he inspected the crane earlier? Why hadn't he noticed the state it was in? Why hadn't one of the airmen reported it to him? It was a terrible failure, and he hadn't yet been here three weeks. He took several lengths of chain with him to the CO's office and laid them on the wooden desk, wrapped in felt to keep them from damaging or dirtying anything. "It should have been replaced long ago, sir." Rhys declared, avoiding the CO's dark, penetrating eyes.

"That's your job, Chiefy."

No words could have hurt more. "Yes, sir. I know that, sir. I'm not trying to make excuses, sir. I should have checked all the equipment thoroughly. I will do so first thing tomorrow. By tomorrow night, there will be no maintenance equipment I haven't personally checked, sir."

"Good," the squadron leader replied and paused. Jenkins stiffened, waiting for the axe to fall. He didn't believe for a minute he was going to get off this easily.

The squadron leader asked, "how is the housing search coming along?"

Rhys caught his breath and took his eyes off the back wall to look at the squadron leader. The younger man looked squarely back at him. "I heard you are looking for a cottage for yourself and your two children to live off-station."

"Yes, sir." Who had told him that? Why? It was nobody's business but his own. "I'm widowed, and I want the kids to live off-station, near a school and shops and that, sir."

"Understandable, but very difficult these days. Ever since we were half bombed out last summer, local housing has been at a premium. It's not just the RAF that is billeting on the local population, the Army has been requisitioning things to defend the coastline and the Navy is inflated to new highs. Any luck yet?"

"Yes and no, sir. I found a suitable cottage, but I can't afford it. Seven quid. And it needs doing up. It's been vacant for a long time."

"Vacant? That's almost a crime these days. Who is the landlord?"

"Ah. I've only dealt with the estate agent, sir, but I was told the landlord was, ah," this was rather embarrassing too, "the Duke of Norfolk, sir."

"Oh, that's lucky. I'll ask Squadron Leader Johnstone of 602 to talk to him about it – he's often invited up to Arundel and is on very good terms with the duke's steward. He should be able to negotiate a discount. Five quid all right?"

"Yes, sir. Of course. Thank you, sir." Rhys wasn't sure what had hit him yet, nor was he at all comfortable with taking favours from his CO.

"I'll need the address," the squadron leader pointed out.

"Of course, sir."

The CO looked about his desk, found a pad of paper and pen and pushed them towards Rhys. Rhys wrote the address on it: Swallow Cottage, Bosham, and returned the pad and pen.

"Bosham? Very nice. I'll get back to you on the cottage as soon as possible. Is everything else all right?"

"You don't know how upset I am about this accident, sir."

"I can guess." There was a tinge of humour in that – just the merest hint.

Rhys didn't know what to make of it. This was a solemn affair, and the squadron leader knew that too. "It won't happen again," Rhys assured him, stiffening to attention.

"Make sure it doesn't, Chiefy."

Rhys saluted, and his salute was returned.

Rhys fled to the mess. It was pitch dark, and sleet was still falling. The Sergeant's Mess seemed almost overheated by contrast, and puddles of dirty water collected in the entrance hall from all the muddy boots. Rhys had rarely felt like he needed a beer as much as he did now, but he decided he'd better ring Ellen first; it was already 9:40.

He hung up his overcoat and went straight to the phone boxes. Ellen didn't answer. Frustrated, he ordered a pint, quaffed it down, and called again at 10:00 pm. Ellen answered after the first ring, and he could tell something was wrong just by the way she said "hello," as if she were anxious.

"It's me, El. Dad. Sorry I'm late. There was an accident, but things are under control now. How are you? Is something wrong?"

There was a telling pause before she said, "no, of course not. There's nothing wrong. Nothing really wrong, that is."

"You sound worried, El. What is it?"

"Owain missed school again today, Dad." She admitted at last.

"Blast the boy! Let me talk to him! Go fetch him and I'll call back in fifteen minutes."

Rhys waited fuming in the box until the fifteen minutes were up and then rang again.

Owain answered in a sullen voice. "Yeah?"

"What's this I hear about you missing school?" Rhys opened without introduction. He wanted to be calm, but he was riled up by the bad day and the wait already.

"I missed geography, that's all. What's the bloody point of geography when I ain't never going to see nothing of the bloody world anyway?"

"Don't you use bad language with me, boy!"

"Why the hell not? You use it –"

"Don't talk back to me! Just what has got into you? Your Mum raised you different and so did I. Bad language isn't going to get you anywhere. Not with me and not out there in the real world. As for missing geography, do you want to end up a school-leaver, no good for anything but stupid, muscle work? This isn't about geography or any other subject, it's about your future. Can't you get that into that thick skull of yours?!"

"Maybe, if you shout louder, Dad."

Rhys was flabbergasted. What could he possibly do with a boy like this? His instincts were to hit him – but fortunately or unfortunately, the boy was miles away. Instead, he found himself shouting louder, just as the boy had suggested. "I'll do better than that! You're going to get what's coming to you as soon as I see you again! If I hear you missed school again, you're going to have to answer to me for it." Even as he said it, he knew how foolish he sounded. What a lot of empty words!

"Piss off, Dad!"

Before Rhys could explode, the receiver was flung down on the other end. Rhys heard a crashing sound, and then Ellen shouting at her brother and Owain shouting back. He tried to attract their attention, shouting into the receiver, but the WAAF at the reception looked over at him, shocked, and he quietened down, steaming with impotent fury. He was going to give that boy what he deserved, whether it made Gladys turn over in her grave or not.

But when he heard a distraught Ellen say tightly into the phone, "I don't know what to do with him, Dad. He don't take no notice of me at all any more," his anger evaporated. Ellen – his self-possessed Ellen – sounded close to tears.

He couldn't be angry with her. On the contrary, she needed building up. He took a deep breath and, with a silent promise to deal with Owain later, managed a controlled tone of voice for his daughter. "Now, don't you worry about a thing, El. It's not your fault. I'm just going to have to come and fetch you down here. I haven't found a place yet, or rather I have but I haven't done it up yet, but I'll get things squared away soon. I promise. Just do your best for a few more days. A week at most." He was making promises he couldn't keep, but what else could he do?

"OK, Dad," his daughter answered bravely.

"I love you, El. Don't you worry about a thing. It's just a phase. I'll sort Owain out soon enough." There was a hard threat in that, but he softened his tone again as he added, "you've done a great job, El. Don't worry, all right?"

"No, Dad. I'll be fine, if it's not for long now."

"No, a week at the most. I'll sort things out."

The operator was demanding more coins. "Good night, Dad." Ellen called without even giving him a chance to put more money in the slot. The dial tone sounded in his ear.

Rhys hung up and just stood in the box, dazed. He had to get the kids here – even if it meant taking one of those terrible flats. But the thought of putting them in another flat now that he'd seen the cottage in Bosham was unbearable. It would only make things worse. Bosham was the right home, and it was right for all of them. But how long would it take the CO to talk to 602's CO, and for him to mention it to the Duke of Norfolk's steward and then – it all felt like a fairy tale. Why should the CO of another squadron request a favour for him?

He wandered into the mess bar in a depressed daze. Propping one foot on the brass rail running around the foot of the counter, he ordered a pint. He was so lost in thought that he jumped slightly when Fogerty leaned on the bar beside him. "What did the CO have to say?"

"What should he say?" Rhys snapped back. "I should have checked every sodding piece of maintenance equipment used by the squadron – and so should Rowe. Things should never have got to this state. I'm not saying I'm blameless, but nor are any of you!" He was suddenly talking to the whole mess – or at least the men from 606.

There was a stunned silence.

Rhys turned back towards the bar and gulped his beer. Fogerty did not leave, and Newbury joined him. Fogerty spoke as Rhys finished his beer. "The Spit will be operational again tomorrow evening."

"It'd better be."

"The engine wasn't damaged much," Newbury put in, "and we've replaced the entire chain on the crane."

"You mean we had good chain just lying around?"

"We can't undo the accident, Sir," Newbury pointed out a touch hotly.

"No, we can't," Rhys agreed and, with a nod, ordered a second pint. Then he turned resentfully on his closest subordinates. They had worked well together so far. He liked both men, but tonight he was feeling betrayed by them. If they'd done their jobs, they would at least have tipped him off that some of the equipment needed a serious overhaul. He was also embarrassed to have the CO involved in something as personal as his housing search. Worse, how could he go and rent another flat without the CO being offended that he hadn't waited for his help? On the other hand, if he waited, Owain might get totally out of hand, and that wouldn't be fair to Ellen.

Angrily he demanded of his subordinates: "Which of you went tattling to the CO about my housing problems?"

The two sergeants looked at one another, and Fogerty replied in a soothing voice, "no need to make a fuss, sir. We didn't 'tattle' about anything. The CO asked how you were settling in. He asked extra about housing. He knows you're a widower with children still in school. He was just taking an interest like he always does. That's the way he is."

"Interfering in my private life is what I call it!" Rhys retorted, grabbing his second pint.

The other two men exchanged a glance, raised eyebrows and then Fogerty shrugged. "If that's the way you see it, sir." They pushed off, leaving Rhys to drink alone. Rhys realised at once that he'd made a fatal mistake: Criticising the popular squadron leader.

By the time he turned in that night, Rhys was convinced he'd made a mess of everything. He'd failed to check the equipment. He'd failed to be on the scene when the accident occurred. He'd let the CO push him into an awkward corner about the cottage. He'd mishandled his subordinates, alienating them without gaining any respect. And Owain was completely out of hand. What was he to do with a thirteen-year-old who talked back to him like that? The only bright spot in his life was Marie. He wished more than anything he could phone her and talk to her right now. Perhaps he could, but then again, it was close to midnight. No, he couldn't do that. It would be rude. She would be in bed, and it wasn't an emergency. What would she think of him?

Uncomfortable, he twisted and turned in the bed, going over all the things that had gone wrong, regretting what he'd done and said, wishing he could start over again. It was very late before he finally drifted off to sleep.

Chapter 6

November 1940

Despite a rough night, Rhys awoke more determined than ever to make a go of things. He made sure he was the first man in the hangar. As the ground crews trickled in, still warming their hands on their mugs of steaming tea, Rhys was already in greasy overalls, clambering about the equipment. He had promised the CO he would inspect every piece of maintenance equipment personally, and in the night, it had occurred to him to do more. Not only would he inspect it, but he would also record the state of repair, what needed to be done and what supplies had to be drawn to bring every piece of equipment back up to standard.

The airmen seeing the Chiefy already at work, were quick to take up their own tasks – in a notably subdued fashion. It wasn't that no one dared talk, but talk was kept to a minimum, and the volume was low. At times it was almost an uneasy whispering.. Rhys felt eyes wandering in his direction again and again. The men were quick to guess what he wanted and tried to supply him with it before he asked. He never had to call a man twice either. They were very readily at hand and quick to do his bidding. It occurred to him that they were expecting him to tear a strip off. They must have heard what he'd said in the Sergeant's Mess last night – or had Flight Sergeant Rowe been one to make life miserable for his subordinates when something went wrong?

Because the hangar wasn't heated, by the time the Salvation Army mobile canteen arrived, he was very hungry and cold. As always, they clustered around the Sally Ann van with their tin plates and cutlery. Rhys was glad to see that Marie was there today – she didn't always come; sometimes she had too much to do at the mission. But the sight of her today was like a breath of warm air. She gave him a private smile, even as she addressed him formally with, "How are you doing today, Flight Sergeant?"

He shook his head, looking her straight in the eye. "There was an accident yesterday. LAC Picket broke his leg when the crane chain broke and a Merlin he was returning to that Spit went right through her wing. You can still see the hole it made." He was pointing, and Marie leaned out of the canteen to get a better look.

She gave him a look of open concern and sympathy that was what he'd both expected and needed. Any other reaction would have disappointed him, but he was grateful all the same. "I'm so sorry," she said aloud. "Is Picket going to be all right?"

"Yes, the MO says he should be, but I've promised the CO to check all the equipment personally today. The chain was completely rusted. It should have been replaced long before an accident like this could happen." Rhys explained.

"Indeed it should! And Flight Sergeant Rowe always pretended he was perfect!" Marie pinned the blame squarely on his predecessor. Rhys appreciated her partisanship; it made him feel more confident.

He could not linger long, however, as there were others anxious for their dinner. He took his plate into his office and wrote on a piece of scrap paper: "Will ring tonight after tea. Try to keep Friday night free." He slipped the paper to her as he returned his plate. She tucked it in her pocket with a smile.

It was a long day, and it was after dark before his list was ready. Rhys dismissed his subordinates to get a meal in their respective messes but remained to transfer his notes from the crumpled and stained pages on which he'd jotted them down to a clean sheet of paper. It was almost 8:00p.m. before he could report to the CO, and he caught the younger man just as he was about to leave his office. At the sight of Jenkins, the squadron leader switched the light back on and waited expectantly.

Rhys handed him the report, explaining what it was.

The CO took it questioningly and started reading it at once. "Well, done, Jenkins," he remarked, still focusing on the contents. Rhys felt himself start to relax a little.

The CO finally set the report aside. "I'll read it properly in the morning, and we'll have to see about the supplies you need. Not all of them will be immediately available, but we should undoubtedly use the bad weather to get as much done as possible."

"Yes, sir. My feelings exactly."

Priestman nodded, adding, "you can have that cottage in Bosham for 5 quid, by the way."

"Sir?" Rhys hadn't been expecting that. In fact, he had been about to say that he would take another flat.

"Johnstone raised it with Norfolk's steward, and he agreed at once. He said you can have it furnished for five pounds ten, if you like – on condition you keep the garden in order. Apparently, the neighbours complained this past summer."

"That's very generous, sir. That would be perfect. I don't know how to thank you—"

Priestman waved it aside. "Norfolk goes out of his way to help all of us here at Tangmere – says it's part of his 'war effort'. With that settled, I hope you'll be able to move your children here before Christmas. Do let me know if you need anything else." He was clearly in a bit of a hurry to get off duty for the night, and Rhys suddenly couldn't wait to call Marie. They exchanged salutes, and Rhys hurried to the Sergeant's Mess.

"Marie? I've got the cottage!" He told her as soon as he heard her voice on the other end of the line. "I don't know what magic the CO used, but he talked the duke down to 5 quid – 5 and 10 furnished. I'll ring the agent tomorrow and see about getting the key and all."

"I'm so pleased, Rhys! I knew it would work out. It's so perfect for you. You'll need help doing it up though. Do you want me to see if I can organise some volunteers? I could ask—"

"No, I'll manage." Rhys was not one for taking help from strangers. It was bad enough he had the CO to thank for the cottage itself. But he rapidly modified his reply, "that is, it would be wonderful if you could keep me supplied with tea and sandwiches while I work."

"I can do better than that," she assured him confidently.

Rhys laughed. She sounded so young in her eagerness. Still, he added seriously, "I don't know when I'm going to have time. There's more to do than I thought, and if the weather lifts, we'll have to service aircraft as well. I'll let you know when I can get away to work on the cottage as soon as I know myself, all right?"

Marie agreed, and he hung up, anxious to call Ellen with the good news, but it wasn't yet nine pm, so he got himself a beer first. Punctually at 9:30 he rang the corner box near his flat and Ellen answered after the first ring.

"Hello?"

"Ellen, I've got wonderful—"

"Oh, Dad!" Ellen cried out. "Owain isn't home yet! I don't know where he is. He wasn't in school again, and now he's not come home. I don't know if he's run away or if something terrible has happened to him. I don't even know where to start looking!" She was clearly on the brink of tears.

Rhys tensed inwardly, but he kept his voice calm. "Now, don't worry, El. It's only just gone 9. No need to assume the worst. Have you been round to the Harrisons?" (Owain's best friend was the Harrison boy.)

"Yes, of course, Dad. He wasn't there. And I stopped in at the Bennet's and Deane's as well. No one has seen him anywhere."

"All right." Rhys was starting to get worried himself, but he told himself not to panic. Owain might be young, but he was resourceful and tough. And what could have happened to him? "Now, El, if he'd been in an accident or something, the police would have contacted you, so I don't want you to imagine the worst."

"But what if he's run away?" Ellen asked in distress.

That was what Rhys feared too – after the way Owain had talked back to him yesterday. "He'll need money for that. Have you checked the sugar bowl?" (They had a glued-together old sugar bowl where they collected petty cash.)

"It's empty!" Ellen sobbed into the telephone.

Now Rhys was concerned. He took a deep breath and ran his finger around the inside of his collar. Where would Owain go? Back to his grandparents in Wales, perhaps? He didn't get on with his maternal grandparents, they were too strict and cheerless, but he liked Rhys' parents. "What are we going to do, Dad?" his daughter asked helplessly.

"First thing is for me to get in touch with your grandparents and see if he's turned up there. I want you to phone me every hour with a report. If he isn't home by midnight, I'll call the police. Have you got the number of the mess reception?"

"Yes, of course, Dad." She sniffled a bit, but that 'of course' suggested she was recovering a little of her self-confidence.

Getting through to his parents wasn't easy as they had no phone and he didn't know the number of the nearest public phone, but he was able to reach the village pub and they sent a boy round to his father. His parents, however, had neither seen nor heard from Owain. Rhys wandered into the mess wearing a heavy frown. He ordered a pint and took it to a side table, still lost in thought about where Owain could be. A mess orderly appeared, "do you want me to bring you something to eat, sir?"

Rhys looked up gratefully. "Yes, if it's not too late?"

"I'll see what I can do, sir." He disappeared and returned with a slab of cheddar, several slices of bread and cold gammon steak. Rhys thanked him heartily and set to work on the meal. At 10:30, the WAAF receptionist called him to the phone. Owain still wasn't home. At 11:00, it was the same thing. The mess was gradually emptying. By 11:30, Rhys was almost alone. Fogerty and Newbury got up to leave, nodded 'good night' to him, and went out.

A second latter, Fogerty returned and stood before his table. "Is there something wrong, sir?"

Rhys started, frowned, hesitated. How could he tell his subordinates about his private troubles? But what if Owain really had run away? Or worse, what if something had happened to him? He'd have to return, and then the others would need to fill in for him. In that case, they'd find out anyway. Rhys was tired and worried. "It's my boy. He isn't home yet."

Fogerty glanced at the clock. "How old is he?"

"Thirteen."

"He's staying with his sister, didn't you say?"

"Yes. It's not a good arrangement, I know. She's too young. He doesn't mind her like he should. But I've only just found a cottage, and it's going to take weeks to get it ready."

"I'm sure we could help there, sir. You'll get it ready faster if we all pitch in. Are the police looking for your boy, sir?"

"I haven't called them yet. I want to give him till midnight to get in."

Fogerty nodded. "Sounds sensible to me, sir." He paused, but it seemed there was nothing more to say. "Well, let us know if there's any way we can help, sir, but I'm sure he'll turn up fine. I used to sneak down to the pub at that age. Played darts for money."

Rhys nodded absently, and Fogerty started to leave. Rhys remembered to call "thanks" after him.

They were closing up the bar. The room was getting chilly. The central heating was off. It was 11:55. Should he ring Ellen? But she would have called him if Owain had arrived. Marie? No, why worry her? She'd be in bed too. But maybe she'd have a suggestion? If only he were at home. He would have gone out and searched the pubs himself – something he couldn't ask Ellen to do.

The telephone at reception rang.

Rhys jumped to his feet. The WAAF answered, looked over at him, nodded, indicated one of the phone boxes.

"Ellen?"

"They just brought him home, Dad." She didn't sound terribly happy.

"Brought?! Who? Why? What's wrong with him? Is he hurt? Where? How bad?"

"He's drunk. He's so drunk he's spewed up all over the front hall. He reeks of gin and he can't stand. It's disgusting!"

Rhys was so relieved he almost laughed, but he caught himself in time. "I know it is, El, but it could have been worse – and maybe he's learnt a valuable lesson."

By the time he got to bed, the sense of relief had been replaced by a nagging sense of guilt that it came to this in the first place. He had to get the kids moved. He had a wonderful place for them now. All he had to do was to get it done up. He paused. Should he really take Fogerty's offer? Or Marie's, for that matter? She said she could organise some help. If he accepted Fogerty's proposal, he'd be indebted to his subordinates. But if he refused, it would be an affront too – just like refusing the CO would have been. He stirred uncomfortably, unable to work out what to do before he fell asleep exhausted.

The next day, Rhys didn't want to wait until Friday to talk to Marie, so as soon as he had a chance to get off- station, he telephoned suggesting they meet that same night.

Hattie was flustered by his call. An amateur jazz band was playing at the mission, and they were expecting lots of customers. "Oh dear!" she exclaimed. "We have this – oh, never mind. Maybe Marion could stand in for me? – no, it's choir practice. She's the organist at St. Andrews. Maybe Emily ... I'll have to call and ask, but she hasn't got a car. I'd have to go and collect her. Oh dear."

Clearly, it was inconvenient, but Rhys was so anxious to see Marie that he hesitated to give in. "I could come to Portsmouth it if helps," he offered.

Hattie couldn't say 'no.' She could not forget how very little time she'd had with Mike. For fear of Lydia's scorn, she had missed opportunities to be with him. She would not make the same mistake again. So she announced, "I'll find someone, and it would help if you could come to Portsmouth." So they agreed to meet at a pub in Portsmouth in two hours.

Hattie then rang her nephew's bride. "Emily?"

"Hattie! Lovely to hear from you."

"Emily, could you do me a favour?"

"Of course. What do you need?"

"I need you to come and help at the mission tonight, for the dance."

"Tonight?" Emily was surprised. "Has something come up unexpectedly?"

"Yes." Hattie hesitated, feeling nervous, even a little guilty. Wasn't she terribly selfish? Well, selfish or not, she was going through with this, so it was only fair to tell Emily the truth. "The – the gentleman friend I told you about. He just phoned and asked me to join him for dinner tonight." Hattie held her breath, hearing in her mind all the outraged remarks her sister would have poured over her. Lydia was sure to remind her that no self-respecting lady would accept an invitation at such short notice; it was demeaning.

Emily was different. Emily had been in her shoes. "I gather he's in the services," Emily observed simply, appreciating how difficult it was for anyone in the military to have control of their time. "How late do you think it will be tonight?"

"Oh, at midnight we throw anyone out who is still here. I could come and pick you up and take you home," Hattie added, unconsciously pleading.

"Yes, that would help. I'll ring Robin and let him know what's happening. What time did you want to pick me up?"

Two hours later, Rhys was sitting at a little round table in a pub crowded with naval petty officers. Marie had suggested it because she knew from her 'customers' that it was a 'respectable' pub, the kind of place where petty officers brought their wives. It had the added advantage of being the kind of place Lydia wouldn't have been caught dead in, while Air Force blue was so rare that Rhys' uniform attracted astonished glances from everyone entering.

Rhys caught sight of Marie standing somewhat uncertainly just inside the door. She looked rather lost – afraid of her own courage. As always when out of uniform, she looked like a vulnerable woman rather than part of an institution. Rhys squeezed out from behind the table and pushed through the crowd to take her arm. She looked up at him with so much relief that it made him feel like a knight in shining armour rescuing a damsel in distress. He led her back to his tiny table, saying as he went, "I like your hair like that."

Hattie looked up at him gratefully but patted her hair self-consciously at the same time. For the first time in her life, she had gone to a hairdresser. They had shown her how to put her hair up in a French twist rather than an old-fashioned bun. "You're sure it doesn't make me look – I don't know...."

"It makes you look younger," he assured her.

Hattie wasn't used to compliments. It embarrassed her to have anyone looking at her so intently. She busied herself with putting her handbag aside and pulling off her hat and gloves. "You look worried, Rhys. Is something wrong?"

Rhys was surprised but pleased that she noticed so quickly. "Yes. My boy, Owain, stole all the petty cash Ellen had saved up over the weeks for an emergency and somehow — Ellen hadn't found out how when I talked to her — he got hold of a bottle of gin. He was brought home by the police, who found him in a park. Ellen was sick with worry, not knowing where he was, and now she's disgusted and angry."

"You've got to bring them here as soon as possible, Rhys."

"I know, but I've got to do up the cottage first. Fogerty offered to help me, but I hate to accept a favour from a subordinate."

"That's not a favour – it's a very nice gesture of help," Marie told him firmly.

"Yes, but he meant asking the lads all to pitch in. That would almost be like ordering them to do it. They might resent it."

"Well, they might if you handle it wrong," Hattie agreed, adding, "but it seems to me if you put it to them the right way, they would probably be just as happy to help out as to sit about in this grim weather doing nothing."

"You make it sound so easy, Marie," Rhys told her, frowning slightly. He didn't think things would be anywhere near as easy as she made it sound. After all, he'd be admitting that he couldn't manage things on his own, that he needed help from his subordinates.

"Well, in my job one gets used to asking for volunteers," Marie told him. "I've found that people can walk past a job that needs doing 100 times without a thought, but if you ask for help, they pitch right in happily. So, I learnt years ago not to wait for people to volunteer but to ask for their help outright."

Rhys considered the woman opposite him, still unsure what he thought. Gladys had been very strict about not taking help from others. Gladys had always warned that accepting help was just as bad as borrowing money: "You never know," she had warned, "when they'll call in their debts."

"If I accept their help, I'll owe them something," Rhys put his thoughts into words for Marie. "They'll expect me to treat them differently afterwards."

"Differently? What do you mean? They can hardly expect special treatment if they all – or at least the bulk of them — pitch in together. Perhaps they will expect you to see them more like individuals afterwards, but I don't see how that is a bad thing."

Rhys continued to look at her with a sceptical frown darkening his face, but he was beginning to see her point of view. Maybe he had been standing too much on his dignity. Maybe it would do them all good if he could relax with them a little, start calling them by their first or nicknames rather than rank or family name. Maybe.

"Tell them I'll be catering the meals," Hattie suggested with a little half-embarrassed smile. "They should like that."

They did. Almost all of the riggers volunteered, and with the weather worse than ever and Bosham so close to Tangmere, they used their 'released' status to do up Rhys' cottage in just three days. Marie and one of her colleagues, the same woman who had been with her the first day, kept the whole team supplied with tea, sandwiches and snacks during the day, and in the evenings, the men went over to Anchor Bleu together, and Rhys bought the first and last rounds.

By the end of the first day, Rhys admitted to himself that Marie had been right. Asking for help from the others had made him more human without undermining his authority. He was still giving the orders and setting the pace. The only disadvantage was that he and Marie had to maintain their façade of polite distance. It was strictly "Flight Sergeant" and "Miss Fitzsimmons."

That was hard sometimes, particularly when Rhys would have liked to ask Marie's advice. She'd been so full of ideas for redecorating when they'd first looked at the cottage together. But wartime shortages meant they didn't have much choice in materials anyway, so he did what he thought best with only the occasionally risked: "Do you agree, Miss Fitzsimmons?"

Marie didn't hesitate to say what she thought, making one or two good suggestions that he readily accepted, particularly in the kitchen. She had a practical approach to things. She was concerned about adequate lighting, working space and convenience rather than decorative effect. Rhys liked that. Of course, in that respect, she was very much like Gladys – and Ellen.

He hoped Marie and Ellen would like each other. They were so different in most ways, but perhaps when it came to practical things like getting a meal on the table, they could find common ground. If Marie could win Ellen's trust, she was sure to be a good influence on her, but he was a little afraid Ellen would keep aloof. She'd never had many friends. They moved around too much, and Ellen kept to herself anyway. When he'd suggested she should have friends and do things with others her age, she answered by saying that he wouldn't want her keeping company with 'silly tarts'. As so often with Ellen and her mother, Rhys hadn't had an answer.

Rhys cast a glance to where Marie was rehanging the curtains, and he had an image of her here with him alone. The thought made his heart beat a touch faster. Perched rather precariously on a ladder, she was stretching up and over, and the back of her skirt was lifted, revealing her thighs almost to the top of her stockings. Rhys couldn't take his eyes away until he heard Fogerty mutter, "not bad for a woman her age, eh?"

Rhys spun about with a hot rebuke on his tongue. He caught himself before he said anything he would have regretted, but Fogerty understood anyway. The senior rigger backed away with a little smile. "Reading you loud and clear, sir. No problem." His eyes were alight with amusement. Rhys knew that the whole squadron would soon know about him and Marie.

For a moment, Rhys was angry, but he asked himself what was so wrong with it? So what if they all knew he fancied her? It wasn't as if they were doing anything wrong? He was a widower, and she a spinster. Yes, they came from different backgrounds, but it occurred to him that it would only increase his status among the "erks," the ground crews, – if he got her.

Most airmen were striving towards something better than what they'd been born to. That was something Rhys had liked about the RAF from the start. Youths might join the army to get away from problems – unemployment, debt, brutal parents, nagging wives or screaming kids — but the RAF attracted the ambitious because its standards and requirements were higher. In the army, the lower ranks needed only the dullest brains and a willingness to obey even the most senseless orders. The RAF required highly trained specialists capable of working independently. Men who had already pulled themselves up a rung or two were far more open-minded about class barriers than those that just accepted them.

Marie descended from the ladder, brushing a loose strand of hair out of her eyes with the back of her hand. She was flushed from the exertion, and she looked very 'domestic' in a flowery apron. Rhys thought she looked like she belonged here. He registered that he was getting serious about her.

She felt his gaze and looked over at him with a question in her eyes. "They look all right don't they, Flight Sergeant?"

"Lovely," he assured her. Their eyes met.

Marie was confused and unsettled by the way he was gazing at her. He was looking so intently that she started to think something must be amiss and tested with her hands that her hair was still in place and then brushed off her apron vigorously. She was sorry that the work was finished. It had been fun spending the days with him, helping out, being part of his life.

Rhys announced, "That does it, lads. Let's pack it in and go down to the pub." Marie and Marion went to get their coats and hats, but when Marion went into the kitchen to collect the empty sandwich boxes and tea urn, Rhys helped Marie into her coat. He hadn't done that the other nights. He was standing right behind her, and she could smell him – sweat and aftershave and hair cream. "Miss Fitzsimmons, I don't know how to thank you for all your help," he said in a normal tone of voice. Then he dropped his voice and added, "how about if I cook you dinner tomorrow night – right here. As a kind of 'housewarming'?"

Hattie looked up at him, almost in alarm. It was not his suggestion that frightened her but her own reaction. Her heart was racing, and she felt quite hot. He was not very much taller than she was, she noticed and standing close behind her, her face was almost at the same level. Their eyes met, and Rhys' were smiling.

"Yes. Thank you, Flight Sergeant. I'd like that very much."

"Shall we say 8:00pm then?" Mentally, he resolved to tell Ellen there was a squadron do tomorrow and that he wouldn't be calling.

"Yes. Yes, I'll be here."

Marion called, asking what was taking so long, and the airmen were watching Rhys with too much amused attention. Marie hastened away with a silly wave of her hand.

Chapter 7

November 1940

Cooking was not one of Rhys' strong points. He had never had to cook for himself until Gladys fell ill. When she first became bedridden, Ellen had been only thirteen. Making meals every night was asking too much of her. So, Rhys had learned to do one or two things himself, sausages, scrambled eggs and the like. That was very different from making dinner for Marie, however.

He was also totally unprepared for the difficulties involved in buying ingredients under wartime conditions. Yes, Ellen had mentioned having to stand in queues and shortages and the complexity of the ration stamps, but Ellen wasn't a complainer. He hadn't realised just how difficult things were. Unable to get what he wanted and baffled about how to cook the obscure things they offered him with closing time rapidly approaching, Rhys ended up with a bag of turnips, spam and spuds.

His efforts to prepare them were even more disastrous than the shopping had been, and when the bell rang at 8:00pm sharp, Rhys was standing in his freshly painted kitchen in his shirtsleeves, sweating profusely in the steam of the boiling pots. "Crikey!" He looked at his watch in dismay, having lost track of time completely. He put the potato peeler aside, washed his hands in the sink, and dried them hastily on a tea towel while looking around for his tunic. The bell went again. Rhys called out 'coming' as he pulled on his tunic and buttoned it on his way to the door.

The temperature had risen about 5 degrees, and it was pouring rain. Rain gurgled down the drains and hissed on the windowpanes. Rhys opened the door, and Marie stepped inside with relief, her coat darkened with wet and her hat dripping.

"What a dreadful night!" Hattie exclaimed to cover her embarrassment. She had never in her whole life gone alone to a man's flat or house before. Mike had been a stranger in England, after all. They had met only in public places – restaurants, theatres, museums, parks, tea rooms and so on or, once, in her own home when she had introduced him to her father. There had never been anyone else until Rhys. But – as Hattie had thought repeatedly during the long sleepless night before – Rhys was a virtual stranger and a man of a different class.

It was the latter fact that made Hattie particularly nervous. She hadn't spent the last two decades working in a Seaman's Mission without learning a good deal about the differences between the classes. Hattie was never blinded by missionary zeal. She had never deluded herself that the working classes were more noble, generous or courageous than other classes. Nor did she view them as pitiful inferiors in need of guidance and care. Hattie quite simply viewed her 'customers' at the mission as men who needed help for one reason or another. This approach had allowed her to see them more clearly than many of her more religiously motivated colleagues. Among other things, Hattie had noted very early on – and when she was still of an age to be embarrassed by it – that working-class men had a much more direct, uninhibited and straightforward approach to sex. Sex was something they liked and something they believed women wanted, and they seemed to resent anything that stood in the way of their getting as much of it as they wished.

Last night as she lay awake in bed, Hattie had managed to remember any number of unsavoury and lurid stories that had made her question the wisdom of coming here tonight. She had asked herself a hundred times what she was getting herself into. She had made sincere efforts to talk herself out of coming. She had told herself she might be accosted, pressured, harassed – even subjected to force. But no matter how hard she tried, she couldn't picture Rhys doing anything to her that she didn't want.

And that was something else that kept her awake last night: The realisation that she very much wanted Rhys to kiss her, to take her in his arms, to ---? Did she want him to make love to her? How could she know, never having made love to anyone? The farthest she had gone with Mike was holding hands and chaste kisses until that goodbye kiss. Suddenly Mike had pulled her into his arms, crushed her to him, and kissed her with a wild passion that had left her breathless and a little scared. She had blocked out the memory of that kiss for a long time, even denying to herself that it had ever happened.

Now she was here. For some reason that she couldn't possibly explain, she thought she might just want Rhys to make love to her. She certainly wanted him to kiss her and hold her.

No sooner had she stepped inside the familiar cottage than she announced in alarm: "Rhys! Something's burning!"

"The spam!" Rhys had forgotten to turn off the gas when he went to open the door. Smoke was seeping out of the kitchen in thin wisps. Rhys plunged into the kitchen and grabbed the pan to take it off the heat. The pan had a metal handle. He burned his hand, and with a loud "bloody hell!" he let the pan drop to the floor. The blackened spam jumped from the pan onto the floor, and the grease splattered all over Rhys' best trousers. He swore again furiously, forgetting Marie's presence altogether.

Hattie took in the scene rapidly. The turnips were in a pot of furiously boiling water that had almost boiled away, and the potatoes were only half-peeled and not even on the heat yet. The spam was burnt to a crisp. "Rhys," she said calmly when his cursing had diminished enough for her to make herself heard. "I think I'd better take over here. Why don't you nip down to The Anchor Bleu and see if they have a spare tin of spam or two?" Hattie was already turning off the heat under the turnips.

Given its troubled start, dinner was astonishingly good, Rhys decided. Marie had brought parsley, mustard and salt and pepper, accurately guessing he would not even have thought of such things. They finished the meal with tinned peaches in milk and then cleared the table. Rhys offered to do the washing up later, but Hattie was already tying on an apron. It was approaching that time when 'things' could happen. Either she would wash up and leave, or – she supposed – Rhys would make some kind of move.

She stood staring at the filling sink as if fascinated by the simple process, still unsure how she would react when he made a move. Wouldn't it be safer to turn him down politely? To tell him she liked her life just the way it was without any romantic complications? But the fact of the matter was she didn't like her life the way it was. She had never really reconciled herself to living alone. All those years when Robin was growing up, she had half pretended he was her own little boy. She had taken a flat with two bedrooms, and one had been Robin's. Lydia let him 'stay the night' whenever it was convenient for her, and Robin had come whenever he could. Because Lydia didn't like travelling, it had always been Hattie who took Robin to the Isle of Wight for his holidays with his paternal grandparents, and Hattie had escorted him to school in the early years. (Later, he wouldn't hear of it, preferring to go on his own.) They had always had a special relationship. Together, Robin and the mission had helped her pretend she was happy.

But ever since Robin had gone to Cranwell, things had changed. After Cranwell, he had served in the Far East. She had seen less and less of him.

He was now twenty-five and married. It was always hard for parents to adjust to children growing up, but most couples had each other after the children left home permanently. Hattie had to face the fact that all she had was the Seaman's Mission – and that was a job, not a family.

It was absurd that she still wanted a family, but just standing here and washing up in the kitchen of this cottage made her acutely aware of just how very much she missed having a family. It was absurd. Who could like doing the washing up? She hated it at home. But it was different here with Rhys beside her, drying the dishes as she handed them to him. It was as if they had been married for years. It felt right.

"Funny to think I've been eating off the Duke of Norfolk's china, isn't it?" Rhys remarked as he rubbed one of the dinner plates dry.

Hattie laughed. "I dare say they aren't from his personal service."

"No, but they belong to him, don't they?"

"Yes, I suppose they must do, if they came with the cottage," Hattie agreed.

She finished and pulled out the plug, shaking off her hands and looking about for a towel to dry them on. Rhys could only offer her the nearly soaked dishcloth. "Sorry. This was all I could find."

Hattie used it as best she could and drew a deep breath, preparing to announce that it was time for her to go.

"I could lay a fire in the fireplace. I mean, I already have laid a fire in the fireplace. I just need to light it." He was gone already, and Hattie stood in the kitchen listening to the beating of her heart. Then she pulled the chain on the lamp over the sink to turn it off and followed Rhys to the parlour. It was chilly compared to the kitchen, which had been warmed by the cooking.

Rhys was on his knees in front of the fireplace blowing on the flames already licking the newspaper crumpled under the carefully laid logs. Hattie tried to consider him objectively. He was rather stocky, even a touch overweight but not in an unsightly way. He was greying. His skin was leathery. And he was very, very masculine.

Lydia had always accused her of having 'crude' taste in men. That was because Mike had been a big man, over six feet tall, with a square face and powerful shoulders. Lydia preferred slender 'poetic' types. Her husband had been almost frail and far too thin for his height.

To stop staring at Rhys, Hattie went to the table and collected their glasses and the bottle of grape juice she had brought as a substitute for wine. She poured it into the glasses and put Rhys' glass down on the side table. She took her glass with her as she sat on the sofa opposite the fire. The fire started to crackle, and smoke curled up into the chimney. Rhys stood, took his glass, and sat in the middle of the sofa. The sofa was large, and they could sit side-by-side without touching, but their legs were just inches apart.

Rhys stared at the flames, but his whole body sensed the woman beside him. He could smell her perfume and feel her warmth. She was dressed as he had never seen her before. When she worked at the mobile canteen, she wore her Salvation Army uniform; on their other dates, she had worn tailored suits, and while helping to do up the cottage, she had worn the kind of cotton work clothes with an apron that Gladys and Ellen wore. Tonight, she wore a classic velvet dress with a sagging neckline and a simple gold chain at her throat. The skirt came well below the knee, the bodice was modest, the sleeves three-quarter length. Nothing about the dress was in any way provocative or even inviting; she was very much a lady. She belonged in this elegant cottage eating off the Duke of Norfolk's china much more than he did.

He glanced over at her a little uncomfortably, wondering if she was thinking similar thoughts. She, too, was staring at the fire and clutching her wine glass filled with juice in her right hand as if she were afraid of dropping it. The image of another Marie flashed across his mind: A frightened young woman clutching her wine glass and trying to explain to him in her broken English that she was a nice girl. She was no whore. She came from an honest family. But the war (la guerre, la guerre)....

"Was there never another man in your life, Marie?"

Hattie started slightly and looked over at him. "A man? You mean someone I was in love with?"

Rhys nodded.

Hattie took a sip of her pseudo-wine and looked again at the fire. "There was an American officer, Mike Polanski. He came from Wisconsin, somewhere on those Great Lakes that border Canada. He was a second lieutenant – Lootenant – as he said it," she added with a little, inward smile.

"And you loved him deeply?" Rhys asked softly.

Hattie shrugged. "I thought I did. He was the most wonderful thing that had ever happened to me. He didn't seem to notice that I was neither a great beauty nor a great heiress. He didn't care about my mother. He was rather awed by my father. His own father was much younger of course — a Polish immigrant to the United States working in a steel mill. By then my father was seventy-five and still dressed like the Victorian he was. To Mike, he seemed like something straight out of a museum, or at least a novel set in the last century." She smiled at the memory.

"And what did your father think of him?"

"My father? My father didn't say. Of course, he found it difficult to deal with a man with such an outlandish accent and brash manners. He didn't know what to make of it all. But Mike was an officer, and he was fighting side-by-side with our troops. Perhaps my father expected — even hoped for — what happened, but if he did, he had the good sense — or kindness — not to spoil my happiness while it lasted."

She looked so sad at that moment that Rhys risked reaching out to her. He touched her shoulder with his hand, and she turned to look at him.

"You're very beautiful, Marie," Rhys murmured honestly. "You must have made your American officer very happy for the last days of his life."

Hattie blushed at the compliment — and the touch of his hand. She shook her head in embarrassment. "I — I'm not sure. I couldn't — you know — give him all he wanted of me. It was all so simple for him. He said that where he came from, if two young people loved each other, then they got married and set up house together and that was all there was to it. He didn't understand why it was so complicated here."

Rhys smiled. "He was right."

His hand had come to rest on her shoulder. It felt warm and reassuring. Hattie smiled at him.

Rhys put his glass aside and moved closer to Marie. He laid his arm across her shoulders. He kissed the side of her head. "You're the most beautiful woman I've ever been this close to, Marie."

"Oh, Rhys! I'm not beautiful at all, and we both know it."

"You are to me," he told her solemnly. He bent his head around in front of hers and kissed her on the lips – very gently, very lightly. There was no pressure and no urgency in his kiss. His moustache tickled her a bit.

Hattie surrendered utterly. She parted her lips and closed her eyes. She hardly dared breathe, and she could hear the pumping of her heart in her ears. Part of her was still afraid, but she knew too that she wanted to take this risk. The worst thing that could happen was that she would be disappointed, and she could live with that.

Hattie self-consciously slipped her arm around his waist. He held her tighter in response, but gently still. His hold on her was so gentle it was more teasing than crushing. It made her long for him to take her more firmly in his arms.

Rhys was lost in memories. Be gentle, the other Marie had begged him. Be gentle, as if she had suffered too much brutality in the past already. He had known it intuitively. She had trembled in his arms like a frightened kitten, and tears had shimmered in her eyes. But he had won her with patience. He had calmed her fears just as you did a child's — with tenderness.

His hand stroked Marie's back slowly, and she let out a little sigh of pleasure. At last, he risked holding her more firmly, but not roughly or demandingly. Marie leaned against him, letting her weight press them closer together. He kissed the top of her head, and she responded by nuzzling her face against his chest. It was a tentative gesture, as if she were uncertain of its effect. Rhys felt his heart soaring in response. All those wasted years with Gladys! He bent his head and found Marie's lips; she parted them again willingly.

Soon they were breathless. Marie pulled back, embarrassed. Her cheeks flushed, and her skin glowed with just a touch of dampness. Rhys glanced at the fire. It was thundering away, casting both heat and light. Marie reached for her glass, wishing it was filled with wine rather than grape juice. Alcohol would have given her more courage, she thought.

Rhys reached out and stroked her arm gently. "There's nothing to be afraid of, Marie. I would never hurt you."

She smiled at him. "I'm not afraid of that."

"What then?"

"I think I'm afraid of losing control of myself."

The answer was so unexpected, Rhys laughed before he knew what he was doing. He cut himself off, afraid she might be offended, but she was smiling at him still. He leaned forward and kissed her on the lips.

"Rhys?"

"Um?"

"You do know I'm an old maid, don't you?"

"Not for long."

"No. Not for long."

Breakfast. The first traces of daylight were still blotted out by the black-out blinds. The cottage was cold. Rhys bathed cold and left the bathroom to Marie while he went to put the kettle on. A quarter of an hour later, she emerged timidly in the doorway — looking rather silly in a cocktail dress at this time of the morning. Yet, nothing had ever been so right. Rhys was sure of it. He took the kettle off the stove, and its scream turned into a whimper. He crossed the kitchen in three strides and took Marie into his arms again. She lay her head on his chest. "I love you, Marie."

She lifted her face to him, and they kissed. "I love you too, Rhys. More than I ever thought possible."

That was it then, as far as Rhys was concerned. They loved each other, and they had made love together. There was no going back, and he didn't want to. It might be a bit tricky with the kids, and her family – especially her sister, who might not like it. But that didn't matter any more. She was his.

Chapter 8

November 1940

"Emily?"

The voice was clearly Hattie's, and yet it sounded strange somehow. "Hattie? Is something wrong?"

"No ... I was just wondering if I could stop by for tea today."

"Of course, you can! You don't have to ask. Four o'clock?"

"Yes, thank you." She hung up. Odd, Emily thought, but then she got on with her chores.

Punctual as always, Hattie rang the bell at 4:00pm. Emily welcomed her in out of a bright, clear, cold day. The weather had cleared suddenly after a night of freezing rain, and Emily had even heard the Spitfires taking off from Tangmere for the first time in almost a week. They had been so low as they raced over Bosham, she had half suspected Robin of leading them, but she wasn't sure.

"Oh! I like your hair!" Emily exclaimed as she let the older woman inside. "You look smashing! Is that a new dress?"

"No, it's ancient – I just shortened the skirt a bit and padded the shoulders so it wouldn't look so old-fashioned."

"It's very flattering. Makes you look ever so chic. Honestly, you look quite different today."

Hattie was about to say, "I am different," but Emily had already turned away with a "do sit down. Tea's almost ready."

Hattie walked over to the table already set for two, a padded cosy waiting for the pot, and she sat down at the familiar table feeling very strange. The mission had been different. The moment she put on her uniform, she had been her old self again. There was so much work to do after the days she'd taken off to help do up Rhys' cottage that she hadn't had a moment to think about herself. But the decision to leave early today and come here had been the right one. She just had to talk to someone about Rhys, and Emily was the only person in the world that she could confide in.

Emily backed in with a tray and set it down on the table, smiling. Teapot, cream and sugar and biscuits. "It feels like ages since we've had a nice chat, Hattie. Has something been keeping you very busy? That gentleman friend of yours, perhaps?"

Hattie blushed like a schoolgirl. "Yes," she admitted, but she couldn't bring herself to meet Emily's eyes just yet. She watched, as if fascinated, while Emily poured a slurp of tea into a cup, decided it was too weak and set the pot down to steep a bit more. She cast Hattie a questioning glance.

It was time to take the plunge. Hattie drew a deep breath. "Emily? What would you say, if I told you I wasn't your maiden aunt any more?" She kept her eyes glued to the pretty, floral tablecloth, but a little smile played around her lips.

Like the cat that swallowed the canary, Emily thought, and then she grasped what Hattie was trying to tell her. She leaned forward and kissed the older woman on the cheek. "I think that's splendid!" She declared. "In fact, I think that's the most wonderful news I've heard since ops stopped for the weather. No, that's not fair. It's much, much more important than that," she corrected herself seriously. "It's absolutely wonderful — and I can see it suits you!"

"Is it that obvious?"

"Well, your hair and the dress and..." Emily cocked her head, "you look softer somehow — younger. You look happy."

Hattie reached out and squeezed her hand in thanks. "I am happy. I don't remember ever being so happy in all my life. Thinking about it, I think maybe I'm even happier than I would have been if I'd met Rhys when we were both young or if Mike had survived the last war. It's largely because I've been alone all these years that I appreciate all the little things."

Emily nodded, smiling. "I know what you mean. Although it's not really comparable, I was already twenty-four when I met Robin, and I felt like an old maid. I was never a great social success and all the opportunities seemed to have passed me by. There I was, out of university, working in a dull job, seeing the same people day after day and still living with my parents. I think I can imagine how you feel after waiting even longer for the right man to come along. It must be rather like finding a rose blooming in November."

Hattie started slightly and looked intently at the younger woman. "Yes, that's exactly what it is: Like a rose in November."

"Now tell me more about your gentleman friend. Rhys, did you say?"

"Yes. Rhys. Oh dear, how can I describe him? He's my age, with dark hair starting to go salt-and-pepper. He wears a moustache. He's very good looking really, for his age and all. Stocky but not fat. But that's not what attracted me to him. It's that he's such a good man, Emily. He's a good father, responsible and caring. He's conscientious and dedicated to his job, too. And he's been so good to me ever since we met, taking me out, treating me like someone special—"

"Which you are!" Emily insisted, pouring the tea, at last, and smiling broadly as she did so.

Hattie watched her, warmed by the younger woman's obvious sincerity. "He's a wonderful lover, too," Hattie confessed softly. "You know, so gentle and understanding of my inexperience."

"I should hope so!" Emily told her, her smile now touched with amusement. "So, when do we get to meet him?"

Hattie looked up, alarmed. "Oh, I can't bring him here! You must promise not even to tell Robin about him."

"But Robin would be so happy for you! Surely you remember all the trouble he got into with Section Leader Brownwell when he told her the WAAFs didn't want to remain virgins for the rest of their lives."

A smile crossed Hattie's face at the memory, but her expression remained serious. "Please, Emily. It's very important that he doesn't find out."

"Why? Is your friend stationed at Tangmere?"

"Yes, he is," Hattie admitted, her expression firm, almost grim.

Emily poured herself tea, giving herself time to think.

Hattie spoke into the silence. "Besides, he has two children — a seventeen-year-old girl and a thirteen-year-old boy, and they haven't been told about me yet."

Emily nodded, and then she looked up and asked intently, "does he want you to meet his children?"

"Yes, as soon as they get here."

"So, he is serious about you?"

"Yes, he asked me to marry him."

"And you accepted." It wasn't a question. Emily thought for a moment and then continued, "If you love him and want to meet his children, why don't you want to bring him home to meet us? Surely you aren't ashamed of him?"

"You know what Lydia is like," Hattie protested.

"Robin and I aren't Lydia, and you're old enough to stop worrying about what your younger sister thinks."

"Yes, of course, but everything has happened so fast. I — I want you to meet him, really I do, Emily. I'm sure you'd like him. But Robin — it just wouldn't be right."

Emily thought about that and drew the correct conclusion, which she kept to herself for the moment, only answering, "It's your decision, Hattie. I'm not going to betray your confidence, but in the long run, if this is serious, which you just told me it was, you can't keep him hidden away from either Lydia or Robin."

Hattie took a deep breath. "I know. But let me take one step at a time. I've only just lost my virginity, after all."

That made them both laugh, and Emily leaned across the table to give her another kiss before remarking, "I think you're misjudging Robin, but take it in your own time."

Rhys caught himself whistling while he helped one of the fitters dismantle a Spitfire engine that was stuttering for unclear reasons, very much to the annoyance of the young pilot who had been forced to return from the first flight in weeks. After what seemed like weeks of sleet and freezing rain, the first day of sunshine had everyone in good spirits. The pilots were like a rambunctious pack of puppies in their eagerness to get back into the air. The ground crews, too, were more than content to be servicing aircraft rather than cleaning and other dull chores. But Rhys knew that none of that would have given him the spring in his step or elicited his rather tuneless whistle if it hadn't been for Marie.

Smiling at himself, he stepped back and wiped the oil off his hands with a cloth he kept in the back pocket of his overalls. His mind wasn't on the work at all. His thoughts kept drifting back to Marie — images of their night together mixing with dreams of what a happy family they would make. He could picture them at Christmas together with Marie and Ellen cooking while he and Owain put up the tree.

Rhys noticed the aircraft's fitter, LAC Cooper, looking over at him questioningly. "You're doing fine, Cooper. No need for me to look over your shoulder," Rhys explained.

The fitter looked astonished and then grinned, "thank you, sir."

The sound of aircraft engines drew their attention, and they automatically looked skywards. It was dusk, and the sky was illuminated a vivid orange colour to the west while the eastern sky was already a bright but darkening blue. The squadron was returning from its last test flight of the day. Only it wasn't coming into land by the look of it. There was no attempt to swing around onto the circuit. Instead, the squadron came down shamelessly low and beat across the field before hauling into a simultaneous loop. The outer aircraft peeled off to the left and right, respectively, in what was called a 'Prince of Wales' formation. Then they were flying upside down across the field, going the opposite way. They rolled off the top of the loop almost simultaneously. The squadron split into two flights, banking vertically in opposite directions and then flew in a wide curve to come charging back at one another head-on.

Rhys noticed that, by now, men were leaving the Nissen huts, hangar and messes and, all around the field, work stopped as everyone watched the display. It was nothing but high spirits, Rhys knew, but it matched his mood so perfectly that he was grateful for it. Over the years, Rhys had seen better displays of team aerobatics. The aircraft on the fringes, presumably the newer, less experienced pilots, missed the timing more than once and lagged noticeably. Around him, the ground crews were cheering on their pilots. "Come on, Billy! Pull your finger out!" One of the fitters growled just behind Rhys, while Foley and Powell (the CO's crew) commented with condescension that "he's really holding back for the sprogs today."

The formation was changing overhead, and Rhys enjoyed the sight of one after another Spitfires flick rolling. He was annoyed when a WAAF tugged at his sleeve. "Flight Sergeant, there is an urgent phone call for you

— from the police."

"The police?" Rhys couldn't make sense of that. What could the police want with him? An accident! Marie! The way she drove, she'd probably had a car crash. He started running across the field towards the mess. By the time he got to reception, he was almost completely out of breath. "There's a—"

The WAAF at reception pointed him towards the phone booth.

"Jenkins!" He gasped into the receiver.

"One moment."

He sobbed for breath, his pulse racing.

"Flight Sergeant Jenkins?"

"Yes."

"This is Chief Constable Kilian of the Salisbury Metropolitan Police. I regret to inform you that your son, Owain Jenkins, was arrested this afternoon for shoplifting. Your daughter, Miss Ellen Jenkins, asked us to inform you. Bail has been set at £5."

"Shoplifting?" Rhys asked, dazed, still trying to get his bearings. Marie was all right, but Owain had been arrested? In Salisbury? "What did he steal? Is it certain?"

"Very. He was observed by a customer and a sales assistant and when arrested he was still in possession of the stolen goods, namely four batteries, two packets of cigarettes and a camera. Furthermore, he resisted arrest, using foul language and attempting to inflict physical harm on the arresting officers. He broke Constable Walker's glasses in the process."

"He's only thirteen," Rhys stammered.

"Yes, and his sister is only seventeen." The chief constable left him in no doubt as to what he thought of Rhys leaving his underaged children to fend for themselves. "We strongly suggest that you take custody of your own children, Mr Jenkins, at the earliest opportunity."

"Yes, of course. I'll come right away. I'll be there...." He looked helplessly at his watch, feeling vaguely sick. He would have to take leave, hitch a ride to Chichester, get the next train, and where was he supposed to come up with the bail? He'd just paid the estate agent the required three months advance on the cottage, not to mention that he'd been living a bit beyond his means to take Marie out as often as he did. He wouldn't draw his pay for another week. "I'll be there tomorrow morning. I don't know when exactly with trains and all, but I'll be there before noon."

"We look forward to meeting you, Mr Jenkins," the constable told him primly and hung up.

Rhys replaced the receiver and stood dazed in the telephone box. How could it come to this? Gladys must be turning over in her grave. The thought of Gladys reminded him of Marie as well — with a slight twinge of guilt, which he quickly repressed. It wasn't Marie's fault the kids had been left motherless at 14 and 10, respectively. Rhys searched his pockets for coins and fed the telephone to put a call through to Marie. She wasn't at the mission, so he tried the home number she had given him. No one answered there either.

Frustrated, Rhys left the phone booth and stood uncertainly in the lobby. He had to get leave to go to Salisbury and bail Owain out. He'd collect Ellen and bring them both back to Bosham at once. He went back into the booth and placed a call to the pub nearest his old flat. He asked them to send someone to tell Ellen to go to the phone box. All that took nearly an hour, but he finally got hold of her.

"Dad! I called you three times last night, and twice first thing this morning! Then I had to go to Salisbury myself. I only just got back."

"I told you there was squadron party, at a pub off station. We weren't back until very late. I slept in. Now—"

She didn't let him finish. "Owain's been arrested. He was stealing, Dad! And then he attacked the constables and broke one of their glasses and they wouldn't release him to me. They want 5 quid for his release, Dad!" Ellen all but wailed this into the telephone. She was so distraught she didn't sound like herself at all. Rhys had never felt like such a failure in his life.

"Don't you worry about that, El. I'll find it. Now what I want you to do is pack up your things and Owain's too. I'm going to bring you both back here as soon as I get Owain out. I'll come and collect you first and we'll go together to the police."

"When will you be here, Dad?"

"I don't know yet. I'll ring you at," he checked his watch, "at 9:30 to let you know. All right?"

"Please hurry, Dad."

"I will. Don't worry."

He hung up and stood, trying to think what to do. Get leave first. No, he'd try to reach Marie again first. He dialed her home number, and let it ring eight times. Still, no answer. He was about to hang up when a breathy voice said, "hello!"

"Marie?"

"Rhys! It's wonderful to hear your voice," Hattie admitted, too much in love to care if she sounded like a fool.

Rhys was too upset for pleasantries. "My son's been arrested for shoplifting. They've slapped on a bail of 5 quid, and I've got to get to Salisbury straight away."

"Is there any way I can help?"

Rhys would have fallen in love at that moment — if he hadn't been in love with her already. "I – I –" he'd almost asked her to lend him £5, but he couldn't bring himself to sink that low.

"Would it help if I lent you my car? You could get to Salisbury much faster that way and it would be easier to bring the kids back as well."

"You are an angel, Marie! That would help me no end!" He hadn't even thought of it.

"I'll drive over to the cottage and meet you there with the car. Then you can drop me at my flat on your way to Salisbury."

"Marie, I don't know how to thank you."

"A kiss would be nice. Do you need help with the £5?"

"No," he decided firmly. He was not going to start taking her money before they were even married. "I'll meet you at the cottage in an hour. I can make a call from there, can't I? To let Ellen know when to expect me?"

"Of course."

Rhys went in search of the CO. He had landed but was still in flying kit surrounded by the pilots. They were discussing their little 'exercise' as the night thickened around them. One glance at Jenkins, however, and he sensed something was wrong. He left the pilots and approached Jenkins, "problem, Chiefy?"

Rhys took a deep breath. "I'm afraid so, sir. My boy, he's been arrested for shoplifting in Salisbury. I've got to go and bail him out, sir."

"Yes, of course. Will forty-eight hours be enough, or do you want seventy-two?"

"Forty-eight, sir. I've borrowed a motor."

"Good. Can you post the bail?"

"Ah – " Jenkins didn't have an answer to that.

"I can give you an advance on your pay, if that helps."

"Yes, sir."

"Come back to my office with me." Priestman turned to the pilots and told them he'd finish the debrief at the mess bar. Then he started walking across the field with Jenkins beside him. Darkness was closing in rapidly, and the eastern sky was already black while the western sky still glowed a sapphire blue. But the temperature had dropped rapidly. Rhys shivered, envying the pilot his fleece-lined, leather flying jacket.

Rhys started to worry about what the CO must think of him with a criminal son. It reflected on his abilities as a father to have the boy in trouble with the police at just thirteen. Shoplifting. Theft. "He's never been in trouble before, sir," Rhys remarked rather lamely.

"You're asking a lot of yourself to be Chiefy of an active squadron while playing both father and mother to teenage children."

"I can't give the kids away, sir!" Rhys replied sharply.

"No," the CO agreed, and they left it at that.

Rhys signed for a £5 advance on his pay in the squadron leader's office and was given a forty-eight hour pass. He grabbed his bike and started peddling as quickly as possible to Bosham.

Chapter 9

November 1940

It was the middle of the night before Rhys arrived at his old flat, but Ellen had left a light on for him. Although she had gone to bed, she had not been able to sleep, and she came down the stairs in her nightie as he unlocked the front door. "Ellen!" He opened his arms to her.

For the first time in years, she ran to them and let him hold her. She was soft and plump and warm, and he was reminded of when she had been two or three before she had become so self-possessed and solemn. No sooner had he thought how nice it was to hold her than she pulled back and started pulling at her nightgown self-consciously, as if there was something to be ashamed of. She straightened her shoulders and announced, "I've got everything packed, Dad." She pointed to five suitcases and a big wicker basket. "I've packed the basket with sheets and blankets and towels and all the food that won't go off."

"Good girl, Ellen," he praised her, longing to touch her again. Last night with Marie had re-awakened his natural inclination to express himself physically. Ellen was screaming for sympathy and reassurance, and he wanted to give it to her, but she had moved back from him already, distancing herself from him.

"How about we have a cuppa before we try to get some sleep? I told the police I'd be at the station tomorrow morning."

"Of course, Dad." She moved ahead of him towards the kitchen and switched on the light as she went in. While she lit the gas and put the kettle on, he took a couple of cups and saucers from the cupboard. He couldn't help but notice how run-down, cheap and – well – ordinary this flat looked compared to the cottage. "You'll like the cottage I've found, El. It's got a big, sunny kitchen with lots of counter and cupboard space."

"Since when did you notice things like that, Dad? Or is that what the estate agent said?"

That hurt Rhys a little, but it had been Marie who had noticed those things and pointed them out to him. To his daughter he just said, "I thought they were important to you. It is also close to the shops. I've found out about a vocational school for you as well, a place that trains girls in bookkeeping, typing, even shorthand and stenography, and how to work telephone switchboards and the like."

"How can I possibly do a course?!" She flung back at him in a tight voice without even turning around. "You see what's happened even with me at home all day! Owain needs someone!"

"But that's the point, El! You can't be responsible for your brother. That's my job. You've got to get some training so you can get a good job, get on with your own life."

He noticed that her shoulders were shaking and realised that she must be crying. He went over and took her into his arms again. She dropped her face in shame. "I'm sorry, Dad. I'm so sorry."

"Hush, El. You've got nothing to be sorry for. You did your best. It's my fault it came to this—"

"NO! No, it's not!" She drew back from him shouting. Her face was bright red, and the tears glistened all down her cheeks and dripped from her chin. "It's Mum's fault! She had no right just to leave us like she did! She had no right to die! It wasn't fair!"

Rhys was flabbergasted. He'd never heard anything so ridiculous. How could anyone be blamed for dying? "Now, Ellen, that's not sensible. Your mother didn't want to die—"

"Yes, she did! She wanted to punish us all for not being good enough for her!"

Rhys could only conclude that his daughter was overwrought. The strain had been too much for her. He pulled her back into his arms and held her tightly even as she made feeble attempts to break free. "Ellen, no one could ever think you weren't good enough. You're the best daughter a man could hope for, and you've done more than most girls would for your brother. And look how you tended your mother when she was ill and how you ran the house all by yourself."

"I was never good enough for Mum," she sobbed into his tunic. "I couldn't cook good enough for her, or clean right or even iron proper according to her. She said I'd never be good enough for a man of my own!"

"Ellen!" He'd never known, never even imagined such a thing. But

Ellen was at last letting him comfort her, so he just stood there letting her sob until she seemed to get hold of herself. Then he gave her his handkerchief.

She blew her nose into it and then remarked a little reproachfully, "it smells of oil and fuel."

Rhys laughed and then kissed his daughter on the nose. "Things are going to be different in Bosham," he promised her, but he didn't dare tell her about Marie yet.

The scene at the police station was terrible. While Rhys paid the bail and signed all the forms and declarations, the constables glared at him reproachfully. He was lectured on his responsibilities and how he was liable for damage done by his underage son. Feeling guilty as he did already, he got a bit huffy at that remark and demanded to know what the broken spectacles had cost, but the police backed down and said they'd let him off this time. Still, Owain would have a 'record'. There were even vague threats that a repeat offence could lead to Owain being removed from his father's custody and sent to a borstal.

Finally, they brought Owain out. He was dressed for school in short trousers, a knitted sweater, and knee-high socks under his winter coat, but having spent the night in jail, he looked rumpled and dirty. His hair was uncombed, and his fingernails were grimy. At the sight of his father, he sneered, "oh, finally remember me, did you?"

"Owain!" Rhys gasped, too stunned to find an answer straight away.

Owain turned to the collected audience of police constables and clerks and announced, "See, that's my dad – more interested in his damned aeroplanes than in me and m'sister."

"That's not true!" Ellen screamed before Rhys recovered enough to say anything, slapping her brother for good measure.

Nothing could have shocked Rhys more. "Ellen! That's enough!" Then he took a firm grip on Owain's upper arm and marched him out to Marie's car. He shoved Owain inside, slammed the door shut and went around to get in the driver's seat while Ellen climbed in the back. They set off in silence.

Rhys had to concentrate on driving in an unfamiliar city. The road signs had all been removed – a precaution taken in the summer when a German invasion had seemed imminent. Now it was just a damned nuisance. Unconsciously he started speaking aloud. "Is this the turn-off?"

"No, Dad," Owain said sullenly, "you're going the wrong way altogether."

"Oh, shut up!" Ellen snapped, leaning forward over the back of the front seat. "You need to go on a bit further, almost to the cathedral, and then turn right onto the Southampton Road."

"Thanks, El."

"The flat is the opposite way," Owain insisted.

"We've packed up and left that flat, Owain," Rhys told him, taking his eyes off the road to watch for a reaction. "I'm taking you to Bosham, to your new home."

"Oh." Owain turned away from his father to look pointedly out the window.

Silence encased them all the way to Southampton, where Rhys decided to stop for lunch. Although it added an hour or more to their journey, they had time, so Rhys drove down to the docks. He parked the car, and they walked down to the quays where countless merchant ships were loading and off-loading their cargoes. Owain's effort to remain sullen was taxed by all the excitement. Rhys took out a packet of cigarettes and shook one out in Owain's direction.

Owain gazed at his father as if he had gone mad.

"Go on. I'd rather you take one of mine than steal them."

Owain gulped and turned away; his ears were bright red.

Rhys stuck the cigarette in his own mouth and lit up, returning the rest of the packet to his coat pocket.

Ellen was staring transfixed at a great ocean liner. "Isn't it beautiful? Just think what it must have been like with fresh paint and coloured lights and classy people going aboard." She had seen the films and the newsreels of ocean liners, but this was the closest she had ever come to a real one. It had been converted into a troop transport, however, and was painted a sombre grey.

They had fish and chips at a little shop just behind the gate to the Cunard Pier and then returned to the car. The silence was less hostile now.

As they passed the turn-off for Portsmouth, Ellen asked rather timidly if they could stop there as well, and Rhys gladly gave in. He was feeling the sleepless night and was very tired. He was not used to driving long distances and glad of the chance to stretch his legs. Portsmouth offered an opportunity for a tea break and some fresh air. He drove as close to the Southsea Esplanade as possible, casting a longing glance towards Eastney where Marie lived, and then led the kids to the Round Tower.

The wind was cold, and the Solent was whipped to a ragged, white-streaked pale green. As usual, many Navy ships swayed uneasily at anchors off Spithead, the waves breaking against their sheer, grey sides. Yet something going on inside the harbour had drawn a rather large crowd. People were still streaming towards the shore, and more and more people joined them on the Round Tower. From inside the harbour came the high-pitched whistle of bosun's pipes and then the deep-throated bellows of ships' horns. Tugs were frothing up the narrow harbour entrance. The Isle of Wight and Gosport ferries hovered at their landings, smoke drifting off their stacks in the wind, but motionless.

Then they saw her: A massive, capital ship with gigantic guns slowly but steadily approached the slender harbour entrance. As she got closer and larger, Rhys thought it would be impossible for her to squeeze through between the stone sentries guarding it. She looked too broad to pass between Portsmouth and Gosport. Along the length of shore to the north, the spectators were starting to cheer and wave. The ship was so close that Rhys could see officers on the bridge wings, binoculars to their eyes, or leaning over the railing to check the clearance. They could hear her engines throbbing. The wash of her wake struck the harbour wall and sloshed back again. The crew was drawn up on deck in neat rows. The wind tugged at their uniform jackets and blew the ribbons on their caps, but the men were as immobile as the towering superstructure that loomed several stories overhead. The whistling seemed to surround them and Ellen and Owain spontaneously joined in the cheering that swept over the entire crowd.

Rhys leaned towards the old man next to him and shouted to be heard above all the noise. "Who is she?"

"HMS Prince of Wales! On her way to reinforce Singapore!"

Rhys looked back towards the great ship, a symbol of Britain's unshaken dominance of the seas and felt proud. Then he glanced at his kids. Owain was leaning out over the railing and waving wildly. With a shock, Rhys realised he was actually smiling.

It was nearly dark, and they were all dead tired by the time they finally reached Bosham, but the mood had changed. After the stop at Portsmouth, Owain seemed to take an active interest in what was passing by the windows. Ellen started asking Rhys cautious questions, including several about the vocational school. By the time Rhys turned into the road behind the cottage, Ellen was leaning forward to peer through the front window, and Owain was leaning forward too. Rhys stopped the car and put on the handbrake. "Here we are."

His children looked at one another, then Owain flung open the door and scrambled out. In a moment, he was lost in the dusk. Ellen got out more cautiously and went slowly up the front path while Rhys went to the boot to unload the suitcases. As he reached the door, Ellen was standing there uncertainly. Owain was nowhere to be seen. Rhys unlocked the door and gestured for Ellen to go in first. She stepped inside and stopped.

"Go on. It's all ours."

Ellen seemed to tiptoe through the rooms, afraid to touch anything. She looked through the bedrooms and then returned to the kitchen and finally ended again in the parlour, where she gazed at the remnants of last night's fire. With a start, Rhys noticed that he had forgotten to clear away the wine glasses. Ellen's eyes found them. She stared and then turned and stared straight at him, a little frown on her face. "Dad?"

For once in his life, Rhys was grateful for Owain's interruption. The boy crashed through the door shouting, "it's right on the water! The sea's right at the bottom of the garden! There are boats laid up in the mud!"

Rhys nodded. "When the tide comes it, it laps at the garden wall."

"Can I have a boat?"

"If I ever work off your bail!" Rhys retorted in a sharp voice, but he wasn't really angry. It was so good to see Owain enthusiastic about anything, and he was grateful Owain had distracted Ellen from the wine glasses.

But Ellen wasn't the type to forget anything significant. She let it go for the moment. They were tired, and they had to unpack. Ellen made them a light dinner that she served in the kitchen. Owain pleaded exhaustion to go up to bed straight after dinner, and Rhys went with him while Ellen did the washing up. She washed the two wine glasses as well. In the morning, Rhys found them waiting beside his place on the kitchen table.

Rhys still had leave. He did not need to report back at Tangmere until the next morning. "Do you fancy going for a walk around the village together," he asked cheerfully as he came into the kitchen. Ellen had an apron on and was already beating powdered eggs with powdered milk. She glanced over her shoulder at him but did not answer straight away.

Rhys sat down warily. He sensed her hostility. Owain flopped into the chair beside him, demanding, "where's the toast?"

"Can't you see your sister's busy? If you want toast, make it for yourself," Rhys told him.

Owain stared at him. "But I don't know where anything is," he protested.

"Neither did Ellen, but she found things. That looks like a breadbasket to me, and I've never seen anything that looks more like a toaster than that gadget there," Rhys pointed to one object and then the other.

Owain opened his mouth to retort and then shrugged and dragged himself to his feet. His expression was habitually sullen, but Rhys was encouraged that he'd done as he was told. "Is there a school here?" he asked, with his back to his father.

"No. You'll have to take the bus to Chichester. We'll go together today, and get you enrolled."

"Can't I look around here first?" Owain whined, instantly rebellious, and was taken completely by surprise when his father said, "yes. I thought we'd go over around midday."

Expecting a fight, Owain was left speechless by this concession.

Ellen came to the table, holding the handle of the frying pan in a hot glove with her left hand as she served the scrambled eggs with her right. She served onto all three plates, returned the pan to the stove and then sat down opposite her father. She hadn't said a word to her father yet.

"Is something wrong, El?" Rhys ventured.

"Don't you think you should tell us about the woman who left lipstick all over the towels upstairs?"

Rhys' hand froze with the egg halfway to his mouth. Then he replaced his fork and sat back in his chair. Ellen was glaring at him furiously while Owain looked from his sister to his father in astonishment.

"Yes, Ellen, I do think I should tell you about her," Rhys managed to answer steadily. "In fact, I want you to meet her, but I thought we should have a little time just the three of us first."

"Just how long has this been going on?" Ellen demanded.

"I don't like that tone, Miss!" Rhys told her defensively. "I don't have to account to you."

"No?" Ellen raised her eyebrows. She had never looked so much like her mother, and Rhys lost his temper.

"No! Your mother has been dead for three years and she wouldn't let me in her bed for a hell of a lot longer than that! It's perfectly natural if I've found someone new. Most men would have found someone years ago – whether they were married to your frigid mother or not!"

As soon as it was out, Rhys regretted it, but it was too late. Ellen gaped at him, and Owain giggled from embarrassment. Then Ellen jumped to her feet and ran out of the kitchen. He heard her run up the stairs and slam the door of her room. "Bloody hell," he muttered and glanced at Owain.

Owain shrugged his shoulders a little helplessly, but he seemed to be enjoying his father's discomfort too, as if it made his own arrest a less serious offense.

With an oath, Rhys threw his napkin down beside his plate and went after Ellen. Standing outside the closed door of her room, he found himself trying to explain. "El, I'm sorry. I didn't mean to insult your Mum. I know she was a good woman. I never cheated on her. Not once in all our marriage. But you've got to understand, I'm – I'm not an old man yet. You and Owain aren't going to be around forever –"

"Now I know why you want me to go to some trade school! Why you want me to find a husband of my own! You want me out of the house so you can – can have your affairs!"

"That's not true! You know as well as I do that I've been begging you to go back to school for years. This has nothing to do with Marie. And Marie isn't an affair. I'm going to marry her."

Ellen answered with a wail of agony. Rhys looked about the narrow hall helplessly. This wasn't at all the way he'd imagined their first day together in the beautiful cottage. He'd thought Ellen would be so pleased. She had been — until she saw the wine glasses.

It was unfair. They hadn't even drunk any wine! And what if they had. Why shouldn't he have a little happiness? What right did Ellen have to make him feel guilty about the best thing that had happened to him in years? Why did she have to begrudge him his happiness? "Ellen! Stop that this minute!"

She wept more loudly.

Rhys looked around again. Owain was slouching at the foot of the stairs watching him. He grabbed the handle of Ellen's door and was astonished to find it was unlocked. He went into the pretty little bedroom with the flowery curtains framing a view over the garden to the bay. He had given Ellen this room because it was the prettiest in the cottage.

Ellen lay on her stomach, sobbing into her hands. Rhys took a deep breath and sat down on the edge of the bed. The bed had a soft mattress, and it sagged under his weight. He stroked Ellen's shaking shoulders. "What are you so upset about, El? Don't you want your father to be happy? Don't I have a right to a little happiness after these last years?" He didn't manage to keep the resentment out of his voice.

"Why does your happiness depend on getting rid of me? What's so wrong with me? Why doesn't anyone want me around? Not even my own father! Everybody just wants to get rid of me. I wish I'd never been born!"

"Oh, Ellen!" He pulled her up off the bed and into his arms, all his resentment against her dissolving again. "That's not true! I don't want to get rid of you. Nobody is talking about sending you away. This cottage is big enough for all of us. I want us to be a real family again, with Marie and you and Owain and me, all together."

"But—but," she sobbed miserably.

"Won't you even give her a chance? She's never had any children of her own. She wants to be friends with you, if you'll let her. She lent me the car to come and fetch you, and she helped do the cottage up. She even found it for us. She isn't going to throw you out."

Ellen risked looking up at him, her breathing irregular and her eyes still wet. He wiped the tears away with his hand.

"Please, Ellen, give her a chance."

Ellen swallowed uncertainly, and then she nodded.

Chapter 10

December 1940

It was Sunday before Rhys could arrange for Hattie to meet the kids. He invited her to Sunday dinner, and Ellen went to no end of trouble to get the rations for a leg of lamb, which she roasted with Yorkshire pudding and peas. The weather was crisp and clear with a brisk wind off the channel. The sunlight poured into the freshly painted cottage, making it bright and inviting. The smell of the roast filled the entire cottage with warmth, and then the bell rang. Rhys answered it.

Marie stood in the door in her double-breasted navy-blue coat and her hat with the half veil and leather gloves. Rhys was so glad to see her here, that he bent and kissed her at once, even before he backed away to let her in out of the wind and cold.

She took off her hat and gloves at once. "I didn't know what to wear," she told him in a low, nervous voice. "I tried three different things, but nothing felt right."

Hattie had been torn between the desire to make herself attractive for her lover and the duty to make herself look 'motherly' for his children. Ever since that night together, Hattie felt twenty years younger. It was inconceivable to her that she was a woman of forty-five. She felt like the heroine in a romance — a woman so in love that she defied all the rules. She was not the least bit ashamed of what she'd done. On the contrary, she was rather proud of herself. She wanted to live her little fantasy of being a young, attractive woman. She wanted Rhys to make love to her again.

But there were his children to consider. Hattie knew how much Rhys loved his children, and she knew that she had to make friends with them, or things would never work out with him. Hattie thought she would have had no trouble if the children had been little. Younger children, who didn't remember their mother properly, could have been won over with sweets and kisses and attention. But Hattie had seen enough teenagers to know they were much more difficult. In fact, she didn't have the foggiest idea what she could do to make two teenagers like her, but it certainly wouldn't be acting as though she were a teenager herself.

Rhys was helping her out of her coat and whispering so close to her ear that his moustache tickled, "I don't care what you wear, Marie — in fact, I think I like it best when you wear nothing at all."

"Rhys!" She flushed not only from his words but because of his hot breath in her ear, and then her eyes fell upon Owain, who was shamelessly leaning against the wall watching them.

Attack is the best form of defence, Hattie told herself, and holding out her hand, she marched straight towards Owain. "You must be Owain."

"Yeah," he admitted standing upright for some reason. He seemed wary, but he did not reject her outstretched hand. He shook it.

"I'm Hattie Fitzsimmons, but your father calls me Marie." Already she felt uncertain again. What did Rhys want his children to call her? Miss Fitzsimmons? Or Marie? Then she realised she did not want them calling her Marie. That was Rhys' name for her; it did not belong to anyone else. So, she added, "why don't you call me Aunt Hattie like they do down at the Seaman's Mission where I work?"

"Hattie? What an awful name!" Owain exclaimed, clearing trying to be provocative.

From behind him, a young woman hissed angrily, "Owain! Can't you be nice just once?!"

"Oh, he's quite right," Hattie agreed, smiling over Owain's shoulder at the plump girl with a round face, flushed from working in the kitchen. She wore a floral-print dress under an apron and was drying her hands on a dish towel. Hattie held out her hand, "you must be Ellen."

Ellen took her hand uncertainly. Hattie felt the sweat and saw the nervousness in the girl's eyes. With shock, she realized that Ellen was at least as nervous as she was.

Hattie chattered to put them all at ease. "Hattie is a horrible name. I've always hated it, which is why I am very pleased that your father calls me Marie." She gave Rhys a private, little smile across both his children, and for an instant, they were naked by the fire again. Then Hattie returned to the present, "but Hattie is what everyone else calls me, so it seems the best solution. Unless you want to call me Miss Fitzsimmons, that is?" The question was directed at Ellen.

Ellen was still 'drying' her hands on the tea towel. "I don't know what would be right, Miss," she admitted self-consciously, with a glance at her father that Hattie couldn't read.

Hattie shrugged, although she felt anything but indifferent, and suggested, "Well, choose what you like best, but don't think you need associate 'Aunt' with any particular intimacy. Sailors who've never seen me before in their lives pick it up from the others and I'm 'aunt' to half the navies in the world."

"Can I come and visit you at the Seaman's Mission?" Owain wanted to know.

"If you want," Hattie agreed at once, "but I'd hardly recommend it. It's a boring place for a boy your age — just a lot of homesick sailors, looking for a hot meal and a place to get away by themselves."

"By themselves?"

"Well, away from their officers and shipmates. Sometimes, being with strangers can be less strenuous than being with familiars," Hattie tried to explain.

"I don't understand," Owain persisted.

Rhys was about to tell him to stop pestering their guest and let her sit down, but Hattie was already answering as she moved into the parlour. Ellen rushed back to the kitchen to look after the dinner, and Rhys decided he ought to see about lighting the fire. Hattie was saying, "well, Owain, I imagine it's not very different from your friends at school. What I mean is, there must be times when you don't want to do what the others are doing. Maybe they want to go to the flicks, but you just feel like staying at home, or maybe they want to go to an amusement park, but you haven't got the money for the tickets. Or maybe they want to play football, but your knee is banged up and hurts. If you're by yourself, you don't have to explain why you don't want to do something; you just do as you please."

To Rhys' utter amazement, Owain was asking another question. "Do the sailors come from all over the world?"

"Well, not from the Axis countries," Hattie pointed out.

Owain laughed, and Rhys gazed over at him in wonder.

Soon Ellen called them to dinner. She had done everything she had ever learned to make the table look 'proper,' but she had more china, linen and more cutlery than she knew how to set. She had been confused by that, at first, and almost opted for just a single knife and fork. Then she remembered an advert in a magazine, which showed a table set for a fancy dinner. She set the table the way it had been set in the picture.

Hattie supposed she would have praised her even if she had just heaped things in the centre of the table, but she found it easy to praise Ellen's efforts, even if they were not having a five-course meal with soup, fish and cheese. The meal, such as it was, however, was excellent, and Hattie had no difficulty making her praise sound convincing. By the time she got up to help Ellen with the washing up, Ellen was less tense than she had been at the start of the meal.

"I can manage everything," Ellen told her, stacking the plates to carry them out.

"I'm sure you can, but why should you?" Hattie countered. "Let me help."

Ellen backed into the kitchen and started to run the water in the sink. Hattie found the apron she had worn almost a week earlier, just where she had left it, and she put it on. Rhys and Owain cleared the table, stacking the dirty dishes on the kitchen table or counters. "Shall I dry?" she offered.

Ellen nodded and pointed to a drawer that was full of neatly ironed dishcloths.

"Good heavens! Do you iron your dish towels? I'm much too lazy."

"My Mum said that leaving anything unironed was like not combing your hair, it showed you had no respect for yourself."

"I see," Hattie answered, suspecting hostility for the first time, "your mother must have been a perfectionist."

Ellen stopped washing and looked over at Hattie, apparently surprised by an observation Hattie found rather obvious. "Yes, I suppose she was," Ellen admitted.

"I suspect that made her a very unhappy person, seeing how much imperfection there is in the world," Hattie concluded almost flippantly. She had long since taken an intense and irrational dislike to Ellen's mother based only on Rhys' rare remarks.

Ellen looked even more surprised. "Yes."

"How sad," Hattie declared.

"What do you mean?" Ellen demanded, frowning slightly.

"Well, I mean, she had a wonderful husband with a steady, respectable job and two fine, healthy children. She had every reason to be happy. So many women of our generation didn't have any of that. Don't you think it's sad that she made herself unhappy by her own intolerance of natural imperfection?"

Ellen had never looked at it like that. She frowned with concentration as she countered, "But Dad and Owain and I did disappoint her. I mean, she hated moving all the time. She wanted Dad to go back to where they both grew up and work in the pits. And Owain has never been good at school, while I'm not much good around the house."

"That's ridiculous! You've taken care of your father and brother all on your own for three years. You cook as well as any restaurant. Good heavens, Ellen, you even have ironed dishcloths!" Hattie held up a stack of the neatly pressed tea towels. She'd expected Ellen to laugh, but the girl only looked solemnly back at her. For a moment, Hattie thought it was hopeless, then she took a deep breath and tried again, earnestly. "Ellen, I want you to try to imagine something."

Ellen was all ears. She did not even attempt to continue washing the dishes.

"When we found this cottage, it had been standing empty for almost a year. There were cobwebs and peeling paint on the window frames and torn wallpaper and dust everywhere! It took all the riggers of 606 Squadron to get the place cleaned up and a friend of mine and I kept them going with tea and sandwiches – just your typical Salvation Army kind of bread and a slab of ham. That's what I'm best at. Then, as a gesture of thanks, your father invited me to dinner here."

"Dad?" Ellen couldn't believe it.

"Yes."

"But Dad can't cook."

"No, he can't," Hattie admitted with a smile at the memory. "When I arrived, smoke was seeping out of the kitchen from the burning spam, and the spuds weren't even peeled yet." Again, the laugh Hattie had expected didn't come. Ellen looked horrified rather than amused. "Ellen, don't you see? It didn't matter! What mattered was that he wanted to do something special for me. We bought more spam from the pub and I did the potatoes myself, and we had a wonderful evening." Hattie added in all sincerity. "It was the most beautiful evening of my whole life, Ellen."

Ellen was still frowning.

Hattie had never encountered anyone so solemn in all her life. Almost in desperation, she tried one last time. "Ellen, your father went to a lot of trouble to do this cottage up for you, but I know it isn't perfect. There's that crack in the bathtub for a start—"

"That doesn't matter!" Ellen told her almost in outrage. "It's the most beautiful place I've ever been in."

"But Ellen, it isn't perfect – and I'm sure the dish towels weren't ironed when you arrived."

"Of course not! I don't expect Dad to do that. It's my job."

Hattie took a deep breath and conceded that Ellen was beyond her reach. She took a plate that had dripped almost dry on the rack and started to wipe it.

Ellen resumed washing. After a moment she said softly, "I – I feel almost like a – a thief. Like I don't belong here – or only to do the washing up." She looked down at her hands, sunk in the dishwater.

"Ellen! What a mad thing to say! Your Dad did it up for you — much more than he did it for Owain. He kept talking about how much you would like this or that. He would never have gone to so much expense or trouble for himself. He has quarters on the station, after all. This cottage is for you."

"Are you sure it isn't for you?" the teenager countered, meeting Hattie's eyes challengingly.

Hattie had never thought of that and started slightly. Ellen saw the surprise and the uncertainty. She looked away and resumed washing. "Up to now, we've made do with flats that weren't half so grand. This is for you because you're a lady."

"No, Ellen. No, it's not." Hattie turned Ellen to face her. "I have my own flat, and my sister has a house in Portsmouth. This is your home, Ellen."

"What is keeping you two so long?" Rhys asked, sweeping into the kitchen.

Ellen jumped guiltily and muttered an apology. Hattie smiled at him. "We just got carried away chatting."

"The fire's going. Why don't you leave that for me to do later?"

"We're almost finished," Hattie insisted.

But Rhys had her by the elbow and was pulling her away, calling, "come on, Ellen."

Ellen didn't follow, and Rhys and Hattie were alone in the parlour. Owain had gone out for a walk before darkness fell. "He loves the sea, Marie. I can't keep him away from it."

"I'm so glad."

"You've been a wonderful success." He was holding her in his arms, content and proud.

"With Owain perhaps. I'm not so sure about, Ellen."

"That's just the way she is – reserved and solemn. You said all the right things and I'm sure she likes you. You'll see."

"She thinks you did up the cottage for me rather than her."

"Well, for both of you."

"Oh, Rhys," Hattie leaned her head on his chest, but he lifted her chin and kissed her. She raised her arms and folded them around his neck to kiss him again. Rhys shifted his lips to whisper in her ear, "I need you, Marie. Stay with me tonight."

She drew back and shook her head, with a quick glance over her shoulder in the direction of the kitchen. "It's too soon. Ellen doesn't feel secure. It wouldn't be right."

"She knows. She won't—"

"No. I can't. I'd feel cheap."

Rhys frowned. "You can't mean you'd feel less cheap in a hotel somewhere—"

"Shhh!" She stepped closer to him again, and his arms closed around her of their own accord. He found it very hard to be close to her without touching her. He wanted to pick her up, take her upstairs and make love to her immediately. "Come to my cottage in Eastney, instead," she whispered.

"Yes. You're right. I'll say I have to get back to the station and come to your flat instead. I'll be there by nine at the latest."

The creak of the kitchen door warned them that Ellen was coming, and they sprang apart, but the look she gave them suggested she had seen what they'd been doing.

Hattie presumed Rhys would have tea with his children before making his way to Portsmouth, but she decided to have a light snack available in case he was hungry. She made a tray with cream crackers spread with butter and liver paste, slices of ham or squares of cheddar cheese. She put this in the refrigerator to keep it fresh, while she set out her best crystal wine glasses inherited from her father. She might not drink wine, but she loved the shape and glitter of the glasses and didn't see any reason not to use these for the grape juice that she put into the decanter. It was a pity she had no proper fireplace, but she lit her candles, and put a record on the gramophone. Surveying the scene, Hattie felt that it was a poor second to Rhys' cottage, but it would have to do.

It was after nine and still no sign of Rhys. Maybe she should check on the bedroom. She had self-consciously changed the sheets earlier and scrubbed the bathroom clean. She had put out clean towels. What else could she do?

She was getting nervous again. What if something had happened to Rhys. Maybe there'd been a scene with Ellen. She was sure to know he wasn't really going to Tangmere. Or what if riding his bike in the blackout, he'd been hit by a car? Hattie felt a horrible flash of premonition. Just like with Mike. She always lost the people she loved: Her father, Mike, Rhys—

The bell rang. She ran back down the stairs and yanked it open. Rhys grinned at her. She flung her arms around him and kissed him with relief.

"If I get that kind of a greeting for being ten minutes late, I might make a habit of it," Rhys teased when she released him at last. He removed his uniform cap and unbuttoned his coat. The skin of his face was scratchy with beard and icy-cold from cycling in the December night. His hands, despite the gloves, were cold too.

"Come in and warm up," Hattie urged, taking his hand and leading him into her parlour.

Rhys stopped to take it all in. The candles, the classical music, the pretty furniture, the crystal wine glasses and decanter. He turned and pulled Hattie into his arms again to give her another kiss. She was, he sensed, as eager as he was. He almost picked her up and carried her to the sofa, but then he thought, why rush it? They moved deeper into the little parlour.

"Oh, the crackers," Hattie exclaimed, annoyed that she had almost forgotten the food. She hastened towards the kitchen, leaving Rhys alone. He spotted a collection of photographs on the mantelpiece and went over to look at them. His attention was drawn immediately to a photo of a distinguished-looking gentleman in tails with a top hat and cane and a young lady hooked onto each elbow. One of the girls was in a lace wedding dress, her veil back over her hair and her new wedding ring displayed on the hand she had hooked over her father's elbow. That must be the sister. So, Marie was the other girl. Rhys leaned closer to get a better look. She was handsome, just as he had imagined. She stood very straight and was notably taller than her plump sister. She wore her hair loosely piled on her head as had been the fashion then. She looked straight at the camera without a smile. Her sister's wedding had not been a happy time for her.

His gaze shifted to the other pictures, and at once, he smiled. The next picture showed Hattie at a beach somewhere with a straw hat, and her skirts hitched up. Here she was smiling. Beside her was a small boy with thick dark hair falling over his forehead, holding a model sailboat and grinning happily. That must be her nephew, Rhys registered, nodding unconsciously. He looked like a nice boy. His gaze shifted further right, and he got a bit of a shock. It showed a pilot in flying kit in front of a Gypsy Moth. Marie hadn't mentioned that her nephew was a pilot. He frowned unconsciously, and his pulse started to race as he turned to the next picture. It showed a Hurricane with an RAF officer standing in front of it, one hand holding a pint of beer and the other sunk in his trouser pocket. The same thick, dark hair fell over his forehead. The same smile. The nephew. Only he was familiar. Very familiar. Too familiar. Distinguished Flying Cross and all. Rhys' throat went dry.

"Here we go!" Hattie announced happily as she returned with the tray. "I couldn't—"

"Why the hell didn't you say something?!" Rhys spun around and shouted at her.

"What?" Hattie stopped where she stood, stunned, uncomprehending.

Rhys' face was livid with rage. "How could you do this?! How could you lead me on?! Deceive me?!"

"Rhys? What are you talking about?"

He shoved past her and plunged into the hall. He grabbed for his hat and coat. "You've been using me! You heartless cow! I was just a toy to you! You knew we had no future together. You heartless cow!"

It hurt so much; he felt as though he were suffocating. He loved her. He really loved her. He wanted to marry her. Everything had been so perfect. Everything had gone so well. The kids liked her, even Ellen. They could have been a real family again. The four of them. In the cottage. How could she do this to him?! "You led me on, you cow! You let me believe we could—"

Rhys couldn't risk saying any more. He yanked open the door and plunged into the darkness. For a second, the light from Marie's house spilled onto the pavement, but then he slammed the door shut behind him. As he charged out into the black night, he tripped over his bicycle. Cursing he kicked it once, then righted it and swung his leg over to mount. As his hands touched the bitterly cold handles, he realised he'd forgotten his gloves, but he could not return to her house for anything – let alone a pair of gloves. He pushed off into the night and peddled furiously. All his dreams gone. Shattered.

He was sobbing. He bent his head against the cold wind and pedalled harder.

Hattie collapsed in the doorway, her back against the door he had slammed in her face. Her premonition had been correct. She had lost him just as she had lost her father and Mike. She was cursed. She could never hold onto anyone she loved. She clutched her knees in her arms and buried her face between them. She couldn't breathe. She closed her arms and knees tighter. She held her breath. But her survival instincts were too powerful. She raised her head, gasping for air.

She would have to go about suicide more carefully, she concluded. She could cut her wrists – lengthways – and then lie down in a warm bath. But she didn't like the idea of lying in all that blood. Nor was it fair to Emily or Lydia, whichever one of them found her and had to clean her up. She could try to get hold of a gun and then go somewhere where the police or a stranger would find her. Maybe the docks or in a railway station? There must be all sorts of guns lying about these days.

Robin had one, for example, she thought with a twisted smile. There would be a certain justice in that. He'd killed her chance of happiness. He might as well provide the coup de grace as well. But, of course, he wouldn't oblige. He would never give her his pistol without having a good reason.

Pills would be easiest, but she would need a prescription. That shouldn't be hard. She wouldn't be able to sleep, so she could get a prescription for sleeping pills and then take them all at once she decided.

That resolved, she pushed herself to her feet and, still dazed, returned to the parlour. The record was going around making a scratching sound. She lifted the arm off the record and unplugged it. She saw the wine glasses and the decanter full of grape juice. A lot of good that would do her! But they were standing on the liquor cabinet. The one full of rum, vodka, gin and whiskey that she kept to offer guests — especially whiskey because that was Robin's favorite drink.

Yes, she thought taking a trembling breath, now she understood him. There were times when the only answer was a stiff drink.

Chapter 11

December 1940

Hattie had never failed to show up at the Seaman's Mission without an explanation before. She was rarely sick, and she always booked her holidays well in advance. Only in the last month had she suddenly become erratic. First, she'd avoided the jazz night at a moment's notice, then taken three days off with practically no warning, and now she simply failed to appear at all. Nor was she answering the phone.

After consulting together, the workers at the mission decided that Marion should go to her house and see if Hattie had taken ill or had an accident. Marion knew where Hattie hid an 'emergency key', so when no one answered the doorbell, she went around to the back, lifted the third brick in the path, removed the key and let herself in. She was shocked by what she found.

Hattie was sprawled out half-dressed in her parlour with an empty bottle of scotch and a partially empty bottle of rum beside her. Marion couldn't believe it. Hattie had been a pillar of the Salvation Army in Portsmouth for as long as she could remember. She had never seen Hattie touch a drop of alcohol — although it was a well-known fact that an alcoholic could only stay dry if they abstained entirely. One drop and relapse was possible — as had apparently happened to their revered Major Fitzsimmons.

Marion got Hattie upstairs and out of her alcohol-soaked dress — a cocktail dress at that! One wondered who she had been planning to entertain and how? Marion got her into bed, although by now, she had come to and kept muttering something about 'sleeping pills'. Could Marion get her some sleeping pills?

"No, you can sleep this off all by yourself," Marion told her firmly.

Then she went back down to the parlour, cleared away the bottles and the glasses. Curiously, although two glasses were in the parlor, only one was dirty. Then Marion sat down and tried to think what to do. She liked Hattie far too much to want to tell the others at the mission what she had found. Besides, something bothered her about the whole scene. She had seen too many alcoholics over the years, and despite the evidence she had cleaned away herself, she didn't believe Hattie had a drinking problem. She had a problem that had driven her to drink, not a drinking problem.

Marion looked around the room again. Candles were burnt down to the candlesticks, the gramophone was unplugged but the record still in place, two glasses. She considered too the cocktail dress, the silk stockings, and the high-heeled shoes that no one at the mission would have dreamt Hattie even owned.

Marion went into the kitchen and looked in the fridge. Cream crackers spread with (now slightly browned) liver paste, ham and cheddar were arranged on a platter and covered by cellophane. She returned to the front hall and found a pair of men's leather gloves.

"Bastard! Whoever he is!" Marion declared.

Marion had been beaten senseless half a dozen times by her husband before she'd had the sense to take refuge with the Salvation Army. She had a deep-seated mistrust of all men. Hadn't her father abandoned her Mum and her when she was only four? Now some man had driven poor Hattie Fitzsimmons to drink — at her age!

Well, she wasn't going to tell the other workers at the mission that either. She went to the phone. There was a little address book beside it, and she quickly found the home telephone number of Miss Fitzsimmons' nephew. She dialled the number.

"Hello?"

"Mrs Priestman?"

"Yes."

"This is Marion Beety from the Salvation Army. Miss Fitzsimmons has taken ill. Is there any way you could come over and look after her a bit?"

"Oh, dear. Of course. What is it?"

"Well, Mrs Priestman, to be honest, I don't know for sure, but I found her lying in her parlour surrounded by an empty bottle of whisky and a half empty bottle of rum. Furthermore, the fridge is full of uneaten snacks and men's gloves are lying in the entry. Now, I'm no police inspector or anything, but in my book it looks like Miss Fitzsimmons had a fight with a gentleman friend that made her very unhappy. Oh, and she wanted me to get her sleeping pills."

"I'll be over straightaway."

Hattie groaned and sank back onto the pillow. "My head is killing me," she admitted in a hoarse, weak voice.

Emily laughed. "I should think so. Two glasses of scotch would have been enough to knock me out. You managed a whole bottle and rum on top. Not bad for an old girl, I'd say."

Hattie opened one eye and squinted at Emily from it. "You know, we don't joke about that. My mother was an alcoholic."

"Hattie, you are not an alcoholic, but I now know where Robin gets his ability to hold his liquor. Would you like some coffee or tea?"

Hattie opened her second eye and squinted from both of them. "Where did you come from?"

"Marion found you and phoned me."

"Marion?"

"Well, they missed you at the mission."

"Oh, God," Hattie groaned. "Now they all know."

"I doubt it. Marion rang me because she didn't want to tell the others. She's going to say you have a terrible stomach flu. Do you want to tell me what really happened?"

Hattie went absolutely still. Deadly still. It all came back to her. She answered very softly. "He left me."

"But why?"

"He found out. About Robin."

"But what difference does that make?" Emily protested.

"Robin is his commanding officer, Emily. He's the new Chiefy."

"I had guessed," Emily admitted, "but if you accept him for who he is, what difference does that make? What did he say?"

"He called me a cow and a liar and accused me of deceiving him, misleading him, leading him on—"

"Oh, Hattie! He's a monster!"

"No, he's not. He's the most wonderful man I've ever met. I love him." Almost inaudibly, she added, "and he loved me."

Emily took a deep breath. She'd comforted enough girl-friends in her college years to know that it never helped a jilted woman to insult the man she still loved. "If he loves you, Hattie, he shouldn't have insulted you like that. You didn't lie to him, did you?"

"I didn't tell him the truth, either. I didn't even hint or warn him."

"How did he find out?"

"He saw the photo, the one taken just after Robin got the DFC."

Emily sighed. "I still don't see what difference it makes. I'm sure Robin wouldn't – "

"Don't you dare tell Robin!"

"Hattie! He's my husband, and he happens to love you very much. He has a right to know—"

"Why? What difference does it make to him?"

"You should see yourself," Emily countered severely. "I've never seen you happier than you've been the last couple of weeks, and I've never seen you fall this low before either. What sort of friend would I be if I were indifferent? And what sort of nephew would Robin be? He looks on you as his second mother."

Hattie reached for her hand. "You're right. So why upset him. I'm so grateful to you for sharing my joy these past weeks, but now it's over. The little episode, just like Mike, is over. Help me forget about it. Please."

"If that's really what you want...."

"Yes. It is." Hattie looked at her steadily, and, with a sigh, Emily accepted it.

But there was no forgetting, not for Hattie. It wasn't just that she had slept with Rhys. Sometimes she even managed to tell herself that didn't matter at all. She wasn't a young girl who was now 'ruined', and she wasn't pregnant either. Yet what Rhys had done was remind her of what she had wanted and what was missing in her life. She couldn't just go back to the way she had been before. The mission was a distraction, but it wasn't rewarding, not any more. She came home in the evening tired, but not fulfilled or satisfied. Every night when she entered her neat little cottage to make her dull dinner alone, she realised it would be the same for the rest of her life. Why drag it out? She didn't want to go on with the charade another minute. Life wasn't fun or interesting or fulfilling; it was simply drudgery.

Furthermore, her life was utterly worthless. She was completely superfluous. Everything she did could be done by someone else — most of it better than she did. If she weren't there any more, people would miss her for a bit, some longer than others, but it would not have a real impact on anyone's life. There were sailors who would turn up at the mission after a long spell at sea and be astonished to hear she was no longer there. They might be sorry for a moment or two, but then they would shrug and carry on. Lydia's shock would far outweigh her grief. She would be delighted to get her hands on their father's beautiful desk, the mirror in the hall, the set of pearls, and various other bits and pieces left from their father's estate. Emily would be most upset — and Robin. But they had each other.

After about a week of thinking about it, Hattie had made up her mind. It was just a matter of finding the best means to carry it out. She started with the chemist, complaining of sleeplessness to the nice pharmacist at the counter. The man was very sympathetic and suggested all sorts of things — don't drink tea after 8:00 pm, have a glass of warm milk before going to bed, even 'a tiny nip of sherry' — but the only products he could sell without a prescription were harmless.

Hattie went to her doctor and told him her problem. The doctor was dealing with twice as many patients as before because so many of his colleagues had been drafted into the armed services. On top of that, Portsmouth was still receiving unwelcome attention from the German Luftwaffe. At the start of the month, there had been three raids in quick succession, and since the raids now came at night, even people not directly affected were dragged from their beds by the air-raid sirens. In short, everyone was suffering from inadequate sleep. The doctor told her in no uncertain terms that whatever sleeping medicines were available had to be saved for the ill and injured who needed them. He recommended taking catnaps during the day, explaining to her that the first four hours of sleep were the most valuable anyway, and she would benefit from sleeping in short spells throughout the day and night. "That's the way soldiers do it, you know." Finally, he sent her out of his office with the parting remark, "besides, you don't want to sleep through an air-raid warning and find yourself the target of a German bomb."

Well, it was an option, Hattie thought and thereafter stayed above ground during all the raids. Yet despite the scores of casualties each raid produced, no bombs fell nearby, let alone on her house. Hattie soon concluded that she couldn't trust the Luftwaffe to take care of things for her either.

That meant finding an alternative method of killing herself. Despite being everywhere, guns were controlled, and Hattie had to admit to herself that she wasn't comfortable with them. She had heard stories of people shaking so violently when they tried to kill themselves that they'd only managed to maim themselves instead. Not something she wanted to contemplate. She could drive her car into a stone wall at 60 or 70 mph, but that too seemed risky. What if she survived the crash paralysed or an amputee? The idea of driving off the end of a pier into the Solent appealed to her, but when she started looking for an appropriate pier, she soon realised that they were all closed to motor traffic. That left inhaling gas or cutting her wrists. The problem with gas was that her kitchen was notoriously draughty. She was not certain the gas would ever reach a poisonous level. The thought of kneeling with her head inside the oven for hours and hours while running up her gas bill for nothing was not appealing either.

She re-examined the notion of cutting her wrists. The tools she needed were cheap and familiar. She had a whole package of razors in the bathroom cabinet. The pain would be minimal, no worse than cutting your finger while cooking. The blood was the only thing that seemed unpleasant, but she thought that lying in the bath, possibly with the water running and the plug out, would reduce the impact. Her blood would get diluted in the bath water and drain out of the tub. When they finally found her, she should be quite bloodless. Yes, that was the best solution.

Hattie felt much better having made her decision. She set about putting her affairs in order both at work and at home. It was now just 12 days to Christmas, and she carefully wrote all her Christmas cards and got them in the post. She paid all her bills, both private and as treasurer of the mission. She went to her solicitor, and together they drew up a last will and testament (in case she was caught in the bombing). She left everything, except the furniture that had belonged to her father, to Robin and Emily. They could either let the cottage or sell it. They could use much of the newer furniture themselves, and the second car would be a big help to Emily. Hattie thought to herself that it was a good thing her faithful golden retriever, Toby, had died last year. Otherwise, she would have worried about him. Lydia disliked dogs, and they were not allowed in Robin's leased cottage. But Toby was dead and buried in the back garden.

Rhys was having a harder time closing the book on the 'affair' (as he tried to call it) than he wanted to admit. Rum seemed to be the only way to put himself to sleep at night. If he didn't fill up on it first, he lay in bed tossing and turning with all too intense images of Marie, soft and naked next to him, keeping him company.

Damn the woman! Twenty bloody years of being faithful to Gladys, three years of absolute celibacy, and when he finally found the woman he wanted, she was off limits. And she knew it the whole time! The cow led him on, let him hope, plan, work his guts out on the cottage. She even let him – the slut! The tart! He said it over and over and over, hoping that if he said it often enough and long enough, he would convince himself.

But it was dangerous to lie awake at night. Sometimes, when he wasn't concentrating on his hate, little images seeped into his consciousness that nibbled away at his heart. Just on the brink of sleep, he'd see her as she smiled over her shoulder from the ladder at the cottage – shy and uncertain and yet so – damn her! Or he'd remember the way she'd competently rescued his disastrous dinner without a word of reproach or even that typically female way of making a man feel stupid for some domestic shortcoming. Or when he worried about how to handle Owain, he'd be reminded of the way she'd tamed the boy with her unruffled candour. There were a thousand little things that reminded him of what he'd lost. If he thought about them, he realised just how hurt and weak he was.

Rhys was terrified of breaking down, of being – and letting others notice – that he was hurt and vulnerable. So, he drank and worked more.

The drinking gave him fierce hangovers. Sometimes he could hardly get his head off the pillow in the morning. It felt as if a vice were slowly crushing his skull. When he tried to sit up, his vision greyed, and he swayed with dizziness. He'd stagger to the bathroom, often stumbling or knocking inadvertently against the hall as he went. Despite a wash and shave, he usually made his way downstairs with his head still throbbing like the unsynchronised engine of a German bomber. Here, he usually declined the breakfast Ellen had taken the trouble to make for him and set off in the frosty pre-dawn with nothing but a sip of tea in his stomach.

The bike ride to the station usually cleared his head, but by the time he arrived, he was starving. The combination of hunger and an obsession with not letting on how weak he was meant that he entered the hangar every morning looking for something that was wrong. He wanted to find fault with someone or something because that was the only legitimate outlet for his pent-up fury. It didn't take long for the atmosphere among the ground crews to reach icy levels of bitter hostility.

Of course, Fogerty and Newbury tried to talk to him about it, but the last thing he needed was them interfering. How could he explain himself? Or had they known all along that Hattie was the CO's aunt? Had they smirked and laughed behind his back while he was courting her? Had they laid bets on when he was going to come out of his cloud and find out? He couldn't trust them any more.

The worst, of course, was facing the CO day after day. There was absolutely no physical resemblance between him and Hattie. There was no similarity of name. And since the CO never came out to the Salvation Army truck (which Hattie — thank God! — never came with any more), he had never seen them together. How the hell should he have guessed they were related?

But when he had to report to the CO or when the squadron leader came over to the hangar for one thing or another, Rhys felt ashamed and resentful. When the CO was friendly, it made him feel like a disobedient schoolboy whose misdemeanours hadn't been discovered yet. On the other hand, if the CO was curt or dissatisfied for some reason, Rhys hatred all but boiled over. Whatever he did or said could not change the fact that Rhys hated him. Rhys hated Priestman because he stood in the way of Rhys' happiness. If he hadn't been there, he and Hattie could have been together.

All was ready at last. Hattie went to the mission for the last time. It was the last Sunday in Advent, and there was carol singing in the assembly room followed by a generous buffet with Christmas 'punch' (non-alcoholic, of course) and Christmas pudding (donated by a local manufacturer).

The mission was exceptionally crowded. Sailors from all over the world, including occupied Europe, seemed to have found their way here for a little Christmas cheer. There were a dozen Norwegians, the crew of a Norwegian gunboat that had managed to slip out with the retreating British naval forces. There were two French fishermen who had helped lift troops off at Dunkirk and then decided to stay in England rather than return to a humiliated France. (They came often because Hattie chatted with them in French.) There were four Dutch sailors who had been serving on a Canadian merchant ship when their country was crushed by the German juggernaut. There were lots of Canadians and Australians as usual, and a smattering of English sailors with no homes to go to for one reason or another.

Despite the best efforts to make it a cheerful and festive occasion, the mood was tinged with melancholy. Everyone here was lonely and homesick, especially if they had lost their homes indefinitely. Nor was there much hope in Portsmouth that night. The RAF might have forced Hitler to delay the invasion, but his Luftwaffe was bombing London and other cities mercilessly. When spring came, the whole, horrible show would probably start all over again: Daylight bombing, fierce dogfighting and eventually the long-anticipated invasion.

Portsmouth was already a favorite target for the Luftwaffe and had endured twenty-eight raids. After a successful landing somewhere on the south coast, it would become a goal for the crack German panzer divisions. The British would fiercely defend it, of course, but Hattie didn't look forward to being part of that piece of history. Better to slip out of the world tonight as planned.

It would have been nice to talk to Robin once more before she left, she thought, as she watched the Norwegians perform a carol together in Norwegian. But she might give herself away because she never rang him at Tangmere. If she rang him now, he would know something was wrong. Better to leave things as they were.

Still, she could put one last call through to Emily, surely? She'd find some excuse, and it wasn't unusual for them to chat now and again with little reason. Hattie joined the applause and slipped out to her office to place the call.

Robin was fed up. After what had seemed like a good start, the new Chiefy had proved a disaster. The accident had been unfortunate, but Jenkins handled it well, and it seemed for a time afterwards that he was settling in well. The crews seemed content, and his own rigger and fitter reported that Jenkins was 'all right'. Fogerty and Newbury were cautiously optimistic.

Then came the incident with young Jenkin's arrest, and since then, the Chiefy wasn't the same man. The mess steward reported he had run up an enormous bill, which he could ill afford after a £5 advance on his pay. More importantly, no one could please him any more. The Chiefy's angry voice taking someone apart was the most common sound in the hangar these days. Even Robin started to dread going over to the workshops. The atmosphere was worse than under Rowe. Now Jenkins had cancelled Christmas leave for two airmen, both of whom earned the time off and had been looking forward to it for months.

Robin sent for Jenkins.

The flight sergeant reported smartly. His trousers had razor-sharp creases. His buttons gleamed. His shoes shone. His salute would not have disgraced a guardsman at Buckingham Palace. "You sent for me, sir!" He was not looking at the squadron leader but a spot over his left shoulder.

Priestman considered the flight sergeant critically for a moment. He remembered their first meeting. He had liked the man instantly, but apparently, his instincts had betrayed him. Jenkins must be very adept at disguising his true nature. That, or Jenkins had undergone a bizarre change. Certainly, there had been a distinct break. All the trouble started after his son was arrested.

"Sit down, Chiefy," Priestman indicated the worn and sagging leather armchair before his desk.

"I'd rather not, sir."

That surprised Priestman, but he could hardly order the older man to sit down. If Jenkins didn't sit, neither should he, so he half-sat on the front of his desk, one leg swinging and the other holding him upright. "Do you remember the day you reported for duty, Jenkins?"

"I do, sir."

"I remember telling you that I didn't expect anyone to be perfect, but I expected you to be honest and tell me if I was asking too much of you or the crews."

"Yes, sir."

"Am I?"

"No, sir. I only meant that you told me that."

"Didn't I ask you to come to me with any problems?"

"Yes, sir."

"Well?"

"I don't know what you mean, sir."

"Jenkins, there isn't anyone on this entire station who hasn't noticed you have a problem. Out with it."

Jenkins stood rigidly where he was and continued to stare at the wall.

"Didn't you get your son out of jail?"

"My son is with me in Bosham, sir, and he is going to school regular."

"So, your son isn't the problem?"

"No, sir."

"Then what is?"

"It's personal, sir."

"It's not personal when every single erk on 606 squadron is suffering for it!" Priestman shot back. "There are two cancelled leaves here on my desk and neither of them is justified."

"Are you saying I'm not doing my job right, sir?"

"Yes, that's exactly what I'm saying."

Robin had the impression that this direct criticism shook the senior NCO, but he did not noticeably change his attitude or expression. At most, he swayed a little in his stance.

After a moment, Jenkins asked without looking at the squadron leader. "Are you going to have me posted, sir?"

"Is that what you want?"

Priestman heard the flight sergeant's quick intake of breath. His hands, so rigidly held at his sides, thumbs on the seams, twitched. His chest heaved up and down. He swallowed. "No, sir."

"Then you have two options: Either you stop taking out whatever it is on my ground crews or you tell me exactly what the problem is so we can try to find a solution to it together. You can think about your options for 24 hours. I want to see you here again at this time tomorrow. Dismissed."

Jenkins snapped him a salute, turned smartly on heel and marched out.

Exasperated, Robin decided to go home early. He grabbed his long white shawl, wrapped it around his neck and then pulled on his greatcoat. He put on his peaked cap and left his office, closing the door behind him. He pulled his leather gloves out of his coat pockets as he went down the hall and exited into the gloom of the short December day. It was the shortest day of the year, and it was dark at 4:00 pm He folded himself into his MG. It was an expensive car that he could not have afforded, but the original owner had been shot down last summer, and his family had sold it for a song.

His thoughts kept returning to Jenkins and his unfortunate personality change. It had been bad enough with Rowe, and he'd been delighted to finally to get rid of the old bully. He'd had high hopes for Jenkins. It didn't make sense that he would have changed this dramatically if things had worked out with his delinquent son. Or had he lied about his son?

Priestman reached Bosham, parked before the church as always and went up to the cottage, still lost in thought. The cottage was wonderfully warm and cosy. He hung up his coat and cap. He could smell something baking in the oven, and called out, "I'm home."

Emily was peering into the oven. She looked over her shoulder with a smile. "You're early."

"Yes, I got fed up with things. Nothing much doing any way. Vodka sour?"

"Thanks. I'll be right there."

Robin returned to the living room and poured scotch for himself and prepared a vodka sour for Emily. She came in, untying her apron and pulling it off over her head. "I've got a problem with the new Chiefy," Robin started at once. "He cancelled leave for two airmen on ridiculous grounds. At Christmas! I feel as though I'm dealing with Dr Jekyll and Mr Hyde! The man was perfectly reasonable for his first month and now he's become a tyrant. Emily, are you listening to me?"

"Sorry, Robin, I'm distracted. I had the most peculiar phone call from Hattie this afternoon. She sounded so distant and then she started talking about her things."

"What do you mean?"

"Oh, how I'd always liked her comfortable sofa, and then, that her pearls would suit me so well. She seemed to have such a hard time hanging up, too. She kept repeating that she was so glad we'd met. That our friendship meant the world to her. It was rather embarrassing, and I tried to laugh it off, but she was so serious."

Robin shrugged. "It's probably just Christmas at the mission as usual – a terribly depressing affair every year because the only people at the mission are people who have no home to go to."

"I suppose you're right, but the call bothered me enough for me try ringing her back. They told me she'd left early, so I tried to phone her at home, twice in an hour, but there was no answer."

"Maybe she's doing her Christmas shopping."

"Sunday afternoon?" Emily countered.

Robin frowned slightly.

Emily was upset enough to admit. "Robin, there's something you don't know. Hattie asked me not to tell you, but you see she's been having a love affair this past month."

"She's what?"

Emily sat down abruptly, clutching her untouched cocktail. "Yes. A real love affair."

"I'll be damned. At her age?"

"She's not that old. I daresay you will expect me still to do it with you 20 years from now."

"Quite right," Robin was grinning now.

"Well, she was so happy and then, well, it ended very abruptly. He broke it off. She was so devastated she drank herself unconscious the night it happened."

Robin was not smiling any more. "Why didn't you tell me?"

"She asked me not to, Robin. She said it was over and there was nothing you could do to help her. She said she wanted to forget it. It's just that I have this horrible feeling. The way she talked to me this afternoon, as though she were saying good bye for good—"

He exploded, "why didn't you say something?!" He ran to the phone and dialled Hattie's number. It rang and rang and rang and rang. "Damn it! Why didn't you tell me! She's tried it before! My God! When did she leave the mission?"

"At 3:30 or so."

He looked at his watch. "We've got to get over there – no, we'll be too late." He grabbed the phone again and rang the police. "This is RAF Tangmere, Squadron Leader Priestman, 606 Squadron. I have reason to believe that my aunt, Miss Fitzsimmons of 56 Gloucester Rd, Portsmouth, may have tried to take her own life. Can you please get over there and check? ... Yes, I'm on my way now. I'll have a key with me. Please hurry."

He was already starting out of the door. "Wait!!" Emily called. "I've got to turn off the dinner." He ignored her, but she ran into the kitchen, turned off the oven and grabbed her coat as she went out of the door. Robin was already turning the MG around in the pub car park opposite. He stopped to let her climb in and then put his foot on the accelerator so hard that the car sprang away to the screech of tyres.

Before they had even reached Chichester Road, Emily was so terrified by the way he was driving in the black out that she shouted at him, "it's not a damn Spitfire! If you keep this up, you'll only kill us both!"

Robin turned and looked at her coldly. "If she's dead, it will be your fault." But he did drive more cautiously.

When they arrived at Hattie's flat, the ambulance was already out front, and the front doors of Hattie's and the neighbour's cottages stood open. The neighbours were gaping. Robin screeched to a halt and jumped out, leaving the car door open. He reached the front door of Hattie's cottage just as the two orderlies emerged with the stretcher. He backed away to let them out. Hattie was covered by a sheet, but her head was exposed.

"Is she alive?" Robin asked. She looked deathly pale, and she was clearly naked beneath the ambulance sheets. Her wrists were bound tightly but blood was oozing into the clean white gauze.

"At the moment, but we've got to get her to emergency as fast as possible. She's lost a great deal of blood. She'll need a transfusion."

"I have the same blood type, A negative. I'll come with you," Robin announced as he climbed into the back of the ambulance. Emily was left to follow behind in the MG.

Of course, Emily couldn't keep up with the ambulance as it wailed its way through red lights and charged like a horse on the way to its barn across the city. Nor could she park in the emergency entrance. By the time she got to reception, there was no sign of either Hattie or Robin. She was told that Hattie was with the doctor, and Robin had given blood. She was directed to a small waiting room with some knocked about, straight-backed chairs around a coffee table with a pile of old magazines on it. She sat down and flipped through the magazines without seeing a thing.

Robin emerged, his tunic hanging from his shoulders, his left sleeve rolled above his elbow. He was pressing a cotton swab to the inside of his elbow joint. He sat down next to Emily wordlessly.

"Robin, she insisted that I shouldn't tell you—" Emily started to explain herself.

Robin's anger had dissipated now that there was still a fighting chance Hattie would live. He nodded, staring at the linoleum floor of the hospital. "Will you please tell me what happened — everything you know."

So, Emily did.

Chapter 12

December 1940

Things were very confused. Hattie had run the hot bath, settled herself in and then cut her wrists. It hadn't hurt much. After the initial, instinctive horror at the amount of blood released, she had slid her hands under the water to lie at her sides, leaned her head against the back of the tub and relaxed in the steam.

Ignoring the telephone that rang downstairs twice, Hattie let her life pass in review as she lay in the bath. She felt it was a good way of taking leave of everyone and everything. Only the memories of Rhys were too painful and had to be excluded. She concentrated on her childhood, when Lydia had still been her sweet little sister, and she had been her father's 'best girl'. She had loved her father dearly. After Lydia's marriage, they had become even closer, but he was over 70 and ailing. It was then that she first thought about suicide. By then, it was obvious she would never find a husband, and she had no training, education or independent income. She did not know how she could live once he was gone, so she had conceived of the idea of killing herself. Then she would neither be a burden to anyone nor have to live alone.

Then Mike burst into her life for a glorious fortnight. Suddenly she had hopes and dreams again. But four months later, he was dead. She briefly considered killing herself immediately and joining him. But then she remembered her increasingly feeble father and reverted to her original plan.

Her father died in late 1922. She laid out the corpse and then took a good bottle of wine to sit drinking with him before going up to do it. One bottle wasn't enough to give her courage, however, so she had opened a second and a third. By then, the wine had touched a well of self-pity. She found herself sobbing uninhibitedly for all she had lost and would never have. That was how six-year-old Robin found her. With increasing alarm he begged her: "Please, Aunt Hattie, please don't cry." Over and over the same words, "please, Aunt Hattie, please don't die."

No, she corrected herself; he'd said, "don't cry," and he'd had a soft, high-pitched child's voice.

"Please, Aunt Hattie, please don't die," the words annoyed her. They were wrong, and the voice was wrong. She opened her eyes in irritation.

He was looking straight at her. Those deep, dark eyes she had so often lost herself in. They widened in evident astonishment and relief. "Thank God! I was so afraid I'd lost you. Why did you go and do such a stupid thing?"

Hattie felt dizzy. The room was white, unnaturally bright, the bed was hard, the sheets stiff, it smelled sterile and disinfected. She felt nauseous. Her eyes rolled back into her head, but she wasn't out. She could still feel his hands clasping one of hers. She opened and looked down at his hands. The discoloured, stretched skin still showed evidence of the burns he'd suffered saving a pilot who had been trapped in his burning cockpit.

"What are you trying to do, cancel kills with saves?"

"The saves are a lot harder," Robin countered, understanding her reference to his 12 recognised victories against the Luftwaffe. "Why did you do it, Aunt Hattie? How could you?"

"What's my life worth, Robin? I'm really very, very tired. it just isn't worth going on the way it is. That's all."

"Emily says you didn't feel this way a fortnight ago," as he spoke, he glanced up at Emily, and Hattie realised she was standing on the other side of the bed.

Hattie turned her head and smiled up at Emily weakly. Then she turned back to Robin, "but that's just it. When I realised what life might have been like, I just couldn't face going on as it was. Is it really so hard to understand, Robin? You have Emily now and you'll soon have children."

"No one can replace you, Aunt Hattie."

"Maybe not," she admitted with a sigh, "but then why would anyone want to? There's no need to replace me when I'm gone."

"You are no more superfluous than any of the rest of us!" Robin told her in no uncertain terms. Then, as if he were afraid he'd spoken too harshly, he added in a gentler voice, "you are out of danger now and you need to rest." He glanced at Emily. "We'll come and visit you again tomorrow."

Robin drew back, and Emily leant down to give Hattie a kiss. "I'm so, so glad we managed to drag you back, even if it's against your will, Hattie. Please give life another chance. We can talk tomorrow about what I can do to help make it more pleasant. There must be something I can do."

Hattie smiled in recognition of her sentiments and nodded as they both turned at the door to wave goodbye. Then she was alone in the hospital room. She closed her eyes.

Unfortunately, she didn't see things any differently than before they'd dragged her back from the brink. She would be much happier if she just died. Of course, it had been nice to see Robin again, but she had no desire at all to return to her flat and the mission or anything. She just wanted to go to sleep forever. If she disconnected the blood being pumped into her arm.... She squinted up at the bag of blood suspended over her but squinting against the light was exhausting, and she felt her head start to spin. Against her will, her eye lids fell shut and she drifted back to sleep, the blood still flooding into her arm.

Rhys was drying the dishes with Ellen in the kitchen. The radio was on. They had listened to the news and then left it on to cover the silence. Ellen had never been much of a conversationalist, but Rhys used to get her chatting by asking her questions. Today he didn't have the energy. The CO's threat to post him had come as a terrible shock. It was a disgrace professionally and personally, it would mean moving again. It would mean giving up this cottage, yanking Owain out of school again and looking for new quarters in some new town. He didn't want any of that.

The humiliation was crushing. Not eight weeks on the squadron and already found wanting. It was a nightmare. And all because of Marie, he thought resentfully. He hated her with all his heart.

He stared at the plate in his hands, remembering how they had washed up together side-by-side before he took her into the living room and made love to her. The memories made his chest cramp. His hands were gripping the plate as if he wanted to break it in two. She had awakened desires and fires in him that he had not known, even as a young man. She had made him feel young and virile, attractive and invincible.

And now, he was nothing but a bitter old man. Worse, he was a bitter old man who was venting his anger on the blameless men under his command. Rhys hated himself so much in that instant that in his inarticulate fury, he tried to break the Duke of Norfolk's china plate in two.

"Dad? What's the matter?" Ellen asked, gazing at him.

He put the plate on the table behind him and took another from the drying rack without answering. Ellen looked at him with big, questioning eyes. "Why haven't you asked Miss Fitzsimmons back, Dad?"

"She's not our kind," Rhys snapped.

"That's not what you thought before."

"Well, I was wrong!" He growled.

Ellen sighed and resumed the washing up. "I hope it's not because of me, Dad. I liked her. And so did Owain."

Before Rhys could answer, Owain appeared at the door to the kitchen. "Dad, there's an officer at the door."

"What?"

"Squadron Leader, to be precise." Owain had been raised in the RAF. He could read rank flawlessly.

"Oh my God." Rhys dried his hands hastily on the dish towel and went out into the living room.

Squadron Leader Priestman was standing inside the door with his cap in his hands. Their eyes met, and Rhys wanted to sink through the floor. He knew, knew everything.

"I've just come from the hospital," the CO announced.

"Sir?"

"The police estimate that my aunt -- who I understand you know quite well -- cut her wrists at 4:45 this afternoon."

"Oh, my God! NO!" Suddenly Rhys realised that he didn't hate her at all. He loved her as intensely as ever. "Marie," he whispered, begging for it not to be true. "My Marie." He would never forgive himself.

Ellen asked in a frightened, distressed voice from behind him. "Miss Fitzsimmons? Are you talking about Miss Fitzsimmons?"

"Yes, we are," Robin answered coldly, his gaze shifting to Ellen in her cotton apron.

Her round face was red and gleaming from standing over the steaming water in the sink. One or two dark curls stuck to her forehead, but her wide-set eyes were full of shock and distress. "Is Miss Fitzsimmons dead?" Ellen asked anxiously.

Robin had expected the question to come from Jenkins and was a bit annoyed that it came from his daughter instead, but he could hardly lie, so he admitted. "No, not yet. When my wife and I left the hospital about an hour ago, she was in stable but critical condition."

Rhys sank onto the arm of the nearest armchair. "Thank God. Thank God for that."

Robin considered him coldly. "Perhaps you'd like to explain yourself?"

Rhys was on his feet at once, and he faced his CO squarely, with dignity and hostility. "It seems you know the facts, sir. What do you want me to explain exactly?"

"Let's start with what your feelings and intentions regarding Miss Fitzsimmons are – or were."

"I – " Rhys had been about to say that he didn't think it was the CO's business, but then again, the young man was also Marie's nephew, and he had just come from her hospital bed. "I wanted to marry her, sir. I introduced her to my kids, and I – I thought she would move in with us here, but that was before I knew she was any relation of yours, sir. As soon as I found out, I broke it off, of course."

"Why?"

"Sir?"

"What the hell difference does it make who her nephew is? Or her father, mother, sister, brother or great-grandfather for that matter?!" Robin had raised his voice slightly but quickly got hold of himself again. "Miss Fitzsimmons is a mature woman who answers to no one but herself. How could her relationship with me have any bearing on what you feel for one another?"

Rhys swallowed, acutely aware that both his children were staring at him. "It wouldn't be right, sir."

"What wouldn't be right?"

"Me, I mean, if I'd married Miss Fitzsimmons, then it would have put you in a very awkward position, sir—"

"Pack it in, Jenkins! I don't need to be protected by you!"

"But, sir, how would it look? People would think I was trying to, I mean...." Just what did he mean? He felt very foolish not being able to articulate it.

"Is what 'people' think more important to you than the love and life of the woman you claim to love?"

"Of course not, sir!"

"It looks that way to me. For the sake of some fictional propriety, you shattered the happiness of an honest, warm-hearted, vulnerable woman. You drove her first to drink and then to suicide. And while we're on the subject, you've tyrannised the innocent men under your command."

Robin set his cap on his head, pulling the visor down low over his eyes. He nodded once to Ellen, then turned and let himself out of the front door.

Rhys was left stunned in his living room. He'd been miserable before, but he now felt like a worm as well.

"Dad, we've got to find out what hospital she's in and go and see her," Ellen decided.

Rhys looked over at his daughter as if he didn't understand what she was saying.

"The squadron leader said she was still alive, Dad. We've got to go and see her." Practical girl that she was, she looked at the clock and announced. "If we hurry, we can just catch the bus to Chichester station and then, the slow train to Portsmouth. I'll run after the squadron leader and ask him which hospital she's in." She was already out of the door.

He would never have made it without Ellen. She found out the name and address of the hospital, made sure they caught the bus and then the train, and once in Portsmouth, she found them the bus that took them to the hospital. It was nearly 10:00 pm. before they reached the hospital, and Rhys was sure they would be told visiting hours were over. But Ellen proved adept at convincing the duty nurse that this was an emergency.

Her father wouldn't be able to get away from his squadron during visiting hours, she explained, and Miss Fitzsimmons had tried to kill herself. It was important that she knew how much and how many people cared about her.

The nurse glanced at Rhys somewhat skeptically, but apparently she liked Ellen because she agreed to see if the patient was awake and, if so, to ask if she was prepared to see visitors. "Whom should I say is calling?"

"Rhys Jenkins." Ellen answered.

The nurse raised her eyebrows at Ellen.

"I'm Ellen Jenkins, but my Dad should go in alone."

The nurse looked back and forth between them, and then disappeared down the hall and into a room.

"Miss Fitzsimmons?"

Hattie stirred uneasily.

The nurse went over to the bed and gently stroked Hattie's shoulder. "Miss Fitzsimmons?"

Hattie opened her eyes and looked up at the nurse. "Yes?"

"There is a Flight Sergeant Jenkins here to see you with his daughter."

"Rhys?" Hattie's eyes widened. "Rhys is here?" She started struggling to sit up, and her hand went to her hair. "I must look a sight," she muttered, looking about for a mirror or a comb or something to help with her appearance.

The nurse laughed and went to the washbasin to get a comb for Hattie. She left Hattie combing her hair and straightening her hospital nightdress and the sheets. She returned to the visitors and announced that they were welcome.

"You go in alone, Dad," Ellen told him with a little shove.

Rhys cast his daughter a last look of helplessness. He felt weak and at a loss. He was afraid to face Marie without Ellen's moral support. His eyes pleaded with her to come with him, but she only smiled and nodded towards the door. He stepped inside and stopped. What could he possibly say?

He looked up and saw Marie. For the first time since the day they met, she looked her age. She also looked weak and helpless in her hospital robe and deathly pale with big bandages on both forearms. Her eyes were sunken in her face. There were dark circles under her eyes, and her lips were colourless, her chin sagged. The sight shocked him, filled him with remorse, and Priestman's description of her as 'a vulnerable' woman came back to him. She was more than that. She was battered, all-but-broken, and nearly dead. And it was his fault.

Then their eyes met. Her eyes looked at him with vibrant hope and fear all mixed together.

Rhys was not conscious of any thought. He was aware only of suddenly having her in his arms. "Oh, Marie! I'll never forgive myself. Never. Even if you forgive me, I'll never forgive myself." He was shaking his head, trying to get hold of himself. His throat was so tight it hurt.

Hattie clung to him, not sure if she should believe this or not. She just wanted to hold him for the moment. Don't ask any stupid questions, she told herself. Don't press your luck.

They remained locked like that for a long time: Rhys standing beside the bed with Hattie sitting upright and resting her head on his chest. Then slowly, Rhys released his grip a little, and so did Hattie. He stepped back and looked at her.

The fear came back into Hattie's eyes.

"Do you still want me?" he asked.

"Of course, I do," Hattie answered, her eyes watering. "You were the one who ran away."

"I'm sorry. I – I was just taken by surprise. I wish you'd told me earlier," he said lamely.

"Then you would have left me earlier," Hattie countered wearily, and Rhys knew she was right.

"I've been thinking. If I ask for a posting somewhere else, then Squadron Leader Priestman won't be my CO."

"Oh, Rhys, that would be too hard on your children. You can't leave them alone again. They like the cottage. Owain even said the school was 'all right'. Why should you leave? Squadron leaders come and go. Robin is bound to get promoted away in the next year or so."

She was right, of course. Why hadn't he thought of it? Twelve or eighteen months facing Priestman every day after this? He dreaded it. But surely it was better than living without Marie for the rest of his life?

Ellen put her head around the door and peeked in. "Please don't make us move again, Dad," she ventured timidly. She had been listening to every word said between them.

They both turned to look towards her, and Hattie held out her hand. Ellen saw the bandages and shrank back for a second, but then she came over firmly, and she did something very unusual for her. She bent and gave Hattie a kiss on the cheek. It was a quick, light kiss that revealed her embarrassment and uncertainty, but the desire to kiss her was there. It brought tears to Hattie's eyes. "Ellen! I'm so glad to see you! I'm so glad you came with your father."

Ellen looked solemnly at her and then nodded to say she believed her. "We came as soon as we heard, Miss Fitzsimmons. I wanted you to know that we – me brother and me – both like you very much. We hope you'll come and live with us in the cottage." Ellen was taking liberties with Owain's feelings. He had never said anything of the kind, but he hadn't said anything against her either – and that was saying a lot for Owain. Besides, at the moment, it seemed more important to Ellen to cheer poor Miss Fitzsimmons up.

Rhys laid his arm across his daughter's shoulders and hugged her to him. He kissed the top of her head. "Ellen, Ellen." He was so moved he could not manage more than that.

The air-raid siren started to wail.

The nurse came in. "I'm sorry to disturb you, but you must get down to the shelters at once." From the hall came shouts and clatter as the staff went through a now well-practiced routine of getting the patients who could be moved down to the cellars. "You can come back again tomorrow," the nurse suggested as she shooed the visitors out.

Ellen managed to give Hattie another hasty kiss and then turned and left the room. Rhys bent and kissed her on the lips. "I love you, Marie. Please...." He didn't know how to finish. Please forgive me, or please marry me, or please don't leave us or please come and live with us. So, it just hung in the air without an ending, while the sirens wailed ever more insistently drowning out all thought.

Hattie squeezed his hand and gestured with her head for him to go. She waved to him as he looked back from the door. Then she lay back on her pillows and drew a deep breath. She hoped the Germans wouldn't get her now when she no longer wanted to die.

From somewhere indefinable, she imagined she could smell roses.

Lack of Moral Fibre

Helena P. Schrader

Lack of Moral Fibre
Foreword and Acknowledgements

The term "Lack of Moral Fibre" (LMF) was introduced into RAF vocabulary in April 1940 to characterize aircrew who refused to fly without a medical reason. The RAF needed a means to deal with this unexpected problem because flying was voluntary, hence the refusal to fly was not technically a breach of the military code. After investing as much as two years into training aircrew, the RAF could not afford the refusal to fly become widespread.

Men designated "LMF" (Lacking in Moral Fibre) faced swift disciplinary action. For the airmen who continued flying operations, the fate of those 'expeditiously' posted for LMF was shrouded in mystery. Rumours spread and legends still abound. The threat of being designated "LMF" acted as a powerful deterrent to wilful or casual malingering. Tragically, the threat of humiliation may also have pushed some men to keep flying when they had already passed their breaking point, leading to errors, accidents, and loss of life.

This novel is based on a combination of first-hand accounts and histories of Bomber Command operations in late 1943 and early 1944, as well as post-war analysis of how the RAF dealt with cases of "LMF." The flashbacks to Kit's operational flights describe targets, routes, tactics, conditions, and incidents from the historical record, although the date, timing and obviously the individuals involved have been changed. The treatment accorded Kit at the NYDN Centre in Torquay (which was an actual RAF establishment) and the opinions expressed by Wing Commander Grace (who was a neuropsychiatrist stationed there during the war) are aligned with the historical record. Dr Grace is the only historical figure in this novel; all other characters are fictional.

I wish to thank all my test readers, each of whom provided unique input based on their respective backgrounds. I am particularly indebted to Leslie Wood (RAF aircrew), Steven Mathews (pilot), Stephen Tobin, John Orton, Hazel Horne, and Diana Page, all of who helped make this a better book.

Cover Image

The photo is a composite image created by Hazel Horne from two photos of the same Lancaster crew. The original photos were provided by the International Bomber Command Centre Digital Archive and belong to a collection of photographs concerning Sergeant William Frederick 'John' Burkitt (1922 – 1944). Burkitt flew as a flight engineer with the No 9 Squadron from RAF Bardney.

Chapter 1

RAF NYDN Centre, Torquay
26 November 1943

"Pilot Officer Christopher Moran?"

The orderly clerk still addressed him with his rank, Kit noted, wondering for how long. "Yes," he answered.

"You're in room 24." The clerk turned to remove a key from the wooden pigeonholes behind him. He handed it to Moran across the reception desk without looking him in the eye.

People had been avoiding eye-contact ever since he'd been posted away from the squadron. The station commander told him to depart as rapidly and discreetly as possible, while his squadron leader reinforced that message with instructions not to say good-bye to any of his former comrades. His orders were to report "immediately" to this mysteriously designated NYDN centre.

It was, however, disorienting to be in what had evidently been a hotel. Although now outfitted with RAF standard-issue furnishings, remnants of its former grandeur lingered in the ceiling mouldings and gracious, bay windows. If it hadn't been sleeting, there might even have been a view down to Torbay. Instead, visibility was so bad that everything beyond the windows was just a blurry white and grey. That backdrop highlighted the gloomy interior. The lobby furnishings were run-down, and four years of war marked the inhabitants, too. Unremittingly dressed in Air Force blue, their averted faces were strained and prematurely lined.

Kit took the key, shouldered his kitbag, and found his way up two flights of stairs to room 24. While the lobby had been overheated, the hall was bitterly cold. He unlocked the door and found himself in a modest room with two twin beds. He was taken aback to find one of the beds already occupied by a man wrapped in blankets.

"Sorry! I must have the wrong room!" Kit started to back out.

"No," a voice rose from the bed. "They double us up like this."

"Oh, of course," Kit nodded to himself. Why hadn't he expected that? He'd expected far worse. He entered and closed the door behind him before introducing himself. "I'm Christopher Moran, but I go by Kit."

"Oliver Huckle, and if you don't mind, I don't want to talk." His roommate rolled over, offering his back.

"Fine by me," Kit muttered. He didn't particularly want to talk himself. He tossed his kitbag on the vacant bed and started unpacking his things. He'd done this countless times on countless RAF Stations for almost four years now. This was just one more move, one more posting. Except it wasn't.

Kit went to the window. Sleet pelted the glass, making a high ticking sound before melting and slithering down the slick surface. His breath rapidly steamed up the inside. Kit raised an index finger to write in the condensation: LMF — for Lack of Moral Fibre.

Everyone knew what happened to aircrew who "earned" that label. They were publicly stripped of their flying badges, their rank insignia, and any ribbons they may have been awarded. Officers were officially court-martialled and lost their commissions. They were shipped off to do menial work, transferred to the infantry, or discharged to work in the coal mines. Their records were stamped in large letters: "LMF" or "W" for "Waverer." Their discharge papers stated the same thing, ensuring problems with civilian employment for the rest of their lives.

Everyone knew of someone who had disappeared down this road to infamy, and no one ever saw them again. What Kit hadn't known about were the NYDN centres, the gateway to LMF hell.

Chapter 2

NYDN Centre, Torquay
27 November 1943

"Pilot Officer Moran?" The Wing Commander looked up from the file on his desk and then stood and held out his hand as he came around his desk. "My name is Grace, Dr Ralph Grace."

Kit's eyes flickered to his insignia as they shook hands. Grace was a doctor, and his hands were icy cold. But then so were Kit's. They didn't go in for much heat at this establishment.

"Have a seat. Would you like some tea?" The doctor asked amiably.

"Not really, thank you, sir," Kit warily eased himself into the comfortable arm chair the doctor had indicated. He was not feeling well; he'd hardly slept. His thoughts and nightmares would have been enough to keep him awake, but it hadn't helped that his roommate also shouted in his sleep.

"There's nothing to worry about," Grace insisted. "I just want to chat with you a bit, go over your case, be sure I've got the facts straight."

"Yes, sir," Kit hesitated and then ventured to ask. "Are you a trick cyclist, sir?"

"A psychiatrist? Yes, I have a degree in psychiatry."

"Is this a hospital?"

"Not exactly. It's a centre where we attempt to diagnose your condition prior to determining a course of action. NYDN stands for Not Yet Diagnosed Nervous. If we determine that you have a psychiatric condition, you will be referred to a psychiatric hospital for treatment. If not, there are a variety of other options."

"I see." Court-martial, public humiliation, the infantry, the mines....

"So," the doctor settled himself behind his desk again and took up the file. "You volunteered for service in September 1939. You were mustered for training as a fitter because you were apprenticed to an engineering firm in civilian life. Promoted to LAC in September 1940, you served with 56 (Hurricane) Squadron, commended and promoted to corporal in March 1941. You transferred to 109 (Mosquito) Squadron in January 1942. You volunteered for Air Crew in August 1942, and on completing training as a Flight Engineer you were promoted to Sergeant and assigned to 626 (Lancaster) Squadron. You completed one full tour of operations in March 1943, you were awarded the DFM and granted an immediate commission. Thereafter, you served in Training Command until October. You had flown six ops on your second tour...." His voice faded away, and he looked up at Kit. He was not avoiding Kit's eyes; he was looking directly at him.

Kit waited.

"Do you want to tell me about your decision to stop flying?"

Kit drew a deep breath. "Do the records show that I flew nearly all those ops with the same skipper, navigator and bomb aimer?"

"No. Do you want to expand on that?"

Kit shrugged and looked out of the window. Visibility was as bad as yesterday, though today it was fog rather than sleet.

The doctor looked down at his records. "I see your skipper was Flight Lieutenant Donald Selkirk. It says here that 'despite being mortally wounded, Selkirk successfully landed his damaged Lancaster at RAF Hawkinge following the raid on Berlin of November 22/23.'"

"You could put it like that," Kit retorted, an edge to his voice like a spark in the cold room.

The doctor looked at him with attentive eyes. "Were you close to Flight Lieutenant Selkirk?"

RAF Lindholm,
Heavy Conversion Unit (HCU),
October 1942

Kit didn't think this "crewing up" was working. It was so typically British — completely disorganised, haphazard, and subjective. It was a perfect example of British "muddling through" and "hoping for the best." Men at the Heavy Conversion Unit were here to train on the heavy, four-engine bombers they would fly on operations. None of them had yet been on operations, and pilots had never had responsibility for a crew before. To make matters worse, a select few of them had been granted commissions, while the bulk of them were sergeants. Yet somehow, informally, just by chatting and doing a little flying together, they were supposed to "sort themselves out" into crews of seven with a pilot, navigator, flight engineer, bomb-aimer, wireless operator and two gunners each. Many crews had already formed tentatively at an Operational Training Unit during training on medium bombers, but Flight Engineers and Mid-Upper gunners came straight to the HCU and had to match up with crews here.

It didn't help that there had been two serious accidents that killed a total of twelve men in this past week. One of those killed had been the likeable young Sergeant Pilot whom Kit had favoured for his own skipper. The accident had been put down to "pilot error" and had wiped out the entire crew. So much for his assessment of pilots! Yet, he hadn't warmed to any of the others.

Kit turned his back on the pub lounge to order another pint at the bar, acutely aware that he was still an 'odd fish' — or maybe neither fish nor fowl. Another man squeezed his way to the bar beside him, and a melodic, faintly Scottish voice asked at his elbow. "You're Kit Moran, aren't you?"

Kit looked over surprised and was discomfited to see that the man beside him was one of the three commissioned pilots. He answered guardedly, "yes, sir."

"Forget the 'sir.' We're off duty. I'm Don Selkirk," the pilot officer held out his hand and it would have been rude not to shake it. Kit was wary all the same. The one thing he hadn't thought about was a commissioned pilot; he didn't like the idea of rank cutting a fissure through a crew whose members depended so entirely on each other.

The pilot officer was slender, dark haired but fair-skinned with grey-blue eyes and the kind of good looks one associated with the British aristocracy. He was also markedly older than most of them; Kit guessed he was already 25 or 26. "Have you decided whose crew you want to join yet?" Selkirk asked casually, while signalling for another drink.

"Not yet," Moran admitted.

"What would you say to joining my crew?" Selkirk asked with a mild smile.

"I hadn't thought about it. Can you give me a reason why I should?" Moran countered. He really did not want a commissioned skipper.

"Well, I've managed to secure the best navigator on the course, Sailor Hart," Selkirk nodded in the direction of a burly, blond and good-tempered Flight Sergeant who everyone knew had been Second Mate in the Merchant Navy before joining the RAF. He too was a good four years older than the others and already married. He was steady, cheerful and unquestionably a well-qualified navigator. That was a good argument, Moran admitted to himself.

Selkirk continued, "Furthermore, if you join my crew, you'll be getting two pilots for the price of one because Teddy Hamed has agreed to be my bomb aimer and he has 62 flying hours. The only reason he didn't get his wings was that he failed the ground exams." Again, Selkirk nodded across the room to where Hamed was sitting with Hart, clearly engaged in a lively conversation.

Moran knew about Hamed as well. He hailed from South Shields and had a strong Geordie accent. Short and dark, his father was a Yemeni stoker with the Merchant Navy, which maybe explained why Sailor had a liking for the lad. Moran knew he'd first trained as a rigger but had been assigned to Training Command where he'd talked his way into a cockpit. He'd shown such aptitude for flying that he'd been allowed to re-muster for pilot training, but his spotty formal education had caught up with him on the ground exams. It surprised Moran that a man like Selkirk would deem the cocky, half-Arab lad from the slums of Tyneside an asset, but it spoke well for the officer.

Moran considered Selkirk more critically. He could not deny that he liked the way Selkirk prised his crew rather than himself. "Who's your wireless operator?" Kit asked.

"Leslie Vernon," Selkirk replied, adding, "and Bob Pickett's my rear gunner." Moran knew them both as they were sergeants like himself and they messed together. He didn't know much about Vernon, who seemed a quiet, introverted type, but Pickett was a Canadian with a reputation as a crack shot.

"Look," Selkirk didn't give Moran the chance to ask another question. "We've been given 48 hours on account of the weather and my parents live only three and a half hours away. My crew and I are going to go for a visit. Why don't you join us? You don't have to commit to the crew just yet. Just come along and see how we get on, eh?"

Moran had nowhere else to go at such short notice, so he agreed.

Ashcroft Park, the Selkirk residence, was imposing: a huge, stone manor, several hundred years old and set in stately grounds. It was furnished with antique furniture, an art gallery of portraits depicting Selkirk ancestors, and other works of art including a grandiose panorama of the Battle of Waterloo — where one of Selkirk's forefathers had fought with distinction, of course.

Yet, the cold formality of the setting was offset by the warmth of the reception. Selkirk's father was a retired colonel with a hearty laugh and a jovial manner, who quickly set the young men at ease. He welcomed all of "Don's friends" with a glass of whisky, while Mrs Selkirk offered smiles and scones, while she expressed her delight at "finally meeting" Don's crew. When Kit and Teddy came down to dinner in battle dress to find the others in dinner jackets and the ladies in evening gowns, Mrs. Selkirk melted the awkwardness by apologising for her thoughtlessness. "We forgot you had no notice and couldn't pack properly."

But the real breakthrough came the next day when Colonel Selkirk took them hunting. Pickett bagged three pheasants, cementing his reputation as a marksman, but Kit caused a greater sensation by bringing down a bird himself — and then admitting it was his first partridge. While the others congratulated him exuberantly, the canny Colonel made the connection between Kit's ease and skill with the gun and his dearth of partridges. With a sly smile he asked, "Just what game did you hunt then?"

"Mostly gazelles, sir," Kit answered.

"Gazelles?" The others exclaimed, confused.

"And the odd ostrich."

"Ostrich?"

"I grew up in Africa, sir," Kit explained. "My father's with the colonial service. He's in Nigeria now."

It forged an unexpected bond. Colonel Selkirk asked Kit to come down to dinner fifteen minutes earlier that evening, and at Kit's appearance, ushered him into his personal study adorned with a zebra rug and a lionskin sofa. He took out an album of photographs filled with his safari pictures. "There's something about Africa!" Colonel Selkirk exclaimed nostalgically. "I was only there a year, but it cast a spell on me. I'd go back in an instant." He gazed out of the darkened window as he remembered. "The silhouette of the acacia trees against the violet sky at dusk, the shades of orange and gold at dawn, the chattering of the monkeys, and the dry, warm wind...." He turned to gaze again at his photos, lost in memories. Then he shook himself loose to ask Kit. "Where has your father served?"

"I was born in South Africa, sir, but spent most of my boyhood in Kenya. My father moved to Nigeria just before I left school...." He let his voice fade, certain that his apprenticeship would earn him no particular laurels with the Selkirks.

"And your father's still there?"

"Yes, sir, he's Regional Commissioner for Calibar."

"Calibar, eh? Do you get back to visit often?"

"I've not been back since the war started, sir."

"Sisters and brothers?"

"One sister, sir. She's at boarding school in Cape Town."

"It must be very hard on your parents, having you both so far away. Mrs. Selkirk and I hate to go more than a month without seeing Don. Thank goodness, Maggie comes home every weekend. With Don going on ops soon, I fear we'll see far less of him. I hope you'll feel that this is your home away from home. You're welcome to come as often as you like — with or without Don."

When the 48 hours were up and they reported back to the HCU, there was no question in Moran's mind but that he was part of Selkirk's crew. It felt like having a family again for the first time since he'd left Africa. On arrival at the HCU, he realized that he'd been absorbed so fully into the RAF since the start of the war that he'd lost himself in a false sense of belonging. The RAF had filled his life with — Kit paused trying to put a name to it. People? Purpose? Excitement? Responsibilities? Self-importance? No, he decided, the right word was 'noise.' His life had been filled with so much noise that he had not been able to hear himself think or feel.

With Don and the Selkirks, Kit felt that he finally found a refuge from the noise, the herd, and the compulsion for conformity. Like a vessel that been thrown blow off course, Kit felt he had weathered a storm and found a safe harbour at last.

NYDN Centre Torquay, 28 November 1943

There were two telephone booths in the lobby of the NYDN centre. Kit closed himself inside one and put a call through to Ashcroft Park. The Butler answered, and Kit recognized his voice from many visits. "Mr. Crowther? It's me Kit."

"Mr. Moran?" Crowther sounded surprised, almost shocked. Surely, he couldn't have heard he'd been posted LMF already?

"Yes, I'd like a word with Mrs. Selkirk, please."

"Mrs Selkirk is in mourning, sir. She is not taking phone calls."

"Please tell her who it is and that there's something I'd like to tell her."

"I shall make inquiries, sir. One moment."

It seemed to take a long time, but finally Kit heard muttering and then Colonel Selkirk spoke at the other end of the line. "Moran?"

"Yes, Colonel, I wanted to—"

"Is it true you've been posted LMF?" An outraged voice demanded on the other end of the line. Before Kit could answer, the Colonel continued indignantly. "I called the station to find out if you were all right and hoping you could give me more details regarding Don's last flight. You can't imagine my astonishment — no, my shock — to hear you had turned lily-livered and refused to fly further ops!"

"Sir, I'd like to explain about that, but not over the telephone. I feel this is something best said face to face—"

"Absolutely not! Selkirks do not socialize with cowards, Mr. Moran. It's bad enough that you're yellow, but, now, after Don has made the ultimate sacrifice? No, absolutely not! The sight of you would be offensive. Can't you see that you are dishonouring everything Don lived and died for? You demean his memory by scorning his sacrifice. I won't have you in this house ever again, and I don't want you contacting Mrs Selkirk either. She is understandably distraught, the sight of you basking in your survival-through-desertion would be too much!"

Kit recognised that it was hopeless. The sense of belonging and support had been an illusion. "I'm sorry," he murmured into the torrent of indignation. "I would have liked to explain...." Colonel Selkirk wasn't listening. Kit replaced the receiver and listlessly turned away. There was no safe harbour, and his last lifeline was severed. He was foundering.

Chapter 3

NYDN Centre Torquay, 29 November 1943

"Have a seat, Pilot Officer Moran," Wing Commander Grace suggested with a gentle smile. As before, Moran settled himself warily into the chair provided. Today, Dr Grace sat on the front edge of his desk in a casual pose. "I'd like to talk a little about your background, home life, childhood — that kind of thing," he announced.

Psychoanalysis, Kit thought resentfully.

"It says here, your father grew up in India, the son of an officer in the Indian Army. Your father volunteered and served in the last war in the Middle East, joining the Colonial Service in South Africa at the end of the war. Is that right?"

"Yes." Kit did not elaborate on his father's pacificism resulting from his war experiences or his break with his parents and brothers, nor did he attempt to explain his father's commitment to doing something positive in the world. His father had gone to Africa because he considered it an 'untainted' continent, not yet mired in the intrigues and corruption that dominated India and the Middle East.

"And your mother was the daughter of an Anglican missionary to the Zulus." Dr Grace paused and looked at Moran as if expecting him to add something. Kit refused to fall into that trap. Instead, he noted, "My grandfather was more than a missionary, sir. He had a PhD in education and believed education was the key to civilization. He was in the process of building a teachers' college for Zulus when he was killed."

"Killed? God heavens! What happened?"

"A motorcar accident. Nothing unusual in Africa. It gets very dark out in the bush and my grandfather's car had poor headlights. Either some animal was sleeping in the road or ran out in front of him suddenly. In any case, he couldn't brake in time and collided with it at a fairly high speed. The collision threw my grandmother clear out of the car, breaking her neck, while my grandfather was trapped in the driver's seat and the steering wheel crushed his ribcage. His lung and heart were both punctured."

"How frightful!" Dr Grace exclaimed with every appearance of sincerity.

"It was probably a hippo," Moran told him clinically. "Most people don't realize how fast they can move."

"How old were you when this happened?"

"Oh, I was already sixteen."

Dr Grace smiled faintly at that and remarked. "I see, already a mature man of world." Kit said nothing, so Dr Grace insisted, "Still, it must have been a shock."

"It was a bit — especially for my mother. She was devastated to lose both her parents at once and so suddenly."

"Were you close to your grandparents?"

"No. They lived too far away. I really only knew them second hand, through my mother's stories. Otherwise, they were a photo on the piano." The photo had fascinated Kit as a child because it showed his grandfather much as God-the-Father was often pictured in Church art and children's books: with long flowing white hair and a chest-long white beard. It also showed him standing beside a shyly smiling black woman, Kit's grandmother.

"How would you characterize your relationship with your parents?" Dr Grace asked.

Kit understood now where the questions were leading: They were going to try to pin the blame for his LMF on his parents, or more specifically on his racially impure mother. Just like them, he thought resentfully, and answered belligerently. "I'm very close to both my parents."

"Can you expand on that?" Dr Grace asked.

Moran shrugged. "My father served as District Officer in a series of places far from major centres of civilization. We did not have access to the usual amenities associated with life in the city, so we had to entertain ourselves. My father didn't have a club, you see, so he spent his evenings at home with his family. He taught me hunting, fishing, bird watching, rowing. We spent pretty much all of our free time together, or that part of it that we didn't share with my mother and sister. Since schools were generally not up to standard, my mother taught me at home using correspondence courses. She introduced me to literature. We read the same books, collecting a library that got bigger and heavier and harder to move from year to year. In short, we relied heavily on one another." Kit left unsaid that his father intentionally sought those out-of-the-way postings to avoid the prejudice, snobbery and slights that surrounded them in places with a large British community.

"You mentioned a sister. Do you have other siblings?"

"Not anymore. My younger brother died of a snake bite when I was eight."

"Good heavens! That's appalling!"

"Sobering. I started paying more attention to my parent's warnings after that." It was the closest thing to a joke that had crossed Moran' lips since his last raid on Berlin. Dr Grace did him the courtesy of a laughing snort before asking, "You were sent away to school, weren't you?"

"At eleven, yes."

"Did you have trouble adjusting?"

"No more than normal. My mother was a trained teacher. She taught in a local school in Pretoria for three years before marrying my father. When it came to studying, she was strict and rigorous. I arrived at school with a head start over the others." Kit's tone dared Dr Grace to challenge his assessment, to imply that his mother's Tswana blood might make her a less competent teather.

"Nevertheless, you were away from your family for the first time. That must have been difficult."

"Most of the boys were away from home for the first time. Most were the sons of colonial and army officers, missionaries, and the like. The school knew how to cope."

Dr Grace looked at Moran as if he thought he was concealing something. Kit was: the racial slurs, the sneers and innuendo of some of the other boys and one or two of the teachers. It had been hard not to be hurt and resentful, despite his fathers' efforts to prepare him for it.

Grace stood and went back around his desk to sit down. He lifted the file on his desk, then set it back down again. "You had an excellent record at school, and not just academically. You played cricket, rowed, won prizes in swimming, track and field...." He paused; his eyes fixed on Kit. "Why did you leave at sixteen?"

"Doesn't it say in there?" Moran snapped back.

"No," Grace replied calmly.

Moran drew a deep breath. "When my grandfather was killed, my parents discovered that he hadn't raised enough donations for his school. He taken loans from a bank to finance it. The bank was about to foreclose and take over the buildings. They had offers from a mining company. My mother was devastated. It was bad enough that she had lost her parents suddenly. The thought of her father's legacy being wiped out was too much. She was inconsolable. My father felt he had to pay those debts, but to do so he had to spend everything he'd put aside for my university studies."

The words seemed to hang in the air for an awkward moment, then Dr Grace asked softly. "Do you resent that?"

Moran looked over at him surprised. "Why should I? He didn't do it without my consent. He asked me if I would let him take the money."

"You were sixteen. Did you have a choice?"

"No. Not if you'd seen the state my mother was in." Moran admitted.

"You must love your mother deeply," Dr Grace noted very softly.

Moran looked over at him sharply and asked belligerently. "Do you find that surprising?"

"Let's just say I'm not sure how many young men would have done what you did — without resentment."

"My dream then was to be a civil engineer. I wanted to open Africa to development by building roads, bridges, dams and airports. I was told that I could do that without a university education, by apprenticing with a civil engineering firm and working my way up. The prospect attracted me. It meant not going back to school, and it meant starting my life straight off. It also meant I'd be earning a wage sooner, too. Perhaps best of all, it entailed going to England. You may not realise that we Colonials tend to think of England as the centre of the world. So, you see, it all sounded rather exciting — starting life as an adult, earning my own salary, and all in a place my parents and grandparents had only dreamt about. It made me feel very grown up." Kit reflected.

"Do you regret the choice you made?" Grace asked.

Kit had to think about that. If he hadn't come to England, he might not have been sucked into the war. But, more likely, if he'd stayed in school and finished, he'd have applied to university in England. In which case, he would have arrived in the UK just when the war broke out. In the circumstances, he probably would have volunteered for the RAF just the same. Maybe he would have trained as a pilot or navigator instead of a fitter, in which case he would probably be dead already. He shook his head. "No, I don't regret it."

But that night he dreamt of Africa.

The transition from waking to sleeping was so gradual that it was imperceptible, leaving the impression of being fully conscious. Only the dark greys of an English night gave way to the golden tones of an African day. A sandy haze washed the sky, darkening the sun to orange, and the scent on the air shifted from wool blankets, coal smoke and disinfectant to dried dung, dust, and sweat. It was Kenya but not anywhere Kit could identify. The people in the village they passed dressed more like Turkana than Kikuyu, but they spoke Swahili.

Kit was on safari with his father, and he was a boy again, no more than thirteen or fourteen. They had half a dozen guides and porters with them, and donkeys for their tent, cooking utensils and the first aid kit. They were trying to find a place to camp, and the villagers kept sending them farther into the bush with large sweeping gestures. Kit was getting tired and thirsty, but they kept hiking, higher and higher.

A snow-capped mountain loomed up ahead of them. "Lion tracks, Bwana!" One of the porters noted pointing in excitement. But Kit's father only nodded indifferently and kept walking in the direction they had been going before. The porter looked back over his shoulder, a frown on his face.

Without transition they were gathered around a campfire where a gazelle roasted over the flames. The fat dripping off it triggered small bursts of light accompanied by sharp spats of hissing. The porters sang beyond the fire accompanied by an oil drum turned into an instrument. The fire and singing kept the predators away, but Kit felt them in the restless darkness surrounding the camp and he was afraid. He tried to inch closer to the fire, pretending he was cold, but his father smiled knowingly.

His father stood and walked toward the darkness and then abruptly flung out his arms and made a loud hissing sound. Something large, silent, light footed and very fast sprang away in the darkness. His father returned to the fire with a smile. "Just a cheetah."

Kit tried to relax. To his father he admitted, "I didn't get much practice with my rifle while at school. I'm not a very good marksman."

"A safari isn't all about killing," Kit's father replied unperturbed.

"What is it about then?"

"For me, it is mostly about observing and enjoying the vast natural world around us."

"The porters say you killed a charging lion," Kit countered in awe.

His father laughed. "It was an old, sick lion — that was why he was preying on people. Humans don't taste very nice and fit lions prefer other meals. This lion was blind in one eye, I think, and certainly limped from an old injury. I shot him because he threatened the villagers — a young boy had been dragged away while herding the goats."

"Why didn't you bring the skin home?"

"It was in terrible shape — matted and scarred. He was a very old lion, Kit, but he must have been fierce once."

"The porters say you were very brave."

"Not really. I had a powerful rifle. If I had faced him with a spear, that would have been brave."

"But lions have been known to kill Europeans."

"Usually when they were behaving foolishly. If you learn nothing else this trip, remember that doing something just to show you're brave is usually foolish."

"But courage is the essence of manhood," Kit protested. "In every African tribe, youths have to pass a test of courage before they are recognized as men."

"Yes," his father agreed cautiously. "That's because in those cultures an adult male is automatically a warrior and so physical courage is the essential prerequisite to fulfil his role in society. In our society, on the other hand, not all men are warriors, and there are many other kinds of courage than the raw physical kind needed to hunt big game."

"What do you mean?"

"Well, for example, standing up for someone who is being unfairly criticized or ridiculed can be just as courageous as shooting some wild animal that is only trying to survive."

Kit caught his breath. "You mean standing up for Mum?"

"Yes, among other things."

Kit looked down remembering all the times at school when he had just let the others insult the natives. Only the Zulus earned a modicum of respect because they were such fierce warriors. The others were dismissed as lazy and stupid. Kit had said nothing, despite knowing that his mother and grandmother were neither.

"It's hard," his father admitted. "It's hard to fight injustice and prejudice and racism — much harder than shooting a wild animal." After a long pause he admitted, "I ran away more often than I stood up to people. It was easier to come here to the bush, to live among people that did not look down on us. However, if you want to have the freedom to live wherever you want and follow whatever profession you choose, you are going to have to learn how to be braver than I was."

"How do you learn to be brave?" Kit asked earnestly, thinking mentally of all the terrible tests the African tribes imposed on their youth.

"By facing things that frighten you. I started going on safari to prove to my peers that I was as brave as they were."

"So, you were afraid of the lion?"

"Not that old lion. On the other hand, one or two hippos have scared me half to death, and I wouldn't want to get too close to an angry elephant either. The point is that by doing things that required physical courage,

I increased my reputation among my peers and superiors. That made it harder for them to demean me for my choice of wife, and easier for me to stand up to them."

The scene shifted without warning again. One of the older boys at school was making racial slurs. Kit, who was wearing safari kit rather than school uniform, raised his rifle and shot the boy's head off. The crack of the rifle yanked him back to the DYND at Torquay. His roommate had thrashed about so hard in his dreams that he'd flung the bedside lamp onto the floor between them. He was panting heavily and staring wide-eyed around the room.

"I'll get it." Kit reached down and lifted the lamp off the floor. He pushed the shade back into place and pushed the switch on the cord to see if it still worked. It did. They lay again on their respective beds and turned their backs to each other.

Kit lay awake thinking about the dream and his talk with Dr Grace. He was no longer sure whether the talk with his father had been a dream or a long-buried memory. The more he thought about it, the more he convinced himself the conversation with his father had been real.

With a shudder, he realized that he hadn't given a thought to his parents when he'd refused to fly ops. Now, as the window gradually became a square of lighter black in the brittle cold of the unheated room, he recognized that his vulnerable parents were going to pay a price for his actions. His "lack of morale fibre" would be interpreted as proof of his fundamental inferiority, the result of his tainted blood. Colonial society would blame his mother, and his father's standing would be undermined — without a single word ever being spoken. The Colonial Service was small, incestuous, and inherently snobbish. There were no secrets in the Colonial Service — and no tolerance for anyone who failed the primal test of physical courage. We aren't really so different from all the African tribes, after all, he thought. In the British Empire, too, positions of respect and authority were reserved for men of proven courage — not those deemed LMF.

Chapter 4

NYDN Centre Torquay,
30 November 1943

The fog was so heavy that it condensed on the windows, and the lights were turned on in the NYDN centre despite it being mid-day. The smell of over-cooked Brussel sprouts and fried spam seeped from the kitchen into the lounge. Kit felt he couldn't face the meal and remained in the lounge. The sound of cutlery and desultory conversation from the dining room formed a dull backdrop to his thoughts as he tried to read the latest news alleging major successes in the assault on Germany's industrial capacity.

Air Marshal Harris, AoC-in-C of Bomber Command, had given an interview to the Times in which he claimed that the combined efforts of Bomber Command and the US Army Air Forces would "create such devastation that surrender would become inevitable." The toll was not "unreasonable" the Air Marshal insisted. Casualty rates averaged between 5% and 6% per raid. That didn't sound so bad — if you only had to survive one raid.

"I believe I owe you an explanation," the voice startled Kit out of his thoughts and he looked up. It was his roommate.

"For what?" Kit asked back.

"I think I've been keeping you awake at night."

"Not when I would otherwise have slept," Kit told him, unsure whether it was true or not. He simply didn't feel any resentment toward the young man who was fighting his own demons.

His roommate sank into the chair next to him. "I just think you have a right to know," he insisted, apparently determined to talk. Kit let him. "You see, I froze. I don't know why. I really don't. There was a burst of flak close by that blinded me for a moment, and then when I looked down into the bombsite again, I — I just couldn't speak. The skipper was asking for instructions, pleading with me to guide him in, but nothing came out of my mouth. I could see perfectly. I could hear the skipper on the intercom, but

I was struck dumb. We had to go around a second time — through the flak. With the rest of the main force turning away, every single German gun seemed to concentrate on us. We made a second run. The skipper called to me. 'Oliver! Are you ready now?' I said, yes, but then — the same thing happened. He started cursing me. Flak was bracketing us, but I couldn't say a thing. The Engineer came forward, pulled me away, flung himself down, called the instructions to the skipper and released the bombs. But, of course, we had to remain steady on course for another thirty seconds for the photos. Just as we started to turn away, a piece of flack penetrated the nose and lodged itself in the Engineer's neck. I tried to staunch the bleeding, but it only made things worse. There was blood everywhere. I was drenched in it. It froze on me. Forever."

Kit had no answer.

He had been lucky with Teddy Hamed. In the mess Teddy could be a bit of a clown. He liked to make others laugh, even at the price of making a fool of himself, and while his sense of humour had been too raunchy for Kit's taste, it appealed to some of the others enabling them to laugh when the tension was high. Teddy played the mouth organ too, something that got on Kit's nerves at first, but after a while he got to like it. What mattered was that Teddy had nerves of steel, no matter how hot it was. Teddy had even been known to crack jokes over the target. Usually, bad jokes that made Kit roll his eyes and sometimes provoked a rebuke from Selkirk, but he never failed them. Furthermore, the photos showed a degree of accuracy that pleased the boffins. Those photos should have gotten Teddy a commission, Kit thought, but his accent got in the way. "They" were never going to give a commission to a lad that said "wye-aye" rather than "aye-aye" or "gan" rather than "going."

RAF Wickenby,
January 1943

"Haway, Kit! The bus is leaving!" Teddy called from the door of the mess. Moran grabbed his Mae West and parachute and dashed out of the door behind Hamed. It was just after 9 pm, and the night should have been pitch dark. Instead, a light snow had covered the airfield with a white blanket that picked up and magnified every fragment of light from the headlights, torches, and the stars themselves. The Lancasters, dispersed around the airfield, stood out black against this lighter background. With their noses tipped up and their twin tail fins low to the ground, they looked pugnacious and purposeful.

The bus groaned around the perimeter, dropping off the crews. When they reached "J" for Jig, Selkirk's crew disembarked. Moran had spent most of the day out at the aircraft. He'd spent so much of his service career maintaining Merlins that it felt strange to surrender the care of the four Merlins responsible for his own survival to someone else. The ground crew had been patient with him for pointlessly looking over their shoulders while they did their work with unquestionable efficiency. Cheerfully but doggedly, they had finally convinced Kit to trust them and get some rest instead. He promised them he wouldn't harass them ever again.

Now, as Moran dropped out of the bus, the ground crew waved and grinned at him. So maybe the day hadn't been wasted after all. Meanwhile, Selkirk led the way up the ladder into the belly of the aircraft, and they spread out to their respective workstations. Bob Pickett turned, climbed over the aft spar, dropped his parachute just outside the rear turret, and folded himself into the tiny, Perspex-enclosed space at the tip of the tail between the tail fins. It was a lonely and bitterly cold station, isolated from the rest of the crew.

Reggie Allwright, their Mid-Upper gunner, was also comparatively isolated. Although closer to the rest of them, his turret was elevated, and his job was to keep a sharp lookout for enemy fighters, so he sat with his head and shoulders in his turret and could neither see the rest of them nor move about. Both gunners wore particularly bulky flying suits with wiring that provided heat when plugged in — provided nothing malfunctioned. Furthermore, their suits could not protect faces or hands, and Kit knew that frostbite was not an uncommon complaint among air gunners.

"Sailor" Hart and Leslie Vernon, the navigator and wireless operator respectively, each had their workstations on the port side of the aircraft forward of the main spar. Both stations were curtained off because navigators and wireless operators needed lighting to do their work, but if a light showed beyond their workspace, it exposed the aircraft to night fighters and reduced the night vision of the rest of the crew.

Moran, Hamed, and Selkirk had their workstations forward in the nose. Selkirk stepped over the controls and settled down into the pilot's seat on the left-hand side of the cockpit while Hamed dropped down the couple of steps into the Perspex-enclosed bubble in the nose of the aircraft where the bombsite and the forward guns were located. Here he lay down on his belly to do his final checks. Moran folded down the seat before the Engineer's station, which was located behind and to the right of the pilot.

From the navigator's cabin came the sound of tools being laid out, while on Moran's left Selkirk was adjusting the cockpit seat. Moran scanned the dials showing oil pressure and temperature, revs and the like. Over the intercom, Selkirk asked the Navigator for the time.

"21:17, Skipper," Sailor answered.

"Time to get started then. Captain to Rear gunner: Comfortable?"

"A-OK, Skipper."

"Mid-Upper Gunner?"

"Yes, sir."

"Navigator?"

"Aye-aye, sir."

"Wireles Operator?"

"Ready, sir."

"Engineer?"

"Ready, sir."

"Bomb-aimer?"

"Canny."

There was a slight pause and then Selkirk asked. "What does that mean, bomb aimer?"

"Fine, Skipper. Everything's fine."

"Ready to start engines, Engineer."

Moran took a torch and flashed it out the window at the waiting ground crew. They signalled back affirmation. Starting with No. 3 engine, Moran flipped the magneto switch to 'on' and primed the engine, pumping ten times. Finally, he lifted the switch guard and pressed the starter button. The engine grunted, belched smoke and the smell of gasoline fumes increased. Then abruptly the engine caught and roared to life. Moran eased back on the power and the engine settled into a steady growl. He repeated the procedure on the remaining three engines. As he did so, he listened to the sound they made as much as he read the luminous dials quivering on the panel in front of him. The aircraft came more and more to life, vibrating more aggressively with each engine. Meanwhile, behind him the hydraulics on the turrets whirred as the gunners turned them back and forth to ensure everything was working correctly.

Moran glanced out of the window. Across the airfield engines were springing to life and turrets swung back and forth as almost forty other aircraft of both No 626 and No 12 Squadrons prepared for a raid on Krefeld. No 626's squadron leader's aircraft A-Able was already edging off its hard standing and taxiing toward the head of the runway. Selkirk asked the crew to check in again and ordered Hamed to take his seat next to the navigator for take-off. After they had all reported back, he flashed his torch to the ground crew to pull the chocks away. J – Jig rolled slowly forward. The way she bounced and swayed betrayed her heavy load: nearly 12,000 lbs of bombs and 2,000 lbs of fuel.

They had not taxied far when, with a high-pitched squeal, Selkirk applied the brakes. Slightly but perceptibly, the aircraft swayed forward and then settled back over her wheels. Ahead of them, the first of 20 Lancasters started to roll down the runway. It lumbered forward as if it was never going to come unstuck from the earth. Finally, it lifted off and climbed gently upwards into the starry night. J-Jig advanced another ten yards and halted again.

They were 18th for take-off, and it was a relief finally to turn onto the runway. Here they sat absolutely still for a moment. Then Selkirk called, "Crew, prepare for take-off. Engineer, flaps 20."

"Flaps 20, sir."

The engines started to howl, and Moran watched the luminous dials recording the increase in revolutions. Finally, the heavy bomber started to roll slowly down the runway. At first, she seemed reluctant to leave home. Gradually, however, the wind rushing under the wings began to lift her up. As if the burden of so much weight had been blown away, the aircraft bounced on the runway. Selkirk held the nose down until reaching 110 mph, then eased back on the control yoke. The needle of the altimeter crept around the face of the dial. Moran risked a glance out of the window as Selkirk banked gently. Spread out below them was the entire station and the surrounding countryside — all clothed in snow except for the remaining handful of black aircraft and the clusters of people standing about watching.

"Wheels up, Engineer," the order came over the intercom.

Moran pulled the lever and watched as the lights changed from green to red before going out. "Wheels up and locked, sir." The engines were still straining hard as they passed through three thousand feet.

"Flaps up, Engineer."

"Flaps up, sir." The aircraft settled down a bit and the noise seemed less mind-numbing.

They steered north as they climbed. Moran concentrated on his instruments. The risk of icing on a night like this was acute. They'd been reminded of it in the briefing, so he watched the engine temperatures like a hawk, adjusting hot air intake and fuel mixture. All went well and they reached the designated cruising altitude of 20,000 feet without incident. Selkirk ordered him to adjust the engines to cruising revolutions and boost.

Meanwhile they turned back for the assembly point. Roughly thirty minutes after take-off, the navigator's radio clicked on. "Navigator to pilot: Steer one-one-two."

"One-one-two, Navigator.... On course now."

That was it. They were steering for Germany on their first operational flight. For the rest of the crew, Moran calculated this was the culmination of roughly two years of training. Ironically, except for himself, the rest had done some of their training overseas — in Australia, Canada, the United States, and even South Africa. Only Moran, because of his trade, had done all his training in Britain.

"Navigator to pilot, turn on oh-nine-five."

"Oh-nine-five, Navigator."

They had just crossed over the English coast, which tonight was white compared to the nearly black North Sea. Millions of ripples on the face of the sea caught the light of a waning and setting moon. These turned the sea from opaque black to a rough, tarnished silver. In other circumstances, it would have been beautiful...

Five minutes before they were scheduled to cross into enemy airspace, Hamed left the navigator's compartment and settled himself in the nose of the aircraft where he manned the forward guns. Once he reported he was ready, Selkirk told the gunners to test their guns. The aircraft shuddered and barked briefly, then all three gunners reported that their weapons were fully operational.

"Enemy coast ahead," Hamed announced over the intercom.

This, too, was a sharp white line against the tarnished-silver sea. An instant later, a score or more lights pierced the darkened sky ahead of them. They swayed and circled, searching for the approaching bombers. J-Jig of 626 Squadron was only one bomber in a "stream" of hundreds. Other aircraft had already entered enemy airspace.

J-Jig's engines growled remorselessly dragging them toward their destiny. Searchlights seemed to surround them, drilling relentlessly through the darkness. Abruptly, a Lancaster on their right was illuminated so brightly that Kit could read the identification numbers on the fuselage: PH-N. That was 12 Squadron, stationed as they were at Wickenby. As the pilot tried to dive out of the blinding light, another spotlight locked on to it and then a third; it had been "coned" by the spotlights.

The anti-aircraft batteries had a clear target. No sooner was the aircraft trapped in the pillars of light, than the flak started bracketing the illuminated bomber. The pilot banked and jinked in a frenzied corkscrew-motion to shake off the lights and deceive the flak. Moran watched, fascinated and horrified, unconsciously urging it to escape by muttering "come on! Come on!" He was rewarded with a flash of light followed by a burning ball of molten red as it exploded. For a split second, the black wings were silhouetted against the inferno that had been the fuselage with the bomb load. Then the broken remnants faded and fell from the sky with the incinerated corpses of seven men.

The bomber stream continued steadily on course.

J-Jig was being shaken by flak. The aircraft was flung both laterally and vertically. One near-by burst sent the Lancaster down 300 feet as if it had fallen into a hole. Hamed yelped so loudly that Moran heard him although he had his microphone off.

A click announced that someone had turned on their mic. Then Reggie's voice came in over the earphones. "Night fighter to port. Attacking another Lanc."

Kit glanced over his shoulder once, but then returned his attention to the dials as he inwardly braced for an attack.

"The Me110 has got his starboard outboard. Lanc's dropping out of the stream." Pickett commented. Adding shortly afterwards, "I've lost sight of him."

Selkirk rolled slightly to enable the gunners to look down better.

"The Hun is still going for him. One of the port engines —" An explosion shook them. No more commentary was necessary. They continued on course.

For a space of five or six minutes, the flak seemed to fade away to practically nothing although it was as intense as ever in the distance ahead of them. They droned closer and closer to the barking flak until it was all around them again. The unnatural but now familiar sensation of being tossed about resumed. A loud crack took Kit's breath away. They must have been hit! His eye scanned the dials. He could see nothing out of the ordinary.

"Engineer, can you see any indication of damage?"

"No, Skipper. How's she flying?"

"Fine."

They flew on. The horizon was gradually brightening. It wasn't just the searchlights and the flak anymore; fires were burning over a growing patch of earth. As they pressed forward, the temperature started to rise in the fuselage and the smell of smoke and cordite filled the aircraft. Selkirk ordered the oxygen increased.

Moran was amazed that the target indicators could be seen against the conflagration. They turned onto their bombing run. Hamed called up the instructions to Selkirk over the intercom, while the intensity of the heat from the conflagration below made Moran sweat. With a noticeable bounce, the bombs were gone, but for another interminable thirty seconds, they continued flying straight and level to photograph the damage. Finally, Hamed announced the photo run was finished. At once, Selkirk banked hard to port and started the journey back to England.

Gradually, they left the noise, light and heat behind, but the increasing darkness was deceptive — or so they had been told. Night fighters preyed on returning bombers no less than approaching bombers.

"Navigator, how long before we leave enemy airspace?"

"Estimate 40 to 45 minutes, Skipper."

Kit switched the engines over to the secondary tanks and did a quick calculation of remaining fuel. Everything looked good.

About a quarter hour later, Hamed came out of the nose and started down the fuselage past the navigator and wireless operator, evidently in need of a piss. Moran preferred to drink less before a long flight than use the Elsan toilet that sat smack in the middle of the fuselage just abaft the aft spar.

Abruptly, a loud tearing sound and a rush of wind buffeted the aircraft, which bucked violently. For a moment, Selkirk struggled with the controls. Only after he had the aircraft back straight and level did he risk calling sharply over his shoulder, "Engineer! What was that?"

"No idea, sir."

"Engines?"

"Smooth as silk. It was something aft."

"Gunners, report in. Are we under attack?"

"Rear gunner here, sir. No fighters in sight."

"Mid-upper gunner, sir. Agreed. No fighters in sight."

"Skipper! Wireless Operator here! Teddy's fallen half out of a hole in the fuselage. I'll try to get him back on board, but don't think I'm strong enough to manage on my own!"

"Kit! Go aft and see if you can help!"

Moran had already grabbed a bottle of oxygen and clipped it to his mask. He took a torch and gestured for Sailor to return to his station. They couldn't afford to have the navigator distracted from his calculations at a time like this. Beyond the wireless compartment, the temperature had plummeted and was bitterly cold. Moran flashed his torch toward the tail as he clambered over the main spar, and his heart stopped. A hole gaped in the floor of the fuselage just beyond the empty bomb-bay. Vernon was kneeling beside it clinging with one hand to the frame of the aircraft and with the other to Hamed. The latter was half in and half out of the aircraft and clasping the base of the toilet desperately.

Kit could see that Teddy's oxygen and intercom had both become disconnected when the fuselage gave way under him. That meant he might black out at any moment. Moran stepped over and around Vernon so he could grab the bomb aimer under his arms. "Ready, Leslie? At my call! Two, six, heave!" Together they hauled Hamed inside with a backward lurch. Fortunately, Hamed was comparatively light because it took all of their combined, panic-boosted strength to drag him fully inside the aircraft. The effort left them both panting, and Moran heard his pulse pounding in his ears.

Eventually, he noticed that Selkirk was calling over the intercom in a voice that sounded increasingly alarmed. "Engineer, report in! Wireless Operator, report!"

Moran plugged his intercom to one of the fuselage sockets and reported, "there's a ruddy great hole in the floor of the fuselage, Skipper. Must have been the crack we heard earlier. Hamed was half out of it, but we've got him back inboard now. We'll get him to the rest bed and hook him back on oxygen again."

Together Vernon and Moran dragged and lifted the unconscious Hamed onto the rest bed. Moran plugged Hamed's mask into the oxygen supply and after a moment he came to.

The teenager was disoriented only for a moment. Then he sat up with a look of horror on his face. He looked down at his groin and his open fly. "Jesus wept, I'm used to ootside netties but they're nivver that fucking cauld. I feel as if I've got a geet big icicle in me drawers." He looked up at Moran, his dark brown eyes wide with panic. "If I've got the frostbite will me cock drop off?'"

Moran didn't have a clue, but he shook his head and advised the teenager in an exasperated tone, "don't worry about that. You nearly went overboard at 20,000 feet without a 'chute! Be thankful you're alive." He pulled one of the extra blankets from its shelf over the rest bed and spread it over Teddy, who was starting to shiver in spasms. On second thought, Moran spread the second blanket over him as well. Then he went forward to the cockpit and stood behind Selkirk until the pilot looked up at him and pulled his microphone off so they could talk without including the rest of the crew.

"I think he'll be all right. Can we fly any lower? It must be 50 degrees below zero back there?"

Selkirk hooked up again. "Pilot to Navigator. Time to enemy coast?"

"Estimate six minutes."

"I'll take her down over the North Sea," Selkirk promised.

The minutes dragged. Searchlights pierced the night ahead of them, marking the coast. For a second, Moran caught a glimpse of a Halifax illuminated by the powerful light, but the pilot jinked and then corkscrewed violently. He escaped the searchlight. "That was well done," Reggie commented from the mid-upper turret having seen it.

Flak was bursting around them again. Without the bombload and with half the fuel consumed, the aircraft was lighter and seemed to get tossed around more than on the inward run. Finally, they passed out over the coast and Kit had the impression that J-Jig sighed with relief. They were over the gleaming black-grey of the North Sea again, and it appeared calm and peaceful. Selkirk eased the nose down to start his descent. "I'm taking us down to 5,000 where the air is warmer."

"Navigator to Pilot: Steer two-seven-five."

"Two-seven-five, Navigator."

At 4:05 am they landed safely at Wickenby. They had successfully completed their first operation. There were just 29 more to go.

Chapter 5

NYDN Torquay,
1 December 1943

It was the first sunny day since his arrival at the NYDN centre and the view from the lobby had been transformed from grim to glorious. Kit went out and walked along the harbour front. He stopped for tea in a quaint tearoom, where a cheerful old lady offered him home-made scones with strawberry jam.

When he returned to the NYDN, he was told by the airman at the desk that Dr Grace was looking for him. He hurried to the doctor's office and knocked on the closed door.

"Who's there?" the doctor asked.

"Pilot Officer Moran."

"Oh, come in."

Kit entered. As usual, the doctor stood and offered his hand before gesturing for Kit to take his usual seat. "I had an unexpected cancellation and thought maybe we could squeeze in an extra chat," the doctor explained.

"Of course," Kit agreed. Despite his initial scepticism, Kit had to admit these chats with Dr Grace didn't seem to be doing him any harm. Grace was never accusatory, dismissive or sarcastic. He seemed genuinely interested in what Kit had to say.

As usual, he started with the files. "According to your files you aren't married."

"No, sir."

"What the files don't tell us is whether you are engaged — officially or unofficially."

"No, sir."

"Have you been seeing anyone special?"

Kit didn't answer immediately.

"You're twenty-three years old, an age in which healthy young men usually have a strong interest in the opposite sex. Although obviously there are exceptions—"

"I'm not one of those exceptions. I've been seeing a young lady regularly." Kit did not want any more strikes against him. He was in enough trouble as it was.

"She wouldn't have had any influence on your decision not to fly additional operations, would she?"

"What do you mean?"

"Well, there are many girls who flatly refuse to get involved with aircrew. The daughter of a family friend told me to my face that she thought any girl who would go out with aircrew was "morbid." Girls may not know the statistics — we try to keep those secret after all. Nevertheless, WAAF with Bomber Command have a jolly good idea that aircrew don't have a high chance of surviving one tour — never mind two. I expect the more intelligent civilian girls can guess too. If nothing else, they know that at present only the Royal Navy and aircrew are facing the enemy day after day. You can't blame a girl for not wanting to see her fiancé or boyfriend killed. Did your girl object to you volunteering for a second tour of operations?"

"She wasn't happy about it," Kit admitted. "In fact, she told me I was stupid and making a huge mistake."

"But you went ahead anyway." It wasn't a question, so Kit didn't say anything. Dr Grace asked gently. "Did your decision to fly anyway impact the relationship?"

Kit thought about that. He wasn't sure. "It was a complicated relationship."

Lincoln,
January 1943

The formal dance was definitely a success. Technically it was a fund-raising event for the Red Cross organized under the auspices of the Bishop of Lincoln, but it had tapped into the craving of thousands of young men trapped on military establishments to socialize beyond the confines of the local pub. Although hosted in the Lincoln Assembly Rooms, the crowd was so large that even this generous venue was overwhelmed by it. There were queues for food, queues for drinks, and the ballroom floor was so crowded one could barely move, never mind dance. The Americans were out in force, of course. With their smart uniforms and deep pockets, they could have their pick of the girls. They were also better at jitterbugging to the fast music that the band was playing.

Kit and Don stood on the fringe of the crowd, drinks in hand, and surveyed the scene. Sailor, being a married man, had opted to stay on the station. Reggie, despite being married, had joined the crowd bent on having a good time. He along with the rest of their crew had hooked up early with some WAAF from a different station. WAAF were less easily bedazzled by the USAAF. Kit and Don, however, were left high and dry, like fish out of water, Kit thought.

Kit knew he was supposed to be enjoying this, but he wasn't. The music was too loud, the room too hot, the beer watery. Then again, not liking things that attracted most of his fellows wasn't anything new to him. In fact, he felt himself right back in school. What surprised him was discovering how shy Don was. He'd assumed that the handsome scion of a wealthy, landed house would sail through any social situation with ease, self-confidence and ready smiles. Don, who was so self-assured in the cockpit, looked even more uncomfortable than Kit felt, and he kept running his finger around the inside his collar nervously.

"Maybe this wasn't such a wizard idea after all," he conceded, looking uncomfortably around the room.

Just then the door opened, and two newcomers slipped in. The girls were evidently taken aback by the spectacle they encountered. They came to an abrupt halt and looked about uncertainly. One pressed a hand over her ear apparently to indicate she found the music too loud, while the other gazed at the frenetic American dancing with a bewildered expression. They were both dressed in full-length evening dresses and high-heeled shoes that looked decidedly expensive to Kit's eyes. One was rather frail with long, light brown hair, and a pleasant but unremarkable face. Kit found her mousy. The other girl, on the other hand, was pleasantly plump and perky. She had dark hair cut provocatively short, and she had a no-nonsense stance.

Don had followed his gaze and asked, "What do you think?"

"I like the dark one," Kit admitted.

Don grinned and clicked his glass with Kit's. "Now that's what I call a mate. I like the other one. There's only one problem: I can't dance whatever-this-thing-is-called."

"Not to worry. They haven't got drinks yet. We can offer to buy them something."

They moved at once, anxious to prevent any of the other unattached males from intercepting their chosen quarry. At the last moment, however, Don hung back a fraction to let Kit make initial contact. "Excuse me ladies, my friend and I were wondering if you might perhaps like a drink?" Kit included Don with a nod of his head.

The dark-haired girl turned to look at them. Her eyes rapidly assessed the young men critically, homing in on their left-breast pockets. Kit saw a frown twitch at her brow, and he thrust his hand at her to stop her from brushing them off. "My name's Kit Moran, and this is Don Selkirk," he indicated Don again.

His brashness earned him a smile of tempered amusement, as the girl took his hand. "Fiona Barker," she introduced herself, turning to offer her hand to Don as well, before adding, "And this is Georgina Reddings."

The slender girl timidly offered a limp hand to Kit, before turning to give it to Don. Kit didn't like girls who shook hands like that — with no conviction or confidence.

When Don's eyes met Georgina's, however, the girl's face lit up with a beautiful smile. Her eyes seemed to grow larger and glimmer with inner fire. Well, Kit thought, Don was very good-looking.

"What are you ladies drinking?" Kit asked before Fiona could revert to her earlier scepticism and withdraw.

"Do you think you could find anything as old-fashioned as cider?" Fiona asked, "or are they only serving those American cocktails?"

"I'll find out," Kit promised, and turned to Georgina for her order. She was still gazing at Don, and he was looking back at her with a soft smile on his lips.

It was Fiona who broke the spell, "Georgina, Mr. Moran asked what you are drinking?"

"I don't mind," she said in a soft, breathy voice. "Sherry perhaps."

"Sherry and cider, then," Kit concluded. "You stay with the ladies, Don, to be sure the USAAF doesn't bounce them."

By the time he returned, Don and Georgina were deep in conversation with one another, and Fiona was looking decidedly bored. She gratefully accepted the cider he brought her, and after taking a sip remarked in a tone that bordered on resignation, "I presume you're stationed nearby?"

"Wickenby, yes."

"And where are you from?"

"Africa."

"Well, that's original!" Her waning interest in him revived noticeably. She reappraised him before remarking, "Big place, though, Africa. Could you be more specific?"

"Do you know it?"

"Only from maps on the wall and travelogues. I'm studying at the Lincoln Diocesan Training College to be a teacher. Geography is one of the subjects I'm training to teach. So, test me. Where are you from?"

"My father's in the colonial service. We moved around. I was born in Pretoria, grew up in different places in Kenya, went to school in Cape Town, and my parents are now in Calabar."

She looked puzzled, so Kit helped her out. "That's in Nigeria."

"What's home?"

Kit had to think about that before admitting with a shrug. "I don't really have a home, not the way you English do."

"Do you find us terribly stodgy and narrow-minded?"

"Sometimes I do."

She laughed at that. "I certainly do! I'd love to go to Africa or India or China. Somewhere tropical and sultry with spicy food, loose, flowing clothes, and fewer conventions — or should I say manners?"

"Oh, every place has its conventions and manners. You just have to learn what they are."

"I suppose so, but listen! They've stopped playing jazz. I could actually dance to this. Shall we?"

Kit wasn't used to women being quite that foreword, but Don was already escorting Georgina onto the rapidly thinning dance floor so he could hardly say no. It was a slow waltz, and Don lost all trace of shyness as he took Georgina onto the dancefloor. Kit didn't think he'd seen anything like it in his life. Georgina seemed to float beside him, her dress swaying and swirling around them in time to the melody.

"I can't dance like that," Kit admitted.

"Never mind. Neither can I," Fiona answered, and they laughed together.

"So where are you from?" Kit asked because he was too busy concentrating on the steps of the waltz to talk himself. Fiona wasn't easy to lead; she seemed to have ideas of her own about where to go and needed a heavy hand to steer.

"Oh, I'm a local girl. Born and raised in Lincoln. If you ever want a tour of the Cathedral, I can do it in my sleep."

"It looks very impressive from the outside."

"Yes, and littered with dead people — sorry, graves, I mean. I'm not at all interested in history, you see. Just dead people. I want to live, travel, see the world."

"Difficult with the war on."

"I know. I hate the war. I hate everything about it. The killing, the destruction, the boring speeches, the black-out, the rationing, the men in uniform — I mean the uniforms, not the men in them," she corrected herself with an apologetic smile.

Kit just nodded and they danced without talking for a few minutes. Then Fiona begged. "Tell me about Africa — especially all the things that most Englishmen get wrong about it."

So, Kit talked about Africa until the music changed to a fast pace again, and then they went back to the side-lines and another drink. Don and Georgina joined them. At the next slow dance, a fox trot this time, Fiona suggested swapping partners; the other three politely agreed.

Kit danced with Georgina and discovered she was feather-light on her feet and completely responsive to his slightest touch. He dutifully asked Georgina where she was from and what she was doing in Lincoln. She replied that her father was a vicar somewhere in Yorkshire that Kit had never heard of, and she had come to Lincoln to attend teacher training college. That was where she'd met Fiona. After that, Georgina asked Kit about his position on the Lancaster. She surprised him by being impressed when he said engineer. "That must be very difficult. My brother is training as a marine engineer, and I can't understand half of what he talks about."

Kit laughed. "That's probably just what he intends. There's nothing really difficult about engineering provided you're interested in it."

"No, I suppose not," Georgina conceded and asked him about his family. She was immediately sorry that they were so far away. "You must miss your parents terribly!"

"I do, but Don's family has been kind enough to adopt me," Kit told her.

"Don seems very nice. Does he have lots of girlfriends?" Georgina asked, looking at him with big, trusting, brown eyes.

"None that I know about," Kit admitted, and Georgina smiled radiantly at that.

For the next hour or so, Kit and Fiona danced together until Leslie and Teddy broke in on them, asking where Don was. Kit stopped and looked around. "He was just here a minute ago. He and his dance partner must have stepped into the foyer to get some fresh air or talk where they don't have to shout." The foyer was farther from the band and only sparsely populated. "Why?"

"Bob's pie-eyed and picking a fight with an American sergeant."

"Excuse me a minute," Kit told Fiona and let the others lead him to the far side of the room where Bob Pickett was indeed making a scene. He was shouting insults at an American sergeant. The latter had raised his fists but was being held back by a couple of his buddies, who were trying to calm him down.

Kit moved up beside Bob and put a hand on his arm. "Calm down, Bob. Let's not ruin a pleasant evening."

"Keep out of this! This Yankee bastard insulted Sally and all WAAF! You should be taking my side, not trying to shut me up!"

Kit glanced at a small group of WAAF standing to one side looking upset and worried. "I am on your side, Bob, which is why I'm asking you to lower your voice and come outside. I don't want you arrested."

"I'm not taking orders from you, Moran!"

"Pickett! You pipe down or you're off my crew," Selkirk's voice cut through the noise of the band and the crowd without him even raising it.

"You don't know what he said, Skipper!" Pickett protested, furiously flinging his fore-and-aft cap on the floor. His face was red, and he was hopping mad.

Meanwhile, an American lieutenant had also arrived and was shoving his sergeant none too gently in the direction of the bar. The sound of the band surged louder and people around them started to disperse. "He said a "Waafery" was just another name for a bordello."

"Did you ask him what unit he was from?" Don replied.

"What?" Pickett frowned at his pilot confused and disbelieving. "I don't even know the bastard's name and I don't care! I just —"

"Believe me, a complaint from our Station Commander to his would hurt him a lot more than your insults or fists could." Don pointed out.

While the Canadian gaped at his skipper, Teddy Hamed offered cheerfully. "I'll gan and get that information now, Skipper."

Don stopped him. "No, you won't. It's too late for now, but next time you all know how to behave, correct?" Don looked from one to the other of them, and they nodded in turn. "Maybe it's time to push off," Don concluded. It was after midnight. "Go out and find the station bus," he urged Bob, Teddy and Leslie. Reggie was nowhere in sight. He added, "Kit and I will join you shortly."

While the others went out to find the bus laid on by the Station, Don and Kit returned to Fiona and Georgina, who were waiting over to one side. "I'm afraid we have to be going," Don announced, "but it would be a pleasure to see you ladies again. What do you think? Would you like to join us for an evening at the pictures sometime?"

"As long as it's not a flick about the war!" Fiona responded. "Something entertaining and distracting, please!"

"Yes, I'd like that very much," Georgina assured Don.

"Is there a number where we can reach you?"

"At the school," Fiona told him. Kit found a pencil and a scrap of paper to write on. Then they shook hands and parted. After that, they started seeing the girls once or twice every week.

Chapter 6

NYDN Centre Torquay,
2 December 1943

Kit went to church on Sunday. There wasn't much else to do. Most of the medical staff had the day off. The 'inmates' (as they called themselves) were left to fend for themselves. Kit was envious of the men who had visitors. Mostly it was family — brothers, sisters, parents, wives — but some had girlfriends. Kit thought about calling Fiona. He'd thought a lot about her since Dr Grace had asked, but he hadn't found the courage to call. He didn't know what he should say to her, either. She knew he was nowhere near the end of his tour and if he said he was off ops and away from the station, she'd know something was fishy. He was going to have to tell her the truth, but he had no idea how she would react. He tried to tell himself that she hated the war so much that she might understand. But what if she didn't? His thoughts kept going in circles as he wandered listlessly about Torquay until he was cold and footsore. He returned to the NYDN centre.

In the lobby, the Sunday papers lay about on the sofas and coffee tables. Most had been read more than once. Sinking down into a comfortable chair he randomly picked one up and found it already opened to an article about an RAF navigator who, after being shot down over Germany, had managed to evade capture.

The story sucked him in. The navigator, the article said, had bailed out on the return from a raid to Essen. Although four of the crew had made it out of the aircraft, they landed so far apart that they never found one another in the dark. The navigator had cut away the tops of his flying boots and started walking towards the coast using the stars as his guide. He slept in barns during the day and walked at night, avoiding all people, until he noticed the signs were in Dutch. He eventually approached a kindly-looking, old woman, and revealed who he was. She brought him to another man who got him aboard a canal barge. Hidden amidst the cargo, the RAF navigator made it almost to the coast. Just short of the harbour, however, the barge owner expelled him and told him to go overland to a small fishing village. No name was given, presumably to protect his helpers.

At the village, the RAF navigator was shown an aged and neglected wooden sailing boat and asked if he wanted to attempt sailing to England in her. As luck would have it, the navigator was an avid sailor who had crewed on a variety of different craft. He jumped at the offer. The Dutch provided him with provisions and water, which were stowed in the boat while he waited for the weather to become favourable. Finally, on a moonless night with enough but not too much wind, he put to sea. With no navigational aids whatsoever, the article stressed, he'd sailed single-handed across the North Sea to make landfall at Ipswich. It was 67 days since his Sterling had been shot down.

Putting the newspaper down, Kit thought, "Sailor could have done that." Sailor had crewed on rich men's yachts to earn extra money ever since he was a youth. He'd sailed around England once. It was his love of sailing that had driven him to the Merchant Navy, and he had loved the life — until the war started. The gruelling business of sailing "convoy course and speed" while around him one ship after another was sunk had worn him down, he said. The U-boat war was like no other, Sailor claimed, because the enemy was completely invisible. One could neither see nor hear a U-boat — until it struck. He'd had a ship sunk under him, and only one of the lifeboats had gotten away. Sailor with a dozen members of the crew had spent four days in that open boat until they had been rescued by fishermen off the Irish coast.

"Still, I would have gone back," Sailor admitted to Kit one night after a few pints in the Mess. "It was Kathleen who couldn't take it anymore." Kathleen was his wife. "You see the convoy arrived on schedule without my ship," Sailor explained. "Kathleen insisted on seeing the escort commander, and he reported they had found no survivors. He also admitted that they had had little opportunity to look. She was left in horrible uncertainty until I finally showed up. She begged me never to put to sea again."

"Do you regret giving up the sea?" Kit pressed him.

Sailor had smiled his broad, slow smile and replied. "I haven't given up the sea, Kit — even if that's what Kathleen thinks. I've just left it temporarily. I plan to go back after the war. When I get my own ship, Kathleen and Hope can come with me, you know. Meanwhile, I'm happier where I can watch Hope growing up, becoming more of a person each day. I'd have missed all that, if I was still going to sea. Each time I came home, she would have been a new person, one who didn't know me or want me around. I've seen that with the kids of other sailors. Besides, with life so uncertain, I value every hour I can spend with Kathleen." He'd grinned and added, "It's because I want to get home to her that I'll always find a course to bring us back."

February 1943

On the outbound leg of their eighteenth operational flight, they encountered severe icing over the North Sea. Although Moran managed to keep the engines from freezing up, the wings became coated with black ice and started to bend visibly. Selkirk had no option but to descend in the hope that at a lower altitude the ice would melt. It did — and flew off the wings and props in huge lumps that crashed against the fuselage like rocks, making almost as much noise as flak.

They never found out what caused it, but when they tried to resume their flight to the target, they discovered that they had lost their wireless antenna. Possibly one of the flying chunks of ice hit the antenna. Alternatively, the weight of the ice combined with the force of gravity during the dive and/or when levelling off had caused it to be torn away. Whatever the cause, they had no radio-based navigational aids or communications. They were somewhere over the North Sea on a moonless night with 12 tons of high explosives in their belly. Landing with that load would be dangerous and it would mean the flight would not count towards their tour. Trying to find the target in Germany without any navigational aids, however, was hopeless.

"I suppose we'd better abort and turn for home. Do you have course for us, Sailor?"

"Mid-Upper to Skipper:" Reggie interrupted over the intercom. "I think I can see another Lanc to port."

Everyone was silent while they searched the darkness.

"Rear-gunner to skipper: I see her too," Pickett called in from the tail.

"Me too, Skipper," Hamed agreed.

"Wireless Operator?" Selkirk asked. "Do you want to try flashing a message to her?"

"I'll try, Skipper," Leslie agreed.

Moran looked over his shoulder as Leslie emerged from his workstation and made his way up to the mid-upper turret carrying a torch and oxygen. Reggie dropped down into the fuselage, while Leslie climbed into the bubble. They waited in tense silence while he flashed a message in morse. The Lancaster beside them answered in the same manner. Leslie activated the intercom with a click. "Wireless Operator to Skipper: it is UM-D-Dog."

"That's Nobby." Selkirk recognized the pilot of the other aircraft. "Skipper to Wireless Operator: See if he can he give us a course."

"To the target or to base, Skipper?"

"To the next turning point and then to target."

There was a moment of silence while the other aircraft blinked at them. Then Leslie reported. "He says: 'Steer One-Two-Two. Follow me.'"

"One-Two-Two. Following."

Selkirk slipped his aircraft behind but to the right of the other Lancaster to avoid the slipstream.

The intercom clicked again. "Wireless Operator to Skipper: UM-D wants to know if we can climb?"

"Until ice forms again."

"I'll pass that on."

They climbed back to 17,000 feet but then ran into the icing conditions and sank down to 16,000. That was not a happy height for getting through the flak, and they sweated it out as they crossed over the enemy coast and met with the inevitable vicious welcome. Fortunately, the target tonight was Bochum, so they did not have to fly far into Germany. Nevertheless, Moran started to feel like the contents of a barman's shaker. They were flung up and down and sideways. Moran kept his eyes glued to the instrument dials, watching for the first indication that one of their engines had sustained damage.

Finally, the fires started to illuminate the horizon and the markers set by the Pathfinders became visible. The heat seeped up with the billowing smoke that enveloped the cockpit in waves. The rancid smell of burning rubber almost turned Moran's stomach at one point. Far ahead an aircraft exploded. Another aircraft peeled off with a burning wing marking its rapid descent into the hell below.

Hamed was in the nose. His voice came over the intercom. "Bomb aimer to skipper: UM-D has its bomb doors open."

"Skipper to bomb aimer: Can you identify anything?"

"Just the markers, skipper."

"That will do. Talk me in."

Hamed took over. This was the worst part, Moran thought, these sixty seconds when they had to fly straight and level. If the searchlights found them now, they were dead. If a fighter found them, they were dead.

The aircraft bounced up as though with relief when the bombs dropped away, and Hamed announced: "Bombs gone."

Now just the photograph.

"Mid-upper to skipper: UM-D is turning away."

"Skipper to Engineer: Kit, can you keep your eye on her so the gunners can watch for fighters? UM-D is our ticket home."

Christ, Moran thought, he'd forgotten about having no navigational aids and the whole trip home ahead of them in the dark. He turned his eyes from the engine dials to rivet them on the Lancaster turning to port in front of them. It was because he was watching her so intently, that he saw a bomb dropped from an aircraft at a higher altitude hit UM-D's wing and tear it clear off. The Lancaster went into an uncontrolled spin. He leapt up from his seat to press his nose to the window, trying to see parachutes as he mentally urged the crew to 'get out, get out, get out!' But the Lancaster was falling away too fast into the smoke and confusion below them. The night was full of flashes of light, smoke and other aircraft. From the nose, Hamed reported they could turn for home, but Moran switched on his intercom. "Engineer to pilot: UM-D is down. We're on our own."

"Pilot to navigator: do you have a course?"

"Steer Two-Eight-Five, Skipper," Sailor answered as if nothing was wrong.

"Two-Eight-Five on, Navigator."

Around them the earth was still on fire and the night was full of lethal metal. Some of it clanged against the aircraft, but no one reported being hit and the engines kept purring in their familiar tone.

After a few minutes of being shaken about, the intensity of the flak eased. They could see the enemy coast ahead, white breakers lighting it up in the darkness. Just another five or ten minutes and they would be safely over the water. "Still two-eight-five, Navigator?" Selkirk asked.

"Navigator to pilot: Steer that until we're over the North Sea. Then I'll shoot the stars."

Shoot the stars? Moran asked himself.

"Will that work at the speed we're flying?" Selkirk echoed Moran's thoughts, scepticism in his tone of voice.

"It should, Skipper. Don't worry," Sailor answered, sounding amused.

Moran glanced at his watch and decided it was time to switch the engines over to the secondary fuel tanks. In doing so he noticed the starboard tank was not full. There was a leak somewhere. He took a torch and shone it along the starboard wing. He couldn't see any major damage, but then neither could he see the underside of the wing from up here. "Engineer to pilot: Nothing to worry about yet, but we appear to have a fuel leak in the starboard secondary tank."

"Understood. Keep your eye on it."

Just then, they slid over the coastline, and the darkness became less intense as the breaking waves provided small squiggles of white across the surface.

"Navigator to pilot: Permission to go to the astrodome to get a fix."

"Granted."

Moran turned to watch Sailor slip out of his workstation, light spilling into the fuselage for a second until the curtains fell shut again. The navigator then clambered up onto the main spar next to the wireless operator's seat and settled his elbows on the rim of the astrodome. He held a heavy, bronze sextant in his hand. Moran found it hard to believe this was going to work, but at least they had perfect visibility. That meant that Sailor could find more than one star to shoot, and that they'd be able to get a ground fix when they crossed back over the English coastline. They'd flown from Wickenby often enough to know the nearby coast.

Longing to see that coastline, Moran turned to look ahead through the cockpit windows and caught his breath. Was that cloud down there? He left his station to stand beside Selkirk, peering into the darkness ahead of them. In the distance —where the horizon should have been a sharp line — there was only a smear.

Maybe it was just some light, high cloud, Moran told himself, and went back to his instrument panel. But the entire aircraft seemed to squirm uneasily. He glanced over his left shoulder at Selkirk and saw him lean forward to switch on the autopilot. He wriggled his shoulders and took his legs off the rudder, swinging them in the air to let off tension.

Sailor dropped back down into the aircraft and disappeared inside his curtained cubicle. After a few minutes he called a new course to Selkirk.

Moran looked forward again. There could be no doubt now. A thick, woolly blanket of rumpled cloud stretched across the sea. If it continued all the way to England, they would have no visual aids to help them identify their position. Worse: without radio communication, they could not contact any station to ask what the cloud base was. They could not put through a "Darky" Call, asking a station to guide them in either. They were either going to have to abandon their perfectly serviceable Lancaster and risk jumping blindly into that murk — or they would have to let down into the cloud without knowing exactly where they were. The chances of going into the sea or smearing themselves across a hillside somewhere were too great for comfort.

The engines droned steadily, bringing the milky blanket nearer with each minute. Moran monitored the fuel consumption. Focusing on calculating the amount of fuel remaining and calculating the minutes of flight it represented to keep his mind off the clouds over England. Meanwhile, Sailor returned to the astrodome to get another fix. They changed course again and repeated the procedure every fifteen minutes.

The time ticked by. The starboard fuel tank was definitely draining faster than normal. "Engineer to pilot: I calculate we have only 30 minutes of fuel in the starboard secondary. There may be some fumes left in the primary tanks — say 40 minutes overall."

"And port tanks?"

"Twenty minutes more."

"Pilot to navigator: Is that going to be enough?"

"Should be, Skipper," Sailor still sounded utterly unperturbed.

They were flying over the clouds now, and Moran's sense of being hopelessly lost increased. The outer starboard engine sputtered. Moran adjusted the pitch and mixture until it resumed its steady droning.

Sailor called out a new course, and Moran looked at his watch. They might be over England – or not. And God alone knew where. If only they knew what the cloud base was....

Selkirk had been in a long slow glide for some time to help save fuel. They were now at 5,700 feet and starting to skim along the top of the clouds. Whisps in various strange shapes swept up like threatening monsters or ghosts. The Lancaster sliced silently through them although, now and then, short spasms of turbulence jolted them. "Pilot to navigator: Do you have an ETA?"

"We should be over Lincolnshire now, Skipper," Sailor reported. "Steer Two-Seven-Five."

Selkirk had evidently left his microphone on because Moran heard him take a deep breath. If he took them into the cloud and it went right down to the ground, they would crash at nearly 200 mph. If they jumped, however, they might still be over the sea and their chances of being found before they froze to death were practically nil.

"Captain to crew: Does anyone want to jump?" Selkirk asked.

"No, sir!" Hamed was the first to respond. One by one the others also opted to stay with J-Jig.

"OK, I'm going into the cloud," Selkirk told them.

They were at five thousand feet when they entered the murk. Moran stared at the altimeter as it unwound. 4,500, 4,000, 3,500 feet. They were still blinded by thick fog. 3,000, 2,500, 2,000 feet.

"Skipper to crew: I can see black through the cloud." Selkirk announced, and Moran realized he'd been holding his breath. Moran looked forward. Sure enough, the cloud was becoming patchy. At 1,800 feet they were in the clear and they were over land, but God knew where. Vernon had come forward to stand behind Selkirk and peer out of the cockpit window, while Hamed had stretched himself out beside his bombsight. Together with Selkirk that made three men scanning the countryside for landmarks.

Moran would have liked to join them, but the starboard inboard engine hiccupped and sputtered, starved of fuel. Moran switched the engine back over to the primary tank and it roared back into life. "Engineer to pilot: Estimate ten minutes of fuel in that engine, Skipper." Even as he spoke the starboard outer engine also lost power and he repeated the procedure.

The intercom clicked. "Rear gunner to pilot: I think I can see runways off our port beam."

They all looked.

Reggie confirmed. "Bob's right, Skipper. There's an airfield out there."

"It should be Faldingworth or Wickenby," Sailor told them confidently.

"Forgive me, Sailor," Selkirk remarked dryly, "but I really couldn't care less as long as we can land there. Engineer: fire a flare to indicate we are in trouble and without communication."

Moran found the very pistol, while Selkirk banked hard to port and pointed the nose for the nearest tip of runway.

"It's Wickenby all reet!" Hamed called up excitedly. "Look! There's the Red Lion and —"

"Pilot to bomb aimer: Got it. Wireless Operator, flash our ID and get permission to land."

Shortly afterwards, the flare path lit up, followed by a green for clearance.

"Prepare for landing!" Selkirk ordered.

There wasn't much time left. They were down to 1,000 feet and sinking fast. The earth seemed to be rushing towards them. Selkirk called for more flaps; Moran complied. Selkirk pulled up the nose and eased back on the throttles. They touched down, still a little too fast, but Selkirk judiciously applied the brakes, and they came to a halt with a hundred yards of runway still ahead of them.

Decorously, they turned the bomber off the runway and taxied back to their familiar hard-stand. Just before Kit could shut down the outer starboard engine, it died on its own accord for lack of fuel. As he turned off its magneto and closed its fuel valves, he felt a shudder go down his spine. His mother would say a cat had just walked across his grave.

Sailor reached the door before Moran and paused to grin at him with the remark, "Home to Kathleen, Kit. I told you I'd get you back every time." Then he stepped onto the ladder and descended to the tarmac.

Kit envied him for having a woman he wanted to return to. Sometimes he thought Fiona might be that woman, but then she'd say something that would make him unsure again.

Ashcroft Park, Easter 1943

Don and Kit brought Georgina and Fiona to Ashcroft Park. Their first tour of operations was over, and they had two weeks' leave that happened to coincide with Easter. Maggie, Don's sister, was also home with three of her university friends. She was reading English Literature at Oxford and had brought along her friend Lucy Edgecomb and two fellow students Paul Thurlow and Weldon Graham. The latter gentlemen were reading law. With a total of eight young people staying, Mrs. Selkirk was in her element. Kit had never seen her so happy.

Kit had warned Fiona that the Selkirks dressed for dinner, and she appeared for evening cocktails in a stunning, three-quarter length, green satin gown with side pleats. Kit was proud to be seen with her. She had also hit it off very well with Maggie, who hoped to teach English literature in secondary school. Georgina, though no less beautifully dressed, seemed shy and unsure of herself despite Mrs. Selkirk's and Don's best efforts to put her at ease.

The weather was unseasonably warm and by popular acclaim, they opted to have cocktails on the back terrace. Colonel Selkirk set up the bar and with expert aid from Weldon produced French 75s and Daiquiris. The sound of ice tinkling in glasses and the high-pitched, tittering laughter of the ladies was like an echo from a different age. "Reminds me of cocktails on the veranda of my lodge in Tanganyika," Colonel Selkirk remarked as he handed Kit his French 75. Kit smiled and admitted, "I was thinking almost the same thing."

"Don," Maggie called from the other side of the terrace, "what was the name of that horrid old professor? The one you were always on about? I'm sure it's the same man who is now tormenting poor Weldon."

Don responded by going to join the crowd gathered around Maggie and soon they were all laughing about something. Kit glanced at Georgina, who like him seemed left out. He gestured with his head for them to join the others.

Weldon Graham was apparently mimicking a professor the others knew and disliked. They were enjoying his satirical performance.

"You'd be marvellous at charades!" Fiona concluded with more admiration than Kit thought justified.

"Oh, yes!" Maggie agreed enthusiastically, "that's a splendid idea! Let's play charades after dinner."

Crowther appeared with a silver tray laden with cream-crackers garnished with pickled salmon. "Our own salmon," Colonel Selkirk announced proudly. "Had a wonderful year so far. More salmon than we can eat. If you like, we could do some fishing tomorrow."

"I've never fished for salmon," Kit admitted as he took one of the crackers, "but I'd be like to learn."

"You'll like it, my boy," the Colonel assured him with an affectionate pat on the back.

"Fishing?" Paul Thurlow asked. "Oh, no! Definitely not for me. Far too smelly and wet." The way he said it made the others laugh. "I think I'll stay at home and amuse the ladies."

"I'd like to go fishing," Fiona announced.

"No, you wouldn't, darling. You just don't know what you're talking about," Paul told her. "I assure you it's boring, smelly and miserably uncomfortable standing about in the water for hours. You'll be wretched and you'll have to soak in a tub afterwards to warm up and get the smell of fish off you."

"Well, I won't know until I've tried it myself," Fiona insisted.

Weldon turned to Kit. "So, you're a friend of Don's, I hear. Trinity College together?" Don had completed a law degree before joining the RAF.

"No, the RAF," Kit admitted.

"Oh." Weldon sounded surprised by that but recovered quickly and asked. "So, can the RAF bomb Hitler into surrender as that man what's-his-name maintains? That's what I want to know. I mean, if we don't do something, this war will go on forever! I was briefly hopeful that the Soviet Union would put Hitler out of action, or the United States would give him his comeuppance, but the Germans are half-way to the Urals and the Americans are getting their ships blown out of the water all across the Pacific. If something doesn't stop the Germans and Japanese soon, I'll have completed my degree and will lose my exemption from military service."

"Well, the Soviets did just destroy an entire German army at Stalingrad," Colonel Selkirk pointed out in an indignant tone that Kit thought had more to do with Weldon's attitude toward military service than what he'd said about the war. "And —

"Oh, please, Daddy! Let's not talk about the war." Maggie interceded, adding pointedly to her guest, "And you, Weldon, should be ashamed! You promised me you wouldn't talk about the war either! This is supposed to be an oasis of peace and sanity,"

Mrs. Selkirk took the opportunity to clap her hands. "Exactly. And now, I think, is as good a time as any to make a special announcement, don't you, Darling?" She smiled at Don and he made a gesture of helpless surrender.

"Ladies and gentlemen, Colonel Selkirk and I are extremely pleased and delighted to welcome a new member to our family." She held her hand out to Georgina, who, blushing, moved to take it. With her arm around Georgina's waist, Mrs Selkirk continued. "Miss Georgina Reddings has consented to marry our beloved Donald." She held out her hand to Don, and he came forward to stand on his mother's other side. Despite being in his own home, Don still looked uncomfortable, as though even this much attention embarrassed him.

"Let's drink a toast to Georgina and Don! What a beautiful couple they make!"

They all happily lifted their glasses and called out "Georgina and Don!"

Later that evening, after dinner, Mrs. Selkirk settled down at the grand piano and played Chopin. She was an excellent pianist, and the room was lit only by a fire in the open fireplace, the candles in the chandelier overhead and candles flanking the sheet music. Because his mother played too, Kit was reminded of home and all the evenings when they had no other entertainment but his mother's music. Gradually, however, even those thoughts yielded to a more profound sense of peace that was beyond conscious thought. The clear notes of the haunting melody and the flickering, golden light from the fire became other-worldly. Kit's breathing grew slower, and he seemed almost to float, disconnected from time and place.

Gradually, however, the magic was disturbed by Maggie and her friends, who were speaking in sign-language to one another, evidently tired of the concert, while Colonel Selkirk snored softly, slumped over in his seat. Even Don looked a little bored. Only Georgina was enraptured by the music, and in that instant, Kit caught a glimpse of what Don saw in her. In her elegant blue gown with a single string of pearls at her neck and the firelight playing across her face, she did not look the least bit "mousy." She was as beautiful in that moment as Chopin's music.

Mrs. Selkirk ended the piece and, with a reproachful glance at her daughter, she closed the keyboard. "Time for charades," she suggested.

Kit had never enjoyed charades as much as he did that evening. They played ladies against gentlemen and the rivalry was delightful, witty, and entertaining. Everyone laughed a great deal. However, when the grandfather clock in the drawing room struck midnight, Colonel and Mrs Selkirk announced it was time for bed. "Anyone for fishing tomorrow needs a good night's sleep," the Colonel reminded them.

"We'll be up shortly," Maggie promised, although Georgina excused herself immediately and followed the Selkirks up the stairs.

"Let's have a nightcap," Maggie suggested, and Weldon obliged by going over to the drinks cabinet to see what was on hand.

"I think I'll turn in too," Don announced and departed.

"That's what getting engaged will do to you," Paul drawled. "Not even married yet, and he's already an old fuddy-duddy."

Kit briefly wanted to point out that Don never stayed up late and never drank too much. Don took his responsibility for the lives of six other men seriously. He felt he owed it to his crew to be mentally and physically fit for each flight, whether it was an operational or training flight. Yet it was obvious that in this company Don's qualities as a Lancaster skipper were not valued. The best Kit could do was stand and depart too.

Fiona stopped him. "Oh, there's no need to go to bed yet! What's the harm in another drink or two? You're not engaged."

"No," Kit sat down uneasily, torn between the desire to back Don and the desire to please Fiona.

"If you drink enough, you'll sleep in and miss the fishing trip," Paul assured Fiona with a smile.

"Rather than fishing," Maggie sat up pertly, "why don't we go for a ride instead? Our neighbours have six or seven hunters and they're not getting enough exercise now that the boys are off serving somewhere." She made a dismissive gesture with her hand. "They'd be delighted to have us come over and take them out. You do ride, don't you, Fiona?"

"I love it, but I didn't bring any riding clothes."

"You might fit into mother's things. I'm sure we can work something out. What about Georgina?"

"She's mad about horses! Owns two of her own, I think, and she hunts." Fiona answered.

"Kit, what about you?"

"I think I'll going fishing instead."

"Suit yourself."

They started chatting about horses and hunting to hounds, something that Kit had never done and had no intention of doing. He started to feel superfluous and out of place again. He emptied his glass and stood. "Well, I'm turning in. See you in the morning."

This time, Fiona stood with him and took his arm. They started up the stairs together. When they reached the door to Fiona's room, he took her in his arms, and they kissed more passionately than ever before.

Abruptly she broke it off and drew back. "Kit, don't take this the wrong way, but I don't want you to get any ideas from Georgina and Don's engagement. Georgina, you know, is the type of girl who thinks a woman's place is at the side of some man. She thinks marriage is the only thing that can give a woman fulfilment." Fiona's tone was bitingly contemptuous. "I'm not like that. I don't want to get married — at least not in the foreseeable future. I want to live first. It's nothing personal. I don't want to commit myself to anyone. It's just that I think there's more to life than being the appendage to some man."

"That's fine by me," Kit told her with a smile and a shrug. "I hadn't planned on proposing." He left her standing in the hallway and walked away unsure whether that was true or not.

Chapter 7

NYDN Centre Torquay,
4 December 1943

Kit had been at the NYDN centre a week. It was getting boring. So boring, in fact, that he found himself sleeping a great deal. It helped that his roommate had disappeared. No one said where or what would become of him. Kit presumed they would billet some newcomer on him, but in the meantime, he had Room 24 to himself. He was amazed to discover that he could sleep without dreams. It was almost like being dead, and when he awoke, he felt both calmer and stronger.

He arrived at his Monday afternoon meeting with Dr Grace feeling almost good. Unconsciously, he smiled as he came in.

"Well, that's better," Dr Grace remarked, returning his smile. "Did something happen?"

"I've been sleeping better."

"That's excellent." The doctor settled himself on the front of the desk, one leg swinging slightly. "What about appetite? Has that returned?"

"Yes, I suppose so."

"You don't have to eat in, you know. There are several good restaurants I can recommend, if you like."

"That's a good idea." Who wanted to sit around in a room with other young men who had failed and were facing a dismal future?

The doctor turned and picked up the files, opening them in front of him. "Today I thought we might talk about something positive. You were awarded the DFM in April 1943. Do you want to tell me about that?"

"Not particularly."

"Why not? Aren't you proud of it?"

"Proud?" Kit thought about that and then admitted. "I was pleased to get recognition for doing my job well. It made me feel good that my efforts had been recognized and appreciated. But..." he shrugged, "I don't understand the system for awarding gongs. It doesn't seem fair. There don't seem to be any objective criteria."

"They are widely seen as recognition of exceptional courage," Dr Grace pointed out gently.

"Courage? Exceptional courage?" Kit asked back as if he couldn't imagine that. Then he shook his head. "That can't be."

"Why not?"

"Well, for example, on my first tour we flew with the same two gunners on all but two flights. One, Bob Pickett, got a DFM, but the other Reggie Allwright got nothing. Yet they were both doing the same job in the same aircraft on the same flights. How can that be fair?"

"There must have been some difference between them."

"Yes, of course. Pickett claimed four German fighters."

"That's very good."

"Yes, it is, but Bob was young, exuberant and ambitious. He was a crack shot. He was a natural gunman and he had exceptionally sharp eyes which he used to good effect. He could identify aircraft that I could hardly see. Most importantly, he wanted to make kills, and he prided himself on his marksmanship. Shooting a Jerry down was important to him. He was cock-a-loop the first time he succeeded — shouting so loudly over the intercom that the skipper had to beg him to tone down. But you know, although we loyally confirmed his claims, we were lying. We were all doing our own jobs. We were still in German airspace. We were surrounded by flak and more fighters were still out there. None of us could know for sure that his 'wild boar' [1] crashed."

Dr Grace raised his eyebrows. "Are you saying you think most medals are given away based on fraudulent claims?"

"That's not the point. It's just that Reggie, our Mid-Upper gunner, was a different sort of man. He was older, more modest, more sober. He never

---

1 Wild boars were day fighters, usually single-engine Me109s that attacked the bomber stream using the light of the flares, searchlights and fires from the bombing, rather than being guided by radar.

claimed anything, but he was up there in that turret for hours. He protected us as fiercely as Bob did, if not better. He was tireless, determined and very focused, but — well — he wouldn't have dreamt of making a claim he wasn't absolutely sure about. In fact, I'm not sure he would have claimed a kill even if he was sure about it. Kills didn't matter to him as long as we got home safely. They certainly didn't 'define' him. But he was every bit as courageous as Bob Pickett. Surely you see that?"

"Yes, I do," Dr Grace conceded. "But at the moment I'm more interested in hearing how you got your DFM — and whether you think you demonstrated courage in the actions noted in the citation."

"Courage?" Kit asked again.

"Yes." Dr Grace met his gaze steadily.

"I thought everyone agreed that I was a coward," Kit rebutted.

"I don't know who 'everyone' is, but I certainly haven't agreed with that. And, not to put too fine a point on it, His Majesty King George VI awarded you a DFM for exceptional courage. Unless you, your skipper, your squadron leader and your station commander all lied about what you did, I'd say the evidence is in favour of you having done something courageous by the standards of your profession — which, I might add, are very high."

Kit looked down at his hands. His fingernails needed filing. He drew a deep breath. "I'll tell you what happened, and you tell me if I was courageous — or just doing what I had to do."

Operation to Magdeburg,
March 1943

They had dropped their load over Magdeburg and just started their run for home, still in the flare-lightened skies over the target, when a 'wild boar' night fighter found them. The tracers lit up the night, slow at first and then faster as they flashed past or thudded into the skin of the Lancaster.

Hamed was firing from the forward gun, Allwright from the mid-upper, and Pickett tried to catch the German fighter as it shot past and turned to make another run. The chattering of the Lancaster's guns and the smell of cordite filled the fuselage. Selkirk took evasive action to upset the fighter's aim, but he circled around again.

On the second run, despite Selkirk's corkscrewing, his cannons found the port outboard engine, and it burst into flame. The fighter passed so close overhead that Moran ducked instinctively even as he focused on cutting the fuel and pumping foam over the burning engine. The extinguisher dampened but failed to entirely douse the flames that soon started to lick along the wing toward the fuel tanks.

The guns shook the Lancaster as the Me109 made a third pass, but all Kit could think about was that if the flames reached the fuel tanks, the whole wing would be engulfed in flame. He opened the secondary tanks to drain the fuel off into the night, and the port inner, starved of fuel, cut out. But the flames from the outer engine were still spreading inward. Moran called to Selkirk. "Engineer to pilot: We have to dive to put the fire out."

Selkirk didn't waste time answering. He kicked the four-engine bomber into a flick half-roll and then pushed the nose down so hard it felt as though they were at the vertical. Although the Me109 tried to follow them down, Pickett got a good bead on him. He pumped enough lead at him for the German to draw back, and then they started spinning. Pickett couldn't fire after that, but they must have looked like they were finished because the Me109 turned away.

Meanwhile, the flames still burned all along the forward edge of the wing. They were small, blue, and the wind was forcing them backwards, but they flickered ominously in the night. Moran glanced at the altimeter, and saw they were eating up altitude at an alarming rate. He returned his attention to the wing. Eventually, the last trace of flame disappeared. "Fire's out, Skipper!" He called immediately.

Selkirk recovered from the spin, but for a horrible moment seemed unable to pull the nose up. It was as if the controls were frozen. The altimeter continued to unwind as the airframe protested with a thousand whines and creaks. This is it, Moran thought. We're going in. He glanced at the airspeed indicator: 320 mph.

Abruptly, Selkirk had the aircraft back under control, and he eased it out of the dive. They were at 4,800 feet and still over land but pointed in the wrong direction: deeper into Germany. With both port engines dead, Selkirk had to gently turn the big bomber around using only his starboard engines. He called to Sailor for a course.

"Give me two minutes, Skipper."

Before Sailor had completed his calculations, the intercom crackled, and Vernon's voice came loud and alarmed. "Skipper! Wireless Operator here! Reggie's been hurt!"

"Can you get him down and to the bed?"

"I'll try."

"Kit, go back and see if you can help."

Moran took oxygen and a torch and made his way back down the length of the fuselage, clambering over the main spar to reach the steps to the mid-upper turret. Wind was howling through a hole in that turret, stirring up tiny cyclones of dust that hit his eyes. The temperature was bitterly cold compared to forward. Pickett had come forward from his tail turret and was standing aft of the mid-upper turret, while Vernon stood forward of it. Together they were trying to ease Allright down.

Suddenly Reggie seemed to drop, knocking Leslie down, and Kit reached out to help. There was blood everywhere. In the darkness it was not red, just wet and sticky. It had splattered and smeared across Reggie's face, but the source was his shoulder and upper arm. The bleeding was so profuse that the heavily lined flight jacket was already saturated. Together, Bob, Leslie and Kit managed to lift Reggie and carry him forward to the rest bed behind the wireless operator's workstation. Once they had him there, they could see bone splinters were lodged in his chin. When they plugged him back onto oxygen, he struggled for breath.

Moran found the first aid kit, while Leslie and Bob tried to staunch the bleeding by wrapping blankets around Reggie tightly. Moran found the morphine syrette and opened Reggie's flying suit to stab the needle into his thigh. Reggie was shaking violently, whether from shock or cold was moot. Bob hooked Reggie's flying suit to the electricity again and connected his intercom as well. "You're going to be all right, Reggie," Bob told him. "You're going to be all right. We'll get you home."

Kit and Leslie used bandages to tie the blankets closer around him, pressing his arm, which had nearly been shot away, back into the socket. From outside the aircraft came the crack of flak. The aircraft dropped like a stone a couple hundred feet, then jinked sideways and started corkscrewing.

"You'd better get back to your gun, Bob," Kit advised.

The rear gunner was torn. He looked at Reggie shaking and pale on the bed, then glanced down toward his position in the tail. Flak burst around them again, briefly lighting up the interior of the aircraft, exposing the metal frame and the various control wires. Reluctantly, Bob nodded and returned to the rear gun.

Kit put his hand on Reggie's good shoulder, and the gunner opened his eyes. "I had so hoped to see Toby grow up," he told Kit. Toby was his five-year-old son.

"You will."

Reggie just smiled sadly and closed his eyes.

"I'm going forward to make sure the skipper doesn't need anything. I'll be back."

Reggie nodded.

Back in the cockpit, Moran first stood behind Selkirk to look forward out of the cockpit window. The Dutch coastline was visible ahead of them. Just another five minutes or so of flak. Then he turned to look out toward their damaged engine and his heart missed a beat. The fire had evidently weakened the engine's housing and the shaking from the flak had torn it loose with each violent jerk and bump. He could see rivets popping and the metal curling down under the weight of the engine.

Moran looked towards Selkirk struggling with the controls, and then returned to his station to check the engine readings. A burst of flak went off right in front of them. The light blinded Kit for a second, and cold air rushed past. The flak must have punched a hole in the Perspex somewhere.

"Pilot to bomb aimer: Are you all right?"

"Wye-aye, sir," Hamed answered.

Moran tried to concentrate on his instruments, but the wind coming from forward was distracting. They needed to plug the holes, or they'd all freeze to death. He looked around and found some packages of "window" they'd neglected to throw overboard on one trip or other. He took these down into the nose, and together with Hamed plugged every hole they could find with them. As they worked, they heard over the intercom, "Navigator to pilot: steer two-five-oh."

"Two-five-oh, navigator. Engineer, I can't get her balanced. It's as though the port wing were dragging."

Moran pressed his microphone and gave Selkirk the bad news. "It is. The outer engine's been shaken loose. It's hanging down several inches."

When Moran came back up out of the nose, Selkirk gestured him closer and unclipped his mask long enough to ask without using the intercom. "Can we make it?"

Answering in the same fashion, Kit told him: "We have to. Reggie can't jump."

Selkirk clipped the mask back over his face and tried to climb, but the Lancaster just wouldn't respond. The best he could do was hold their altitude at 4,000 feet and Selkirk was fighting hard to keep the heavy bomber on course. His breathing was so heavy that Moran could hear him, and his leg seemed to tremble in spasms.

Moran got up and looked more closely at Selkirk's legs. Something glistened in the dark, below his knees. He unclipped his mask with the intercom. "Have you been hit?"

"My left leg is peppered with shrapnel from that flak burst that almost hit our nose."

Moran's first thought was that he should bandage the leg, then he remembered they'd just used up all their bandages on Reggie. How stupid of them.

Selkirk spoke into his thoughts, "Go check on, Reggie."

Moran did as he was told, thinking he'd check again for another roll of bandages.

The gunner was still lucid. "How bad is the damage, Kit?" He asked, as Kit rummaged through the first aid bin.

There were no more bandages, but Kit found another dose of morphine. He pocketed it as he reported to Reggie, "we've lost both port engines, and the Lanc won't climb above four thousand feet."

"The rest of you'd better get out," Reggie suggested.

"Are you crazy? We'd be dead in minutes down there. We'll make it."

"Toby wants a pony," Reggie answered. "I promised him one for his sixth birthday. That's only five months away. My Dad has been looking for something suitable." Reggie had grown up on a farm, and his father still ploughed with horses. "Maybe Dot will let him live with my parents," Reggie speculated. Kit knew that Reggie's wife Dot had threatened to leave him more than once, and Reggie had been cheating on her regularly. The only thing holding them together was their son Toby. "I think Toby would be happy there."

"Reggie, you aren't dead yet."

"It's a terrible thing to kill a man, Kit."

Moran didn't know what to say to that.

"Doesn't it ever bother you that we are killing people? I tell myself they are Nazis and all, but there must be little boys like Toby down there too."

"Yes, I expect there are," Moran admitted.

"They killed my grandmother. Back in 1940." Reggie spoke slowly, with long gaps between the phrases. "Just an old woman. Living in a cottage. Middle of nowhere, really. Maybe the bomber was lost. It was cloudy. They told me. Maybe he pitched his bombs. Because he was in trouble. Didn't want to crash-land with the bombs. I don't know. Made me angry. At the time. Thought I'd get even."

Damn, damn, damn, Moran was thinking. It was their 30th operational flight. Their last. They had almost made it....

"Bomb aimer to pilot: there's a convoy down there. I just counted 27 merchantmen and five escorts."

"I see her," Selkirk's voice sounded strained and faint.

"Skipper, Sailor here: If we jump alongside her, we'll almost certainly be picked up. Leslie's got the VHF frequency for alerting Navy rescue. I'm happy to hold on to Reggie and make sure he makes it down all right."

"We'll get his chute clipped on and jump together," Leslie joined in.

"I can hold him up once we're in the water," Sailor continued. "I've done it before." Kit remembered Sailor saying that when his ship had gone down, he'd kept an injured crewman from drowning by holding him upright for several hours until they were picked up by the only lifeboat that got away.

"Reggie? It's your call. Do you want to try jumping with Sailor and Leslie, or stay with me and the aircraft?"

"You're going to fly her home, Skipper?" Reggie asked over the intercom, but his eyes were directed at Kit. The Flight Engineer nodded.

"I'm going to try," Selkirk answered, adding, "but we've lost both port engines. You may be better off taking your chances with Sailor." He said nothing about his own injuries.

Reggie shook his head to Moran, removing the mask to mutter. "I can't swim, Kit. Never learnt. I'd panic down there. If the skipper is going to try to land, I'll take my chances with him."

Moran pushed the mic button. "Flight engineer to pilot: Reggie's staying with you."

"Understood. Wireless operator, give our position to the Royal Navy. Anyone who wants to jump, go aft now. You too Hamed. Use the aft hatch all of you. I'll hold her straight and level until you're all safely out."

At once, the doors to the tail turret opened, Pickett backed out, grabbed his waiting 'chute and came forward. He bent over Reggie and declared. "You can trust the Skipper, Reggie. He'll get you home. I'll come and visit you in sick-quarters as soon as the fishheads put us ashore!" He sounded cheerful enough, but he wasn't lingering either. With his parachute already clipped in place, he returned to the entrance on the port side of the aircraft and jettisoned the door. A gust of wind immediately sucked anything not pinned down towards the tail. Pickett stepped out and the tail of the Lancaster lifted slightly.

Meanwhile, Leslie had come out of his station. "Kit, come here!" he ordered. Moran joined him at his worktable. He'd written down the frequencies for Wickenby and Oulton, as well as instructions for making a "Darky" (emergency) call. "Oulton's closer," he stressed. "And in case your Morse code is a little rusty. This is our call sign. Got it?"

"I can manage."

"Good luck!" Then Vernon took his parachute and moved aft to follow Pickett out of the aircraft.

Sailor was next. "Leslie's right, Kit. Oulton is closer. Here's the latest course for it. ETA twenty minutes or a little more. If you miss it, there are three more stations just slightly further inland. Give a 'Darky call' and see who answers. Have them shoot a flare to show you exactly where they are and then aim for it."

Moran nodded.

"You understand don't you, Kit? I've got Kathleen and Hope to think of."

Moran understood perfectly. If it hadn't been their last operational flight of the tour, it might have been different, but the thought of dying now, at the very last minute, was too much. "Of course," he answered. "Go."

Teddy Hamed shook his hand as he went by, and patted Reggie on the shoulder. Kit wasn't sure, but he thought the teenager was fighting back tears. He could feel the Lancaster lift as each of them stepped out into the night sky. Kit followed them until he was about three feet from the open door, then he went down on his knees and waddled forward until he could see out of the open door. Four parachutes hung in a ragged line, drifting gracefully down toward the convoy. As he watched, a searchlight swung up from one of the escorts and found one of the parachutes. He could hear a loud siren bleating, and one of the escorts veered away from the convoy in the direction of the parachutes. They were going to make it.

He fought his way back up the length of the fuselage, clambered over the main spar. He put his hand on Reggie's shoulder as he passed him without stopping. As he entered the cockpit, Selkirk called out. "Who's there?"

"It's me, Don."

"Kit? Why didn't you jump?"

"Because you can't bring this crate safely home on your own."

Selkirk didn't answer. Moran stood directly behind him, and realized Don's gloves were dark and wet, evidently from touching the wounds in his leg. "Do you want morphine for the wound?" Kit started digging in his pocket for the syringe.

"No."

"Then at least put it on autopilot steering two-two-oh, that's the course for Oulton, and save you strength for landing."

"The autopilot can't cope with two engines out on the same side. She takes constant rudder."

"OK. I'm going down to the bomb aimer's compartment. I can reach up and hang on to the rudder bar from there for a bit. You need to save your strength for landing."

Moran did as promised. It was a strange feeling hanging onto the rudder bar and gazing out of the glass nose as the North Sea inched by below him.

When the English coast came up, Selkirk called, "I've got her, Kit. Go back and give a May Day call."

Moran released the rudder bar, climbed back through the cockpit to the wireless station and put out the May Day call, requesting a flare. He next checked the readings on the dials at his own station. The starboard engines were working perfectly, and they had enough fuel for another forty minutes, maybe more.

He took his torch and flashed it along the damaged wing to see how things looked. The surface was charred. The outer engine was still hanging down several inches, but not noticeably more than before. Finally, he went back to Reggie. "We've got the coast in sight."

"Good show," Reggie answered in a whisper.

"You aren't slipping away from us, are you?" Kit asked.

Reggie shook his head. "No. I've got to give Toby his pony."

"That's right."

Moran went back to the radio. Someone was trying to raise them in a voice that sounded slightly alarmed. "Come in UM-J-Jig. This is Oulton. What is your condition?"

"This is UM-J-Jig. Port engines u/s. Skipper wounded. Other wounded on board."

"UM-J-Jig. You are very faint. Can you repeat, please?"

Moran did and again requested a flare.

He was given a slightly different course, which he passed on to Selkirk.

Shortly afterward, Selkirk reported seeing the flare, and Moran returned to the cockpit to assist with the flaps and undercarriage. Before going forward, he checked once more on Reggie, strapping him in for landing.

"OK, Reggie?"

"In view of the circumstances, just dandy."

"We're almost there now."

Reggie nodded.

When Moran reached the cockpit, they were down to 2,000 feet, and the flare path was lit up ahead of them. Selkirk said tightly. "Kit, I need you to throttle back the engines and give me flaps 10."

Moran obeyed, trying to ignore the fact that the aircraft was yawing badly as Selkirk fought with the controls. He lowered the undercarriage from his own station, and then turned his attention back to the throttles.

The runway lights rushed toward them, but they were much too high. This wasn't going to be a landing; it was going to be prang. Without awaiting Selkirk's order, Moran pushed on more flaps. Selkirk tried to lift the nose and stall out over the end of the runway. Moran instantly ducked down behind Don's seat and clung to it as they crashed. The next thing Moran knew, they were in a flat spin with pieces of aircraft and rocks crashing against the outer skin, metal screaming and the whole world shuddering around him. After an eternity, the aircraft came to rest, leaning at an awkward angle. The only sound was of something dripping somewhere — and the howl of the approaching meat wagon.

"Don?" Kit looked up and saw Selkirk sitting hunched over the steering column. But at the sound of his name, he roused himself. "I'm fine." He pressed the mask to his face and called into the intercom. "Reggie, are you OK? Reggie?"

There was no answer. "Kit, go back and see about Reggie."

With difficulty Moran worked his way back toward the bed. The Lancaster seemed to be bent. "Reggie? Reggie?"

"I'm here, Kit," Reggie answered. Apparently, it was only his intercom that wasn't working. "Did the skipper make it?"

"Yes."

A brilliant light flashed inside, nearly blinding Moran. It was a torch held by a medic at the door. "Hello? Hello? Anyone alive?" A voice asked.

"Yes. Two wounded. One here and the skipper in the cockpit. The other four crewmen jumped on the skipper's orders."

The medics climbed in through the crew door with a stretcher.

They had done it. They had completed thirty operational flights.

Selkirk was awarded the DFC and promoted to Flying Officer, while Moran was given the DFM and recommended for a commission. Reggie Allwright lost his arm and was invalided out of the service.

Chapter 8

NYDN Centre Torquay, 6 December 1943

The sun was out again, and Moran went for a long walk beside the shore before his next session with Dr Grace. He used it to try to sort things out in his own head. He was feeling increasingly confused about what he was doing here and why. If they were going to humiliate and discharge him, why not just get it over with? Or was he truly mad and he just didn't recognize it?

He arrived at the doctor's office with wind-ruffled hair and flushed cheeks.

"Been out for walk?" Dr Grace asked cheerfully on seeing him.

"Yes. Sometimes I feel as if the sea air can blow the cobwebs from my mind."

"Did it?"

Moran shook his head, "not really."

"Maybe I can help shake them loose," Dr Grace suggested.

Moran nodded. Talking did seem to help.

This time Dr Grace did not start with his medical records. Instead, leaning back in his chair with his hands clasped behind his head he remarked. "One thing that has struck me about you, Pilot Officer Moran, is that you have a very strong inner compass. You go your own way, it seems to me, regardless of what the world around you thinks or does."

Moran was inwardly startled by the observation. It hadn't always been that way. As a child, yes, and when he first came to England largely because he didn't have any choice. He was so different from everyone else. But when he first joined the RAF there had been a period when he had been happy to submerge in the crowd — maybe because it was the first time he could? In England no one knew — and he wasn't sure they would have cared — that his grandmother was African. Only slowly had he become conscious that "fitting in" was play-acting. He was different from the others no matter what he pretended. When he'd found Don and the Selkirks, he had believed he could be himself again. In answer to Dr Grace he said simply, "I suppose so."

"So why did you volunteer?"

"For what? The RAF?"

"Yes, let's start with that. You had a good job, earning a reasonable wage — for your age and qualifications. Why give that up to become a lowly erk? I don't think in your case it was because it was what everyone else was doing."

"No, it wasn't that everyone else was doing it, but by then I'd been an apprentice engineer for two years and I'd become disillusioned with civil engineering. The work itself was quite interesting, but I'd learnt that very few civil engineers work on daring, innovative or important projects. They do what they are paid to do, and most of the time that is boring work like pedestrian bridges, flyovers or suburban drainage ditches. I was already thinking about changing to mechanical engineering, and I thought aerial engines would be particularly interesting. I just hadn't worked out how to go about escaping the job I was in.

"When the war came along, it acted like a catalyst. After all, no one could object to me signing up with the RAF. Besides, it was history in the making. I mean, who doesn't want to take part in history? I certainly did. I also thought Hitler needed to be taught a lesson and was happy to do my part to achieve that aim. Last but not least, I expected conscription would come eventually and I didn't want to land in the army."

"That makes sense," Dr Grace agreed nodding, and then asked evidently somewhat surprised, "So, you never particularly wanted to fly?"

"I didn't say that. I would have liked to learn to fly, but the recruiter said there was a very long list of young men seeking flying training and that it might be many months before I was called up. On the other hand, due to a shortage of fitters and riggers, I could start right away if I mustered for training in either of those trades. That suited my impatient nature." Moran smiled deprecatingly.

"How old were you?" Dr Grace asked.

"Let me see, September 1939, I was 19."

"I haven't met a lot of patient 19-year-olds in my life," Dr Grace remarked, and they both laughed. When the laughter died away, Dr Grace noted, "However, that begs the question, why did you volunteer for aircrew a couple of years later?"

"That was more serious," Kit admitted.

"Meaning?"

"By then I'd watched a lot of young men die." He paused before adding, "I think pilots underestimate the degree to which ground crew get attached to their pilots. I joined 56 Squadron at the tail end of the Battle of Britain. No. 56 Squadron had been pulled out of 11 Group on September 1 — an indication of how badly they'd been mauled. The Chiefy was — how do I word this? — he was like a boxer who'd taken too many blows. The younger blokes told me stories too — bit by bit, at odd times, over a pint. And then it happened to me.

"I'd been looking after G-George, which was regularly flown by a young Sergeant Pilot. He was a fresh young man, about my age but with a lot less experience in life. He used to ask for my advice on how to chat up girls!" Moran gave a half laugh and shook his head at the memory.

Dr Grace did not interrupt him, just let him talk.

"They called him Dobby for some reason. He had a wonderful, crooked smile that lit up his rather ugly face, and he couldn't seem to keep his hair out of his eyes. He was addicted to Black Cats — the cigarettes — but never lit up without offering me one. I liked him without reservation, and I would have lied for him if he'd let me." Feeling that required an explanation, Moran added, "There was a flight which he broke off because he thought his radio was malfunctioning, but he'd simply hooked it up wrong. Pete, the rigger, and I were willing to say we'd found a problem, but he wouldn't have it. He was a good bloke." Moran fell silent.

"And he bought it," Dr Grace concluded.

Moran nodded. "The squadron was scrambled and disappeared. After about forty-five minutes, we ground crews started to interrupt whatever we were doing and emerge onto the field. We hung about, watching the sky. Dobby had tossed me a nearly empty packet of Black Cats as he mounted, so I snitched one and lit up, keeping down wind of the hangar and bowsers. Eventually, we heard the engines. You could tell right away there were too few of them. I dropped and crushed the cigarette and scanned the sky more intently. Finally, we saw them and counted eight Hurricanes. Then another two lurched in, one gushing glycol. But two were missing and G-George was one of them. Dobby's Flight Commander saw me standing there looking bewildered, and he walked over. 'Dobby won't be coming back,' he told me. I must have looked upset because he added, 'It wasn't anything you did. The 109s fell on us out of the sun, and the leader with his wingman picked on Dobby. Between them they got the fuel tank.'" Moran paused and Dr Grace chose not to say anything.

"I was assigned a new aircraft the same day, and a week later there was another fresh young pilot flying it regularly. He was nice in a different way. Very quiet and conscientious. He sometimes asked me to explain things about the engine to him. He seemed anxious to know how to handle an emergency. I gave him some tips about fuel mixtures and whatnot. Told him what to worry about. He only lasted a couple of months before he was killed in an accident.

"I thought things would be better with a Mosquito Squadron, but while the casualties were fewer, it meant we had more time to get attached to our pilots before they went for six."

Moran went silent after this remark, so Dr Grace posed his question again, "and, yet, knowing the risks, you volunteered for aircrew. Why was that? What were you hoping for?"

"Nothing. I had interesting work. There were dances, flicks and musical shows every week. Girls were plentiful, if you weren't choosy and only interested in a good time for the moment. I was getting steady promotions and pay raises, and I didn't have any worries: a roof over my head, plenty of food, and skills that I knew I could eventually use in civilian life. When I thought about my father's stories from the last war, it didn't feel like war at all. Not that he'd talked a lot about his war experiences, but he'd said enough to make me know that what I had as an RAF fitter was jolly good."

"But not good enough, apparently," Dr Grace observed.

"It was a good life, not a satisfying one."

"What's the difference?"

"I didn't feel good about myself."

"About yourself?"

"I felt I wasn't doing enough."

"What? But as a fitter you were doing a vitally important job." Moran stared at him, so Dr Grace expanded on his statement. "If you'd been an entertainer for the troops, a batman, a supply clerk or the like, I might be able to see your point of view. But an aircraft fitter is a highly skilled and critical job, a job that contributes every bit as directly to the war effort as flying."

"I'm not saying the job isn't important. I'm talking about my sense of self-worth. I didn't like feeling inferior."

"Inferior? To whom?"

"Aircrew."

"But fitters are far more qualified than air gunners or bomb aimers, for example."

"Yes, but at some point, I started to ask myself how I could go on living my safe and comfy life while other men were putting theirs at risk. Why should they risk their lives and not me? I started to ask myself, if I wasn't man enough to do what they did."

"Are you suggesting that courage is the measure of a man?"

"Isn't it?" Moran shot back. Their eyes locked for several seconds.

Gently, Dr Grace shook his head and with a small smile replied. "I'm not prepared to make that judgement. It seems to me there are many other admirable, manly qualities: honesty, trustworthiness, diligence, compassion, charity, a sense of responsibility for those less fortunate or less powerful than ourselves. I'm sure there are many more that I can't think of at the moment."

"Undoubtedly, those are all fine qualities. Yet, strip away the cultural niceties, and look at the core of how we define a man. From the Iliad and the knights of the Round Table to Nelson at Trafalgar, courage is the essential characteristic of a hero, isn't it? A hero can be poor, ugly, even lame, but he cannot be a coward."

"And you wanted to be a hero?"

"No. I didn't want to be hero!" Moran spat back angrily. "I didn't delude myself that I was exceptional in any way! I just wanted to show to myself that I could face the same risks as those young pilots who had died in my aircraft and the other aircrew I saw going out every might."

Dr Grace nodded. Drew a deep breath and got up to go back behind his desk. He sat down. He clasped his hands together, his elbows on the desk. "You certainly proved all that — with your first tour: 30 operational flights, several of them very difficult. DFM. Why the second tour?"

Moran was reminded that he'd been asked that once before.

Ashcroft Park,
Late September 1943

Kit got leave at short notice and Don didn't, so Kit went to Ashcroft Park alone. On arrival, he discovered that Colonel and Mrs. Selkirk were rushing off to visit a relative who'd had a stroke; they wanted to give his wife some moral support. The Selkirks assured Kit he was perfectly welcome to stay, adding Maggie was expected later in the day so he wouldn't be entirely bored. It was too late for a change of plans anyway, so Kit settled into his room and then took the Selkirk dogs for a walk. It was a splendid autumn day with the trees starting to turn shades of gold and rust, but the grass still green.

On returning to the manor, he found that Maggie had indeed arrived and been informed of his presence by Crowther. She seemed happy to see him, saying she'd dreaded a boring weekend since none of her friends from Oxford had been able to join her. "Lucy seems to be getting awfully serious about Paul," she complained. "They do more and more things on their own, leaving me out."

"And you aren't that keen on Weldon Graham?" Kit asked without thinking.

"Weldon? I don't know.... Do you think we're suited to each other?"

"I don't know him well enough to judge."

"Oh, you sound just like Don — evading straight answers. Let's have a cocktail. Can you make a Mint Julep?"

"No, but I could manage a Gin and Tonic, a Cuba Libre or a Vodka

Sour — assuming your father's drinks cabinet is adequately provisioned."

"I don't think he goes in for Coca Cola, but we should have gin, tonic, vodka and lemon juice. I'll have the vodka sour."

They moved into the well-appointed "smoking room" that also contained the expansive drinks cabinet and bar. Kit, feeling a little like an impostor but encouraged by Maggie, opened the cabinet and found the ingredients, while Maggie asked Crowther to bring them ice.

As they settled onto the couch to sip their drinks, Maggie remarked, "I haven't seen much of Fiona recently. Aren't you seeing each other anymore?"

"Oh, we still try to meet up now and again, but it isn't as easy since I was posted to Training Command. Don's hoping to get us posted back to 626 Squadron, however. If so, we would be close to Lincoln again."

"Are you serious about this second tour?" Maggie asked as if she couldn't believe him.

"Yes, of course."

"Why?" Maggie asked bluntly. Then before he could open his mouth to say anything, she demanded in an aggressive tone. "Don't you ever think about what you're doing? I mean, dropping tons of high explosive on people's heads."

Kit was taken aback by her attitude and the vehemence with which she spoke. He knew she would not have dared ask such a question in her father's presence, and he suspected she had not subjected Don to her outrage over bombing either. He was the target of her anger because she didn't particularly care what he thought of her. He tried to answer calmly. "We target military installations and war industries, things like aircraft and tank factories, U-boat pens, synthetic petroleum and rubber plants, steel mills and ammunition depots."

"Yes, and what about all the workers at those plants that just happen to be in the way?" Maggie added.

"We bomb at night."

"How civilized! So, you kill people in their beds rather than while they're standing up at the assembly line."

"At least we aren't targeting cultural monuments like the Nazis did."

"Ah, yes, the Baedeker Raids, a justification for lowering ourselves to Hitler's level," she retorted sarcastically.

"We're not intentionally targeting the civilian population."

"Tell that to the people of Hamburg!"

"Look, Maggie, I don't think there's anything pretty about a fire storm. I've seen what London looks like, and Coventry too. I know what bombs can do, but we don't exactly have much alternative, do we? We can't defeat a continental power like Germany with our Navy. Our army was expelled from the continent in just six weeks after the Wehrmacht struck and is now helpless — unless you count a sideshow like North Africa. A bombing offensive is all we have. Aerial bombardment is a dull weapon. It's not precise. There is collateral damage. There are civilian casualties. I know. But it also happens to be the only weapon we have that can hit Germany at this moment. What would you have us do? Just sit back and let Hitler have his way on the Continent?"

"Frankly, I don't know," Maggie retorted belligerently, "and I don't think it is my job to know either! What I do think is that our leaders ought to have been cleverer than to get us into this mess in the first place!"

"You're probably right," Kit conceded, conscious that he was getting angry despite his best intentions not to, "but it's a little too late now! We've got this ruddy war, and we've got to find a way of ending it to our advantage."

"I don't see what's wrong with letting the Russians and Americans do the fighting. They have more resources."

"If you think you'd like the world that emerges from a Soviet victory, I think you're deluding yourself."

"We'll still have our Empire and America to keep the Soviets in check," Maggie countered. "That's the whole point, really. Let the Soviets and Nazis fight it out amongst themselves until they're both exhausted and bankrupt. Then we can pick up the pieces and rebuild the continent in a way that will keep both Russia and Germany down."

Kit didn't have an answer for that. He was an engineer not a politician. So, he opted out of the discussion altogether. "I don't think either of us is going to be forging British policy any time soon, so I think I'll just have another drink. What about you?"

"Oh, yes, please!" She held out her glass with a sweet smile that implicitly asked his forgiveness for her remarks. She was a lovely girl in her own way, and Kit wondered vaguely why he wasn't attracted to her. Maybe because he feared that he'd lose the Selkirks' good will if they thought he had his eye on their daughter. They liked him well enough — but not as a son-in-law. His tainted bloodlines would never pass muster.

He brought Maggie her refill. She had kicked off her shoes and curled her feet under herself on the sofa. She looked up at him with wide eyes as he handed her her drink.

"You know, Kit," she started in a gentle, reconciliatory tone, "I'd like you so much better if you didn't do what everyone expected of you."

"What do you mean?" He was genuinely puzzled.

"I mean, this volunteering for a Second Tour. It's so, you know, 'good form' and 'doing one's bit,' isn't it?"

"Is that the way you see it? That I'm just a useful idiot doing what's expected of me?"

"I wouldn't have put it that rudely, but, be frank, aren't you doing this just because it's expected of you? I mean, if you're brutally honest with yourself, isn't this more about proving something to your fellow officers and society at large? Isn't it, deep down, about living up to other people's expectations rather than acting on your own convictions?" Her eyes bored into him, demanding honesty, but they were not hostile eyes. To his surprise, he felt a surprising warmth in them, as though she genuinely cared.

"Well, since you put it like that, I suppose you're right. I am trying to live up to expectations, but not those of the RAF or the general public."

"Whose then?" Maggie asked confused.

"I volunteered for a Second Tour because your brother asked me to."

RAF Witchford,
Early-July 1943

Having wangled postings as instructors to the same HCU, Selkirk and Moran occasionally flew on the same training flights. Today's roughly eight-hour training mission entailed flying over two designated "points" at set times before swinging out over the North Sea where they were "intercepted" by fighters from a nearby RAF fighter OTU before finally returning to base.

For the early part of the flight, Selkirk kept Moran, the trainee pilot and trainee engineer busy by giving Moran pre-arranged signals to tinker with the engines causing first one and then another to fail. The trainees had to respond to these simulated "emergencies," receiving tips and advice as appropriate.

After making a turn with two engines out on the same side, the trainee navigator had to re-calculate their course to the second of the "targets." Only after passing this did Moran relax. Feeling like an airline passenger, he had time simply to enjoy the beauty of England in summer from the air. Selkirk suggested they lie down in the bomb aimer's bubble, where Selkirk pointed out various landmarks to Moran, who was not as familiar with the United Kingdom as the Englishman.

Once they crossed over the North Sea, however, there was nothing to see but water, so they returned to the cockpit. Moran squeezed behind the trainee engineer, scanning the dials for any sign of trouble. He was startled when the intercom switched on. "Mid-Upper Gunner to pilot: Aircraft to starboard, low."

"Low?" The pilot glanced up at Selkirk who was standing behind his seat. "I thought the day fighters tried to bounce us from above?"

"They're supposed to, but if they're scrambled late, they don't have time to gain height," Selkirk reminded him.

"It's not a fighter," the gunner's voice broke in on them. "I think it's a Flying Fortress, and it looks beaten up."

"Let's go and have a look," Selkirk suggested.

The pilot looked up questioningly, "Do you want to take over, sir?"

"Yes."

The trainee pilot put on the autopilot and climbed out of the pilot's seat, allowing Selkirk to take over the controls. Selkirk adjusted the seat for his height and then switched off the autopilot. He put the Lancaster into a gentle bank to starboard, while Moran scanned the sky. Sure enough, an American B-17 Flying Fortress was dragging itself across the sky from the Continent. Even from a distance, they could see the port outboard engine was charred and hanging down slightly while the starboard inboard engine had been feathered. The bomb aimer's bubble was completely shattered, probably from flak.

"Pilot to wireless operator: See if you can pick up communication from a Flying Fortress at this position."

"Yes, sir."

Selkirk intercepted obliquely, so they swung in slightly behind the Fortress and flew alongside her port side to get a comprehensive look at the damage. The tail was in tatters, the waist guns hung down, unmanned. Holes had been punched along the length of fuselage, obviously from a fighter, and a huge, charred gap yawed abaft of the wings. The hole in the fuselage was large enough for two or three people to stand up in. Moran guessed the aircraft had caught fire at this point and burnt for some time. As they came abreast of the cockpit, they saw the pilot slouched to one side, apparently dead or unconscious.

Selkirk dipped his starboard wing and sideslipped down to come up on the other side of the Fortress. The co-pilot's head turned in their direction. He put his hand to his headphones and shook his head.

"Engineer to pilot: I suspect he's got no wireless," Moran concluded. "The fire was where the Fortresses have their radio operators, and there's nothing that looks like an antenna anywhere."

"Pilot to wireless operator: Make a May Day call on the behalf of the Fortress," Selkirk ordered. "Pilot to crew, can anyone read her ID?"

"Rear gunner to pilot: There's an A inside a triangle on her tail."

"Pilot to wireless operator: Report that and see if we can find out more about her."

"Yes, sir."

"Bomb aimer to pilot: Have you seen that nose?"

"Jesus Christ!" Someone exclaimed. The Perspex glass around the bomb aimer's position was completely shattered and metal fragments were bent inwards.

"If I remember correctly," Moran called in, "the Americans have the navigator down there directly behind the bomb aimer. I don't think either of them had much of a chance of surviving whatever hit that nose. He probably doesn't have a clue where he is."

"Wireless Operator to pilot: the symbol on the tail denotes USAAF 91 Bomb Group, stationed at RAF Bassingbourn. They were sent out to Schweinfurt today."

Selkirk flew in closer to the Fortress. "Moran, signal to him to follow me."

Moran moved up to the port window and made gestures to encourage the Fortress to follow them. The co-pilot nodded and gave them a thumbs up.

Selkirk pulled ahead but slightly to starboard of the Fortress so it wouldn't be flying in the Lancaster's slipstream and then called. "Pilot to engineer: "Let's reduce power to 70% and see if we can match speed with the Fort. Keep close watch on the engine temps and adjust the cowling flaps as you need."

"Reducing power to 70%," Moran answered.

After watching the distance between themselves and the Flying Fortress for several minutes, it appeared that they could in this manner fly as slowly as the Fortress.

Satisfied, Selkirk switched on the intercom again. "Pilot to navigator: Get us a course to the nearest RAF station."

"Navigator to pilot: The nearest station is Coltishall. That's a fighter station and only has grass runways."

"Pilot to navigator: Where's the next bomber station with concrete runways?"

"Navigator to pilot: That would be Downham Market. It's roughly 50 miles farther inland."

"Pilot to engineer: What do you think, Kit? Can he make it?"

"Can you fly us over and under his wings so I can assess the damage to his fuel tanks?"

Selkirk throttled back practically to stalling speed so that the Fortress crept up on him again. "Signal for him to keep flying straight ahead."

This done, Selkirk dipped a wing and sideslipped for a second time under the B-17, then flew back across the top of the Fortress before resuming his position ahead but slightly to the right of the B-17. "Well, what do you think, Kit?"

"He's leaking some fuel from that damaged port outer, but he's not going to need that anyway. The starboard tanks are intact. My guess is that he's got the fuel to make it to Downham Market. On the other hand, he obviously has seriously injured crewmen on board. Thirty minutes longer to hospital could be fatal."

"Understood," Selkirk answered, but the tone of his voice suggested he was not convinced. Moran knew what he was thinking. Crashing on landing would almost certainly be fatal. Kit knew that Don would make the decision for the B-17 as if it were his own crew. He would make the best decision he could, right or wrong, but it was hard not knowing what the injuries were or how the aircraft was flying. Furthermore, there might be damage to the hydraulics. There was no certainty the flaps would work, or the undercarriage would come down.

"Pilot to navigator: I'm going to try to make Downham Market. Give me a course there."

"Yes, sir.' After a pause while he did the calculations, he reported, "Navigator to pilot: Steer two-oh-five."

"Two-oh-five." They banked onto their new course, and the Flying Fortress followed them.

The sun was slipping down the sky bathing the English countryside in golden light. There was not a cloud in sight. At least that would help with the landing, Kit thought, but after another ten minutes or so, the American co-pilot started to have trouble maintaining altitude and course. Moran could also see other men moving around in the cockpit. The aircraft jinked.

"Engineer to pilot, the B-17 co-pilot is trouble. I think he's passed out at the controls. Other crew men are trying to pull him out of the seat."

The B-17, meanwhile, had gone into a shallow dive and was veering increasingly off course to port.

"Pilot to navigator: Distance to Down Market?"

"Another twenty miles, sir. Ten minutes."

"Navigator, is there any airfield nearer? Anything?" Moran could hear the guilt in Selkirk's voice, the fear that he had made the wrong choice.

The B-17 was starting to roll over to the left. It appeared to be on the brink of falling into a spin. Abruptly, the wing came up again, and the aircraft was back under control. "Engineer to pilot: It appears that the pilot has been revived and has taken over."

"Wireless Operator to pilot: I have Downham Market flying control. I have advised them of the situation. We and the B-17 are cleared to land."

Selkirk put the Lancaster into a descent while Moran waved to the men in the B-17 cockpit and pointed downwards. They nodded and waved back. Selkirk lined up on the longest of the three runways and took the Lancaster down, touching very lightly near the start of the runway and rolling as far as he could.

No sooner had they touched down, than Moran stood and looked backwards out of the cockpit glass. He riveted his eyes on the American four-engine bomber, which was flying erratically. It swooped up and down like a sparrow as it made its final approach. The undercarriage came down at the very last minute, but the flaps did not look fully extended. Someone hauled back on the throttles too abruptly, and the engines sputtered. The big bomber fell out of the sky, and the undercarriage collapsed under it. On its belly, it tore down the runway striking sparks and losing pieces until it came to a crooked standstill about two hundred yards from the end.

With sirens and flashing lights, two ambulances and a fire-engine dashed towards it. Selkirk turned off the runway and taxied along the perimeter track to the place nearest the wreck. Here he stopped the Lancaster and shut down the engines. "I'm going to see how many of them made it," he announced.

They all piled out of the Lancaster after him, Moran close on Selkirk's heels. They crossed the grass to the broken American bomber. It had not burst into flames yet, although the smell of aviation fuel filled the air. The fire engine was hosing foam over the wings to make sure nothing ignited, while the 'body snatchers' from the ambulances were already at work removing injured crew men. There didn't seem to be anything the Lancaster crew could do to help, so they hung back and watched.

Then one of the Americans noticed them. He limped over, holding his right elbow in his left hand. "Are you the Lancaster crew that led us in?"

"Yes."

"Thank you, guys! We never would have made it without you. I'm Clark Bennet, Waist Gunner. I'd shake hands, but I can't move my right arm."

"Glad to meet you. What about the rest of your crew? How many injured did you have on board?"

"The bombardier, wireless operator and the other waist gunner were dead before you found us. The navigator is in bad shape. God knows if he'll make it. Both pilots took shrapnel, but they were conscious, so I guess they'll make it. The rest of us are OK."

"The injured will get medical attention immediately," Selkirk assured the American. "You'd better go and board the ambulance yourself."

"Yeah. Will do." He started to turn away and then thought better of it and turned back. "Hey, can you tell me who you are and where you're from? I'm sure the Lieutenant will want to know."

"We're from RAF Witchford, a Heavy Conversion Unit. We were on a training flight. Name's Selkirk, Flying Officer Donald Selkirk."

"Pleasure to meet you, sir. If you don't mind me saying so, you looked like the Archangel Gabriel, when you came in on our beam like that. Until you guys showed up, I'd lost all hope of feeling land beneath my feet ever again. I swear, it was like Christ walking on the waves of Galilee!"

Selkirk smiled at that, and they all murmured something about it being nothing. The American grinned and ran to catch the ambulance, which was starting to pull away from the Fortress. They watched him scramble into the back with the aid of one of the medics and then both ambulances wailed their way back toward the sick quarters. For a few seconds longer, the RAF crew stood staring at the wreck of the B-17, each lost in his own thoughts.

Six weeks later, five Americans turned up at Witchford asking to see Flying Officer Selkirk and his crew. It was the two pilots and three of the air gunners from the Flying Fortress they had guided home. They wanted to take Selkirk and his crew out for a drink.

Selkirk explained that the crew of the Lancaster had been in training and already moved on to their operational unit, but he found Moran and together they gave the Americans a tour of the station and a short "joy ride" in a Lancaster. The Americans were a little shocked by how cramped the Lancaster was, but impressed with its power and manoeuvrability. It helped, of course, that this Lancaster wasn't carrying her payload.

By then they were all hungry, so they sought out the closest pub that did bar meals and ordered the first round. In the atmosphere of the pub, they talked less "shop" and started to reveal more about themselves. The Flying Fortress' captain was a First Lieutenant by the name of Beauregard "Beau" Middleton from South Carolina. He hailed from a military family going back to the Revolutionary War. ("When we had the bad sense to be fighting each other," he told them with a grin.) He was clearly well-heeled and wouldn't let his gunners put their hands in their pockets to pay for a drink, much less a round. His co-pilot was from Chicago, Illinois and had quit college to join the Army Air Force the day after Pearl Harbor. The three gunners hailed respectively from Pocahontas, Iowa, Belfast, Maine and Sacramento, California, a farmer, lobsterman, and a salesclerk.

Suddenly there seemed so much to talk about: the different routes that had brought them together, their shared love of flying, their desire to knock Hitler down and out, their hopes for a better future after the war, and the girls they'd left behind or had found in a strange land. When they couldn't put off their departure any longer, the Americans staggered a bit unsteadily back to their jeep and ended the evening with an invitation for Don and Kit to visit them at their base. The RAF officers readily agreed.

Roughly two weeks later, Don and Kit took a Lancaster on a "test flight" over to RAF Bassingbourn. They'd called the day before and Beau had assured them that would be fine. They knew something was wrong, however, as soon as they found the field almost empty except for two B-17s being serviced on hardstandings. Reporting to Flying Control as required, they were told that Middleton's aircraft had been hastily added to a mission when one of the aircraft slated to fly had become unserviceable at the last moment. The entire Group was airborne on a mission to Munich but should be returning in the next hour or so. The RAF officers were invited to wait in Flying Control.

At first, they chatted easily with the controllers, radio operators and Flying Control Officer. They were still happily exchanging and comparing experiences and procedures, when the first returning Flying Fortress called in. Immediately, all the small talk stopped as everyone focused on the returning aircraft.

Unlike the RAF, the USAAF flew in formation, and tried to maintain formation not only to the target but back again as well. The idea was that the Flying Fortresses with their nine guns would be able to support one another and discourage fighter attacks. The concept had rapidly proven faulty, but the USAAF was a highly disciplined force.

As Selkirk and Moran watched, a great air armada of four-engine bombers lumbered toward the airfield. The formation was still recognizable, and so were the gaps. Aircraft were firing flares to indicate injured on board, and the radio in the control tower crackled with captains calling in for emergency landings. The aircraft without emergencies stacked up in a slowly spiralling flock over the airfield, while the lame-ducks and those carrying wounded crew landed first.

Kit always remembered what followed as a "slow horror flick." One badly damaged aircraft after another set down on the runway, often bouncing or skidding. One veered off the runway and ended in a crumpled heap. Another had no landing gear and opted to land beside the runway, tearing up the turf and flinging stones and clumps of grass into the air. Aircraft landed with burned-out engines and shattered gun turrets, with shot-up rudders and punctured wings. Ambulances seemed to be darting about everywhere. Finally, the controller informed the Group Leader that undamaged aircraft without injured on board were cleared to land, and one after another they settled on the runway with neat efficiency.

When the last aircraft was down, Selkirk and Moran asked which aircraft belonged to Middleton. The controller checked and pointed out one of the undamaged aircraft that was slowly swinging onto a hardstanding in answer to the signals of the ground crew. They were told to go ahead and welcome Middleton home. They left Flying Control and started across the busy airfield, surrounded by the fierce roar of aircraft engines, the higher-pitched grinding of jeeps engines, and the wail of sirens.

Abruptly, Selkirk stopped in his tracks. "Did you count the number of damaged bombers, Kit?"

"No, I lost track."

"Thirteen."

"How many didn't make it at all?"

"Five. Ten crew in each. Fifty men who won't be at the mess tonight."

"And how many took off?"

"I didn't ask."

"We can ask Beau," Kit suggested and resumed walking, but Don caught his arm and stopped him. Kit looked back at him questioningly. Don met his gaze, and there was something frighteningly otherworldly about the look in his eyes. Kit shivered in the summer's heat.

In a low, tense voice Don announced, "I don't think we should allow the Americans to fight our war for us, Kit."

"It's their war too," Kit countered.

"American cities haven't been bombed. They aren't at risk of invasion."

"Maybe not, but Hitler declared war on them, and I, for one, am glad he did. I feel a lot more confident of victory with them on our side." Kit nodded toward the B-17s.

"Me too. But I can't hide behind them either. Can you?" When Kit said nothing, Don added. "I have to do another tour, Kit." Still, Kit said nothing. "You'll be with me, won't you, Kit?"

"Of course."

Chapter 9

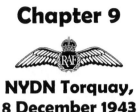

NYDN Torquay,
8 December 1943

Kit had mail. Three letters. Two were addressed to him at the HCU and had been forwarded, but the other one was addressed to the NYDN Centre at Torquay. He recognized the handwriting on all three. His parents had written to HCU, and their letters were post-marked in late October, before he started his second tour. The third letter was from Lincoln, post-marked only three days ago, and it was addressed in Fiona's handwriting.

Kit's heart beat faster as he withdrew to his room, which he still had to himself. He closed the door behind him and sank down into the sole chair. He put his parents' letters aside and held Fiona's message in his hand, his mind filled with images of their last enchanted afternoon in Cambridge. They had hired a punt and "punted" on the Cam just as people did in novels and films. It had been warm and sunny and infinitely peaceful. Fiona had worn a short-sleeved, cotton frock that fluttered in the gentle breeze. She'd taken off her sandals to let her bare feet trail in the warm water of the river. Kit had almost proposed to her then and there, but something had held him back. Cowardice perhaps.

He couldn't forget what she'd said that day at Ashcroft, although she'd seemed eager to spend the weekend with him in Cambridge. The night before they had gone to a student production of "The Importance of Being Earnest" and laughed themselves silly. Everything had been so harmonious and natural as though they were meant to be together.

Fiona was different from all the other girls he'd been out with. As an apprentice and erk, he hadn't taken girls seriously, and he couldn't remember the names of most. Then it had all been about having a good time and seeing how far they'd go. With Fiona, he wouldn't have tried anything inappropriate. It wasn't just that she was a nice girl, but she was so sure of what she wanted — and what she didn't.

Was it possible that she, who hated the war so much, would understand what he'd done? If she did, it would make all the difference in the world. If Fiona stood by him, then he would be able to face whatever

315

they decided to do to him. And why would she write, if she didn't want to offer him her support? It would have been so much easier just to pretend he no longer existed.

Fortified by these thoughts, he turned the envelope over and opened it with his pocket-knife. He unfolded the letter written on pretty, pale-blue paper.

Dear Kit, it opened.

These last two weeks have been the most terrible of my life. I have watched Georgina sink in a flood of her own tears, hardly able to breathe for grief. She is wasting away for lack of food and sleep, and nothing will console her.

Watching her, holding her, trying to comfort her has made me realise how terrible this thing called 'love' really is. My beautiful friend is being destroyed by it. I know that she will never be the same. Oh, I know, time heals all wounds, but Georgina will bear the scar of what Don has done to her for the rest of her life.

*Not only **a** scar — I fear it will be an **ugly** scar and one that she wears on her forehead for all to see. I hope that the time will come, when she realizes that the only one to blame for her misery is the man who so callously shattered her happiness with his selfish ego! Don and his pretensions of being better than everyone else! His anachronistic, aristocratic notions of 'duty' and 'honour' have killed a beautiful, fragile, and utterly selfless butterfly."* Fiona's anger was evident in the deep grooves her ball-point pen had impressed upon the heavy stationary.

Watching Georgina suffer, made me see more clearly than before why I would not and could not ever commit myself to you. I am determined not to let you break my heart and scar me for life. The best way to ensure that doesn't happen, is never to see each other again.

It makes no difference to me that you don't share Don's class delusions of superiority. Nor does it matter that you have refused to fly any more operations. Georgina tells me such a refusal is very serious and could result in some sort of disciplinary action. I hope that whatever they do to you isn't too terrible, because I think you are only being sensible not to want to fly any further operations.

However, I told you before you started this second tour that I thought it was foolish and unnecessary. You wouldn't listen to me. It hurt me terribly that you insisted on doing this thing that I knew was wrong for you. And though I did not see it at once, I now know that our relationship was doomed the moment you would not listen to me. In that moment, you put your self-image as some sort of storybook hero ahead of a meaningful relationship with me. It doesn't change anything that you have now learnt the hard way that I was right.

So, this is good-bye, Kit. I honestly wish you all the best. At least now you won't die for some silly dream of being a hero, and maybe next time you'll listen, when a woman tells you something for your own good.

Sincerely, Fiona.

Kit stared at the letter for several moments and then folded it together and slipped it back inside the envelope. He sat in his cold room staring at nothing for a long time. At first, he felt completely numbed, but gradually he became aware of the cold and the discomfort of sitting too long in one position. He shifted himself in the chair, but the emptiness remained inside.

After a while, he registered almost clinically that he had never expected Fiona to be sympathetic. He had only briefly imagined that she might be. He supposed that knowledge dulled the pain a little because he had no sense of betrayal — just inevitability. Still, her letter had left him without even a dream to cling to.

His eyes fell on the forgotten letters from his parents, and he reached out for his mother's letter first, confident that his mother would stand by him in everything no matter what he did. He needed a little of that boundless, maternal love at the moment.

His mother wrote in a very neat, disciplined and exquisitely legible hand — just as she taught her pupils.

Dearest Kit, My heart,

Today the goats were loose again, and I thought of you. I almost thought that I saw you in your school uniform trying to herd them back to the pen, and they were bleating and running away from you on their short little legs, then turning to mock you from the windowsills.

Sometimes I wish you were still that little boy whom I could hold in my arms or that you would sit beside me on the piano bench and play duets with me. I find myself playing this or that just so I can hear you playing in my mind. I've started rereading all the books we read together, too, the ones we loved best — 'Heart of Darkness,' 'For Whom the Bells Toll,' 'Crime and Punishment,' and, of course, 'Lord Jim.' I have just finished re-reading 'Lord Jim' and cried myself silly at the end as I always do.

Yet I am so proud of the young man you have become. I'm sure from beyond the grave both your grandfathers would be proud of you too. I was tempted to send a copy of your photograph and the DFM citation to your uncle Charles Moran. He was so pompous towards your father because he had no medals, and here you are a proper warrior, proud and straight as a spear, with a medal after just three months of combat. I keep that photo you sent in your officer's uniform with the silver aircrew badge on your chest here on my desk where I look at it a hundred times a day. You make me so proud — and so afraid, my darling.

When I read that you had volunteered for a second tour, I trembled as badly as if the old gods had come out of hiding. That is not something a missionary's daughter should admit, but in the night, I heard the voo doo drums in the hills. It seemed as though many evil spirits were at large in the darkness of the night, and I was so frightened your father had to hold me all night long.

My darling, my heart, when two Zulu warriors contend, then the man with the greatest courage and skill wins. But when a Zulu warrior faces a machine gun, courage and skill are of no use to him. Forgive me if I speak foolishly or ignorantly, but I cannot see how skill and courage can shield you from the German guns that light up the night as you described in one of your letters. It was just luck that you were not hit during your last tour. And now you must be lucky thirty more times. Isn't that asking a lot of God?

Oh, my dearest, my fear for you was so great that in the darkest hour of the night I wanted to slip out to the witch doctor and beg him to cast a spell to protect you. Fortunately, I was too frightened of the darkness to act upon my shameful and superstitious wishes. By the morning, I had regained my faith in Our Dear Lord, and I say with all my heart 'Thy will be done.' I will put my trust in the mercy of the Lord and beg you to do the same.

Now, I shall say no more. Forgive you mother for being frightened and foolish and not quite as 'British' as she should be. If only I had the chance to come to England and see it at first hand, I'm sure I would be fortified and be able to banish the silly remnants of my African superstitions. I shall continue to nag your father about a trip. Meanwhile, write as often as you can. I live for your letters and for the day when I shall hold you in my arms again.

Your ever-loving mother.

Kit folded and replaced the letter in its envelope, but he did not set it aside. He sat holding it as he remembered his mother's grief at the loss of his little brother and the sudden death of her parents. In both cases, even as she grieved, she had accepted the Will of God as only a missionary's daughter can.

What he had done, however, was an act of Free Will. To remove himself from the dangers and risks of flying was not just a cowardly refusal to do his duty and be a man, it was also a cowardly refusal to surrender to the Will of God. In so doing, he had robbed his mother of the solace offered by believing that his fate was God's will.

With a deep sigh, Kit set her letter aside and resignedly turned to his father's letter with little hope of comfort any more. His father's missive was short as always, just one page, front and back.

Kit,

We have just received your letter announcing your decision to volunteer for a second tour of operations. By the time you receive this, it will be too late for you to alter that decision, so I must accept it.

Yet, even if I can change nothing, I want you to know that I wish I could have been near enough to talk to you about this decision. It reminded me of things I saw in the last war. I regret I told you so little of what transpired and what I saw then. I feel I have failed you. I should have explained more. I should have been more honest with you. Most importantly, I shouldn't have let you go away at 16 and a half.

When I look back on my life there are few things that I truly regret. I don't regret coming to Africa or making a career in the Colonial Service. I don't regret the break with my bigoted parents and self-satisfied siblings. I certainly don't regret my marriage to your wonderful mother. But letting a 16-year-old go out to face the world on his own was a cruel and selfish thing. I should have kept you with me for another two or three years. And I should have talked to you more.

But it can't be undone. That is the worst of it. We can't undo our misdeeds. We can only bear their consequences with as much dignity as we can muster. For me, that means living with this awful fear that I shall never see you again, never hear your voice, your laughter, never share another sundowner on the rooftop terrace or another campfire on the banks of Lake Victoria, watching the otters play....

Remember, whatever happens, Kit. You are loved by your mother and me. Do not think you must be particularly brave or daring. Leave that to young men who aren't so well loved. Do what you think is right. That is enough. And write as often as you can.

Love, Dad.

Kit read the last paragraph twice, and it sent a chill through him. It seemed as though his father had anticipated his actions. It was as though his father had expected him to refuse to fly at some point. Suddenly, too late, his brain was filled with vague recollections of isolated sentences dropped at seemingly random times. Hints, half-uttered and unexplained like: "Courage, Kit, isn't always what you think it is." Or: "War is a terrible thing. I wish I'd had the courage to turn my back on it."

Suddenly, for the first time in years, Kit wanted fervently to talk to his father. He thought if they could just sit down and talk, man to man, about everything, maybe he would come to terms with what he had done. Maybe he wouldn't feel so guilty, ashamed and worthless.

Chapter 10

NYDN Centre Torquay, 9 December 1943

A brisk knock on the door was followed by a voice calling, "Pilot Officer Moran? You have a visitor."

Kit was at the narrow, upright desk trying to draft a letter to his parents. "A visitor?" he asked startled, twisting around bewildered. It was Sunday. The only day visitors were allowed.

"Yes, sir. A young lady."

"I'll be right down!" Kit promised, despite feeling disoriented and confused. If the orderly had announced an "old lady" it might have been Mrs Selkirk, who (Kit secretly hoped) might not be as harsh a judge of what he'd done as the Colonel. Or it might even have been his mother, who had wanted to come to England for years. But a 'young lady'?" Had Fiona changed her mind?

He looked at himself in the mirror and realized he'd shaved badly, and he needed a haircut. He looked as run-down and second-rate as he felt. He found a comb and ran it through his hair as best he could. Then he changed into his other tunic, which had been hanging out and wasn't as rumpled. Thus dressed, he cautiously descended the stairs to the lobby. On the third step from the bottom he paused, still in the stairwell, to scan the room systematically — rather as one did the sky for enemy fighters.

It was nearly empty, except for a hefty middle-aged woman talking animatedly to one of his fellow inmates, an old couple sitting side-by-side looking frightened, and a frail, hunched figure in a dowdy tweed coat looking out the large bow window with her back to him. It certainly wasn't Fiona. He stopped breathing, afraid of who he thought it might be.

She felt his eyes and turned around. It was Georgina.

Kit stepped down the remaining stairs and crossed the room to her in a state of sheer terror. He found it hard to swallow, and he only managed to croak out, "Georgina," as he stopped three feet away from her. At this distance, he could see her whole face was slack and her eyes were swollen and red. She wore no make-up or lipstick.

"Kit." Her eyes seemed to search not just the surface of his face but to peer deep into his mind, heart and soul. At last, she asked very softly, "How are you?" Something about her tone or inflection made it sound as if she sincerely wanted to know.

Kit shrugged. "I'm all right. Do you want to go somewhere for tea or something? I'll get my greatcoat." He didn't give her a chance to answer. He turned and fled back toward his room, taking the steps two at a time.

Five minutes later, he was back. He opened the door for her and escorted her to his favourite tearoom with the cheerful old lady and the best homemade scones and jam. It was so warm here that the windows were steamed up on the inside. He took Georgina's coat and his great coat to hang up on the stand. Georgina was wearing a navy-blue skirt and cardigan over a white blouse; very prim and sober. She also wore black cotton stockings and flat, black shoes with straps on them, almost like a nun. When the waitress came over, Georgina tried to smile, but her hand shook in spasms as she tried to hold the menu. Only after the tea was served, did Georgina speak again. "Kit, I thought you might want to know that Sailor is going to be all right. Or did they tell you that already?"

"No, they didn't tell me. And Leslie?"

"He's out of danger now. I think Kathleen said he was likely to be invalided out, but he's going to survive."

So only Don had died. The best of them. The one with the most to give the post-war world. Furthermore, Don's death had destroyed not only his own life but Georgina's as well. In a fit of guilty candour, Kit burst out, "I wish I could have died in Don's place, Georgina."

Tears flooded her eyes, but she shook her head. "Don't say that."

They both looked away and pretended to eat scones. Georgina pulled herself together first and asked, "Are you all right, Kit?" How was he supposed to answer that? When he said nothing, she pressed him, "What are they going to do to you?"

"I don't know. I don't think they've decided yet. I have regular talks with a doctor, a psychiatrist, and apparently, he makes a diagnosis of insane or not. Or, anyway, determines what sort of person I am and what sort of treatment I deserve. It doesn't matter." He paused and then realized it was more than that. He added, "I don't matter."

Georgina took hold of his hand and made him look at her. She met his eyes and told him firmly. "You mattered to Don."

It was like a kick in the gut. Winded, he shook his head. "Georgina, what do you want from me?"

"I want to know what happened. On that last flight. Tell me. Everything."

RAF Elsham Wolds, 22 November 1943

It was Berlin again — "the Big City — and the route was long. Bomber Command wanted the bomber stream to fly across Denmark, down the Kattegat to cross over the German coast between Rostock and Stralsund. They were then to continue on a south-easterly course for forty minutes before turning back toward Berlin on a dogleg course that took them to the German capital from the northeast. Once they reached the outskirts of Berlin, they were expected to cross the city from northeast to southwest, dropping their load on the north-eastern sectors of the city. After the bomb run was complete, they were instructed to fly roughly west-by-west-southwest on a course calculated to take them south of the industrial centre of Hanover before bending on to a course designed to guide them north of the Ruhr. The final leg of the route was due west over Holland and the North Sea. The Main Force, to which Selkirk's new squadron, 103, belonged, was due over the target at 22:35. Take off was at 18:15.

There was some light lingering in the west as Y-York took to the air under the command of Flight Lieutenant Donald Selkirk. With him on this flight were Pilot Officer Moran, Flight Engineer, Flight Sergeant Teddy Hamed, Bomb Aimer, Pilot Officer "Sailor" Hart, Navigator, Flight Sergeant Leslie Vernon, Wireless Operator, Sergeant Neal Ramsey, Mid-Upper Gunner, and Sergeant Sam Rhodes, Rear Gunner. It was a bitterly cold night, crystal clear with excellent visibility under a sky so brilliantly star-studded that Vernon joked with Sailor he'd get confused if he tried to shoot the stars.

Hamed muttered, "if we have to ditch or jump in the North Sea, we'll freeze our bollocks off faster than those silly sods on the Titanic."

Although the Germans jammed the signals from the Gee radio grid from the middle of the North Sea, navigating was easy with this astonishing visibility. So easy, in fact, that Sailor raised the alarm almost at once. "Navigator to pilot: Winds must be substantially more than forecast. We're far south of our dead reckoning course."

"Can you correct for the actual winds and give me a new course to re-join the stream?"

"I'll take another fix and make an estimate, Skipper."

A couple of minutes passed, then: "Navigator to pilot: My calculations put the wind at close to 100 mph."

"That can't be. The Met said 40 to 45 mph."

"I know. I was at the Navigators' briefing. Met got it wrong."

"You want to plot a course that corrects for 100 mph winds?"

"Do you trust me or not, Don?"

They could hear Selkirk draw a deep breath before he ordered, "give me the course."

Even with the adjustment, they crossed the coast south rather than north of the distinctive island of Sylt, which they readily identified below them. This meant they were totally off course.

"Can anyone see any other Lanc, Hallifax or Sterling out there?" Selkirk asked.

"No' a thing, Skipper," Hamed answered first, followed by the gunners who chimed in with the same answer.

"Engineer to pilot: These winds are buffeting every bloody aircraft up here, friend and foe. I think we can assume there is no concentrated bomber stream anymore."

"Agreed. Pilot to navigator: Give me a new course — calculating for 100 mph winds — to take us north of Kiel and across the Baltic."

Tensely they swept over the neck of land that was either Germany or Denmark until they reached the glimmering silver of the Baltic Sea. Here they picked up landmarks on the coast that verified Sailor's estimate of the winds, but they felt utterly alone in the sky as if the winds had swept the rest of the more than 800 bombers to oblivion.

As they turned south for Berlin, however, the fierce winds were on their tail, pushing them southwards. Sailor warned that they would be over the target as much as 30 minutes early. Hamed pointed out that if that were true, the Pathfinders wouldn't have laid down the target indicators yet. So, Selkirk throttled back and started flying long, slow zigzags across the sky to the north of Berlin to slow their southward progress. This had the advantage of giving the gunners a better view below and behind them. Yet the sky remained eerily empty until Ramsey reported: "Flares! Mid-Upper gunner to pilot: Flares to starboard."

Selkirk banked the heavy bomber toward the flares. "Pilot to navigator: How many minutes to target?"

"Eight to ten minutes if we go straight in."

"Please give me a time hack."

"22:15."

"Wireless operator to pilot: Bomber Command has moved Zero Hour forward by five minutes."

They heard Selkirk sigh over the intercom as he swung out in another lazy sweep away from the target.

"Berlin looks — Sorry — Rear gunner to pilot: Berlin looks like it's on fire already."

They turned back toward the city which was, they noticed, partially covered by cloud. This layer of rumpled fluff was rapidly turning red and yellow as if there was an inferno burning underneath. Had the other bombers gone in early? Had the raid been moved forward not by five minutes but by fifteen?

Without comment, Selkirk turned back toward Berlin and opened up the throttles. Suddenly another Lancaster cut across their bows no more than 100 feet away. They missed the tail fins by what felt like inches. It happened so fast that no one aboard Y-York had a chance to say anything.

After Moran's pulse had returned almost to normal, a cold fear settled on the back of his neck. The winds had disrupted everyone's navigation to the point that 800-something bombers were scattered all over the sky and flying every which way to try to get back to the target for Zero Hour. He supposed that made the risk of collision about 800-times higher than during a normal operation.

The closer they came to Berlin, the more confused the picture became. Rather than clear target indicators, there appeared to be two different flare paths, leading in divergent directions.

Hamed was the one to figure out what was going on. "Skipper! Ignore the flares at 2 o'clock! Them's a German diversion! Can you see? Them's some Jerry bomber laying 'em out."

"Well done, Teddy!" Selkirk praised.

They followed the Pathfinder flares. Strangely the searchlights, which usually didn't bother on a cloudy night, were probing the under-bellies of the cloud. Here and there they broke through a gap in the clouds to light up a cone of night sky, but it was impossible for them to coordinate and triangulate on a bomber. Which seemed like a good thing until Teddy called up from his bubble. "Bomb aimer to the rest of ye: the light below the cloud is like background lighting at a puppet show! I can see dozens of Lancs out there — perfect silhouettes against the light — and so can the 'wild boars.' We might as well be naked on a big stage!"

"There they are! Seven o'clock." Rhodes called from the tail followed by the chattering of his guns.

The fighters were, in fact, all over the place, and soon the sky was illuminated by the flames of burning aviation fuel as one after another RAF bomber ignited.

Y-York lined up on the bomb run. Hamed was calling out: "Left. Left. Steady. Right. Steady."

Just then, a wild boar homed in on a Halifax flying to port. First one and then a second engine burst into flame. The Halifax veered sharply toward Y-York, and Selkirk just managed to avoid a collision by yanking the Lancaster upward and banking away.

"You call that straight and level, Skipper?" Hamed shouted furiously. "This is supposed to be—"

The rest of his words were lost in the explosion that erupted with such violence that the Lancaster's tail was flung upwards. Then they started to dive. Before Selkirk recovered control, they were engulfed by waves of molten smoke washing over the Lancaster from behind them. Bits and pieces of debris rained down on their fuselage. They all heard Sam Rhodes yelp.

As soon as Selkirk had the Lancaster back under control, he called over the intercom. "Pilot to rear gunner: Are you all right?"

"Rear gunner to pilot: Yes and no. I haven't been hit, but we just lost one of our tail fins and the turret's jammed."

Moran stepped behind Selkirk to watch as he tested the ruder and elevators. The aircraft responded, and Moran breathed again. Then Selkirk looked up at him. "Go back and see if you can mend whatever's wrong with the turret."

Moran took oxygen and a torch. He squeezed past the navigator and wireless operator's stations, Hamed announced, "Well, we really buggered up that bomb run, Skipper, so noo we have to do it all again."

"This is like being naked in the middle of Waterloo Station and hoping no one will notice us!" Neal Ramsey commented as Selkirk banked the big bomber to circle around to the start of the bomb run again.

Leslie grumbled over the intercom. "As if anyone could hit the target on a night like this! There are bombs going off over 100 square miles down there!"

"Harris will grouse about the bomb pattern again, no matter what we do," Sailor added.

"That's enough chatter, chaps." Selkirk told them off.

Meanwhile, Moran had clambered over the main and rear spars to reach the tail. On his way, he noticed there were some small holes in the fuselage, apparently caused by the Lancaster that had exploded so nearby. The tail of the aircraft also appeared to be vibrating more than normal. At the very end of the tail, Moran was confronted not by the doors to the turret, but the side. He plugged his intercom into one of the sockets and called, "Flight engineer to rear gunner: What position is the turret in?"

"It's turned to port, and I can't turn it back."

"Have you tried hand cranking it?" Moran asked.

"Of course! That's the first thing I did. It won't budge."

This was not good. Because the turret was too small to accommodate the gunner in his parachute, the parachute was left just outside of the turret, in the tail of the fuselage. In an emergency, the gunner had to extricate himself from the turret, clip on the parachute and evacuate via the side door. Alternatively, he would reach into the fuselage and grab his parachute before turning the turret to one side and falling backwards into space. If he could not realign the turret so its armoured doors opened into the fuselage, however, Rhodes had no way of being united with his waiting parachute.

From the nose came Hamed's instructions to Selkirk, "Right. Right. Steady. Steady, man." The Lancaster bounced upwards, and Moran sighed with relief even before he heard Hamed announce. "Bombs gone."

Sailor provided the course for the next leg of their journey, while Selkirk kept the aircraft straight and level for the photos. Moran registered that they were still bucking the winds, which were howling back through perforated skin of the tail frame. The temperature was almost unbearable. "Engineer to rear gunner: Is your electric heating still working?"

"Oxygen and heating are fine. The turret just won't move." Rhodes apparently made another attempt to move it because Moran could hear the humming of the motor, but the turret didn't budge. He flashed the torch over the equipment looking for a hydraulic fluid leak but found nothing. The most likely explanation was that some of the debris from the exploded Lancaster had lodged in groove along which the turret slid. "Engineer to Pilot and Rear Gunner: I don't see any way I can repair this — short of trying to break into the turret with an axe."

"I'm all right for now," Rhodes responded. "Let's just get home as fast as we can."

The problem with that was that those 100 mph winds were now head winds. Their ground speed had been reduced to what felt like a crawl. Returning to his station in the cockpit, Moran watched the engines guzzling fuel for far too little progress.

Agonizingly slowly, they clawed their way past Hanover, but found themselves passing directly over Muenster, rather than north of it. That put them over the city's air defences. For a moment they were caught in a searchlight, but Selkirk corkscrewed out of it, diving sharply downwards. That brought them into the range of the flak, however, and the next thing they knew a burst of flak had fractured the Perspex and punctured small holes in the floor of the nose. Unfortunately, one piece of shrapnel lodged itself in Hamed's foot. It wasn't a fatal injury, but painful and bloody nevertheless.

Selkirk ordered Hamed up out of the bubble, and Moran dropped into the nose to help take Hamed's arm over his shoulder and drag him up the steps and down the length of the fuselage to the rest-bed. There he gave Teddy some morphine.

They were now over Holland and Selkirk asked for an updated ETA.

"Seventy-five minutes if we can maintain speed and course made good," Sailor answered.

"Engineer to pilot: Oil pressure dropping on number three engine. I think it must be leaking oil."

"Keep your eye on it."

They flew on until the sky abruptly went white with a flash of light. Like a giant light-bulb going off in the dark, it exposed a Lancaster on their left and an Me110 flying below and slightly behind it. The Me110 had set the petrol tanks on both wings of the Lancaster alight with its fixed, upward-firing guns — the so-called "Schraege Musik". The brilliant white flash was rapidly replaced by the yellow-orange light of burning aviation fuel as both wings of the Lancaster became engulfed in flames. A body dropped almost instantly out of the Rear Turret and hurtled towards the earth, but Moran had no chance to see if the parachute opened. The Me110 had seen them in the flash of light and throttled back to subject them to the same treatment.

Selkirk saw what was happening in the same instant as Moran. He dipped the Lancaster's wing and turned toward the fighter, shouting over the intercom. "Upper gunner: Night Fighter port low!"

The manoeuvre was so unusual that it caught the Me110 pilot off-guard. His "Schraege Musik" 20mm cannon were fixed and all he could do was turn inside the Lancaster, ranking it with fire as he shot past. The Lancaster vibrated with the recoil of both guns since, as luck would have it, Rhodes was frozen pointing to port and could also open fire. Flashes of light suggested that the night fighter took some hits. It certainly dived away and did not come back for more, but its cannon had done enough damage already.

Moran didn't immediately realize what had happened. Selkirk ordered, "Crew: report in." Although from the sound of his voice, Kit suspected he'd been injured, he couldn't judge how badly. Sailor, however, had been flung from his seat and was crawling to Leslie, who had collapsed onto the floor. Moran reached Leslie at the same time Sailor did. He was bleeding profusely from a wound in his belly and writhing in agony, his face already bathed in sweat. Moran went for the morphine, while Ramsey dropped down from his turret to help. Together, they got him onto the bed that Hamed vacated long enough for them to get Leslie stretched out and settled.

Leslie was shaking, sweating and whimpering. Although he had not taken a direct hit from the fighter's cannon, shrapnel fragments had apparently punctured his abdomen. Moran left him in Hamed's care to find out how seriously Sailor had been hurt. Ramsey, meanwhile, returned to his turret to keep a look out and try to defend them.

Sailor had dragged himself back onto his seat and was trying to concentrate on his charts, which had smears of blood on them. He greeted Moran with the words. "We're less than an hour from England. We can make it, but only if you help me."

"Where are you hit?" Kit asked him.

"In my side, but it's not going to kill me. Get on the wireless. We should be in range of the Gee grid soon. The wind is dropping and starting to veer wildly. If we get this wrong, we'll go into the drink, and none of us will make it."

Kit nodded, but he looked back toward the cockpit, worried about Don. On the other hand, by the way the aircraft was flying, so straight and level, Selkirk appeared to be in complete control. He twisted to look over his shoulder at his own instrument panel. The oil pressure on Number Three engine had stabilized, although the engine was running a little rough. They were getting low on fuel, but not desperately so. Again, he looked towards Selkirk. He clicked on the mic and called over the intercom. "Don? Leslie's unconscious and Sailor wants me to help him. Can you manage?" he asked.

"Yes," Selkirk answered. His voice was no longer strained. It was extremely calm and strangely disembodied.

Moran turned his attention to helping Sailor work out their position. He frequently looked forward through the cockpit window to judge their progress, and now and again checked his instrument panel. The autopilot light was on, which made sense. Selkirk needed to save his strength for landing, but for now everything seemed fine with the aircraft.

The sight of the English coastline outlined by white breakers sent a surge of relief through him, only to be followed by a superstitious fear that they might still crash. They were so close to salvation, yet many crews had been killed landing damaged aircraft on their return. God, let us get down safely, he prayed, telling himself that with excellent visibility and the Lancaster behaving like a lady under Selkirk's firm and calm control he had nothing to fear.

As soon as the coast slipped under their wings, Moran put out the "Darky" call. Hawkinge airfield answered, switching on all their lights. It was a fighter field and had no concrete runways, but the Lancaster seemed fine.

"Pilot to engineer: Flaps ten." Selkirk seemed to speak directly inside his head rather than over the intercom.

Moran folded down his seat and prepared to assist with the landing. Selkirk's orders came through without a trace of urgency or distress. He asked Kit to manage the throttles. Kit eased them back, lowered the undercarriage, and extended the flaps even further. They were lined up perfectly on the runway and came across the perimeter fence at less than one hundred feet. Selkirk reduced speed, and the heavy bomber settled back onto the earth like a graceful bird. It didn't even bounce. It was one of the best landings Moran had ever experienced in a Lancaster.

Braking gently, Selkirk brought the Lancaster to a stop at the far end of the field and then with a sigh sank back in his seat and leaned his head on the headrest. Moran jumped up to shut down the engines then made his way along the length of the fuselage, climbing over the main spar, to meet the medic at the door of the aircraft. Ramsey reached the door ahead of him and opened it, while Rhodes had opened the armoured doors of his turret and dropped to the ground without waiting another moment. A medic came into the Lancaster and Moran greeted him with: "The wireless operator and navigator are seriously injured, the bomb aimer has a foot injury, and the pilot is also wounded, I'm not sure how badly."

The medics acknowledged and told Moran to get out as he was now in their way. He glanced over his shoulder up the narrow fuselage toward the cockpit, but the medics were right. So, he climbed out of the aircraft and stood to one side as first Vernon, then Sailor and Hamed were brought out. They were all loaded into one of the ambulances and whisked away.

Finally, the two medics who had gone to the cockpit came out with their stretcher. They seemed to be handling it a bit roughly as they climbed down.

Kit called out sharply, "Careful! That's my skipper."

They stopped and looked over him. On the face of the nearer one, Kit saw an expression of astonishment that rapidly composed itself contritely. "I'm sorry, sir. Your skipper is dead. He was hit in the chest by cannon fire. He must have been killed instantly."

"No!" Kit corrected him. "He flew us back!"

The look they gave him was pitying. Then one of them said soothingly, "Whatever you say, sir." His tone suggested he thought Kit was out of his mind.

Chapter 11

NYDN Torquay,
15 December 1943

Dr Grace opened the session pleasantly as he usually did with "Pilot Officer Moran, you've been with us almost three weeks now, and I have to tell you," he parted his elegant hands helplessly and then folded them together again with a sigh, "I can't find the slightest evidence of mental illness. In fact, I would venture to say that you are one of the sanest young men I've talked to in a long time."

"Well, you are working at a mental institution, so you probably aren't talking to a normal sample of the population," Moran countered.

Dr Grace laughed shortly but sobered rapidly. "The point, I'm afraid, is that in the absence of a clear mental disorder, you cannot be admitted to a psychiatric hospital."

"That's just as well," Moran agreed. "I'd probably go mad there."

Dr Grace leaned back in his chair. "I have to admit I'm somewhat surprised — but glad — to see you can face the future with this degree of levity."

"I think it's called 'gallows humour', sir."

"Hm." Dr Grace thought a moment and then admitted, "Moran, I can't make a recommendation about your case unless you are more candid with me about why you refused to fly on November 23. I know you don't want to talk about it, but you have to tell me what happened."

Moran drew a deep breath. "There's not that much to it. Returning from the operation to Berlin on November 22, we landed at Hawkinge at roughly 2:30 am on the morning of November 23. I learnt on arrival that my pilot — and friend — Flight Lieutenant Selkirk had died, apparently immediately after landing the aircraft and thereby saving the lives of all aboard. Three other crewmen, and friends, were injured on that flight, two critically.

"The three of us who were not injured had to take trains back to RAF Elsham Wolds in Lincolnshire. We spent most of the night sleeping in railway stations in our flying gear or standing up in over-crowded trains. Apparently, no one in this country thinks bombing Berlin is important enough to give up their seats to tired aircrew returning from an op there!"

Dr Grace grimaced and shook his head in sympathy.

Moran continued, "We reached Elsham Wolds roughly twelve hours later. I had only been in bed about two hours, when I was told I was slated to fly as engineer with a sprog crew that same evening. I was not amused, but it wasn't until they opened the curtains at the briefing and it was yet another run to Berlin that I balked."

Dr Grace did not have to urge him to explain himself. Moran suddenly wanted someone to understand. "It was as if bloody Butcher Harris was punishing us for not hitting the target in a tight pattern the night before — as if we were to blame for the 100 mph winds, and for Met getting the forecast wrong and sending us all over the sky! We're not people to Harris — just tools to prove that bombing alone can force Germany into surrender.

"He could have given us a night off to recover. Or he could have sent us against a different target — something closer and less hotly defended like Bielefeld or Muenster. Sending us back to Berlin the very next night was too bloody much to ask!"

Dr Grace didn't answer for several minutes, during which time Kit started to become uncomfortable. All the rumours about what happened to men like him who "lacked moral fibre" crowded his brain.

Finally, Dr Grace drew a deep breath. "It is probably immaterial that I agree with you. I make no pretence of understanding the strategy behind our bombing campaign. As for asking you to go, my understanding is that many squadron and group leaders feel that crews that have undergone a traumatic experience need to be sent out again immediately in order to prevent the trauma from taking root. It's the same principle by which a rider who is thrown from a horse is told to get back on immediately. It's well known that if they don't, the fear of riding can become overpowering. It is equally true, that many pilots who have crashed need to overcome a fear of flying again. It has been proven that that fear increases rather than decreases with time. So, it seems to me there was some justification for the actions of your CO. Would you agree with that?"

Moran nodded stiffly.

"Now, let me ask you this — a purely hypothetical question, you understand. Could you imagine any circumstances under which you would be willing to fly operations again?"

"With a skipper I knew and trusted? Tomorrow."

Dr Grace nodded but remarked with a mildly reproving smile. "That may be just a wee bit over-zealous, Pilot Officer Moran."

"Maybe, but you did say the question was hypothetical."

Dr Grace smiled in acknowledgement, but then turned serious again as he leaned forward, his elbows on the desk and his hands clasped. "Colleagues of mine and I have been looking at the evidence, and we have come to the conclusion that the tours of duty are too long and the breaks between tours too short. Aircrews are all volunteers who are, with very few exceptions, men of not just average but superior dedication and character. Nevertheless, as a colleague of mine put it, courage is like money in the bank. If you use it up more rapidly than you can replenish it, you will eventually have nothing left."

Kit wasn't sure he understood what Dr Grace was saying. The wing commander seemed to be implying there was nothing fundamentally wrong with him. Indeed, he seemed to suggest he had nothing whatever to be ashamed of. "I'm not sure I understand what you're saying, sir."

"Nothing very complicated, Pilot Officer Moran. I'm simply saying that on the afternoon of November 23, 1943 your personal reserves of courage had been wiped out by a severe blow — the loss of your close friend and skipper on an operational flight the previous day. You needed time to recover your confidence, your equilibrium, and indeed your physical health. You also needed time to grieve. You were a wreck when you arrived — in case you didn't notice."

"Are you saying, sir, that you don't think I'm lacking in moral fibre?"

"A ridiculous term with no medical basis whatsoever. It was nothing but an administrative solution to an unexpected problem: the refusal of volunteers to continue to volunteer in certain circumstances. As volunteers you could hardly be subjected to the full weight of the military code. Yet you had, temporarily at least, lost the confidence of your commanding officers and needed to be removed from active duty."

"That doesn't entirely answer my question, sir. I understand that for you the term LMF isn't scientific or medical or however-you-want-to-word it, but it does describe aircrew who have failed to do their job, doesn't it?"

"Failed? Do you feel you have failed, and if so, in what way?"

Kit was bombarded with emotions and confused by his own thoughts.

"Isn't it true that the only way in which you have failed is in not living up to your own expectations? Is it not your high standards — as a member of an elite military force — that trap you into thinking that you have failed?" Grace paused and then continued, "Objectively, you have done a great deal more than 99% of the British population. Many would say you have indeed 'done your bit.'"

"What 'many' say isn't really the issue, is it? The question is what does the RAF say? What do you say? It seems to me that my future is very much in your hands, Wing Commander." Moran was deadly serious.

Dr Grace shook his head. "Not really. As I noted at the start of this talk, you are clearly not mentally ill, so transfer to a psychiatric hospital is not an option. On the other hand, almost everything else is possible. You are a trained fitter. If you choose, I can recommend that you be re-mustered as a LAC Fitter. You would lose your commission and aircrew status, but you would also never have to fly operations again." Dr Grace paused, watching for a response. Moran shook his head only once but decisively.

"At the other extreme, you could agree to return to operations and resume your second tour."

"Is there anything in between those two options?" Moran asked cautiously.

"Yes, you can volunteer for another kind of aircrew. You would then be sent to train as, say, a navigator or wireless operator, and on successful completion of training would arrive at your new squadron from Training Command. None of your new comrades would ever need to hear about your short stay at a NYDN centre, unless you told them. During training, you'd have time to rebuild your reserves of self-confidence and come to terms with your losses."

Kit had to admit that sounded remarkably attractive. It was an honourable option that enabled him to salvage something of his self-respect. "Did you have any particular recommendation in mind?" He asked cautiously.

"I'd suggest flying training."

That surprised Kit. "Flying training? Why?"

"Well, let's start with the fact that you've already flown Lancasters, haven't you?"

"What makes you say that, sir?"

"It's only hearsay, I suppose, but I've been told that many Lancaster pilots turn the controls over to their flight engineer now and again, so another crew member would be in a position to fly in an emergency. Didn't Flight Lieutenant Selkirk do that with you?"

Moran smiled sheepishly as he admitted, "well, yes. He even let me land once. It was a a bit of a prang and we got an awful ticking off for it."

"Hm." Grace commented. After a pregnant pause, the doctor came out with. "Contrary to your own account, Moran, the medics at Hawkinge are convinced that you landed the Lancaster on your last flight. They claim Selkirk was long dead." He paused, waiting for a response, but Kit said nothing.

Grace took a deep breath and continued. "In my humble opinion, Moran, you'd make a first-rate skipper. You demonstrated the necessary qualities on the flight you earned the DFM and again on Selkirk's last flight. Furthermore, flying training is the lengthiest and so it would give you the greatest amount of recovery time. Many pilots now take part in our Empire Training Scheme, which entails sending trainee pilots overseas for the early stages of training. South Africa is one of the regions handling a large number of aspiring pilots."

"I'd like going home," Kit admitted, and he risked looking at Dr Grace with something bordering on hope.

"I thought you might. Then may I recommend that you be accepted into Flying Training immediately?"

Moran nodded vigorously. "Yes, sir."

Smiling broadly for the first time in their acquaintance, Dr Grace brought his hands together and announced, "Excellent. I am delighted with your attitude, Moran."

"When will I know, if I've been accepted?" Moran asked cautiously.

"If I recommend it, acceptance is only a formality. I don't think it will be more than two or three weeks before you hear officially. You will jump the queue for training, as well, since your familiarity with engines and operations makes you a safer bet than green youths of unproven character."

"Meaning I'll start flight training soon?"

"Well, it might be a month or more before a slot is available," Dr Grace admitted, but Moran wasn't really listening anymore. The one thing he hadn't been prepared for was a second chance. The thought of flying training and going home preoccupied him until he realized that Grace was saying something about immediate leave. "I don't see any reason to keep you around this depressing institution. How would you feel about leave starting tomorrow morning until you receive orders to report for your initial flying training?"

"Is that supposed to be some sort of punishment, after all?" Moran lashed out with so much vehemence that Dr Grace flinched visibly.

After a moment in which the question hung in the room embarrassing Moran, Dr Grace patiently answered, "No, that was supposed to be a gesture of good will, Moran. Most people like getting leave."

"Most people have somewhere to go!" Kit snapped back, the conversation with Colonel Selkirk and Fiona's letter mocking him.

"Ah." Dr Grace opened the drawer of his desk and passed a letter across the desktop.

Kit stared at it.

"It is from Mrs. Kathleen Hart. She wrote asking me to release you over Christmas so you could be with her and her daughter during the Holidays. She said with her husband in hospital, your presence would do wonders to cheer them up. She also says she's planning a large Boxing Day dinner and has invited a long list of people who she says want you to be there. Go on! Open it up and read for yourself."

Kit felt more confused than ever. He hardly knew Kathleen Hart, Sailor's wife. Warily he opened the letter addressed to the "Senior Medical Officer handling the case P/O Christopher Moran" and skimmed the text. As Dr Grace had reported, Kathleen requested his release "for the holidays" and said his absence from the Boxing Day dinner would be "sadly and sorely missed" by "Reggie and Toby Allwright, Teddy Hamed, Sam Rhodes, Neal Ramsey, and Georgina Reddings." Kit folded the letter back together and looked guiltily at Dr Grace. "I'm sorry I snapped at you like that."

"No need to apologize, Pilot Officer. I've been trying to tell you that you need a rest — and I don't mean sitting around agonising over what you did or didn't do as you have been for the last three weeks. Does this letter change your attitude about immediate leave?"

"Yes, sir."

"Good, then I think everything's settled." He got to his feet and held out his hand. "In case we don't see one another again before you leave, it's been a pleasure getting to know you, Pilot Officer Moran. I wish you the best of luck for the future."

Moran stood and took the doctor's hand. "Thank you, sir." They shook hands.

At the door, Moran stopped, turned around and saluted smartly.

Historical Note

In the post-war era, popular perceptions conflated LMF with "shell shock" in the First World War and with the more modern concept/diagnosis of Post Traumatic Shock Syndrome PTSS. In literature — from Len Deighton's *"Bomber"* to Joseph Heller's *"Catch 22"* — aircrew were increasingly depicted as victims of a cruel war machine making excessive and senseless demands upon helpless airmen. Doubts about the overall efficacy of strategic bombing, horror stories depicting the effects of terror bombing on civilians, and general pacifism in the post-war era have all contributed to these clichés.

In reality, LMF was a more complex and nuanced issue. Historical analysis of the records show that over the course of the war, less than one percent of aircrew were posted for LMF. Furthermore, while nowadays LMF is most commonly associated with bomber crews, the statistics show that only one third of LMF cases came from Bomber Command. Surprisingly, fully another third came from Training Command, while Fighter Command and Coastal Command had their share of cases as well. Significantly, only a tiny fraction of those initially posted away from operational squadrons were ultimately designated LMF or the equivalent. (The term used for describing aircrew deemed cowardly varied over time, including the terms "waverer" and "lack of confidence.") Last but not least, the process for determining whether aircrew were LMF or not was far more humane than the myths of immediate and public humiliation suggest.

While the decision to remove a member of aircrew from an operational unit was an executive decision, applied when a member of aircrew had "lost the confidence of his commanding officer," the subsequent treatment was largely medical/psychiatric. Thus, while a squadron leader or station commander was authorized — indeed expected! — to remove any officer or airman who endangered the lives or undermined the morale of others by his attitude or behaviour, the man found LMF at squadron level was not automatically treated as such by the RAF medical establishment.

The medical and psychiatric officers at the NYDN (Not Yet Diagnosed Nervous) Centres (of which there were no less than 12) were at pains to understand the causes of any breakdown. They did not assume the men sent to them were inherently malingerers or cowards. On the contrary, as a result of their work they made a major contribution to understanding — and helping the RAF leadership to understand — the causes for aircrew behaviour. These included not only inadequate periods of rest, but irresponsible leadership, lack of confidence in aircraft, and issues of group cohesion and integration. As a result of their interviews with air crew, the medical professionals were able to convince the RAF leadership to reduce the number of missions per tour in Bombing Command and to exempt aircrew on second tours from LMF procedures altogether.

The psychiatric professionals increasingly came to recognize that "courage was akin to a bank account. Each action reduced a man's reserves and because rest periods never fully replenished all that was spent, eventually all would run into deficit. To punish or shame an individual who had exhausted his courage over an extended period of combat was increasingly regarded as unethical and detrimental to the general military culture." [Edgar Jones, "LMF: The Use of Psychiatric Stigma in the Royal Air Force during the Second World War," The Journal of Military History 70 (April 2006). 456]

Meanwhile, roughly one third of the aircrew referred to NYDNs returned to full operational flying (35% in 1942 and 32% in 1943-1945), another 5-7% returned to limited flying duties, and between 55% and 60% were assigned to ground duties. Less than 2% were completely discharged.

Wing Commander Grace was a neuropsychiatrist stationed at NYDN Centre Torquay during the war. All other characters are fictional. However, the raid on Berlin during which the bomber stream encountered winds in excess of 120 mph and became widely dispersed occurred on 24/25 March 1944. Also, the incident of a heavy bomber making a "perfect landing" after the pilot was dead is historically documented. The bomber involved was a B-17 of the 8th Air Force and the bulk of the crew had bailed out during the return trip. Nevertheless, the aircraft landed at its base with a severely wounded tail gunner still at his post — and a stone-cold dead pilot.

HELENA P. SCHRADER

342

Glossary
of RAF WWII Terminology

A/C: Aircraft.

Ace: A fighter pilot who has an extraordinary number of victories; in WWI this as "over five" but in WWII the number was not really defined.

Ack-Ack: Friendly anti-aircraft guns (as opposed to Flak — enemy anti-aircraft guns).

Adj.: Short for adjutant, the administrative assistant to the commanding officer of a squadron.

A/G: Air gunner.

Airscrew: Complete assembly of three or four propellers, hub and spinner.

Aircrew: Men who served in aircraft, regardless of their specific trade (i.e. pilots, observers, navigators, bomb-aimers, wireless operators and air gunners).

Angels: A term used in airborne radio communications to designate altitude. One angel equaled 1,000 feet, e.g. angles twenty was 20,000 feet.

AOC: Air Officer Commanding a Group.

AOC-in-C: Commander of a Command (e.g. Bomber Command, Fighter Command, etc.).

Armourer: Ground crew responsible for bombs, defensive ammunition, flares etc.

Arse-end Charlie: In Fighter Command an aircraft that flew behind a section, flight or squadron weaving back and forth to see the enemy better; in Bomber Command the rear gunner.

Availability, Squadron or Flight: The status of a squadron or flight requiring pilots to remain on the station but not at the dispersal hut or in flying kit yet ready to take off in roughly 30 minutes.

Bag: To collect or secure, including illegally.

Bags of: A large quantity, as in "bags of fun" or "bags of flak".

Bale or bail out: To abandon an aircraft using one's parachute.

Bang on: Right on.

Battle dress: Woolen working uniform.

Bandit: Enemy aircraft.

Beat up: To fly very low.

Belt: Travel at high speed.

Best blues: Dress or parade uniform.

Binder: One who nags or bores.

Binding: whining or complaining.

Bits and pieces: a crashed aircraft.

Black, a: as in "put up a black", doing a bad job of something.

Black out: To lose consciousness due to the force of gravity or "g".

Blitz time: Time for aircraft to be over the target.

Blood wagon: Ambulance.

Bloody: At this time a fairly heavy-duty profanity.

Blotto: Drunk.

Bods: Short for "bodies" and used to refer to personnel.

Body-snatcher: Stretcher bearer, medical orderly.

Boffins: Scientists.

Bog: A latrine.

Bogey: Unidentified aircraft.

Boomerang: Return to base due to technical difficulties before reaching the target.

Boost: The amount of supercharging given to an engine to increase power.

Bounce: A surprise attack, usually from above, and/or out of the sun.

Bowser: Tanker used to refuel aircraft.

Brass: Senior officers.

Brassed off: Extremely annoyed or unhappy.

Brevet: Cloth insignia worn over the left breast pocket of the uniform (battle dress and dress blues) to indicate status as aircrew and trade. Pilot's brevets had two wings. All other aircrew had one wing attached to a circle with a letter designating their trade, e.g. "N" for Navigator, "AG" for Air gunner, "E" for Engineer etc.

Brew up: To prepare a pot of tea.

Browned off: Same as brassed off.

Brown jobs: Army personnel.

Bull: The formalities of the service, e.g. parades, salutes, etc.

Bumpf: Useless paperwork.

Burton: (As in "gone for a Burton") killed in action.

Bus: Aircraft.

Buster: Use maximum boost/speed.

Buy it: Killed in action — past tense is "bought it".

Cart, in the: To be in trouble.

Chain gang: Aircraftmen, general duties.

Chairborne division: RAF personnel working in offices (also wingless wonders and Penguins)

Cheesed off: Fed up, bored, had enough.

Chiefy: Flight Sergeant.

Chop: (As in "get the chop") to be killed in action.

Circuits and bumps: In training, the act of landing and immediately taking off again to practice landings and take-offs.

Civvy street: Civilian life, before and/or after RAF service.

Clapped out: An aircraft or person nearing the end of its useful life.

Clock: Airspeed indicator.

Clot: Idiot

Cloud x/10: Cloud cover described as a percentage of the sky covered, e.g. 10/10 complete cloud cover, 5/10 50% cloud cover etc.

CO: Commanding Officer.

Cockup: A disorganized mess.

Cookie: A 4,000 lb bomb creating a surface blast.

Coned: Multiple searchlights fixing on a single aircraft.

Corker: A woman.

Corkscrew: Evasive maneuver to disrupt the aim of flak, searchlights and night fighters.

Crabbing: Side-slipping usually on landing or approach.

Crate: An aircraft.

Crumpet: A woman.

Curtains: Killed.

Cushy: Something comfortable.

Dalton Computer: Early mechanical handheld computer used in air navigation.

Darky: Call sign of an emergency channel to help aircraft find nearby airfields or get navigational assistance.

Deck: The ground

DFC: Distinguished Flying Cross for officers only in WWII.

DFM: Distinguished Flying Medal for NCOs and other ranks.

Dicey-do: A particularly dangerous operation, comes from "dicing with death."

Dim view: (As in "take a dim view") to view with skepticism or disapproval.

Dispersal: Area on an airfield to which aircraft are dispersed to protect against enemy attack.

Dispersal hut: A small building close to dispersed aircraft with lockers for clothing, tables, chairs, camp beds, and a phone connection to the control room. In Fighter Command pilots on readiness waited in or around the dispersal hut waiting for a "scramble."

Ditch: To crash-land on a body of water in an emergency.

Dicky or 2nd Dicky: Co-pilot, second pilot. Since the RAF discontinued the practice of assigning two pilots to an aircraft early in the war, pilots only flew "2nd Dicky" for specific reasons. Most common was for a pilot arriving at his first operational squadron to fly 2nd Dicky with an experienced pilot on one operational flight before flying his first operation with his own crew.

Dicky Flight: A training flight for inexperienced pilots.

Dicky seat: The fold-down seat used by the second pilot

Do: An event, action in the air, an operation.

Drink: A body of water

Drome: Aerodrome, airfield

Driver, airframe: Derogative term for the pilot used by other aircrew.

Duff: Bad or not accurate.

Dust up: Heated action, aerial combat.

Elsan: Chemical toilet carried on aircraft

Erk: General term for ground crew from the Cockney pronunciation of "aircraftman."

ETA: Estimated time of arrival

Fishheads: The navy

Fitter: Ground crew responsible for engines — more qualified than a "mechanic"

Flak: German anti-aircraft guns (derived from Flug Abwehr Kanonen).

Flame float: Small incendiary device that could be dropped from the flare chute to measure wind speed and direction.

Flamer: An aircraft shot down in flames.

Flaming: Mild, all-purpose expletive.

Flannel: To bluff, to deceive.

Flap: Unnecessary excitement or panic.

Flare path: A row of lights marking the boundary of the runway for take-off and landing.

Flat out: As fast as possible.

Flat spit: To be bewildered, confused, at a loss.

Flight: Subdivision of a squadron. In Fighter Command, each squadron had two flights of six aircraft designated "A" and "B" and usually commanded by a Flight Lieutenant; in Bomber Command each squadron had two flights of six to eight aircraft, also designated "A" and "B," ususally commanded by a Squadron Leader.

Flying Brevet: See Brevet.

Fruit salad: A large number of ribbons denoting decorations (worn under the flying brevet).

Gee: An early form of radar-based navigational aids.

George: The automatic pilot.

Gen: Information (from intelligence).

Get cracking: Get moving.

Get one's finger out: To hurry up or pay attention.

Get some in: Get some experience.

Get the drift: To understand.

Gone for six: Dead.

Gong: A medal, decoration.

Green: Untried, inexperienced.

Gremlin: A mythical creature that lived on certain aircraft and caused malfunctions at inconvenient times.

Green, in the: All engine control gauges reading normal. (A needle in the "red" indicated a malfunction).

Green, get the: To receive permission. Originated from permission to take off as indicated by a green light flashed from the caravan beside the runway by airfield control officer.

Grief, come to: Get in trouble or crash.

Hack: An aircraft used for general duties.

Half-pint hero: Boaster, braggart.

Hare after: To pursue.

HCU: Heavy Conversion Unit, a training unit dedicated to training aircrew on the heavy (four-engine) bombers.

Hedge-hopping: Flying so low an aircraft looks like it has to hop over hedges.

Hit the silk: To bail out, parachute.

Hold the can: To be responsible.

Hoof it: To walk.

Humid: Without personality.

Hun: A German.

Illuminator: An aircraft tasked with dropping flares to illuminate a target. Load ca. 54 flares.

Jankers: Punishment, extra duty.

Jerry: The Germans.

Jink: To take evasive action.

Kill: A victory, a downed enemy as in "a fighter pilot needed five kills to become an ace"

Kip: Sleep.

Kite: An aircraft.

Laid on: Supplied, as in "extra beer was laid on."

Let down: To descend.

Line abreast: To fly wingtip-to-wingtip, on a broad front.

Line astern: To fly nose-to-tail in single file, one aircraft after another.

Line shoot or shooting a line: Exaggerating, bragging, fabricating.

LMF: Lack of moral fibre.

Look See, A: Reconnaissance.

Lose your wool: Lose composure.

Low down: Inside information.

Mae West: Inflatable life vest worn over flying kit.

Maggie: A Miles Magister training and communications aircraft

Meat discs: Metal ID worn by all aircrew, "dog-tags" in USAAF.

Mess: Dining room, bars, and quarters for personnel, separated by rank: officers' mess, sergeants' mess and other ranks mess.

Met: Meteorology Officer.

MIA: Missing in Action.

MO: Medical Officer.

Mob: The Royal Air Force.

MT: Motorized Transport.

MU: Maintenance Unit, where aircraft that could not be repaired at squadron/station level were sent for more extensive maintenance and repairs.

NAAFI: Navy, Army, Air Force Institute, an organization which attempted to bring comforts to crews to raise morale. Mobile canteens provided tea, buns, cigarettes and the like.

Natter: Chatter, talk.

NCO: Non-Commissioned Officer, in the RAF, Sergeant or Flight Sergeant

Odd bod: Any spare personnel, particularly crew member left over after the rest of the crew had been killed or finished their tour.

Old Man: The squadron commander

Op: Operational flight

Ops Room: Place where information was collected, tabulated, and operations planned and controlled.

Orbit: To fly in circles, usually over an airfield or a marker.

OTU: Operational Training Unit, a training unit where aspiring pilots few operational aircraft/service aircraft for the first time, having previously learned to fly on training aircraft.

Pack up: To break down.

Packet, to catch a: To receive something unpleasant such as flak or a reprimand.

Pan out: To happen

Panic: Intense flap.

Panic bowler: Steel helmet worn during air raids.

Pancake: To land.

Pansy: Effeminate.

Party: A sexual experience, or an air battle or any difficult experience.

Pasting: Punishment.

Peel Off: To turn away from a formation.

Penguin: Derogatory term for non-flying personnel.

Perspex: Comparatively shatter-proof, transparent material used for windscreens, cockpit hoods and gun turrets.

Pickled: Drunk.

Piece of cake: Easy.

Piece of nice: Anything very pleasant or attractive.

Pie-eyed: Drunk.

Plaster: To bomb heavily and accurately.

Popsie: A girl, girlfriend.

Prang: An accident.

PSP: Perforated or pierced steel planking, steel mats used for runways, hardstandings and taxiways instead of concrete.

Quack: Derogatory term for the Medical Officer.

Racket: Swindle, scam.

Readiness, Squadron or Flight: The status of a squadron, flight or section requiring pilots to remain at the dispersal hut in flying kit ready to take off in a short period of time, usually 10 to 15 minutes.

Recce: Reconnaissance flight.

Rick view: To view with pleasure.

Rigger: Ground crew responsible for airframe.

Ropey: Bad, no good, duff, decrepit, doubtful.

Saturated: Without personality, even worse than wet or humid.

Scram: To leave in a hurry.

Scramble: Get airborne as quickly as possible.

Scrambled eggs: Braid on a senior officer's hat.

Scrap: To fight, aerial combat.

Screw: Propellor.

Scrub: Cancel.

Shakey-do: see "dicey do" — a particularly dangerous operation.

Shot down in flames: (In addition to the literal meaning) to be reprimanded.

Skipper: Pilot/captain of an aircraft and crew leader.

Sky Pilot: A chaplain, priest.

Smashed: Drunk

Smashing: Marvelous, super.

Snappers: Enemy fighters.

Snogging: Kissing.

Soaking glass of wet: A gin.

Soggy: Description of when an aircraft that does not respond properly to the controls.

Sortie: One aircraft doing one trip, e.g. if eight aircraft take-off on an operation, that is eight sorties, if twelve aircraft scramble to intercept a raid that is twelve sorties.

Sozzled: Drunk.

Spill the beans: To disclose information.

Spoof: A diversion.

Spot on: Same as "bang on", precise.

Sprog: Someone fresh from training without experience. Also used in "sprog crew" to mean an inexperienced crew.

Squirt: A quick burst of gunfire.

Stand-by, Squadron or Flight: the status of a squadron or flight requiring pilots to be in their cockpits with engines ticking over ready for immediate take-off.

Strip, to tear off: To be severely reprimanded by a superior. Refers to having one's rank insignia stripped off to denote a demotion.

Stooge: To idle around, an uneventful sortie.

Streamlined piece: A slim, lovely woman.

Take the day off: Never mind, something's not important.

Tallboy: Bombs developed by the British engineer Barnes Wallis, which penetrated below the earth and exploded after a timed delay causing an earthquake effect. The bombs weighed 12,000 tons and were custom made. A Lancaster bomber could carry only one at a time.

Tally ho!: Enemy in sight

Through the gate: Flying at maximum power.

T.I.: Target Indicator, colored flares dropped by the Pathfinders to identify targets, used after April 1944.

Ticket: Pilot's certificate.

Ticking over: An engine running slowly and using little power.

Tick off: To reprimand or criticize.

Tracer: A type of machine gun round that glowed showing the direction ammunition was going and allowing a gunner to adjust his shooting. Usually, every fourth round was tracer.

Twirp: Same as clot and twit, idiot.

Twit: Same as clot and twirp, idiot.

Upstairs: In the air.

U/S: Unserviceable.

UXB: Unexploded bomb.

Vic: Flying formation of three aircraft, with the middle aircraft forward of the flanking aircraft.

Waffle: An aircraft out of control, losing height or not on a steady course, or a person not giving a straight answer to a question.

Washed out: To fail, particularly in training when qualifying for a trade.

Wet: Without personality, boring.

Whack: An attempt

Whiff: To take a breath of oxygen.

Window: Strips of metal dropped from bombers to confuse German radar.

WingCo: Wing Commander.

Wizard: Excellent.

Biography

Helena P. Schrader

Helena P. Schrader is an established aviation author and expert on the Second World War. She earned a PhD in History (cum Laude) from the University of Hamburg with a ground-breaking dissertation on a leading member of the German Resistance to Hitler. Her non-fiction publications include *Sisters in Arms: The Women who Flew in WWII*, *The Blockade Breakers: The Berlin Airlift*, and *Codename Valkyrie: General Friederich Olbricht and the Plot against Hitler*. In addition, Helena has published nineteen historical novels and won numerous literary awards. Her novel on the Battle of Britain, *Where Eagles Never Flew*, won the Hemingway Award for 20th Century Wartime Fiction and a Maincrest Media Award for Historical Fiction. RAF Battle of Britain ace Bob Doe called it the "best book" he had ever seen about the battle.

With the *Grounded Eagles Trilogy*, she explores the fate of two secondary characters from *Where Eagles Never Flew* in greater detail and in the third tale introduces a new character, who will be the central figure in her next book, *Lancaster Skipper*.